WHERE FIRES BURN

SMOKE AND SHADOW
BOOK 1

VERONICA CASTILLO

PRICKLY PEAR

Book Cover by Miblart

Illustrations by Atticus

First edition 2024

For Eric and our boys.
And to Maria

Comanche may die today, tomorrow, ten years.
When the end comes, then they all be together again.
I want to see my mother again.

QUANAH PARKER, December 4, 1910

Part One

1

June 1837

Bridget crept through the cramped wagon, careful not to knock over any grain sacks and wake up her sister. She searched in the dim light for the water pail, but her bare foot found it first and sent it clanging against the wagon's wooden frame. She winced and rubbed her toe. "Darn blasted bucket."

"Mrs. McDougal says, 'ladies don't curse,'" Maggie muttered from under her blanket.

"Hush, go to sleep." She tucked the worn quilt under her sister's chin.

"Where you goin', Briddy?"

"To fetch water and start breakfast."

Maggie's face brightened at the mention of food. "Does that mean Papa's comin' back today?"

To stall for an answer, Bridget set the pail upright. "We're doing just fine without him, aren't we?"

Maggie sat up and the creamy curls around her face bounced like a spring. "Can you drive the team? What about wild animals? And

Indians! Papa says Comanche roam in the south and they're anything but friendly. What if they got him?"

Got him. Killed him. Scalped him. Any one of those and they'd be done for sure. "Hush! He'll be here soon. I'm sure of it." She patted her sister's leg. "I'll take the gun with me. Ain't no Indian or toothy critter gonna get you, or me, or even Papa. He's too quick and too smart."

"Not when he's been drinking." Maggie ducked her head like she did when she'd taken the Lord's name. Or the Devil's. It was true that drinking made Papa mean, and he drank often. Bridget's hand went to rub the ox whip welts on the back of her legs. She hadn't meant to spill the sack of grain. It tipped when she went looking for her powder horn.

"Quit worrying. Sun's not up yet so get some sleep, and then I'll make us some johnny cakes. If you're lucky, we'll have some fresh meat to go with." She stretched above a tower of crates for her father's breech-loading carbine. Her fingers curled around the barrel, and she pulled it down, hugging it to her chest like an old friend. She set it by her feet and reached for the pouch with lead and caps, and the powder horn.

Maggie frowned at the gun. "Be careful, Briddy, and come back soon. I don't like being in the wagon all alone."

With a sigh, Bridget sat beside her sister and set the carbine across her lap. Even though they both grew up quick after Mama died, Maggie was only seven. Natural for her to be afraid, but who would listen to Bridget's own fears? She ran her fingers along the wooden gunstock, over the carved initials. E.M.O. Emmet O'Connell. Papa had left the carbine with her while he took his newer rifle, but he should have been back by now.

"Everything's going to be fine. You're safe as long as you stay in the wagon," she told Maggie. "Do you remember the song?" She sang the line Mama used to sing. "Tis the last rose of summer, left blooming alone."

"Who would inhabit this bleak world alone?" Maggie finished.

Bridget tucked a lock of Maggie's blonde hair behind her ear. "You won't be alone long. After breakfast, we can braid hair."

"Promise?"

"Let's pinky it."

They hooked little fingers and pressed thumbs together to seal the promise. "Pinky pinky, bow-bell, a promise to keep but never tell," their voices said in unison.

"Sleep now, back in two shakes." Before Maggie could ask more questions, Bridget grabbed the pail and hopped from the wagon with the carbine tucked under her arm. Outside, the camp was coming to life with women lighting breakfast fires, babies crying for milk, and men's voices murmuring in hushed tones. The aroma of coffee and bacon made her tummy rumble. She ought to hurry, but first she followed Papa's warning to always check her surroundings.

With the pail hooked on her arm, she shaded her eyes from the hazy glow of the rising sun. Sweeping hills stretched for miles around the cluster of wagons, mules, and horses camped at Lower Cimarron Spring. Sunlight spread over wind-swept grasses, turning them from dull gray to tipped with fire, like an amber quilt thrown across the landscape. In such an open space, how could any creature hide from view? When the caravan first set for the frontier, she'd hoped to see a wild Indian, but with Papa missing, such a silly idea had turned to dread.

Two men walked the camp perimeter holding long rifles on their shoulders. There weren't many men left and each took his patrol seriously. The wagon party arrived a week ago, but their hopes had withered at the sight of the dry stream bed. With horses, mules, and oxen days from death, Papa and some of the men-folk had ridden out to find another water source. Two days later, rain had filled the riverbed and the men should have returned.

With a last glance around the camp, she headed down a grassy slope to the shallow stream. She hopped over cow patties and watched the Doyle twins roll hoops in a race. No time to join them. After passing through tall reeds and shrubs, she arrived at the creek where women were collecting water or washing clothes. Rust-colored and bitter, the stream trickled over ruddy sand and rocks. She set the carbine down and dipped her dusty feet in the water. Dragging the pail, she let it fill and poured chilly water over her gangly legs.

"Take care not to get your father's gun wet." Mrs. McDougal pointed to the carbine. The stock had slipped close to the edge.

Bridget picked it up and laid it in the crook of her arm. "This here's my carbine."

Busybody McDougal placed a hand on her hip and turned to the other women. "What kind of father leaves his two daughters alone in Indian country?"

Bridget scrunched up her nose. "You shut up about Papa. He trusted me to take care of Maggie. Besides, I'll be twelve next month. I'm not a little girl."

"You're not grown, and you shouldn't be playing with gunpowder."

"I'm not playing." She hugged the rifle closer. "I know how to shoot."

The woman snorted and continued to pound her laundry.

"Old gossip." She stood, gathering the power horn, pouch of lead, and her tin of percussion caps. She strode away until the other women shrank into the distance.

What did nosey Mrs. McDougal know anyhow? Her aim was almost as good as any of the men. Papa made her practice until she could load and fire the weapon in a matter of seconds. If she shot a rabbit, or better yet, a deer, that'd shut her up.

The sun was getting warm, so she gathered her long copper hair from her hot neck and continued downstream. Maybe a buck would be taking a drink, and she could put a ball of lead right in the heart. Wouldn't Papa be proud when he came back? As she trudged along the shore, she collected flat stones that fit into her palm. Ten skips were her best. With tall reeds at her back, she flung rocks into the water and imagined each one a perfect shot into a large buck.

A burst of gunfire jolted her out of her daydream, and she jumped, looking through the grass. Dust rose above the camp in a cloud, like from a stampede of horses. Beneath the popping gun blasts, strange cries and whoops split the air. Women and children screamed. Oh, dear Lord. Maggie!

She snatched the carbine and sprinted upstream until she remembered Papa's warnings not to be an easy target out in the open. She hugged the riverbank and inched forward. Shrieks and cries grew louder. One of those shrieks could be Maggie. She bit her lip and willed herself not to cry.

As she crept along the stream, the water became tinged with red. She trembled and peered through the tall grass. The sight forced her to a stop. Women lay motionless with arrows and lances protruding from their bodies like porcupine quills. Their clothing lay torn and strewn about, and their legs spread open in gruesome poses.

Through the growth up the slope, she spotted mounted men. They raced their horses through the camp carrying bows and lances. A few sat still on their restless war ponies, as though waiting to kill anything that moved. Their nearly naked bodies glistened with sweat, grease, and bright paint, both fascinating and repulsive. A blood-chilling war cry sliced through the heavy air, a sound more terrifying than the screams of agony.

She ducked down and covered her eyes. Between her fingers came flashes of people dragged and trampled by horses. Scalped and skinned, bodies pinned to the sides of wagons with lances. Limbs cut away, ripped clothing and flesh. Such cruelty could only mean Comanche.

And Maggie? Remembering her promise, she raised her head. Her heart pounded to the drumbeat of hooves as she squinted to find their wagon among the chaos and spotted Maggie crouched inside, huddled beneath the quilt. Their eyes met and Maggie screamed. She threw off the blanket and crawled out.

Bridget waved her hands to tell her to stay put, but Maggie bolted into the open. A fierce-looking warrior with long streaming hair spotted her and pointed his gray horse in her direction. He drew his bow, the arrow tracking her sister to see where she'd run. His dark eyes surrounded by black paint locked onto Bridget. Her blood froze.

He shouted to his companions and another Indian urged his mount forward. This man's upper body and face were smeared with red.

Hands shaking, Bridget lifted the carbine and took aim at the red-painted warrior. A man on horseback made a frightening target compared to a deer, and the idea of taking a human life sent bile into her throat.

She fired but missed when the red warrior dropped alongside the neck of his horse. Then came a sharp, heavy twang as his arrow struck the ground in front of her, its force so great most of the shaft buried into the hard soil.

Ducking further down the slope, she fumbled to reload. With trembling hands, she tried to place a percussion cap. Maggie screamed, and Bridget peered up. The red warrior, still hanging from the side of his horse, reached out his arm and snatched her sister like a rag doll and galloped away. He passed her to another rider and then Maggie was gone, disappearing on the back of a horse into a crowd of warriors.

Forgetting everything she'd be taught, Bridget screamed, making herself the next visible target.

Red warrior spun his horse, facing her. The first man, the fierce-looking one, kicked his heel into the flank of his iron-gray stallion and both men rode forward, bows drawn, and arrows notched.

She clutched the cap in her fist, gathered her skirts, and charged through the stream behind her. Arrows flew past. Hooves splashed in the water, and tiny bells tinkled. She resisted the urge to look over her shoulder and kept running. Across the opposite bank, her bare feet pounded the dry earth, but the drenched layers of her dress stuck to her legs. Grass grew past her shoulders, whipping her face and blocking her view. There was nowhere to go, nowhere to hide where mounted men couldn't find her, but she hurried onward.

An arrow pierced through her leg, and the force of its impact crashed her to the ground. Sharp pain gnawed up her thigh as she lay in stunned shock. With a shaking hand, she pulled up her skirts and let out a yelp when the wet cloth yanked on the shaft. The arrowhead protruded from her thigh, pinning her dress to her leg. Her vision threatened to darken, but she forced her eyes to watch her pursuers through the grass.

Red Warrior was the first to get close enough to reveal the triumph in his eyes. Her fear grew to bitter anger and desperation. She raised the loaded carbine, set the cap, and found her target. This time, she wouldn't miss. The shot blasted through his chest, and his body crashed to the ground as she scrambled to escape horse hooves flying past.

The other man yelled, both a war cry and one of rage. Fierce One's gray horse slowed to a trot, but he still approached. His hateful glare stole what was left of her courage. She reached for the pouch of lead, but her hands shook so badly she dropped it in the tall grass, open and spilling.

Throbbing pain and tears blurred her vision as she searched the ground. Her fingertips touched lead. She grabbed the ball and struggled to load the gun, spilling the powder as she poured. She raised the stock to her shoulder. A third warrior had joined the pursuit. Everything about his appearance was just like Fierce One, only he was clutching a stone club.

She swung the barrel back and forth between the two men, wondering if she was seeing double. The one with the club was further away, but his galloping horse was closing the distance. Fierce One's horse came at a lope, but his erect posture displayed deadly confidence. He barked a warning at his companion, but the stone-club warrior did not slow.

Her arms trembled, weak from pain and loss of blood. She took aim at the stone-club warrior with the galloping horse. Her eyes met his, a mirror of the same desperate grief and loss. Before the stone club came swinging at her skull, she pulled the trigger. Hot gases burst from the chamber, burning her fingers and singeing her hair and in the same moment, the man's skull burst in fragments of brain and bone, spattering her face and arms. The club and his body thumped beside her. Vomit surged up her throat as she watched the man's bloody eyes soften and go blank.

She clutched at clumps of grass and tried to crawl. The arrow in her leg twisted in her flesh. Bridget could go no further. She rolled onto her back and held the gun by the barrel, like a bat ready to swing.

Fierce One dismounted in one swift movement and strode closer.

She scooted back. "Don't come near me, heathen!"

His answer was to draw a large knife from his narrow waist. Other men gathered around, holding weapons and shouting.

Were the others now dead? Papa? Mrs. McDougal? The Doyle Twins? And where was Maggie?

Tears filled her eyes. Papa was never coming back. Maggie was gone, and everyone was dead. She was alone.

The warrior stopped. He towered above her. The sun behind him darkened his figure into black shadow. He pointed his knife, and she raised the carbine. If she was going to die, she'd die fighting.

Strange voices filled her ears. Laughter mixed with wails of anguish. Her head spun, and the images before her blurred. Leather and long hair. Feathers and paint. She smelled sweat, buckskin, gun smoke, the sharp tang of blood, and something fragrant she couldn't place. She put out her hand as if to stop the world from spinning. The laughter grew louder, but the warrior stood still, watching. The last thing she remembered was his face as he came toward her.

So strange, he wasn't much more than a boy.

2

Bridget's arms ached and couldn't move. A foul-tasting cloth smothered her mouth, and her entire body jostled in pain. When she opened her eyes, she couldn't see past the blindfold covering them. Her head pounded, but her injured leg had gone numb. Everything came back in a rush of panic. The attack. Maggie running and being snatched away. Three men chasing her down and the one she couldn't kill.

Her body tensed, making her limbs throb. By the odor of dung and sweat, the touch of hide, and the rough rocking of her body she guessed she'd been tied across the back of a horse.

She made a muffled cry and struggled to break free, but a quick jab in her side warned her it was futile. Nothing to do but pray.

Lord, please help me. Give me strength and give me courage. If not for myself, then so I can find Maggie. I beg of your mercy, Lord. Amen.

Terror, hunger, and exhaustion battled her ability to remain alert. The next several hours were a mix of unknown sounds and constant pain. Hours seemed to stretch into days, but she lost all sense of time. The endless riding with only the briefest stops were beyond the endurance of normal men or horses. The warriors couldn't be human, but beasts. How could anything else survive?

The horse stopped and her captor slid off. He conversed with his companions in a low voice. No light came through her blindfold, so it had to be nighttime. Perhaps they'd break long enough for a proper rest.

She listened to the sound of feet shifting in rocky soil, then pausing. The tension in her binds released as he cut her from the horse. She dropped to the ground. Despite being unable to see, and with hands still bound, she scrambled to her feet to run. As soon as she put weight on her injured leg, her face struck the ground with a yelp. Dirt filled her mouth and her nostrils burned with the odor of horse dung.

The warrior grabbed her hair and yanked her up. He half-dragged her while she stumbled and stretched out her arms in an attempt to keep balance.

"Please... Let me go, please."

He spoke sharply and lifted her onto another horse.

"No, no! I can't go on." She tugged at the binds. The blindfold slipped, but she could only make out a faint outline of the man struggling to tie her down. A strange scent hit her nose and she recognized it as Fierce One. She thrashed her arms and legs, attempting to kick him, hit him, anything.

His fist raised and struck her. Her ears buzzed and sparks of color flashed behind her eyelids. When she gasped, he shoved another water-soaked rag into her mouth. Why bother keeping her alive? She sucked on the moisture, fighting to stay conscious, but losing.

In her sleep, she dreamed. Her mother sat on the edge of the bed in their little cabin back in North Carolina. Golden blonde locks cascaded down her shoulders as she read from an old book. Heroes defeated villains and rescued maidens. Children went on adventures and came back safe and sound. Good defeated evil, true love always prevailed, and everyone lived happily ever after. Except when they didn't.

"Mama, are you going to die?"

"My darling, Bridget. You have to be strong. Take care of Maggie. She won't understand. Take care of your father too."

"But, Mama..."

"Please, Bridget. Promise me."

"I will, Mama. I promise."

She awoke to find herself on solid ground. Her head pulsed with her heartbeat. She tried to sit up, but the ache in her arms and legs made movement difficult. As her eyes adjusted to the dark, she pulled up her skirts to reveal a bandage tied around her wound.

A low fire burned nearby, its faint light revealing that she was inside a circular, hide-covered tent. Wooden poles formed the frame and assorted items hung from ties or lay about at the base. Across the fire sat two human figures, but beyond, an opening of some kind, an exit.

One person spoke and stood, growing tall into a young woman. She left through the round door. The second woman was middle-aged with huge round cheeks. Her dark hair was tucked behind her ears and fell just past her wide shoulders in thick hanks. An animal hide dress covered her ample body, with colorful designs on the shoulders and cinched by a belt with a large knife at her hip.

Eyeing the knife, Bridget drew up her feet, ready to run. "Let me go, you heathens! Why have you got me here? You're murderers! Let me go!" Her dry throat scorched her words. She grabbed a piece of wood from the fire and brandished it at the woman. "Where's Maggie?"

Big Cheeks called out and a man rushed in, ignoring her puny weapon. He had the same young face as Fierce One, but without the black paint, she couldn't be sure. He gripped her arm with fingers like iron and she dropped the stick. His fist came at her head and her world went black.

The door flap opened, and a bright shaft of light fell across Bridget's eyes. She squinted and buried her face in the rough ground, worsening her throbbing headache.

Hands dragged her from her small refuge, and she kicked out and screamed. Big Cheeks and a younger woman held her arms and legs with surprising strength. She stopped struggling when an old woman's face loomed close. Dark eyes filled sunken eyes sockets, making the old woman's face look like the dried apple doll Maggie used to play with. The sudden memory of her little sister brought fresh tears to her eyes.

The old woman spoke in a calm tone and wiped Bridget's face with a moist cloth that smelled dizzyingly fragrant. Although the cool cloth was soothing, she turned her face away, lowered her eyes and scowled. The old woman just smiled.

When the woman tried lifting her tattered skirts, Bridget slapped her hand away. "What are you doing? Leave me alone." She fought to free her arms and kicked out with her feet. The two women yanked her into obedience, sending shots of pain through her leg. She gasped and lay still.

15

Old One lifted her dress again and examined her wound. She spoke to the other woman in a language which sounded rhythmic and singsong. A shaft of light hit Old One's face to reveal the deep lines on her face framed by stringy, gray hair cut short to the ears. She removed the bandage and cleaned the wound with a damp cloth like the one she used on Bridget's face. Then she wrapped fresh bandages around her leg.

Watching the woman work in slow but skillful movements, Bridget's fear subsided to curiosity. Long gashes marred the old woman's arms, and two of her fingers were missing the last joints. The wounds were crusty and scabbed with dried blood, only a few days old.

Who would cut off an old woman's fingers?

Old One finished her work and released Bridget's leg. She sat dumbfounded, wanting both to flee and to have her continue with her ministrations. Unable to question these women, and helpless to escape, she burst into gulping sobs.

Old One patted her foot and placed a rawhide strip of food and a bladder of water on the ground, then left with the others.

Bridget stared at the food for a long time, hunger battling her fear. At last, she reached for the flat piece of rawhide and lifted it to her face. A small pile of mash looked like corn. She poked it then licked her finger. Tasted like corn, too. Papa had said Indians on the plains followed herds of buffalo. They couldn't possibly stay in one place long enough to grow corn.

Next to the corn was something far less familiar. It was dark and mashed into a block shape. She sniffed again. It had the odor of meat mixed with another substance, maybe berries. She tore off a small amount and touched it to her tongue. Didn't taste unpleasant, so she put the piece into her mouth. Chewing slowly at first, the savory flavor melted over her tongue.

Before she knew it, she'd devoured everything on the 'plate.' She quickly set to the water and gulped it down then leaned against one of the sturdy frame poles. The pain in her leg had diminished to a dull ache. After a bit of rest, she could walk on it. She'd escape as soon as she got a chance.

Loud wails awoke her. She shivered in the dark. The fire and blanket were gone, and tight ropes bound her limbs. Cries of anguish echoed in the distance while drums beat, slow and mournful. She trembled and curled up like an armadillo. Were other captives being tortured? More awful screams cut through the drums, but they didn't sound human.

The air filled with the smell of smoke, burning flesh and hair. Flames crackled and she imagined the heat of what had to be a great fire. Horses whinnied, a great number of them by the sound of it, with more screams. She struggled with her ties, but they wouldn't budge. One voice rose louder than the others, someone consumed by pain.

Devils! Only a demon could produce such a sound.

The voice grew louder until it changed, becoming more like the howl of a wolf. It rang into the night until at last, it faded and died. She sat and waited, expecting at any moment someone would come and drag her to that fire and make her scream that same horrible cry, but alone she remained.

The next morning, a hand shook her awake. She drew away and Big Cheeks laughed like a mockingbird. "Where's Maggie?" she asked again, but these people couldn't understand her questions.

Big Cheeks set down another large, flat piece of rawhide laden with food and Bridget sat up, seeing her hands were untied. She rubbed her wrists and stared at the offering. The food from the day before had been good, but remembering the demon sounds in the night, perhaps it was poisoned. She'd rather die than give in to kidnappers and killers. She turned her head away and bit her lip to fight the welling tears.

Big Cheeks made her mockingbird laugh, then ducked out through the round door.

It didn't make any sense. The Indians had cruelly attacked and murdered, but they were giving her food and treating her wounds? Was she a prisoner held for ransom? She picked up the tray and threw it across the room.

Night came. Without a fire, there was no light, so she waited until she could make out the black shapes of various objects inside the tipi. No one had entered or left in many hours. Her captors probably kept her in an unoccupied shelter while the women lived elsewhere.

Heart hammering against her chest, she struggled to rise and stood unsteadily on her injured leg. One step and she almost fell until she gripped one of the poles. When balanced again, she continued. Each step was torture, but she had to make it outside.

At the door flap, she paused and listened for sounds of movement or life. Dogs growled in the distance, and a baby cried. People were probably awake, but hopefully they were far enough away not to see or hear. Satisfied no one was close, she opened the flap and stepped out.

It was the first time she'd truly seen the camp, catching only the briefest glimpses each time one of the women came and left. She hadn't expected there to be so many houses, but aside from the hide-covered, cone-shaped lodges, there were a few low, brush shelters.

Seeing the size of the village, her confidence shrank. Maybe she should return to the lodge, but then came the whinny of a horse. Indians on the plains were supposed to have large horse herds. Her bad leg wouldn't take her far, but if she could steal a horse, she could ride her way to freedom.

She crept behind the lodge, limping her way in the direction of the horse whinny. She stayed behind the lodges in the shadows cast by the moon, but not too close in case someone inside would hear. The further she got, the quicker her pace. Laughter burst from the lodge up ahead. The amused voices sounded like company gathered for a good time, an unexpected sound in a place full of enemies.

She froze, unsure whether to turn back or to continue ahead. The horse whinnied once more, like a calling, then another loud burst of laughter arose. Those chattering coyotes wouldn't hear her over their own noise, so she shuffled past. She was almost behind the next lodge when someone opened the flap and came out into the night.

She gasped. The figure stood with his back to her, facing up to the sky. He took a deep breath and turned. His head arched high as he followed a shooting star course its way across the dark vault above. He stopped, facing the very direction Bridget stood.

She became a statue and hoped in her stillness and shadowed hiding spot he wouldn't notice her. Her legs ached and her knees trembled, but she dared not breathe.

Dear God, please don't let me fall!

If he didn't look away soon, she wouldn't be able to hold herself up any longer. At last, he turned away and strode in the other direction. She released her breath and lowered herself to the ground. She'd crawl if she had to.

She inched toward the horse tied just ahead. Its ears flicked in agitation, but she couldn't resist the splendid strength and beauty. The horse appeared almost black in the night, but up close she could see the coat was dark gray and a male, a stallion. He snorted and stamped his hooves.

"Whoa, there. Easy boy." She reached out her hand to let him smell her, hoping he wouldn't bite. He let her stroke his muzzle. "You're not so mean, eh?" She bent to unhobble him, then used his solid flank to draw herself to a stand. Rather cooperative for a stallion. She patted his back. How could she get on without a saddle?

Those warriors at the wagon raid had maneuvered themselves on their horses with ease. The red painted man had picked up Maggie while holding on with his legs. Oh God, Maggie!

She scanned the painted lodges in the dark. There were dozens of them, maybe even a hundred. Was Maggie even there? How would she even find her? She sank against the horse's side. Freedom was within her grasp, but she couldn't leave her little sister behind.

The horse stepped away and Bridget lost her one-footed balance and hit the ground. A pair of blue-beaded moccasins appeared on the flattened grass. Her heart stopped and she looked up. At the same time, the warrior grabbed her arms and lifted her.

"No!"

It was her last fight. She thrashed, struggling to free herself from his hard grip. She bit at his hands, kicked at his legs and scratched at his face. One of her ragged and torn fingernails caught on his brow. She raked her hand down with all her strength, gouging his face and nearly scratching his eye. He growled and threw her down. She tried to scramble away.

A foot stomped between her shoulders and pushed her onto her belly. The solid weight of a warrior's body pressed on her while he tied her arms. She tried to turn, but he gripped her legs and tied them as well.

"Damn you!" She twisted her body around and tried to kick with her joined heels.

He was too quick and grabbed her ankles. He then pinned her shoulders, crushing her arms agonizingly behind her while he sat on her knees. She was immobile.

For the first time, she stared at her captor directly. Dark eyes shone from a smooth lean face. His skin glowed a rich brown, flawless but for the red streak from temple to chin where she scratched him. Loose, straight black hair fell across broad shoulders, long enough to land upon her arms as he leaned over her.

She took in the vaguely familiar decoration on his leggings and the hilt of the knife sheathed at his waist. Then that strange, fragrant scent filled her nose, sending a new wave of panic through her already overwhelming fear. He was the same young warrior from the raid, Fierce One.

Fear condensed into hatred, for Papa who was probably dead. For Maggie's sake. For being unable to kill him like she did the others. He held her gaze, equal contempt radiating from his dark eyes, before he stood and left her helpless upon the ground.

Their scuffle had alarmed the occupants of the nearby lodges. They gathered around and spat curses at her. Others laughed and threw rocks and sticks, striking her already sore body. One person landed a kick in her gut, and she doubled over in pain. She gasped for breath. Her fingers dug into the soil. Perhaps she could dig herself a grave.

Big Cheeks and the other woman from the lodge pushed through the crowd. They lifted her and carried her back.

"Please." She couldn't muster a struggle. "Just let me go. What do you want with me? If you won't let me go, then kill me, please."

The women threw her down upon the hide blanket and spoke curtly before they left.

In the oncoming days, she remained bound and tied. She ate and drank without hands and fouled herself. After three days, she stopped fighting and stopped eating. They wouldn't let her go, but they couldn't make her live.

3

Mouse strolled under the morning sun along the familiar paths of the summer camp. She headed toward the edge of the village, where other women worked on cleaning the remaining hides from the last hunt. Her moccasined feet hardly made a sound in the dewy grass, but her deerskin dress swished against her legs, and the elk teeth sewn along the yoke and skirt rattled, soft and pleasant to her ears.

Children and dogs wrestled in the dust, while elders sat in the shade against their backrests, where they smoked and talked in muted tones. Many of the younger men scouted for buffalo, while others gambled in Ferret's lodge or repaired weapons and tools for the hunt they hoped would come.

Female voices grew louder, high-pitched tones with tittering laughter. Her grandmother, Winged Woman, sat with Laughing Bird and Squirrel in a less crowded area, perhaps so other women couldn't eavesdrop.

"*Haa maríawe!*" Mouse sat beside them and opened her rawhide parfleche.

"*Maríawe,*" Winged Woman said.

The other two women greeted her in turn. She took out her hide scraper and examined the tool for wear. The blade needed sharpening, and the wooden handle was loose, but it would serve for today.

She helped her grandmother scrape bits of flesh and fat from the huge buffalo hide staked between them. The scraps would be used for tanning, glue, or even to make a broth in winter if food was scarce. The older women returned to their conversation.

"The fire-headed one will not eat then?" Winged Woman asked her husband's second and third wives.

"No, she made faces at me." Laughing Bird, the second wife, leaned over a wide deerskin and rubbed a brain mixture into it to loosen the skin fibers.

"She's not grateful to be alive," said Squirrel, the youngest wife.

"I think she wishes to be dead." Laughing Bird paused to stretch her back. "I wouldn't want to be alive if I was taken by white-skins."

"The white-skins are cruel. They wouldn't let you live," Squirrel said between breaths as she scraped at her deerskin.

"Then they are kind!" Laughing Bird's round cheeks stretched tight, and her large body jiggled with laughter. "Truly, it must be better to be dead." She reached for a piece of dried meat in a pouch she had brought with her. "Maybe Lone Wolf was wrong to bring that girl here."

Mouse paused at the mention of her cousin, and the talk which hinted at what white-skins had done to their people. The southern bands often fought the Texians, but her people rarely encountered attacks from white-skins, until recently. But it was taboo to speak of the dead, and no one would explicitly mention the men and women killed in those battles.

Winged Woman spoke again. "We don't know if Lone Wolf made the right choice, so we'll see what happens."

Mouse continued her work without comment. Her grandmother had made the surprising choice not to torture or kill the white-skin child, something they often did with captives, unless they were adopted. But no one wanted to adopt *that* child.

When the sun was low, Mouse helped prepare the evening meal by crushing mesquite beans with green corn and added broth from her grandmother's pot to make a watery mash. As the only granddaughter, it was her job to help with domestic tasks, but she didn't mind. She looked forward to the day when she would run a household of her own.

Winged Woman stirred a pot of stew and addressed her husband, Red Hawk, civil leader of the band of *Kotsoteka*, the Buffalo Eaters. "The fire-headed one has decided to die," she told him and brought the ladle to her lips to taste the stew. "Shall we help her finish the job?"

Her grandfather was sitting against his willow backrest, cleaning his pipe with a piece of soft suede cloth. After many heartbeats, he set down the pipe, leaned forward, and took a deep breath. "If you want to kill her, then kill her already, but I think the fire-headed girl is well named. She fought well against Lone Wolf. If she hadn't been hurt, his strength alone wouldn't have been enough to restrain her."

"Laughing Bird and Squirrel are strong. They work well. I don't need more help," Winged Woman said. She flexed her hands and rubbed the joints of her missing fingers.

Her grandfather laughed. "That's the first time you have spoken well about those two. Laughing Bird is idle and talks too much, while Squirrel is slow."

Winged Women set her hand on her hip. "If you think so, why did you marry them?"

"A man with so many mouths to feed needs many women to help." He slipped the pipe into its beaded case. "Besides, you and I both enjoy Laughing Bird's jokes, and Squirrel does the best quillwork. She doesn't mind the unpleasant chores."

"She won't have to anymore."

"Precisely. I allowed Lone Wolf to bring the fire-headed one so you three would have less to do. Maybe then you'll be able to sit with me and bring me comfort in my old age." He stretched his legs in front of him.

"If she doesn't die," Winged Woman said. "We'll still have to tame her and teach her to work."

"Send Mouse." He used his pipe to point at Mouse. "Perhaps the girl is tired of seeing old faces." At this, Winged Woman hit Red Hawk across the back with her stir stick, but he only laughed again.

Mouse sat rigidly and bit her lip. Captive children were usually meek and soft, and more so the girl children, but *that* girl, with eyes like spring grass, wasn't like the others. She had fought and even killed grown men. What if she attacked? What if she tried to run?

"Will you go see the white-skin captive?" Winged Woman asked.

"What can I do?"

"Your grandfather is right. The girl needs to see someone closer to her own age. Maybe she'll feel less threatened and be more willing to cooperate. Will you help her?"

They awaited her response, looking as though they had asked her to fetch water, and not visit a wild, murderous foreigner, but she couldn't refuse their request.

"I'll go."

Mouse stood outside the spare lodge where the white-skin captive was being kept. With a quivering hand she opened the lodge flap and entered, carrying a rawhide bowl of supplies. The stench of filth and urine burned her nose, and she grimaced. Why hadn't anyone taken the girl to the stream to wash? Perhaps that was her first duty.

At her approach, the white-skin turned, showing a gaunt face and green eyes full of misery. Mouse crept forward and handed the girl a moist rag from her bowl. The child raised a hand to take it, but her arm quivered and dropped. Seeing how weak she was, Mouse gathered her courage and brought the damp scrap of soft deerskin to the girl's forehead. When it seemed like she wasn't going to bite, she gently bathed her brow.

The girl closed her eyes and moaned. Droplets of moisture trickled down her cheek, either tears or water from the rag. The girl hadn't the strength to run, least of all attack, and the poor thing needed to get clean. Mouse set down the rag and gently pulled the girl to her feet. The captive could barely walk and leaned heavily on her shoulder.

When they reached the open air, others stopped to watch. She ignored them and continued through the village while supporting the thin girl. They passed numerous lodges, spread far to the horizon across the thick buffalo grass. Ash and elm dotted the landscape, as well as oak trees clustered together. Scrub brush and cottonwood grew

27

dense near the banks of the lazy river, glistening in the afternoon sun. Several children followed them.

"Ugh, she stinks!" Deer Tail held her nose.

"Look at her hair. It's so ugly!" Lizard pointed a stick at the girl.

"Are you going to drown her in the river, like a weak puppy?" Deer Tail asked.

"No, of course not," Mouse answered.

"Why not? What good is she to us?"

Mouse paused to consider, unable to come up with an answer. "What good are you? Want me to drown *you* in the river? Go play somewhere else." The children hung back but continued to giggle. The captive hardly looked at them.

She carried the girl past a group of young men and older boys. Lone Wolf stood in the middle, taller than the others. He was the only one who didn't look away as the men averted their eyes in shame and embarrassment for the girl's pitiful state.

"That's my cousin," Mouse explained. "He brought you here. He's young, but brave so many follow him. He's Red Hawk's grandson and only by their kindness are you still alive." The girl managed to lift her head and stared. Fire burned in her eyes, but she made no effort to leave Mouse's side.

They reached the water's edge and the women who were washing huffed their disgust and cleared away or went further upstream. Mouse removed the girl's tattered and filthy clothes. She hardly resisted, as though she didn't care whether she got washed or *did* drown in the river.

"You're so pale," Mouse whispered. She'd never seen a white-skin up close before. If she hadn't known any better, she would have thought the child a ghost. As quiet as she was and with that empty stare, she might as well have been.

Her eyes landed on the funny brown spots on her ruddy arms and face, then noticed the bruises. Blue and purplish green, they stood out against her pink-white skin. The girl was tall, but skinny and hairless. She must have been no more than ten or eleven winters. Hardly young enough to be taught their ways.

She lowered her into the water, but the girl pulled free and let herself sink below the surface. Maybe she was just wetting her hair, but when she didn't come up, Mouse waded in and pulled her out. The girl scowled and sputtered water. She spoke angry words that cut her ears.

"Do you want to wash yourself?" Mouse asked.

The girl's lip quivered in response and red-rimmed eyes blinked. She turned her head to look around, at the cottonwoods, the rocky shore, and the field of grass beyond. Her hand flattened against the current, as though testing its speed.

"Don't try and swim across. You'll drown." She remembered Deer Tail's comment about weak puppies.

Muttering to herself, the girl's head fell back as she let herself float, eyes focused on the cloudless sky above while her arms drifted at her sides. What could she be thinking? Plotting revenge or had they broken her?

Once the girl was properly soaked, Mouse scooped up a handful of sand and took hold of the girl's skinny arm. She pulled away but Mouse held the arm firm. "You clean your skin, like this." She swirled sand along the pale skin until it shone pink and raw. Since the girl had stopped resisting, she continued scrubbing along her shoulders while the girl hunched her back.

Next, she dipped her head to wet and clean her hair with the yucca root and juniper wash someone had left on the shore. The light suds loosened the dirt and grime until her dull hair became a fiery gold.

She brought the girl back to the bank to let her dry in the sun, while she smoothed out an old, but mended gown from her supplies. The girl sat with her knees drawn up and rested her head on her arms. She allowed Mouse to dress her then returned to her perch.

Since her arms were tired and her own dress was soaked, Mouse joined her for a rest. The girl's bright hair was almost dry, but it lay in tangled curls. Would she let her comb it out?

The girl suddenly turned and spoke, and Mouse startled at the harsh sounds. She stared at the girl's expectant face and pleading green eyes. "I don't know what you're asking." Maybe she just wanted to know what was going to happen to her. "When you're stronger, they will want you to work. You will work hard. You belong to Red Hawk and Winged Woman, but you're not adopted. You're not their child. You're nobody's child, but they will feed you. That's the best you can hope for."

The captive gave a reply, again with the sharp words. Mouse frowned. "You seem strong and brave. I don't doubt you will try to escape again, but if you do, they will kill you."

After they returned to the lodge, the girl curled up against the back cover, tugging the old dress over her knees. She really was like a puppy, one that had been scolded with its tail tucked under.

The lodge still smelled so Mouse gathered up the soiled bedding. She tidied up the rest of the lodge before leaving with the mess and returning with clean bedding, food and water. Remembering what Laughing Bird had said, she remained to make sure the girl ate. She picked at her food and scooped up a few bites.

Satisfied she'd done all she could, Mouse got up to leave. As she reached the lodge door, she heard the girl's voice and turned back. Though she couldn't understand the words, there was no mistaking that look of gratitude.

It was early evening and the sun had dipped below the prairie line, making long shadows of the lodge poles on the ground. Mouse returned to her family's lodge, finding her mother, Quick Hands, and her father, Two Horns, already engaged in their evening meal.

She sat in her spot in front of her bedding and her mother handed her a stick of roasted deer meat before continuing to put away her cooking tools. "We heard you went to see the white-skin girl."

"I did. She was in a bad way." She bit into the juicy meat, then wiped the grease from her chin.

"Will she live?" her father asked. He swept his long braids over his shoulders before chomping into his own portion of meat. Three empty sticks lay on the ground in front of him.

"Yes, but I'm not sure how willing she is to work." Even as weak as she'd been, the girl had shown signs of her obstinance. Once she was strong again, she'd probably try to fight.

"What does that have to do with anything? She's a captive. She will work or she'll be beaten," he said matter-of-factly.

Mouse pictured the girl's bruises and cringed. If only she could talk to the girl, convince her to cooperate for her own good.

Her mother gave her father a nudge. "What did they say at the council? Were there many men?"

Women weren't allowed at council, but like many husbands and fathers, Two Horns always reported the details to his wife and child.

"Most of the men came. Red Hawk had bad news. Or good news, depending on whether you're anxious for battle." He took a long drink from his bowl of water and belched, then made a show of looking in the pot for another choice piece of meat.

Mouse groaned and gave her father a playful shove. He often kept her and her mother waiting when he had something exciting to share. "What happened?"

He acted like he forgot what he was talking about. "Oh, yes. Well, while a few men were out scouting for buffalo, they spotted a trail of smoke, just south of where we raided the wagon camp."

"More white-skins?" Her mother's voice wavered. She came to sit beside Mouse.

He nodded. "Scouts discovered a group of hair-mouth men. They weren't soldiers, but we think they found the remains of the raid. They might be tracking us."

Mouse trembled at the idea of more white-skins coming into their lands. "What's going to happen? Are our warriors going after them?"

"Your cousin plans to lead a war party, but Red Hawk disagrees. He wants us to move camp at dawn."

Quick Hands scowled. "You should've told me that first. Now we have to pack."

It would mean an early rise and lots of work to dismantle the lodge and build a travois. Mouse planned to tell one of the boys to fetch their packhorses. She'd be glad to leave though. The further away they could get from those hair-mouths, the better. No more reasons to mourn.

Her father leaned forward. "Daughter, I thought you might be interested to know, several men were in disagreement about whether we should leave the white-skin girl behind."

She lifted a brow. "You mean, they want to give her back to the hair-mouths."

He shook his head. "Just leave her. Maybe they'd find her, maybe not."

The girl would die left out on the plains, especially in her state. She shouldn't care. That girl was dangerous, but a nobody. "What reasons did they give?"

"Most think she's too old and won't fit in with us. The whites are determined to recover their people, and they won't quit. Her presence will bring them to our hunting grounds."

It was true, but Lone Wolf had gone to a lot of trouble to bring her if they were only going to let the girl die. "Did anyone argue for keeping her?"

Two Horns took another bite. She summoned patience while her father chewed and swallowed, then licked the grease from his fingers. "Some did, like Badger."

Her face warmed at the mention of Badger, recalling his pleasant face and sturdy body. She tried to concentrate on her father's words through thoughts of her cousin's best friend.

"Badger agreed that older captives don't adapt well to our ways, but also reminded everyone that no man can tell another what to do, and no one can decide for another what to do with his horses or possessions. 'Why do we talk about this girl when she's not our concern?'"

Whenever Two Horns quoted the other men, he changed the tone of his voice to mimic them. She hid a smile at her father's imitation of Badger's confident manner. "Did anyone agree with him?"

"He was just showing his support for Lone Wolf."

She smiled. "He would, those two are like brothers."

Her father's eyes narrowed at her comment, and she blushed. Two Horns didn't like Badger, but she could never figure out why.

"And Eagle Beak? Did he say anything?" Quick Hands whispered.

Two Horns took a breath. "No. He didn't go. He's still deep in mourning."

Mouse hung her head and picked at a clod of dirt stuck to her leggings. "What did Red Hawk decide?"

"He said the girl has the heart of a warrior and we need as many warriors as possible. He believes she can learn the ways of our people, so she's going to stay with us."

She breathed a sigh of relief and shoved the empty stick back into the ground. The girl was going to stay. If she was going to work for Red Hawk's wives, then they should probably find a way to communicate.

4

A finger poked Bridget in the side. She sat up and blinked in the dim lodge. "What do you want?"

The blurry figure of Big Cheeks squatted beside her, becoming clearer as Bridget's eyes focused. The woman leaned forward, her face wide and faintly lined, especially around her mouth. A strip of red highlighted the center part of her hair. Was it blood?

Bridget scooted away. Why couldn't it be the pretty girl who helped her bathe and dress? She'd even prefer the Old One who had tended her wound.

Big Cheeks reached out with her thick arm, scarred with lines, and rattled Bridget's injured leg. She made a motion with her hand, an unmistakable signal to rise.

Hiding her flush of shame, Bridget removed the blanket covering her, feeling naked with only the thin hide dress the girl had given her.

Big Cheeks grunted dismissively and tossed her a pair of moccasins. They were huge and stank like rotten cabbage, but having nothing else, Bridget put them on. She tried to stand. Her leg shook with pain, but she must not show weakness.

Her captor ignored her pain and pointed to the lodge cover, waving her arms as she headed out the door. What did it mean? Bridget followed the woman outside.

Pink light glowed in the east, signaling dawn, but the air was already warm and heavy with dust and noise. Women and children hustled about, removing the outer coverings of their lodges or tying the poles onto pack-horses.

"Are we moving?" If they took her further away, she'd never find her way back. She planted her feet, or foot since the injured one couldn't take much weight. "I'm not going anywhere."

Big Cheeks grabbed Bridget's arm and yanked her to the side of the lodge. She demonstrated the removal of a stake which pinned the cover to the ground. Bridget shook her head again and backed away, but the woman gripped her arms, speaking roughly until she crouched and started pulling out the stakes. They were going to work her like a slave.

In a matter of minutes, the Indians were packed and ready. There were scores of families and hundreds of people, but they headed out as the sun showed its edge. Her father would have been impressed with such efficiency. A pang of heartbreak for her family stopped her short, followed by the memory of the bodies at the wagon camp. She needed to find Maggie and escape.

Big Cheeks gestured to an old swaybacked mule, surrounded by a cloud of gnats. The mule flicked its ears, scattering a few flies.

Bridget shook her head. "I'm not getting on that thing."

With a string of sharp words, Big Cheeks shoved her toward the mule. Pain shot through her injured leg and once again she faced the challenge of pulling herself up without the use of a saddle. She gripped the dirty mane and hopped, swinging her foot to try and get her leg over the mule's back. When it seemed like she couldn't make it, Big Cheeks shoved her into her seat.

"Thank you," she said out of habit, then pressed her lips together. For once, she was glad the woman couldn't understand her. None of those people deserved her gratitude.

After tying the mule to her own horse, Big Cheeks mounted and followed the rest of the travelers. The flea-bitten animal staggered into an uneasy gait, and she fought to keep her balance. She shifted into a better position and adjusted her grip. Her bare legs itched against the rough coat.

Old One, who had tended her wound, and a younger woman rode ahead. An elderly man on a fine-looking stallion rode in front. She couldn't see his face, only his gray hair hung tied in two long braids, wrapped with fur. He wore a hide shirt and leggings. A quiver hung from his shoulder, a shield on his arm, and a long lance in one hand. He laughed at something the Old One said.

Heat rose to her chest from their show of humor. How could they be happy when she was a captive? Her eyes burned and she mashed her lips together so she wouldn't start blubbering.

Maybe she could find Maggie in this crowd. She glanced in every direction in search of anyone with pale blonde hair, but only found black and deep brown. Looking over her shoulder, the sight stole her breath. Growing clear in the dawning light, a brown and white spotted mass flowed as one living being along the ground. It gathered and reshaped, fluid as starlings across a golden sky. Clouds of dirt billowed in the air. The ground rumbled under pounding hooves to which her heartbeat in time.

"So many horses," she whispered.

A fast horse was her only means of escape. She could try to get free from Big Cheeks but had no way to cut the rope running from her mule to the woman's horse. She tried to reach the knot, but slipped each time she bent forward. If she was this bad at riding bareback, the mule was useless as a means to freedom. Besides, how could she leave without Maggie?

The path left by the horse herd would allow her to find her way back, but back to where? She didn't know the way to the wagon camp. She'd heard rangers sometimes found captives and returned them back east. Perhaps they were looking for her. She needed to remain watchful.

Almost everyone sat on a horse or mule. Women, children, and older people rode in the center while mounted men flanked either side. Like the old man, they carried lances, bows, and other weapons, but were otherwise unburdened. Each time a warrior raced past, she hunched her shoulders and braced for an attack, but the men showed no interest in her. They shouted at each other, or laughed at jokes she couldn't understand.

The mules and horses dragged long poles tied on either side like a sled. Between the poles, branches had been tied into platforms holding bundles of blankets and stacks of rawhide containers. Small children or elderly people sat on some of the platforms under arches of curved branches, like a wicker cage.

As they traveled, the Indians chattered and laughed. They exchanged smiles and jokes along with bits of food, although neither friendship nor sustenance was passed her way. Their calm and cheerful demeanor sharply contrasted against the evidence of cruelty she'd seen with her own eyes, and she hated them for it.

She dozed under the heat of the sun and the rhythm of the mule's sway. They'd been traveling nonstop, all day. She struggled to keep her eyes open, afraid she'd miss her chance to escape. Her stomach rumbled with hunger and her mouth parched with thirst. If only they would stop for a rest.

A group of children stared and whispered as they rode past. She sneered at them, until one girl caught her eye. Like Maggie, she had piercing blue eyes and blonde hair, almost white, but long hours under the sun had left her complexion as dark as the other children's.

"What's your name?" she asked. "Did they take you too?"

The girl stared back and smiled.

"It's okay, they won't understand us," she whispered.

The girl giggled and rode away. Bridget's gaze followed until it met with the familiar but foreboding figure of Fierce One on his gray stallion. He held a bow and arrow in his fist and his dark eyes narrowed. He must have seen her talking to the little girl.

Her face and chest grew flushed with heat. Even if she couldn't kill him, she couldn't let him intimidate her. She lifted her chin, set her mouth in a hard line, and managed to hold his steady glare. But memories from the attack, the screams, bodies and blood filled her vision and she broke eye contact. She was a coward, and a fool. He wanted her to be afraid, but she'd nearly gotten away. Did he still have that scratch? She glanced back.

A thin red line ran from one corner of his eye down his cheek, and she huffed in satisfaction. His mouth curved up in a sort of smile.

Arrogant ass. She glowered until he turned his gray horse and went on his way. His voice, low and clear, faded in the distance. Was he *singing?*

The moving band of Indians split up as small groups of families broke off onto their own paths. Bridget's heart sank. The trail would divide and any rangers who might be following wouldn't know which way to go. She watched the little blonde girl leave with a group headed south. Meanwhile, her captors led the way northeast.

Evening came and the group set up camp. Big Cheeks took a large stone and used it to grind dried corn she'd piled on a flat rock with a shallow dip. She handed the stone to Bridget and pointed to the partially ground corn.

For the briefest moment, she imagined smashing the stone against Big Cheeks fingers, hopping onto one of the horses, and taking off like the wind, but with her injured leg, she'd take a few steps and fall. Or get caught. Or she'd make it to the horse only to be stopped by one of the more experienced riders, which was pretty much anyone in camp.

With a sigh, she gripped the stone and dropped it on the kernels. Most shot out and scattered in the dirt.

Big Cheeks let out a stream of words which were obvious scolds. She collected the spilled kernels and dumped them back in the 'well.' After picking out grit, she held Bridget's hand over the stone and made the careful twisting motions needed to properly grind them, letting go once she had the hang of it. Every now and then, she sprinkled pecans for Bridget to crush along with the corn. Then she mixed the grounds with broth and formed round patties, directing Bridget to do the same. Big Cheeks' patties were even and flat, while hers came out lopsided.

Although the work was new, she went through the motions without further protest. If she did exactly as they showed her, perhaps they'd leave her alone. Wishing for death had been selfish. Her little sister needed her. Food would keep her strong until she could figure out how to escape.

Big Cheeks placed the patties to cook on hot stones beside the fire. Once the meal was ready, she served the old man while the other women gathered around to eat. Bridget debated whether to join them, but Big Cheeks waved her away, flapping her hand with a scolding tongue, like she was an unwanted pet. Alone in the dust behind the lodge, with one misshapen patty and a tiny chunk of meat, she sat, savoring her meager meal and the solitude. Her mind receded to memories of her former life while around her strange sights, sounds, and smells tried to break through her daydreams.

Angry voices awoke her, coming from outside the lodge. Maybe a ranger had come to rescue her. Unable to resist, she crawled over to the door to see. She paused when her foot stopped short, the jerking motion accompanied by a dull rattling sound. A rough rope, dangling with deer hooves, stretched from her ankle to Big Cheeks' chubby wrist. The woman continued to lay snoring.

Unable to reach the door, Bridget lifted the edge of the cover and peered outside. A group of men stood beside the old man's lodge. They held weapons and their bodies were painted with the same hideous designs as during the raid.

Fierce One stood among them and her heart stopped. He spoke to the old man, his voice mild. The old man replied with more anger, and they stood facing off a moment before they suddenly embraced. She averted her eyes from the strange display of affection until she heard the group dispersing.

The warriors joined the group of nearby horses. An older boy held the reins with clear agitation, his eyes wide with fear. One man, large and bulky with his face painted black and white like a skunk, patted the boy's cheek and made a curt comment. The boy laughed and the warriors mounted their horses. They took off in the direction everyone had traveled earlier that day.

Where could they be headed for battle? Had a rescue party come for her? Were those men heading out to stop them? She could try and escape, but if she was wrong, she'd die of thirst or starvation on the open prairie.

She watched the men disappear into the night, her hope of rescue vanishing with them. Fresh tears stung her eyes, and she curled into a ball and returned to sleep.

When morning came, the camp moved on. Bridget had little trouble doing her part to take down the lodge. Big Cheeks and the other women gave her approving glances and spoke in pleasant voices. A tiny rise of pride grew in her chest, but she forced it down and focused on her contempt.

Why were they being nice? They killed her family yet seemed to act as though it never even happened.

The group stopped and unpacked all their belongings unlike the few needed supplies as before. Big Cheeks directed Bridget to help set up lodges, then sent her to the empty one. Grateful for the chance to be alone and free of work, she limped inside, but the sound of beating drums and singing had her sitting in front of the door.

A crowd of people stood around a fire. Men with drums and long sticks sat at one end, while other men danced within the circle. Stripped of all but their breechcloths, their bodies were covered by colorful painted designs. Many of the dancers wore a furry hat with horns while others carried lances or bows and shields. They leaped and spun in a display of great athleticism and coordination. The men with weapons pretended to kill the ones with animal heads.

At first, she watched in horror. Their dancing confirmed what she had been taught: that Indians were heathens and devil worshipers. The scene brought back awful visions of the raid. Was she about to be sacrificed to the devil gods? The more she watched, the more she could see the men were not imitating a battle. It was a hunt. Beside the drummers, a group of women rose and fell in a small dance of their own. They cheered for each kill and added their own chorus to the drummers' song.

Her head and feet bounced with the intoxicating rhythm. She searched for familiar faces, finding the young girl who had washed her at the river, the one with long dark hair and eyes like wells of ink. Eyes that were kind among all the judgment and scorn. The girl left the circle and came over. She spoke and held out her hands.

Bridget recognized one of the words. It must mean buffalo, as it was repeated often in the presence of meat. The dance had something to do with the buffalo she had yet to see. Her portions of meat had gotten smaller and smaller, until that morning when she had only been given corn mush.

Willing to do anything to eat meat again, she put her hands in the other girl's. The girl led her to a less crowded area of the circle, where she proceeded to demonstrate the simple movement of the women's part of the dance. While she side-stepped, her feet rose onto her toes, then back to the ground.

The simple dance looked easy, but the pain in her leg was a reminder of her limitations. Fighting the shame for participating in such a heathen ritual, she attempted to copy the girl's movements. She smiled at her feet, then looked up to meet the girl's wide grin.

I wish I knew her name.

At the same moment, the girl pointed to herself, saying, "*Nu nahnia tsa Kahúu.*"

"I don't know what you're saying."

The girl bent to the ground, took a stick, and drew a small animal in the dirt.

"Is that a mouse?"

The girl repeated the word while alternately tapping herself on the chest and pointing to the drawing.

"Is that your name? Mouse?" The girl continued to gesture, then stopped and sighed. She put her hand to her mouth, as though thinking.

Her small body and quick movements *were* like that of a mouse. Bridget repeated the word several times in her mind before attempting to form the strange sounds. It was hard to make her mouth copy that of the girl's.

"Kahoo?"

The girl laughed, shook her head, and said the word again. Bridget tried once more. After a couple more tries, the girl grinned.

"*Kahúu,* Mouse." Her first Comanche word.

5

O utside the lodge, women chattered with excitement, and Bridget caught the word for buffalo repeated in their conversations. While the women prepared for some mysterious event, the men stripped down to their breechcloths, out in the open, in front of God and everyone. She blushed but couldn't help but watch while they painted themselves and their horses. Their rough fingers traced jagged lines in bright yellow and crimson onto brown spotted rumps, or ringed soft horsey eyes with white.

Once ready, the men mounted their decorated ponies, carrying bows and lances. Women and elders gathered to see them off. A strong odor hung in the air, as though they were camped in a cow shed.

She spotted Mouse, got up from her spot in the dirt, and walked over. "*Kuhtsu,* Buffalo?" she asked.

"*Haa,*" Mouse said. It must mean yes. Her black eyes shone with excitement in the morning sunlight. She left Bridget to join her mother and the other women who ducked into their lodges and brought out rawhide pouches and tools made from bone or antler. They tied spare poles to their ponies and followed the hunters.

At Big Cheeks' command, Bridget mounted the mule and joined the group. They followed up a steep hill and when she rounded the other side, her eyes widened. The horse herd had been a marvelous sight, but the herd of buffalo stretched in an endless wave of brown shaggy humps. Their stench filled her nostrils, making her gag.

The hunting party spread out, flanking the herd. The mass of animals began to move, slowly at first, then thundering loud. Men raced alongside, darting in and out among the animals while they loosed arrows. If she hadn't seen their cruelty, she'd admire their skilled and fluid movements, but she buried that feeling below disdain.

As soon as the hunt started, the women followed at a distance. Dark spots of dead buffalo lay scattered over the prairie and the women spread out to start their butchering. Big Cheeks dragged Bridget into the commotion and shoved a knife at her. The weapon was old and the blade so dull and worn it was practically useless. Could she use it to escape?

She wouldn't get far on the mule, and it'd be futile to try and hide the knife. Big Cheeks was watching from the corner of her eye, as though testing to see what she would do. If she failed now, she'd never get another chance to gain trust. It was better to let them think she'd forgotten about escaping, then make a move when they didn't expect it. Funny thing was, she was already starting to forget.

Following Big Cheeks's guidance, she shoved the knife against the tough buffalo hide. Nothing happened, not even a puncture. Big Cheeks let out a burst of laughter. It was obvious she'd been made the wrong end of a joke.

"Why you...!" She bit her lip to hold in the insult. Big Cheeks had a well-sharpened knife in her hand.

It wasn't fair. They expected her to help, but what was she supposed to do with a useless knife? She'd butchered pigs and goats before, but nothing as large as a buffalo. Blood drained from a slit in the animal's throat and pooled into a rawhide bowl. She eased the blade into the slit at an angle, separating the flesh from the hide and pulling on the skin with her other hand. It came away as she tugged, and she smiled with satisfaction.

While she helped remove the hides, the women split open the carcasses and emptied the insides. Steaming intestines, slippery stomachs, and livers so deeply red they were almost black slid onto the grass. Big Cheeks and the other women consumed the raw organs with eagerness. Hunters joined them, sucking on the entrails draped around their necks. They dribbled bile onto bloody livers and bit into them with relish.

Her stomach roiled from the smell, and she covered her nose with the collar of the old dress. Big Cheeks passed her pieces of raw kidney but she scrunched her nose and turned away. Nor would she drink the warm blood collected in a rawhide bowl, although she did try the clumps of clotted milk from stomachs of calves, feeling nostalgic for her old dairy cow.

Once the carcass was empty, Big Cheeks showed her how to cut long, flat strips of meat and lay them on a sheet of rawhide. The juicy red piles stirred her hunger. Those bits of meat she'd been given a few days before had tasted delicious. Keeping that thought in her mind, she got to work, but two boys would grab at the pieces she set down, then dart away laughing as they ate.

She sneered at the filthy urchins, giving a particular stink eye to one boy who'd come by her pile multiple times. "Smelly goat head! I hope the Devil makes a ladder out of your bones and uses it to pick apples.

In *Hell's* orchard." It felt daring to say those words, especially when Papa wasn't there to punish her for swearing.

The boy made a face like a snake and snapped back words that sounded equally scathing. Huffing, she gathered up the skirt of her old dress, ready to chase him. She'd taken three steps before Big Cheeks grabbed her collar and yanked her back. She smacked her cheek with the flat of her knife and shoved her to the ground. The woman made a comment to the boy and smiled at him. He laughed, smirking as smug as a rooster.

Bridget got to her feet and shot the woman a glare. Big Cheeks brandished her sharp knife, but she stood her ground. "Why should I do all this work if those boys are going to ruin it?" And why was she being punished when she was doing exactly what she'd been told?

The knife swung closer, about to expose her insides. Bridget backed up but bounced against something solid. She turned to find another woman behind her. This woman was immense in size. Her hair was loose and greasy, and she smelled worse than the cabbage moccasins. In her hand, she held one of the quirts she'd seen the men use to spur their horses to faster speeds. Its long-braided lashes dragged on the ground.

Bridget tried to run but the huge woman used her wide belly to knock her to the ground. A glimpse of the quirt came only seconds before the lashes hit her back. She gasped at each agonizing hit, each sting echoed by the next lash that came again and again. She tried to crawl away, but Big Cheeks grabbed her hair and neck, holding her in place.

"Stop! No more, please!" She pressed her face into the already bloodied ground, mixing in her own tears and spittle.

It wasn't the first beating she'd endured, but the others had been deserved. She'd been wicked and disobedient, and Papa had been teaching her a lesson. Sometimes she didn't think she always deserved such a harsh punishment, but it was hard to argue with Papa.

But these women were evil and cruel, just as devilish as the men in their company. She hadn't done anything wrong, as far as she could tell. Simply by existing, they'd found fault with her. She was the enemy and there was nothing she could do about it.

Her hands gripped the earth, and she prayed to endure this beating like she had Papa's punishments. The lashes stopped. She peered over her shoulder through strands of tangled hair.

Huge One sat in the grass, gasping for breath. She leaned on one hand and wiped at her sweaty brow. At her command, the people watching grabbed her arms and sides and struggled to bring her to feet. Was she about to strike again? Bridget tensed, but Huge One staggered away and the others went back to work.

Rising on shaky legs, she bent an arm to feel her back. The old dress was ripped in a few places and her back was sticky with blood, but the skin was only open in a few places. The wounds weren't as bad as she felt, and the pain paled in comparison to the humiliation. Usually, she could lick her wounds in private, or sometimes with Maggie's help, apply a bandage, but she stood in the grass among the laughter and teasing jaunts of the same children who were to blame.

Big Cheeks continued to cut strips of meat like nothing had happened, though she probably wouldn't be giving Bridget a knife. The woman used hand signals until Bridget understood she was supposed to take the loaded mule back to camp. Wiping her nose, she took the reins and limped to the main camp. Flies buzzed as much around her as they did the meat-loaded mule.

No one noticed her tears as she hung the strips on a wooden rack. Why would anyone offer sympathy? She was nothing and no one.

When the others returned, the old man sat in front of his lodge along with other warriors. They cracked open bones and sucked out the marrow, as indifferent to her as they were the flies. Whenever the old man spoke, everyone stopped to listen. If he was the chief, no one would go against him to help her.

She glanced at the three women who bustled around to feed the man and his guests. Old One must be his wife and the others were probably daughters, but as the women passed him, he patted their rumps and made comments that made others laugh. She didn't need to speak the language to know the nature of those comments. She'd heard Indians often had more than one wife, sinful heathens.

That night, she lay on her stomach and tried to sleep despite the sting in her back. Someone entered the lodge, and she stiffened. Another beating? But it was the girl again, Mouse. As the old woman had done before, she lifted Bridget's tattered clothes and brought a cool cloth to her wounds.

Bridget remained frozen until the gentle touch and the unexpected kindness broke through. One by one, her muscles gave way, and her body sank into the bedding. She sobbed as Mouse stroked her hair and murmured in rhythmic words. A song.

A memory of her mother sprang forth, a voice singing her to sleep. It'd been so long since she'd experienced a mother's nurture. How strange that she should be kidnapped and taken by savages in order to experience it again. Did the person who had Maggie treat her with care?

She sat up. "Do you know where my sister is?"

Mouse shook her head, but it only meant she didn't comprehend.

Bridget grabbed the piece of rawhide that had been her plate and a piece of charcoal from the fire. On it, she drew two figures, one shorter than the other. She pointed to the taller one, then tapped her chest. "This is me." Then she pointed at the smaller image. "This is Maggie, my sister. Where is she?"

Mouse's eyes widened with understanding. She took the charcoal and drew what looked to be a man and a woman. Then she circled the figures along with the one of Maggie.

"Are you saying Maggie is with these people? Who are they? Can I see her?"

Mouse glanced out the door, then set the rawhide aside. She said a few words Bridget didn't know, then hurried out.

"Wait, come back." But Mouse was gone.

The next day, Big Cheeks gave her a brief lesson on how to scrape flesh and fat from a buffalo hide and tossed her a tool. She made a few swipes with the blade, wincing from the pain in her back with each movement. If she failed at this, what sort of beating would come next? What would it take for them to kill her?

The sun beat hot on her back and her brow dripped with sweat as she worked. She hummed the song Mouse had sung the night before. It brought little comfort. When she was finished, the hide came out gouged and uneven, with areas so thin she could see the hair on the other side, and other places where the skin was still thick and fleshy.

Big Cheeks scolded her for her poor efforts, waving her own scraping tool, but a beating never came.

Mouse approached, the decorations on her dress making a soft rattle. She took her own tool from a pouch and demonstrated the correct way to hold it. She placed the scraper against the hide, emphasizing the angle with a few words and a flourish of the hand, then made smooth, even strokes.

"You make it look so easy." Bridget picked up her scraper and copied Mouse's movements. Her strokes weren't as nice, but it was an improvement. "*Urako*," she whispered, which she'd learned meant thank you.

Mouse prattled on in Comanche while they worked in tandem. She tried to get Bridget to repeat the names for the things around them, but after a few failures, Bridget held up her hand, pointed to herself, and said, "My name is Bridget O'Connell."

She tried the same technique the girl had before, tapping her chest and repeating her name, but Mouse remained silent.

"You won't say it, will you? What's wrong? You'll teach me your language, but you won't even learn my name? Can you at least tell me why I'm here? Where's my sister? What's going to happen to me?"

Mouse chewed on her lip and looked over her shoulder at Big Cheeks and the other women.

Bridget dropped her voice to a whisper. "Will you help me escape? I need a horse. You know, a horse?" She drew one in the dirt, trying to remember the word for the animals so abundant around them. Mouse grabbed her hand, stopping her. Her thin brows furrowed in sorrow, but her mouth was set in reproach.

"What is it?"

She put her finger to Bridget's lip, an unmistakable signal of silence. She then jumped to her feet and scurried away. As Bridget's eyes followed, they landed on the three wives, who'd obviously been listening, spies who made sure Mouse's friendship came with limitations.

———◆———

Mouse and her parents joined Red Hawk and his three wives outside their lodge, enjoying a second round of feasting after the successful hunt. They had delicious roasted meat with honeyed broth and boiled wapato roots mixed with late spring shoots.

When a lull in the conversation left everyone quiet, Two Horns said, "My daughter has told me she's been teaching the fire-headed one the tongue of our people."

"We've seen them together," said Deer Hoof, one of Red Hawk's daughters. Everyone looked at Mouse and she prepared herself for their admonishment. Her grandparents had asked her to help, but perhaps she'd done too much.

"We should all be glad for this," Red Hawk said and looked at Mouse. "I hoped you would be able to soften the hard heart of the white-skin child."

She relaxed at his smile. "I don't know if her heart has softened," she said, "but when we talk together, she's pleasant enough, but... she's sad. She wants to know where her white sister is."

"Did you tell her anything?" Winged Woman asked.

Mouse wondered how much to say. It wasn't as though she'd really revealed much. "We can hardly understand each other." She understood why it was necessary to keep the girls apart. They'd adapt quicker and forget their old ways, but was it so wrong to have explained that the yellow-haired girl had been adopted?

"She has much to learn, and she may still be angry," Winged Woman said, "but I think she will be able to become *Nʉmʉnʉʉ*, one of the People."

Mouse smiled, imagining the hot-tempered girl as one of them. She'd like to braid her wild red hair.

"Do you think we should give her a name?" Red Hawk asked.

"I thought she already had a name," Two Horns said. "Fire Girl."

Red Hawk smiled, "That name is good for her. It matches her looks as well as her nature. *Kuuna Tuepɨt.* Fire Girl."

"Are we adopting her then?" Winged Woman picked at a bone.

Mouse twisted the fringe of her dress around her fingers. If Red Hawk adopted the girl, her life would get much easier. Sharp Mouth wouldn't dare beat her again.

"I've thought about it," Red Hawk said. "Eagle Beak, my cousin's son, has asked about taking Fire Girl. Since his daughter is gone, he needs another woman to help with the baby. He can't afford a second wife, so he's offered to raise Fire Girl as his own. I told him I'd have to ask you, my wives, since you have depended on her help already. Would it burden you if I let Eagle Beak take her?"

Winged Woman didn't answer immediately, and Mouse said a quiet prayer. Eagle Beak and Pretty Robe were honorable and kind. They'd shown no hatred towards the white-skin girl though they had every reason to. Sending the girl to them would be even better than Red Hawk adopting her himself.

Laughing Bird opened her mouth, about to protest since she'd been the one to use the girl's help the most, but Winged Woman shot her a look that made the woman's jaw shut and her round cheeks jiggle. Even if she had spoken up, it would have made little difference. Laughing Bird and Squirrel might have been younger, but first wives were often favorites, and Winged Woman was especially so to Red Hawk.

"It will be good if Fire Girl becomes Eagle Beak's daughter," Winged Woman said. "She can help them and perhaps they will be of help to her."

Mouse released the coil of fringe from her fingers. The decision was final. Eagle Beak would adopt Fire Girl.

6

B ridget chewed on her dry lips as she limped after the old chief. They passed several lodges and racks of drying meat. The smell brought moisture to her mouth which she eagerly swallowed to wet her parched throat. The summer sun beat down and she shaded her eyes to keep him in sight. "Where are you taking me?" she asked, knowing he couldn't understand. Was she going to be beaten and tortured? Were they finally going to kill her?

He hadn't bound or restrained her in any way. She could run, get to one of the horses like she'd planned, but although she could walk short distances, running was still too difficult.

The old chief stopped before a lodge she'd never seen, an eagle with outstretched wings painted on its hide cover. A stocky, middle-aged man with slightly bowed legs came out. Behind him came a woman carrying a baby in a wrapped bundle. They didn't look dangerous. In fact, both smiled at Bridget, and she tried to make out the words of their conversation with the chief.

The bow-legged man gestured to a couple of horses tied nearby but the old chief shook his head. He gave Bridget a curt nod, then walked away.

"Wait? Are you leaving me here?" She turned to follow. He was her enemy, but at least he was familiar.

The woman with the baby reached out for her hand. Bridget pulled away, but the woman' expression gave her pause. Kindness shone in her eyes. The hold on her hand was gentle, and without threat. Her cropped hair and the fresh wounds on her arms were like Old One's, the woman who first tended her leg wound.

"*Ihka*," the woman said and gestured with her hand.

Bridget understood enough to know she had been invited into the lodge, so she followed the woman inside.

The space was sparsely furnished, though orderly and clean. Towards the rear sat two backrests and a few stacks of robes, and along the edge lay several pouches and containers. The inner lining was painted in bright red and yellow. If circumstances had been different, she might have called the home cheerful.

The bow-legged man pointed out a simple reed pallet with buffalo blankets.

"*Nohrʉna, ʉpʉi sikʉ*," She caught him saying the word bed and sucked in her breath. Did he expect her to lie with him? Had she been traded to be the man's wife? She'd heard of such horrors before.

The kind woman raised her eyebrows at the man in a look she remembered her mother giving her father when she thought he was mucking things up. The man shrugged and left the lodge.

The woman spoke again, but in words too quick to catch. She handed the baby to Bridget, who scrambled to get her arms around the bundle before the woman joined her husband outside. Their hushed voices carried through the opening.

"Now what?" Bridget held the baby with outstretched arms and tried not to look at it. The child whimpered, getting ready to cry. If she didn't calm it, the husband might return to punish her like Papa did whenever Maggie made a fuss.

Pulling aside the soft doeskin blanket, she revealed a pair of huge brown eyes. The baby appeared to be between six months and a year, with two tiny teeth in his lower gums. No longer whimpering, the baby stared back with equal curiosity. She smiled and grazed his plump cheek with her finger. The baby rewarded her with a happy squeal and a drooly smile.

The Kind Woman returned to the doorway and beckoned with a crooked finger. Still confused about why she was there, Bridget sighed and carried the child out with her. Once outside, Kind Woman turned Bridget around and tied the baby to her back using the straps attached to the firm cradle board.

"What are you doing?" She flinched since her back was still sore. Why was this woman putting her in charge of a baby?

The woman gripped her shoulders and spoke in a stern tone, forcing Bridget to stand still. She repeated the words in a softer voice as she tied the straps, but it wasn't clear whether she was talking to her or the baby.

Kind Woman gestured once more. "*Ihka,*" she said, urging Bridget to follow.

Bridget gritted her teeth but obeyed. It was getting tiresome, always following people and doing what she was told.

The woman led her to a grove of mesquite trees full of green pods. A trickling sound from the nearby creek reminded Bridget of her thirst, but she didn't know how to ask for a drink.

Under the spotty shade, women sat in a circle, sewing what appeared to be a new lodge cover. They glanced at Bridget and made comments to each other, but their faces were not unfriendly.

Kind Woman sat with them and patted the ground next to her. "*Ihka̱ karʉ.*" She held up a bone awl and pointed to a hide marked with a dotted pattern along the edge. With the point of the awl, she dug into one of the impressions until the end poked through the other side.

They wanted her to sew. Bridget had never been very competent at sewing.

She took the awl from Kind Woman and copied the task. Wiggling the awl back and forth, she pushed against the tough leather. It wasn't as easy as the woman had made it look, but finally the awl poked through.

Kind Woman made a sound of satisfaction and set to work. She took a coil of sinew string from her tool pouch and put it in her mouth, then picked up a sliver of bone and threaded it with the end drawn from between her lips. She used the needle to sew the hides together, pulling lengths of sinew from her mouth as needed.

Bridget continued to poke more holes, but it wasn't long before her fingers began to ache. Still, she kept at the task. It was better than scraping hides.

The women continued their conversation, ignoring Bridget, which suited her fine. As she listened to the women's chatter, she pictured sewing circles back in North Carolina where women pieced calico into a patterned quilt. *Sometimes, no matter where you go, folks are the same.* The thought surprised her as soon as it came.

After poking the last hole in the hide, she set it down in relief. Kind Woman handed her a fresh one with marks all around the trimmed edges.

"How many hides did it take to make a lodge cover?" she mumbled under her breath.

Kind Woman gave her the sort of look that suggested she understood Bridget's meaning even if she didn't know the words.

Bridget picked up the new hide and continued to work.

After five more holes, she sensed eyes on her and glanced up. A woman joined the circle. It was Huge One who'd lashed her with the quirt. She stared at Bridget with malice then turned to a friend beside her, whispering something that made the other woman laugh into her cupped hand. The remark had obviously been at Bridget's expense.

She fumed and tucked her legs under, ready to run or fight, but the woman picked up a hide and focused on her sewing. The other women settled back into their work, showing no sign of immediate threat. She examined each of their faces. Which ones had hit or kicked her when she almost escaped? Which had laughed when Huge One had lashed her. Had Kind Woman joined in?

She was sitting with enemies. Yet sewing, with one of their babies on her back. She met Kind Woman's curious eyes. There was understanding and patience in those eyes. She ducked her head and concentrated on the awl. Maybe these women, all but Huge One and Big Cheeks, weren't so terrible. Fierce One, though... he was the worst. If only she could dig the awl into *his* hide.

All morning long Bridget worked the awl. The baby mostly slept until Kind Woman loosened the strap and took the baby out. She took a small amount of meat from her pouch, chewed it, and then slipped the mush into the baby's mouth. He smacked his lips and gummed the meat.

Bridget held in a grimace of disgust.

"*Tuhkapu*?" Kind Woman asked, using one of the few words Bridget had learned.

She accepted the portion of meat and while she chewed, the baby stared with wide eyes. He opened his mouth like a bird waiting to be fed. His eagerness turned to frustration, and he whimpered. With a guilty pang, she fished out a bit of the mashed meat and scrunched her nose while she pushed it past his lips.

Kind Woman laughed, then she quieted, and her eyes shone with emotion. Her brows drew down with sudden sorrow. She wiped her cheeks and went back to work.

Her odd reaction left Bridget mystified, but everyone and everything around her was a mystery. She resumed her work and when at last she was allowed to stop for the day, her fingers were sore and bleeding.

Kind Woman brought Bridget indoors and removed the cradle board from her back. She told Bridget to sit while she rummaged through a stack of containers, then produced a small tin. She picked up Bridget's hand and applied a sweet-smelling salve to her sores, using a delicate touch as she smoothed the ointment over her fingers.

Bridget tensed, still unused to such displays of care. She stared at the recent wounds on the woman's arms. They were in neat lines, like carefully cut rows of anguish. Her chest panged with surprising sympathy.

The woman sensed her gaze. She pulled her hands away then brought out a container of ground corn and another of dried herbs to prepare the evening meal.

Bridget searched for a word Mouse had taught her, and when she recalled it, she pointed at herself and said in Comanche, "*Tʉkʉman-inʉ*."

The woman gave her a wide-eyed stare, but grinned and nodded. She sat on the bedding and changed the baby's swaddling.

Bridget wasn't sure why she'd offered to help instead of waiting for orders like she'd done with Big Cheeks, but this woman wasn't like Big Cheeks. She was gentle and patient and clearly grieving for someone.

After removing ashes from the fire pit outside, Bridget blew on the still-warm embers. She took strips of meat from the drying rack and dropped them into the pot hanging over the fire, then added water from bladders hung near the doorway and sprinkled in crushed herbs. While the stew heated, she mixed broth with the ground corn and patted the mixture into round cakes, making sure they came out well-shaped, unlike her first attempt. She set them on flat rocks beside the fire to cook. After the food was ready, Kind Woman directed her to bring the meal inside.

Soon after, the bow-legged man entered the lodge with another, younger warrior. They greeted the woman, and the young warrior went to the baby and stroked his cheek. He had the hard and calloused hands of a man used to rough work, hands that took lives without mercy, but there was no question of the love he displayed. She watched his blank face crack with grief that he quickly smoothed away before joining the other man.

Kind Woman spoke to her husband in earnest, no doubt telling him about Bridget's successes that day. The bow-legged man gave Bridget a satisfied smile and told her to sit. The chief's family had never allowed her to join them for meals, but her status was still unclear. Was she a slave or something more?

The brief calm became disrupted by the young warrior's disdainful glare. He seemed just as hateful as Fierce One, but she remembered the way Fierce One had given her that smug smile when she stared him down. She didn't have the courage to glare at this man now.

After they ate, Bow-legged man reached behind his backrest for a long case, then slid out a pipe and pouch of tobacco. Kind Woman immediately got to her feet and took Bridget's hand, leading her out. They took the baby with them, while the men remained inside to smoke and talk.

The woman ducked into a lodge next door. It was becoming clear that most men had their own lodges separate from their wives, especially if they had more than one. But what happened when men and women wanted to sleep together? She blushed and forced the indecent thought away.

She lay on a pile of bedding while the woman took the baby out of his board and sang and crooned to him. She closed her eyes, listening. The woman's voice broke, as if she was crying, but Bridget pretended to sleep, wondering who it was that deserved everyone's grief.

It'd been less than a month since the wagon raid and the couple continued to treat her with kindness. Most people had accepted her and no longer worried she was about to be killed or beaten, Bridget focused on learning about the people around her. She could speak enough to have her needs met and ask simple questions.

Bow-legged man and Kind Woman became known by their true names, Eagle Beak and Pretty Robe. Their grandson was Round Eyes, and the young warrior, Fox Laugh, was the baby's father recently widowed. Anytime she tried to ask what happened to the baby's mother, Pretty Robe would hush her and not speak of it.

Each morning, Bridget went to the river to collect water. She strolled along the flattened grass of the camp, carrying empty bladders to fill. A group of dogs ran past, followed by young children who almost knocked her over.

"Careful," she said in Comanche.

A boy turned and grinned. "Sorry, *Kuuna Tuepït*."

She paused, struck dumb not only by the boy's polite response, but by the name he'd called her. She opened her mouth to ask him, but the children had already run ahead.

She continued to the edge of camp, where the grass reached her knees. Heat prickled her skin, adding to the already numerous freckles and peeling sunburn. She passed under a grove of pawpaw trees, their bright green leaves providing welcome shade. She picked one and crushed it between her fingers, wrinkling her nose at the smell that reminded her of rotting meat.

Heading down the slope to the stream, she spotted Mouse among the other women and girls completing the same chore.

"*Haa maruawe!*" She greeted them as friends, though she didn't know the other girls' names. They were a few years older, like Mouse, but not quite women.

Mouse gave her a friendly smile. "This is Antelope and Rain On the Lodge."

Bridget smiled politely but the girls exchanged smug glances, then gathered their things to leave. The one called Antelope whispered to Mouse as she left, but it was too quick to catch.

She turned to Mouse. "They don't like me."

"They don't know you."

"Who is *Kuuna Tuepit*?"

Mouse pointed to Bridget's chest. "*En tzaré Kuuna Tuepit.*"

"*Kuuna Tuepit*," she repeated. "*Kuuna*, that's fire... Oh wait, I get it. Fire, like my hair." She laughed then touched her hair to show she understood. "And *Tuepit*, that's girl, like you and me." She pointed to Mouse and herself.

Mouse giggled, a sound like rippling water. "Not just your hair." She tapped Bridget's forehead.

"Yes, that too. I was always told I had a temper," she said in English.

Mouse's fingers pressed on her lips, a sign of silence.

When she took them away, Bridget added in Comanche, "I must speak like *Nʉmʉnʉʉ*?"

Mouse nodded, "*Haa*, Yes."

Bridget frowned. She didn't want to upset Mouse, but she didn't want to become an Indian. "I will try," she lied.

After she filled her water bags, she and Mouse started toward the lodges. Since there were no adults around, none of Red Hawk's wives to spy on them, she grabbed Mouse's hand and searched for the right Comanche words. "Where is my sister?"

Mouse pursed her lips and made the same search with her eyes for spies. "Your white sister is not with this band, but she is well-cared for."

"But—"

"You mustn't ask about her. If you ever want to see your sister again, then you must forget her. Pretty Robe and Eagle Beak are your family now. Be grateful for their kindness." Mouse squeezed her hand, both in reassurance and to signal she would say no more. "I must go."

What did Mouse mean by forgetting Maggie in order to see her again? She was grateful Pretty Robe and Eagle Beak were kind to her, but not everyone was kind. Besides, Maggie was her sister. She promised to protect her.

Since there was nothing she could do at the moment, she headed back to the lodge. A group of women cut off the path from the opposite direction. It was Sharp Mouth, the Huge One who'd beaten her and Big Cheeks who she now knew was called Laughing Bird.

Sharp Mouth curled her lip in disgust. "Here comes that Nothing Girl," she said to Laughing Bird.

Despite her apparent acceptance, insults were still commonplace, like the way Antelope and Rain On the Lodge had snubbed her. She ignored them, especially since Laughing Bird was one of the chief's wives.

She tried to hurry past, but Sharp Mouth bumped her arm, causing her to drop her skins and spill her load of water. The women laughed and continued down the path.

"Bitter hags," she mumbled. The skin on her back remembered Sharp Mouth's lashings. She wanted to pummel the woman, but Eagle

Beak might punish her if she did. He'd never threatened her, but he was still a warrior, and she was afraid to test him.

She sighed, returned to the stream, and refilled her bags. When she approached the lodge, Eagle Beak stood outside with the young warrior, Fox Laugh. The men argued. She couldn't make out the words but read the sharp tone and stern faces. Fox Laugh gestured in her direction. He glared, spoke curtly, then strode off.

Once they were gone, she refused to meet Eagle Beak's eyes and find his own hatred. It didn't take much to remind her of the raid, and that each of the men she encountered were likely ones to have been there fighting and killing the people she once knew. She left the water with Pretty Robe and hurried out to collect firewood.

After the day's encounters, she wouldn't be surprised if she ran into the tall warrior with the gray horse, Fierce One. She hadn't seen him since the night he left with the other warriors. At least she didn't have to worry about his intimidating stare, but one day he might return, and she would be ready for him.

7

December 1837

Winter approached with its chill. Outside the lodge, the last leaves clung to dark oak branches, shivering in the icy wind. Fire Girl finished the last stitches on a pair of winter moccasins lined with rabbit fur. She surveyed her quillwork on the instep, and content with her skill, put them on Round Eyes' feet. After placing him back on the pile of buffalo robes so he could play with the toy horse Eagle Beak had fashioned from a piece of wood, she built up the fire that had nearly died.

Pretty Robe entered and looked at the child. "You finished the moccasins. They look good."

"Thank you. I'm surprised they don't look lopsided."

"It's well that you finished. Red Hawk has decided to break camp tomorrow, then we'll go to the winter camp."

Bridget's fist tightened on the piece of kindling. They'd be moving again. Every time they did, she was further and further away from where she last saw Maggie.

"You worry," Pretty Robe said. "I know Eagle Beak hoped for one last hunt, so we'd have enough food to last the winter. We shall manage with what we have."

Managing was all she'd been doing for the last few months. The tiniest hope that someone would find her still lived in her heart. She fed her hopes with the idea that long as the camp remained within a certain distance of where the wagons had been raided, she might be rescued, but Pretty Robe and Eagle Beak couldn't know she still thought of escape.

She tucked a loose strand of hair back into her braid. "We shall have enough, I think."

The next morning, she helped her foster parents load pack horses for the journey. Eagle Beak said they were headed to a small range of mountains in the northeast. As they traveled, she looked over her shoulder at the path behind them, but a dusting of snow drifted and covered the trail, as though no one had passed through.

The journey was slow and noisy, and cold winds plagued them. Pretty Robe had given her a small buffalo hide to wear as a robe for warmth, but the chill found its way through gaps in the hide. After three days they reached the mountains. A ridge of reddish gray rocks formed jagged peaks, while the surrounding land rolled with bluegrass dotted with black oak and juniper.

Eagle Beak followed the rest of the travelers and Fire Girl maneuvered the old nag along the stoney path behind him, winding around boulders and thorny prickly pear.

Other bands had already set up camps deep in the valleys, hidden from view until they were far within the granite ridges. A narrow creek carved its way through slabs of rock, and lodges lined the shore until they disappeared behind a bluff.

People hurried to the arrivals, greeting each other with hugs and laughter. While they reveled in their good humor, her hopes shrank. If anyone was still looking for her, they'd never find her in those mountains.

"Our people, the *Kotsoteka,* Buffalo Eaters, will be camped with the *Yamparika,* the Root Eaters," Eagle Beak explained. "Everyone is happy because relatives and friends who haven't seen each other since spring are now reunited."

Something about the reunion made her anxious but she couldn't place her misgivings, nor did she trust her voice, so kept silent and watched the greetings.

Red Hawk, the old chief, moved through the crowd with unusual determination, He called a name, "*Ata Esa,* Lone Wolf."

A tall young warrior, stepped from the crowd, the one who'd captured her. The two men grasped each other's forearms in a formal greeting, then embraced tightly.

She pressed her hand against the horse's withers to steady herself, lowering her head so Eagle Beak and Pretty Robe couldn't see her flushed face. She'd almost forgotten about Fierce One, or wait, his name was Lone Wolf. Hope took a final breath, and all her hatred returned like fuel thrown onto a fire.

"Are you unwell?" Pretty Robe asked.

Bridget forced her face into something neutral. "I'm fine, *Pia,* Mother. Only tired from all this riding. Where are we setting up camp?"

"Let this crowd disperse. Then we'll find a clearing," Eagle Beak said. "After everyone is settled, we'll join Red Hawk in his gathering lodge for a feast."

"Why with him?" she blurted.

Eagle Beak's eyes narrowed at the panic in her voice. "I forget you're still new to our customs, but Red Hawk will host a feast after reuniting with his grandson after all these months."

"No, *you* forget," Pretty Robe said, "Lone Wolf left before Fire Girl became our daughter. She doesn't know him."

It was an odd thing to say, since Lone Wolf had been the one to bring her there, but it was true. She didn't know him at all.

Fire Girl followed Eagle Beak and Pretty Robe to Red Hawk's lodge for the welcome feast. Lone Wolf sat at Red Hawk's right, in a place of honor. As soon as she entered, the weight of his presence pressed on her chest. She struggled to breathe, caught in the memory of him standing over her with his knife, tackling to hold her down when she'd come so close to escape.

People talked while they ate, but she didn't listen to the conversation. All she could think about was how she could get a hold of that knife and plunge it into Lone Wolf's chest. Her attention shifted when she heard a word hardly ever spoken among The People. *Taibo*, white man. She turned to the speaker, a large, muscular warrior called Badger.

"We came upon the hair-mouths in the afternoon, so we waited until dark," he said. "Only one of them kept watch, so Big Tooth put an arrow in him, but he screamed like a coward and woke up the others. They came at us with their guns." He paused to take a large bite of meat, but the audience waited in silence for him to continue.

71

It was painful to wait, and Bridget's heart pounded her in her chest so hard she wondered if everyone could hear the drumming. Would those white men come for her?

"The battle wasn't long, but the hair-mouths fought well. We didn't lose anyone, but Turtle was wounded." He winked at a young man sitting across from him, the boy she'd seen guarding the horses the night the warriors left. A fresh scar marked his shoulder.

"Maybe we should call you, Hides in His Shell," Badger said. The men laughed, but Turtle scowled. "Anyway, we had trouble getting out of there. We decided to split up, staying in other camps for the rest of the summer." He held up a large pistol and a rifle. "We took their guns and extra powder." The listeners responded with chattered excitement. She'd not seen many firearms since coming to the People.

Badger then tugged at a decoration on his and Lone Wolf's shirts, "Look at the scalps we took. They look good on him." The lodge shook with laughter.

"Then I'm glad you went after those hair-mouths," Red Hawk said. "Our tracks are long gone and there will be no one to find our people." The guests nodded and murmured their relief.

Now she knew what the warriors were doing that night. They'd left to kill a group of men tracking them, tracking *her*. It was Lone Wolf's fault. He stole her and made sure no one would ever find her again.

She clenched her fists and fought the tears threatening to fall. She searched for a face that recognized her awkward predicament, but no one paid her any mind, except for the one person she wished never to see again. He gave her a look bordering on sympathy or was it just mockery? Since no one else seemed to care, she rose and hurried out.

As she wandered through the camp, she hid her face deep into her buffalo robe against the cold. She entered an area where another band had set up their lodges. Most people were inside where it was warm, giving her much needed solitude. She sat on a fallen log, coated in a layer of frost.

If only she'd escaped sooner. If only Eagle Beak and Pretty Robe hadn't been so kind to her, she might have had more determination to leave. Lone Wolf's return gave her plenty of reasons, but now she'd have to wait until spring.

The sound of a shifting lodge door caught her attention. A child came out, wrapped in a robe, probably on her way to relieve herself. Bridget watched with little interest. The robe slipped and before the child could readjust it, Bridget caught a glimpse of the face and a lock of fair hair.

"Maggie!" She jumped up and ran over, then dropped to her knees and hugged the girl. "Oh, you're alive," she said in a loud whisper. "You've no idea how happy I am to see you, little sister! This is a miracle."

"Bridget?" Maggie said. "I thought you were dead for sure."

"Well, I'm not. Come over here and let's be quiet." She gripped Maggie's hand and led her over to the log. "Listen, I've been thinking about getting outta here, and now that I have you, I know for sure we can leave—"

"But Briddie," Maggie said. "I don't wanna leave. I like it here, and where would we go anyways?"

Unprepared for that response, Bridget sat dumbstruck for a moment, staring at the sister who was *not* her sister. Maggie wore a red stripe of paint in the part of her hair, which wasn't as fair as it used to be, darkened with grease and charcoal. Long beaded earrings hung from pierced earlobes.

Bridget grew hot with anger. "Maggie! How dare you say such a thing. These people, they killed Pa. They killed everyone and took us away. Don't tell me you've forgotten that."

Maggie looked down. "I know, Briddie. It's just...we don't have anywhere to go...and they're nice to me."

"Well, me, I'd rather die than stay here a moment longer." She let the tears fall. "They beat me and put me through all sorts of suffering."

Maggie looked up. "They still doing that to you?"

"Well, no, not anymore, except for this one woman... but I know the man who took me. He's a scoundrel and I hate him."

Maggie stared at the ground.

"Oh Maggie, I can't leave you here, but I can't stay neither. There were some rangers, and we could've been saved, but they killed them, and that scoundrel wears their scalps. Scalps, Maggie!" She shook her sister's shoulders "They're heathens. Don't you remember your learning? We can't stay."

A couple emerged from the lodge where Maggie had come out. The father called to her, using a Comanche name. Bridget debated whether to take off with her sister or not, but Maggie broke free of her grasp and ran back into the lodge.

"Maggie!"

The man stared hard at Bridget. "You are not to come back here. Leave my daughter alone and go back to your own family."

"Maggie is my sister," she stammered in English. "She is my family," she said again in Comanche.

"She is *nuumu*." He stepped out threateningly. "If you try to take her, I will kill you, or I'll tell Red Hawk, and he will kill you. Now go."

She could hardly breathe. She'd found her sister, but Maggie had become one of them. While she... what was she now?

Defeated, her feet led her back to her own lodge. She could never escape in the winter and perhaps they'd make sure she never found Maggie again. At least her sister was alive and safe, even happy. Maybe Maggie had a point... No, that was impossible. It would be sinful to stay, but it was hard to hate the kind faces before her, and their kindness was infectious. She would save her hatred for Lone Wolf and Sharp Mouth and wait for an opportune moment to get her revenge.

At the winter camp, Fire Girl's chores were few, so she had enough leisure time to visit Mouse. With her friend, she rarely thought about escape or revenge. Mouse taught her games and told stories about Coyote and his clever ways, or of Big Cannibal Owl who haunted the mountains and stole wicked children. The story Fire Girl liked best was about a girl who loved a star but transformed into a bush to be with him.

"This way, she could forever be under the desert sky and see the star she loved," Mouse said. "But when the star saw what she had done, he leaned down over her. He leaned so far, he fell from the sky. His light shattered into tiny pieces, coating the leaves of the shrub with white. His body transformed into purple flowers. This plant still grows in the desert. It is the purple sage."

In the second month of winter, a fierce storm hit, covering the camp in a blanket of snow. The following morning, Mouse took Fire Girl to a nearby slope where they played with other young people and children, throwing snowballs and sliding down a hill on a sheet of rawhide. For a time, she was too carefree to consider herself a captive.

She plopped onto a boulder, warm from exertion but chilled in her fingers and toes. She had stuffed her moccasins with rabbit fur and buffalo hair, but the damp seeped through.

"Rub them with beeswax mixed with grease," Mouse said. "They won't get so wet."

She smiled and squeezed Mouse's hand. "How did you get to be so clever?"

"It's not cleverness. Everyone knows how to keep their moccasins dry."

Every day she learned something new, but also came to realize how much she didn't know.

She watched a boy slide down the slope. Two older boys on either side lifted a rope between them just as the sledder came past. His neck hit the line, knocking him back and the other boys laughed.

"Did you see that?" she hopped to her feet. "Where are their fathers? Someone should punish them."

Mouse frowned. "Punish them? What for?"

"That was mean. How else will they know it was wrong?"

Mouse lifted a brow. "The boy they knocked down burnt *his* little sister with a hot coal two days ago." She pointed at the boy running with the coiled rope while the one who was knocked down chased after him. He caught up, shoved him into the snow, and kicked him in the gut before striding away. "See, looks to me like each one got what they deserved."

"But—" Fire Girl looked around. There were adults in the area, but none seemed concerned with the children's actions. Back home, all those boys would have been whipped and sent to bed without supper. The memory of her own harsh whipping from Sharp Mouth's quirt made her back tingle. "Then how come last summer, I was beaten when I didn't obey Laughing Bird, but the boys who stole meat weren't punished at all?"

Mouse gave her a look of sympathy, placing a hand on her arm. "That was before you were one of us."

"But those boys stole from me."

"How can they learn to sneak up on an enemy and take his horse if they don't practice? You should have done a better job of guarding the meat."

She crossed her arms. "Are you saying I should have punished them myself?"

"Maybe." Mouse glanced at the sun. "I must go home. I promised Quick Hands I would prepare the evening meal." She bundled her robe tighter around her as she trudged away through the snow.

On her way home, Fire Girl gathered wood for Pretty Robe. She ventured toward the outskirts of camp where wood was still plentiful. The snow crunched under her feet while she searched the ground. She didn't notice Sharp Mouth, Laughing Bird, and one of their friends until they stood in front of her. No one else was around.

"Look at you, too stupid to stay alert when walking alone. Don't you know any better?" Sharp Mouth said.

The memory of Sharp Mouth's quirt lashes froze her limbs.

"Perhaps she thinks her skin will hide her, pale as it is," Laughing Bird added.

"It's not pale, see how red and patchy it is?" The third woman laughed. "How can something that ugly hide anywhere?"

Bridget flinched. She hated being reminded of her ruddy skin.

Sharp Mouth sneered, making her cheeks puff up and her eyes shrink into tiny slits. "She couldn't stay hidden when Lone Wolf found her."

Tears burned at the corners of her eyes. How dare they bring up her capture. "Shut your stupid mouth!"

"What can you do? We can say what we want about you. You're nothing. You think you can become *nuumu*, one of the People, but you will always be nothing," Sharp Mouth said.

Rage boiled in her chest. She dropped her load of wood, all but one stout branch, and charged the large woman with the force of her hatred. The woman stumbled back, lost her footing on the ice, and went down. Fire Girl slammed the branch into her face with a satisfying thump.

The other two stood dumbly aside, mouths agape. She was gangly and bony, but she was tall and had grown strong. She beat Sharp Mouth's face with the branch, ignoring the others and hardly noticing when Laughing Bird ran yelling for help. The wood snapped, becoming useless. She tossed it aside, staining the snow with red, then dropped to her knees to use her small but hard fists. If only Laughing Bird could get the same treatment, and Lone Wolf with that stupid smile of his.

People clustered around, watching and laughing until Sharp Mouth screamed. Then someone dragged Fire Girl off and dropped her onto the hard snow. She lay there panting.

Others lifted Sharp Mouth to her feet. Fire Girl glared, narrowing her eyes until Sharp Mouth turned away and wiped at her bloodied face. The spectators departed, leaving her alone and without another glance. This time there were no teasing taunts or laughter. No one was going to beat her in return?

Her hands ached, throbbing, and the knuckles bruised and bloody. She stumbled to her feet and trudged home.

When she entered, Pretty Robe sat with Eagle Beak, Round Eyes in her lap.

"We heard what happened today," Pretty Robe said. It never took long for gossip to spread.

Fire Girl wiped the wet from under her nose, smearing blood onto her mouth. She licked the blood away and prepared for admonishment and whatever punishment awaited. She cringed, remembering Papa's belt lashes and Sharp Mouth's quirt, but that never hurt as much as the words that came with. Hot-headed. Insufferable. Useless. Worthless. Nothing. The same words she heard in the snow.

But instead of anger, Eagle Beak's eyes glinted with amusement and his mouth twitched to hide a smile.

Pretty Robe patted the space beside her. "Come and sit with us. You must be hungry." She handed her a strip of dried buffalo.

Fire Girl took it and sat. "You aren't angry?"

"Why should we be angry?" Eagle Beak said. "Did Sharp Mouth deserve her beating?"

She deserved that and more. Lone Wolf, too, but she simply said, "Yes."

He shrugged. "Then there's nothing to be angry about."

"I don't think we'll be seeing much of Sharp Mouth for a while," Pretty Robe said. "Or Laughing Bird."

"Good," she blurted, then covered her mouth. Better not to push her luck.

Eagle Beak laughed, and Pretty Robe reached for her hand. "Let me take care of those wounds for you. You'll still have to collect double the firewood tomorrow."

If that was the worst of her punishment, she'd gather a whole forest for Pretty Robe, her mother.

8

Spring 1838

The morning spring air chilled Fire Girl's forearms where they peeked out from beneath her old thin robe. She took a breath to settle her anticipation. Eagle Beak had spoken to her days before about teaching her how to use the bow. Her initial surprise was overcome with a feeling of pride and relief. They trusted her, but more than that, they saw her as an asset.

She followed her foster father to the edge of camp, leading an ancient mule loaded with supplies. She hoped Eagle Beak planned to make a trip of it and use the time to show her how to track prey, find water, and other skills for survival in the open plains. She smiled with pleasure when he cut two ponies from his small herd.

"Are we going far then?" she dared to ask.

"You need to learn how to ride."

"I can already ride."

Eagle Beak's mouth set in a serious frown, but his eyes twinkled with amusement. "You ride clumsily, like the hair-mouths. No daughter of mine will ride so poorly. You need to learn how to ride like one of the People."

Her heart skipped. Eagle Beak had never before referred to her as his daughter, and she'd never had the courage to call him Father. Guilt crept into her conscience. It had been almost a year since she joined the People, but her loyalties were still torn.

She nodded in acceptance of his criticism. She'd been envious of how well the People rode horses. Determined to learn how to handle a mount with equal ease and grace, she would make Eagle Beak and Pretty Robe proud.

After watching the way he mounted his horse, she tried to copy his fluid movements. While he made it seem effortless, she strained to pull herself up without the aid of stirrup or saddle. She followed his instructions to grip the horse with her legs and used the same squeeze to get the animal moving.

They rode in silence until they came to a copse of birch trees in the shallow before a small rise. Behind her, only lodge pole tips were visible in the distance. It was the first time she'd gone so far from the camp, and the idea of riding away to freedom briefly crossed her mind.

Eagle Beak's stoney expression suggested he knew her thoughts. She smiled, realizing she valued his opinion and desired his trust. He continued to give her a stern look and brought his horse beside her, so they were knee to knee.

"There are tracks nearby. Can you find them and tell me which animal they belong to, and how long ago it passed?"

Her natural father had taught her to read the tracks of deer, bear, wolf, and fox. Such a simple task would be easy to complete. She started to dismount but Eagle Beak waved his hand.

82

"Do it from your horse."

She hesitated. Could she find the tracks without being able to look closely at the ground? But she understood his reason. It'd be better to be able to spot animal signs from horseback in case there was danger and she'd need to ride away quickly.

She glanced at the ground from her position, and seeing nothing, turned the horse and scanned the area they'd passed, being sure to follow the path Eagle Beak had taken. She retreated about twenty paces before she stopped. As expected, Eagle Beak offered no help, and his face revealed nothing.

Copying her father's expression, she set her mouth in a determined frown and returned the way she had come. She passed Eagle Beak and looked to each side.

The grass to her right was shaded a darker color than the surrounding area. Dew had been wiped from the blades, leaving the grass slightly bent in a different direction. The animal had passed while the grass was wet, only hours before.

Her triumphant smile gave way to a frown. The tracks were obvious, and she'd failed to see them right away. Moreover, she still had to determine the animal.

Following the narrow path, she considered its width. The creature had to have been small. Not a bear or a deer. The body was low enough to cause the grass to bend. A fox maybe, or a wolf?

She'd yet to discover any prints but had an idea. So early in the spring, the animal might be shedding its winter coat. If she found any loose hairs sticking to the wet grass, that would help her to determine the type of animal. Once she knew what to look for, it wasn't hard to find. The hairs were light gray, almost white, and black at the tips. Wolf hairs. If only she could find actual tracks, she could confirm it.

She squinted to look closer at the ground.

"You can dismount now," Eagle Beak said.

She jumped down and peered at the trampled grass. There wasn't enough exposed soil to show a true print, so she turned her head to examine the ground at an angle. A few places showed where the grass had been compressed and enough time had passed that it had sprung back, but not completely. The size of the tracks was about the size she'd expect for a wolf's paw, though she'd never actually seen a wolf before. Didn't wolves usually travel in packs? Two animals would trample the grass like that, but anymore and she'd expect the path to be more worn.

She turned to Eagle Beak and grinned. "Two or more wolves passed this morning, not long after dawn. They headed south, toward the river perhaps?"

He nodded. "There were three of them, one a pup." At her look of surprise, he smiled. "Come, I'll show you how I know."

He pointed out the tracks she had missed. The faintest trail in the grass ran in a meandering pattern, zigzagging across the path left by the adult wolves. He even found a tiny paw print in the mud.

She listened to everything he had to say with rapt attention. By now, her real father would have ridiculed her mistakes, criticized every wrong move, but Eagle Beak spoke with patience and care. If she learned from him, perhaps she could survive in this world after all.

Fire Girl and her father spent more time discussing tracking before Eagle Beak brought out the small bow he'd made for her, and a simple quiver with several different types of arrows.

He explained the purpose of each. The hunting ones had narrow heads, easily removed from the bodies of deer or buffalo. The thin ones were for antelope, slender and swift to bring down such fast and delicately framed prey. He had a few war arrows too, their heads broad and barbed, meant to inflict as much damage and pain as possible.

"See these grooves?" He showed her the long channels carved into the lengths of the arrow shafts. "This is for the blood to drain, so your prey dies quickly."

She rubbed her thigh to feel the old scar through her thin dress, then pulled her hand away. It wasn't the time to think about those memories.

Eagle Beak strode further down the field and set up a few buffalo chips he'd brought along. "Try to hit these targets with your hunting arrows."

She'd never used a bow before but had seen enough to know how to hold it and draw the shaft back.

"I designed the bow so it doesn't require much strength to draw it, though that means it won't shoot as far," he explained.

She still had to strain to bend the bow far enough. Her arms shook with exertion and her fingertips ached against the sinew string. She released the shaft, not really surprised when it fell short and far to the left of its target.

"Try again, but this time, bring your hand all the way to your jaw, and keep your wrist straight."

The arrow traveled straighter, hitting closer to the target. She drew another from the quiver and aimed. The shaft landed just to the left of the buffalo chip. She made one more attempt. The arrow pierced the chip, crumbling it.

Though he wasn't smiling, Eagle Beak's eyes lit with approval.

The next two days they practiced, and soon she was aiming at moving targets, a small hoop he rolled along the ground. She also worked on her riding skills and tracked a deer, which Eagle Beak killed. After several more lessons she was sure she'd be able to contribute to the family's food supply.

When they returned to the camp, she went to visit Mouse. The older girl begged to see the bow and quiver, looking them over with eyes of admiration. "You're lucky Eagle Beak has taken his time to teach you how to hunt. Not many men would bother to train their daughters, but then again, Eagle Beak has no son."

"Do you know how to use a bow?" she asked.

"Not really."

"Would you like to? I'm sure Eagle Beak wouldn't mind. Then we could hunt together."

Mouse looked doubtful. "I'm not sure I want to. Besides, it's important you have Eagle Beak's complete attention."

Her meaning was unclear, but she wasn't surprised by her response. Mouse was a timid sort of girl, though she had strength of a different sort.

"Come," Mouse said. "We're moving camp tomorrow, and I want to gather as much clay as I can before we leave this site."

She and Mouse carried rawhide containers to the banks of a shallow stream where they collected white clay to clean teeth and clothes, to use as paint, or even as a cure for an upset stomach.

Mouse offered the latest gossip. "While you were gone, Yellow Bird got married."

"To whom?" Fire Girl said, not really caring, but trying to be polite.

"To Big Tooth. He's a friend of Badger and Lone Wolf."

She tensed at hearing the name.

"Soon, all of those men will be married," Mouse continued.

Her friend's voice carried a note of concern. Mouse was fifteen, a prime age for marriage in the customs of the People. She clearly hoped to attract a husband, someone in particular even, and she wouldn't have a hard time doing so either with her thick black hair, glossy eyes, and rich complexion. Meanwhile Fire Girl was an oddity with her unruly hair and freckled nose, but why should she care how she looked?

Nevertheless, she immediately felt pale and ugly, dimming her pride over learning the bow.

9

Summer 1838

Fire Girl strapped on her skinning knife and slid her bow into its case before looping the quiver over her head. She grabbed a water container and sack of food she'd packed the night before. Crouching next to Eagle Beak's bed, she shook his arm. "Father, I'm ready. Let's go."

Eagle Beak jerked awake, then relaxed and groaned when he saw her. "Didn't I tell you yesterday? I can't go hunting today. I promised Two Horns I'd help him break in his new horses." He rolled over, turning his back to her.

She opened her mouth, then swallowed an irritated response. "Can I go on my own?" The question was a risk, but worth taking if she could kill a deer on her own.

Eagle Beak sat up and she held her breath, waiting for his reply. He looked her up and down, as though assessing her clothing and gear. She wore a too-small dress as a tunic and had cut herself a pair of leggings and breechcloth from Eagle Beak's old clothes. Her chin bore three red lines she had painted with Pretty Robe's vermilion.

"Take the nag." He pulled the robe over him and returned to sleep.

Her breath blew out in relief. She grabbed a bridle and a long loop of rope, then ran out of the lodge toward Eagle Beak's small herd. The sky was still dark and many of the horses were asleep. The old mare stood under a dead oak tree. She was one of their packhorses, slow but strong. If only she'd thought to ask to borrow one of his better horses. Eagle Beak was tolerant, but she didn't dare take a horse without permission.

She patted and rubbed the mare while feeding her clumps of sweetgrass. She strapped on the bridle, then grabbed a handful of mane, right above the withers. After a couple hopping steps, she jumped, throwing one leg over the horse's back. She almost slipped off but gripped the mane and shifted her bottom up and over.

If only Eagle Beak could see her mount the horse without multiple attempts.

She rode southeast from camp. The prairie rose and fell in rounded hills, dotted with scattered oak trees and timber. The ground sloped into a grove of cedar, where a shallow creek ran south through the trees and deer came to drink. She headed down the slope, then walked the horse to the stream.

When the mare had finished drinking, she took the horse back to the edge of the wood and hobbled it with a piece of the rope. "Okay, Nag, here you can reach the grass," she said, then heading back to the shore.

She followed the creek in the center of the shallow water, away from where she had moved through the brush and spread her scent. Cold water seeped through her moccasins, freezing her feet as she stepped over the slippery rocks.

As she crept along, she glanced into the wood on either side, keeping an eye out for a deer path. Above the cedar branches, the cloudy sky turned purple with crests of orange as the sun peeked from the horizon. She'd better find a path soon or it'd be too late for deer. At last, she found what she was looking for, the narrowest break in the woods and a thin depression in the soil where the grass grew short. She retreated several yards away and hid in the brush.

The wait wasn't long, and if she hadn't left as early as she did, she would've missed the deer. It was a buck, young but with a fine set of antlers. It paused and sniffed the air.

Winds, please don't change.

The deer bowed its head to drink. Moving slow and quietly, she raised her bow and took aim. It wasn't the best angle. The buck was facing her slightly, increasing the chance she'd hit the sternum. If the deer turned, she could get her arrow deep into the ribcage.

She held her breath and waited. The buck turned exactly as she'd hoped. She released her breath with the arrow. It struck just above the front leg crease, right at the heart. The buck leaped across the stream and took off several paces before dropping dead, its blood spilling from the pierced artery.

Waiting for her heart to stop pounding, she sat back in the brush. It wasn't the first time she'd killed a deer. She'd hunted before, with her white father, but making the kill with a bow felt significant.

She moved to kneel beside the buck. "Forgive me for taking your life. Your meat will feed my family and me. Your skin will make us clothing to keep us warm. Your organs will make us strong, and your bones will find use as tools. Thank you for these gifts."

From her sack, she withdrew a small pouch of tobacco then took out a pinch. She lifted her hand and sprinkled tobacco the four directions, then to the Earth and Sky, to give her gratitude. The dried leaves crumbled as she released them from her fingertips.

"And thank you, God, for keeping me alive and giving me the strength to survive."

She grasped the arrow and pulled it free. Blood rushed from the wound and the smell filled her mouth with saliva. After making an incision in the underside of the buck, she reached inside to pull and cut free the warm liver. She hungrily brought it to her mouth and took a large bite. The rich metallic flavor settled onto her tongue, nourishing. She took several more bites before wrapping it and the rest of the organs in a large scrap of hide brought for that purpose.

Seeing the buck lying there, she questioned her preparations. The air was thick with the odor of blood, which she regretted wasting, and it was larger and heavier than she estimated. How was she going to get it back to camp, especially before the meat spoiled or attracted predators? She could build a travois, but she hadn't brought a hatchet, and the trees were too thick to cut with her knife. Even the saplings were too large. She cursed herself for not planning well enough ahead. Next time, she would do better.

She found saplings strong enough to fashion into travois poles, but possible to cut down. Using a heavy rock with enough of an edge to function as a blade, she hacked at the saplings until they broke free. Sweat dripped from her chin and her hands bled from a few broken fingernails by the time she finished.

Using her knife, she removed most of the branches and leaves. She took the branches and tied them with long strips of peeled bark, fashioning a platform on which to carry the buck, but still had to get the carcass onto it. Rolling it proved useless, as it was too heavy, and the legs got in the way. Nervous to leave her kill lying in the open, she ran to get the nag.

She tied the rope to the buck and the other end to her horse and had it drag the carcass onto the platform. Then she tied the buck down and the travois to the mare. It wasn't the best-looking contraption, but it would have to do. Too much of the morning had passed, her muscles ached, and her stomach rumbled with hunger, but she paused to go to the stream to wash her hands and face.

Her reflection startled her. The red lines she'd painted on her face were gone and her complexion was flushed with exertion and too much sun. The dress clung to her sweaty skin and hair poked out from her braids in messy tangles. She took out her braids and shook them free, preferring to leave her hair loose rather than trying to rule it again.

She grabbed a piece of pemmican from her pack to chew while she walked the nag out of the wood. The travois bounced and rattled over the rocks and uneven ground, but it would hold. They reached the flatter ground of the prairie, just at the edge of the trees.

The village wasn't visible from where she stood and there wasn't a soul in sight. For a moment, it seemed she was the only person on earth. It was the first time she'd traveled away from the camp on her own. She was completely free. If she wanted to, she could keep riding eastward and no one would know. At least, not right away. Would anyone bother to come after her? What reason would they have? Perhaps they'd mind if she stole a horse. The nag was old, but capable. Although, maybe she didn't need the nag.

It'd be a shame to leave the buck she had worked so hard for, but she knew enough to be able to find water and food on her own. She could survive for a long time if necessary. If she followed the creek southward, it would eventually join a river, perhaps the Red River, and she could follow that east. She'd have to hit a town or settlement after that.

And then what? What would happen once she joined the white civilization? She was thirteen, almost a woman to the People, but whites would consider her a child. She'd be put in the care of strangers, or worse, in an orphan asylum. They'd never allow her the freedoms she had now.

While it was true, as a girl, she didn't have the same liberties the Comanche boys and men had, she had far more independence than she ever would back east. Orphan girls usually became housemaids or worse. She'd be doomed to subservience for the rest of her life, never to speak her mind, never to do as she pleased, and forced to clean up after others. Would she ever again watch the sun rise across the open prairie?

Then again, was it better to be a captive? Was she still even a captive? Eagle Beak and Pretty Robe cared about her, perhaps even loved her, but the Comanche had killed and tortured her family and friends. How could she remain with them? What did that say about her if she stayed? Was she capable of that kind of forgiveness?

And what about Maggie? *Maggie has a new family now. She doesn't need me.*

Still divided by her thoughts, the ground began to shake. Clouds of dust and grit formed, rising, blinding her, and making her cough. A wall of sharp animal odor hit her nose, and she gagged. The animals themselves rushed past. First one, then another, and soon many at once. Their huge, brown, shaggy bodies thundered along the ground.

She stepped back and watched the buffalo make their way alongside the creek. She was deep enough into the brush that she was unlikely to be trampled, but she hid behind the trees. It was the closest she had been to a live herd, and the sight left her awestruck.

Whoops and cries of hunters turned her attention to the rear of the herd. Their voices grew louder as they came into view. She watched them, mesmerized. The riders rode as though they and their horses were one. The well-trained mustangs darted and wove through the crushing bodies of buffalo, as though they followed commands communicated by the very thoughts of their riders.

The men themselves seemed frenzied with their cries of exhilaration. It was clear they were in it for the pleasure of the ride and not because they needed to hunt.

The herd thinned and the riders disappeared into the distance. She was sorry to see them go. She'd not been able to pick out one man from another, as they had passed in a blur. Their half-naked bodies and painted horses were difficult to distinguish among the buffalo and dust.

There was little choice but to head back. The buck needed to be butchered, and her father would expect her soon. No doubt the warriors' trained eyes didn't miss her.

As she emerged from the wood, the hunters returned. They paused in a line and at a barked command, the horses sprang into a race back along the trampled ground. One rider outpaced them all.

His iron gray stallion thundered past at a dizzying speed, leaving the others far behind. Once he'd passed, he slowed, turned, and shouted at his friends, taunting them. At an unseen command, the gray horse raced back toward the start before the rest had even reached the end. He dropped to one side of his mount and stretched out his hand to snatch something from the ground. When he reached his friends, he spun in his seat and sat backward, holding out the object. It was a single, pink, prairie rose.

She couldn't see the other men's faces but imagined they must be rolling their eyes. He stuck the rose into one of his braids and galloped across the field. The others followed and each performed stunts and tricks, trying to outdo each other. They stood on their horses or swung under them. While at full gallop, they'd swoop to the side, touch the ground, then swing up again.

She watched with a mix of disdain, curiosity, and envy. The men made each of their tricks look easy, but she learned it came from years of training and practice. As soon as boys were old enough to sit on a horse, they learned to ride. Soon after, they'd learn how to control their horse to do the most daring maneuvers, but it wasn't simply for show.

Horse and rider needed to be able to respond to the deadly requirements of battle and hunting. Plucking a flower from the ground while hanging off a galloping horse required strength, dexterity, and superior balance, but it wasn't enough to grab something small like a flower. Each man was expected to be able to lift a body from the ground, such as a fallen warrior. It was disgraceful to leave a man behind in battle, dead or alive.

By now she had identified each of the hunters, and she wanted to be far away from them. Lone Wolf didn't often wear his hair braided, but she should have known that gray horse. She also should have guessed that he would be the one to show off his exceptionally fast and well-trained mustang. The other men, Ferret, Big Tooth, Buffalo Horn and Badger waved and rode over to her.

"Did you kill that buck?" Badger asked.

"I did." She responded without stopping but sat straighter on her mount.

"And you built that travois on your own as well, I suppose," Badger added.

She expected the men to be critical of her handiwork, but Badger's expression showed approval. Perhaps they hadn't expected a white-born girl to be so resourceful.

"Can I get a better look?" The question came from Buffalo Horn, Badger's brother.

By now she had little choice. Ferret and Big Tooth had maneuvered their horses in front of hers, and Badger sat mounted beside her. Though he was the largest man of the group, his friendly demeanor made him the least intimidating. Nevertheless, she moved her hand to rest on the hilt of her skinning knife.

The men hadn't shown any threat, but she couldn't help but feel uncomfortable around them. Every one of them might have taken part in the raid on the wagon camp. They weren't just hunters, but warriors, killers. She swallowed hard.

Lone Wolf hung back, his horse restlessly prancing about, as though he had better things to do than talk with an adolescent girl, even if she had killed a large buck. She couldn't decide if she was relieved or offended by his lack of interest.

Buffalo Horn dismounted to examine the buck. He was younger than Badger but probably only a year or two older than Lone Wolf.

He wore his hair like the others, in two thick braids with a scalplock of eagle feathers attached to a thin plait at the crown of his head. He had a large aquiline nose and part of his left ear was missing at the top edge, probably shot off in battle. She supposed most women would consider him handsome but wasn't used to thinking of men in that way.

He finished examining the buck and grinned. A few of his teeth were crooked but somehow it added to his appeal. She couldn't help but blush as he smiled at her.

"You killed it with a single shot, a perfect shot." He sounded genuinely impressed and her blush deepened. The other men looked at her with esteem. He moved closer to stand at her side, and his eyes scanned over her. "Would you hunt buffalo?"

"My father says I'm not allowed." She shifted in her seat and gripped the reins.

He grunted. "Eagle Beak is right, but I think you could, with the right training of course." He continued his visual assessment, pausing at her hand on the hilt of her knife. The look in his eyes changed, something on the edge of menacing, but there were still signs of amusement and curiosity dominating his stance. Nevertheless, she wished to get away. She sensed another pair of eyes watching intently and her discomfort intensified.

"I could take you hunting. I could come by tomorrow morning. You'd need a better horse though." He frowned at the old mare.

Before she could respond, Lone Wolf whistled to his companions, urging them to continue their game. His face showed impatience and annoyance, but she used the opportunity to seek an escape.

"I need to hurry back before the meat spoils."

Ferret and Big Tooth rode away. She urged the old nag forward and headed back to camp as quickly as the rickety travois allowed.

She wished she hadn't looked back, but she did. Buffalo Horn still watched her, and Lone Wolf on his mustang behind him, watched them both.

She skinned the deer and was cutting off strips of meat when Pretty Robe arrived with a full basket of wild grapes and plums. Round Eyes clung to her dress, his face and hands smeared with fruit pulp and juice.

"Looks like we'll be eating well today." Pretty Robe set the basket down. "Let me help you."

After they finished butchering the deer, Pretty Robe roasted hunks of meat on sticks while Fire Girl prepared the hide. Most of the fruit was reserved to make pemmican with the dried meat, but she scooped a few handfuls into a rawhide bowl to eat with their meal.

After Eagle Beak returned from training horses, he asked her to retell the events of her hunt. He listened closely, asking questions while his face glowed with pride at her achievement. Since he was in such a good mood, she decided to ask him about buffalo hunting. The last time she brought it up, he had given her a stern 'no,' and reminded her that buffalo hunting was a rite of passage for young men.

"Father, while I was bringing the buck home, I met some of the men." She paused. "Buffalo Horn offered to take me on a buffalo hunt." She held her breath for his reaction.

Eagle Beak scrunched his face. "What's this about hunting buffalo?"

"Buffalo Horn said he'd take me."

"When did you speak to Buffalo Horn?"

She masked her annoyance that her father hadn't been listening. He obviously was still glowing about the buck, but she regretted even bringing it up. "He was there when I took the buck from the woods. I ran into him and the other hunters, and they saw the carcass—"

"What other hunters?"

"Badger, Ferret, and Big Tooth."

"Was Lone Wolf there?" Pretty Robe asked. "I saw him leave with them this morning."

She stifled a groan of irritation. "Yes, he was there, but he didn't seem interested."

"As I've said before, you may not go," Eagle Beak said. "It's too dangerous and there are other risks. Buffalo Horn should know better. I'll speak to him myself." He got up to leave, seeming more bothered than she'd expected. It was clear she'd reached the end of her leash.

Pretty Robe sat beside her. "I don't know if it's so wrong for a girl to hunt buffalo. You seem capable enough, but probably not with Buffalo Horn. Lone Wolf would have more to teach you."

"No!" Her voice even startled herself. "I mean, not with Lone Wolf. Nevermind, forget it. I didn't really want to hunt buffalo anyway." She stared at her lap.

Pretty Robe tilted her head. "Did you really want to go with Buffalo Horn?"

"No, it's not that I wanted to go with him. I just..." She couldn't explain it. Buffalo Horn had scared her, so why had she asked?

"You want to prove yourself," Pretty Robe said.

Fire Girl lifted her head. It was impossible to hide anything from this woman.

Her mother moved closer, stroking her hair and face. She was still unused to the affection, but relaxed into the embrace as tears began to well.

"You don't have to prove anything to anyone, my daughter. In many ways, you already have. You're brave and strong. We all know it. I think, sometimes, you wish to be a man. A man is not better than a woman. We each have our strengths. You can be strong and brave, but you can be gentle too. There is strength in that as well."

"I don't know what to feel anymore," she choked out.

"A flame burns right here." Pretty Robe tapped her chest. "Why do you think we named you Fire Girl? But you mustn't destroy everything in your path. Burn strong, but steady." She pulled her closer. "I know you still carry so much anger, but don't let it consume you."

Fire Girl stared into the embers in the center of the lodge. Pretty Robe's words echoed in her mind. She understood the message but had no idea how to accomplish it. Seeds of anger were all she had left of the father who had vanished and the sister she didn't know how to find. If she let the anger go, it would be like forgetting them. Even the memories of her mother were slipping away.

The next day, she went hunting alone again, to the same spot as before. The morning passed, but no deer came by the creek. Defeated, she returned home.

As she walked toward the lodge, she remained distracted by thoughts and absent from her surroundings. As she was about to open the door flap, she collided into a man exiting the lodge. First came the solid wall of sinuous muscle, then the force of that recognizable scent.

She stepped back, drew her skinning knife, and pointed it at Lone Wolf.

He stood there, staring as she retreated another step. It was the closest she'd been to him since in the days right after her capture. All her fear and terror from that day came rushing forth. It was her chance. If she moved quickly enough, she could take her revenge, but she remained frozen in place.

For several moments, the only movement was his hair as it blew gently behind him in the breeze, the slight rise and fall of his chest, and the pulse at his throat. His features had become sharper, angular, losing all traces of boyhood.

His eyes darted to the blade in her hand, then he straightened his stance ever so slightly. She could see the shift in his muscles as he readied himself for her next move. Her grip tightened around the knife. She had no chance against him in strength, speed or skill, but she had righteousness and justice on her side.

"Go on then," he said at last. His voice was so low she had to strain to hear him. Was he daring her, or giving permission?

She met his eyes again, finding something there she hadn't seen before. It wasn't hatred or anger or fear. There wasn't even the hint of conceit or disdain, but she couldn't place the emotion. Whatever he was thinking, it gave her pause.

He must have sensed her doubt, because the tension faded, he dropped his shoulders and walked away. She watched his confident stride and tried to blink away the hot tears of shame. She was a fool and had missed her chance.

Inside the lodge, she found Eagle Beak seated inside, cleaning his pipe. He glanced up. "How was your hunt?"

She hid her face and sat in the shadows. "There was nothing today."

"Don't look so miserable. There will be many other hunts. Even the best hunters come back with no prey at times," he said.

It would be better to let her father think she was upset about her failed hunt than to know what really bothered her, so she didn't argue.

Pretty Robe swept open the door as she entered. "I saw Lone Wolf leave the lodge. It's been a long time since he made a visit. What did he want?" Her eyes flicked over to Fire Girl, then back to Eagle Beak.

Fire Girl tensed. Her mother had seen? Was she going to tell Father? Eagle Beak smiled wryly. "Oh, he just came to ask for something."

"Ask for what?" Pretty Robe sat to tend the fire.

"Just... something of ours."

Pretty Robe and Eagle Beak exchanged funny looks. "Did you agree?"

Her father finished cleaning his pipe. "We came to an agreement, but it won't be ready for a few more years anyway." He put the pipe in its case, signaling to his wife he would say no more about it.

Fire Girl couldn't care less about what Lone Wolf wanted. She was just glad Pretty Robe wasn't going to bring up the incident outside, at least, not now. In any case, she wouldn't be punished for it. Maybe it was like what had occurred with Sharp Mouth. Maybe they felt Lone Wolf deserved to be threatened. No, he deserved far more than a threat, she just didn't have the courage to deliver the proper vengeance, but next time, she'd do better.

10

F ire Girl strolled up the slope from the creek carrying waterskins. She'd been swimming with Mouse and her damp hair cooled her back from the late summer heat. The band had moved further southwest in pursuit of buffalo herds and the land was drier and flatter than their usual hunting grounds.

As she entered the village, she passed a group of boys playing with leashed crickets, betting on which insect could leap the farthest. A few girls sat nearby with dolls and toy lodges, playing house.

Two-year-old Round Eyes stood on the edge of the cluster of boys, penis in hand and urinating on a trail of ants. He glanced up and waved with his other hand. Urine dribbled down his leg as he toddled up to her.

"Do you want some water to replace that puddle you made?" she asked.

He tilted his head back and opened his mouth like a baby bird. She poured him a drink, then sprinkled water on his legs and feet to wash him.

"Where's your grandmother?" she asked him.

"Home. She said to come."

Hopefully Pretty Robe wouldn't need her for too long. She wanted Eagle Beak to show her how to hunt pronghorn antelope since their grazing grounds weren't far from camp.

Fire Girl found Pretty Robe in the lodge, sitting beside a pouch of sewing tools, her arms full of garments. "We have work to do."

"Can I go hunting first? If I wait any longer, it'll be too late in the day."

Pretty Robe gave her a patient smile. "Your hunting achievements are well appreciated, but your other skills need refining."

Fire Girl scowled at the bag of tools. "I can sew. I can quill."

"You can, but your stitches are too large and uneven. You only quill simple designs." Pretty Robe held up a shirt Fire Girl had sewn for Round Eyes to prove her point. The stitches were loose and crooked, and she'd quilled a striped design on the shoulders, unlike the more detailed patterns her mother used on Eagle Beak's clothing.

She huffed and crossed her arms. "But it's too hard."

Pretty Robe looked undaunted. "Exactly why you need practice. You may still hunt with your father, but you'll also work with me."

All that day and the next, her mother showed her patterns which she had to copy with dyed porcupine quills. She also brought out her precious stash of trade beads and demonstrated how to stitch them onto moccasins and clothing.

After a month, Fire Girl stopped following her mother's patterns and invented her own designs. She created scenes of sunsets and wild horses on parfleche cases, quilled landscapes she saw while hunting on the prairie, and beaded color combinations of plants and flowers she found that pleased her. Sometimes her mother would be confused by designs which didn't follow tradition or custom.

"What is this supposed to be?" Pretty Robe held up a bag with a cluster of red beads in the center.

"It's a flower. A prairie rose. I wanted it to be pink, but we don't have pink beads."

"And these, right here?" She pointed to the corners of the bag where Fire Girl had sewn beads of yellow and orange.

"Those are flames. That way, everyone will know the bag is mine." She smiled, hoping to avoid her mother's disapproval.

Pretty Robe frowned. "I suppose you could use it to store your medicine."

"My medicine?"

"Yes, things that give you power and strength. Plants for healing and preventing illness." Pretty Robe sighed. "There's so much I must teach you. I forgot you missed out on so much. Tomorrow, I'll show you which plants you should store in your bag and what they do."

The next day, Fire Girl wandered the fields and woods with her mother. Pretty Robe showed her how to find wild bergamot for fevers, yarrow for cramps or wounds, and honey locust for indigestion. Despite spending her days with Pretty Robe, gathering food and plants, preparing meals, and working to make clothes and other items, her early mornings were still spent on hunts with Eagle Beak. By midsummer, she had a new appreciation for the People's way of life. Everything she needed was at hand. Everything had a purpose, working harmoniously together, and she was a part of it.

On a sweltering summer morning, Fire Girl lay prone in a dry stream bed beside Eagle Beak, hidden from a herd of pronghorn grazing beyond a high riverbank. In the same position for too long, she fought the urge to fidget or talk. According to Eagle Beak, pronghorn were not only fast, but incredibly skittish. High winds made them nervous, so they had to remain silent and still until the winds died and the animals relaxed. But her muscles had gone stiff, and rocks were digging into her elbows. She had scrapes on her forearms from when they belly-crawled after leaving the horses a hundred paces behind them. If her father was uncomfortable, he hid it well. He hadn't moved or changed his expression since they started. Suppressing a sigh, she summoned the will to show the same patience.

Instead, she daydreamed of startling the antelope herd so she could witness their speed. She could chase them on horseback, feel the wind on her face, and see the prairie fly pass in a blur.

The air settled into a light breeze. Eagle Beak waved a stick with a long strip of calico tied on the end. He made it disappear and reappear above the grass until the antelope moved closer. Skittish, but curious to a fault.

She peered over the bank to watch them approach. Three bucks grazed in a group. Thorn-shaped prongs extended from their short horns. She pressed her lips together to keep from laughing at their little brown and white bodies like barrels balanced on spindly legs.

Eagle Beak made a low hiss, the signal for her to take her shot.

Caught unprepared, she grabbed her bow. Her heart pounded as she drew the arrow, and let it fly at the closest buck. The arrow pierced the buck's neck, a bad shot. The antelope snorted and took off, scattering the herd in a panic.

She scrambled to her feet, barely coming to a stand in time to watch the antelope bound over the prairie, flashing their bright white rumps as they disappeared into a cloud of dust.

Eagle Beak grunted in annoyance, then whistled for the horses.

"I'm sorry. I wasn't ready."

"You should always be ready," he said without looking at her.

He mounted his horse, and she did the same, following him as he galloped after the herd.

The sun had reached its zenith when they found the antelope lying alone, almost invisible in the field of grass. If it weren't for Eagle Beak's keen eyes, following spots of blood, they would never have found it.

The buck lay half dead, wheezing its final breaths.

"Finish it," Eagle Beak said.

She drew her knife and started to kneel by the buck's head.

"No," Eagle Beak said. "He could kick you or bolt up. Both men and animals can be most dangerous when facing death. Use your bow."

She drew an arrow from her quiver and notched it. As she pulled the string, she sighted down the length of the shaft, aiming at the heart. The buck stared at her, the whites of its eyes showing. A memory leaped into vision. The arrow shaft became the barrel of her carbine, and the buck changed to the face of a man, strangely familiar. She pulled the trigger, and his face vanished in red.

She blinked and the image was gone. Her hands shook and bile rose into her throat. By some miracle of muscle, memory, and proximity, she released her bowstring, sending an arrow into the buck's heart.

That evening, Pretty Robe showed her how to prepare the meat in a stew. "Antelope can be sweet and delicious, but not when they run."

She hung her head and finished adding the wild onions she had chopped into the pot.

Pretty Robe smiled. "Don't worry. This stew will make the meat tender again, and some people like antelope no matter how they get it."

Eagle Beak ducked into the lodge with Fox Laugh. Her throat tightened. Fox Laugh hardly visited, and whenever he did, his animosity made her feel small and frightened, like when she first arrived in camp.

Round Eyes hurried to his father, arms outstretched, and Fox Laugh swept him up. The only time she saw him smile was when he was with his son. "You're growing into a strong warrior," he said.

The boy's grin reached his ears. "Grandfather says I look more and more like my father every day."

Fox Laugh's face darkened, only for a moment, then another smile replaced the frown, less genuine than before. "I'm sure you do, Round Eyes, but when I look at you, all I see is your mother."

The air in the lodge thickened with tension. She watched the faces of Pretty Robe and Eagle Beak, searching for clues to the grief and loss of which they wouldn't speak. It was insensitive of Fox Laugh to mention their dead daughter so casually. Then again, perhaps a man could choose when to bring up the memory of his own wife.

Fox Laugh still hadn't acknowledged her presence, and she moved to the back of the lodge while Pretty Robe served the men. Buffalo Horn entered the lodge soon after. He pulled Round Eyes into his lap. After taking a few bites, he wiped his mouth with the back of his hand. "Eagle Beak, you're going to have to have fend suitors off this girl soon."

"Oh, I don't know. Fire Girl is capable of fending for herself," Eagle Beak said.

Fox Laugh grunted. "What man would want a wife who hunts? That's his duty. What will he do? Change a baby's swaddling?"

"She'll give him hides to flesh," Buffalo Horn said, "then drag him into the lodge and ride him until he's worn out from all that work." He laughed, shaking Round Eyes off his lap and then slapping his knee.

Fire Girl hopped to her feet. "Then it's a good thing I can take care of myself, if I'm such a threat to your manhood!"

"See what I mean?" Eagle Beak said with a chuckle.

"Fire Girl, sit down," Pretty Robe said as she passed her a bowl of stew. "These men are just teasing you. Both know quite well there are plenty of women who hunt and raid." She gave Fox Laugh and Buffalo Horn a hard stare, long enough to wipe the smug looks from their faces.

She admired her mother's quiet way of influencing people and felt ashamed of her outburst. She sat. "Did you say raid? There are women who fight?"

"Now you gave her ideas," Eagle Beak said to Pretty Robe. "You will not be joining any battles, my daughter."

Fire Girl picked at her bowl of food. Maybe Eagle Beak's first daughter had died in a battle. That would explain the mood and Fox Laugh's bitter comments. If only she had the courage to break taboo and ask Mouse about what happened to her.

The next day, she was kneeling beside the lodge, fleshing the antelope hide, when Eagle Beak hurried over. "Quick, gather any spare buffalo robes, whatever we don't need."

She dropped her flesher and stood. Neighbors hurried from their lodges with armfuls of hides. They loaded them on travois, chattering excitedly.

"What's happening?"

"A caravan from Mexico is here."

Traders? Someone who could take her home? She kept the thought locked in her head and hurried to gather whatever spare buffalo hides they had, which weren't many, while her heart hammered in her chest. It had been so long since she'd seen anyone outside the People, and traders presented a chance of rescue, but if Eagle Beak and Pretty Robe let her see outsiders, then either they knew she wouldn't leave, or they knew she had nowhere to go.

Pretty Robe arrived with Round Eyes on her hip. She handed the toddler to Fire Girl. "Stay close to your father, and do not talk to any of the traders." She paused with a tilt of her head. "You don't speak Spanish, do you?"

Fire Girl shook her head, certain her voice would reveal apprehension.

"Good, but even so, don't speak to them. *Ho-say* is fair, but I don't trust all of his men."

Ho-say. José. She tucked that name away, adjusted her hold on Round Eyes, and followed her parents in the direction of the crowd.

There were too many people gathered to get a clear view, but she caught glimpses of carts, mules, and several men. They wore light-colored cotton trousers and loose-fitting shirts and all, but one wore wide-brimmed hats. Instead, he wore a bright cloth tied around his head.

The men spoke a mix of Comanche and what she assumed must be Spanish, using hand gestures to fill in where words could not. Red Hawk did most of the talking, speaking to the man with the bright cloth. Lone Wolf stood beside him, also speaking in a mix of Spanish with the People's language, helping other men and women make their trades.

Her hope died when she saw him. If the Mexicans were friends with Red Hawk and his grandson, they would be of no help to her, even if she could ask for it.

She stepped back, moving toward the rear of the crowd. Round Eyes squirmed in her arms. "I want to see," he complained.

"No, we don't need to see. This is no place for us." She lost Pretty Robe and Eagle Beak in the crowd and headed back to the lodge.

That afternoon, her parents returned with their arms full of items, grinning with excitement.

"The Comancheros were fair with us today," Eagle Beak said.

She forgot her earlier apprehension and looked over the new goods, which included a metal pot, a ladle, a bag of white sugar, and hunks of bacon.

Eagle Beak unwrapped a cloth bundle and held up a small flat disk. "These are *tortillas*, made from corn, like the cakes we make, but this is much tastier than the corn from those stinking Pawnee."

Round Eyes toddled over to see the rest of the items, including a knife and iron tools her father needed. Pretty Robe snatched the knife from him and addressed her husband. "Are you going to show your daughter and grandson the gifts you have for them?" Her eyes twinkled.

"Something for me?" Round Eyes clapped his hands together.

Eagle Beak sat between her and the boy, then produced a color-fully painted wooden spinning top. He demonstrated the spin on the smooth surface of his tin of bear grease. Round Eyes squealed with delight and promptly snatched it mid-spin.

While Round Eyes tried, and failed, to spin his top, Eagle Beak withdrew a small cloth pouch from the sleeve of his hunting shirt. "This is for you." He handed it to Fire Girl.

She opened it, finding a silver bracelet. As she took the bracelet from the pouch, it tinkled. Tiny cones hung from each link of silver. They caught the firelight, bright and sparkling. Her vision blurred and she struggled to speak.

"How did you—"

"Don't worry about how." He smiled.

They had so few robes to bring to trade, and Eagle Beak didn't own many horses. She had no idea how he'd been able to afford the bracelet in addition to all the items he had brought. The act of generosity and affection was too much to bear. She threw her arms around his shoulders.

As soon as she did, she started to pull away. She'd never hugged him before. They hardly ever had any physical contact, but his arms embraced her in warmth.

"Thank you," she whispered in his ear. She hoped he knew the thanks wasn't only for the bracelet.

Cold winds came and the People moved to the winter grounds in the Wichita Mountains. Fire Girl finished quilling a new bag for Mouse, made from the skin of the first antelope she killed that sum-mer. She meant it for storing paints and the little mirror Two Horns had given Mouse after his visit with the Mexican traders.

After gathering the bag and her robe, she crouched near her stored belongings. Inside her medicine bag, she found the little pouch with the bracelet. She didn't often wear it, since it was too big for her wrist, but couldn't resist putting it on.

The bracelet jingled when she stood, making her smile. She wrapped herself in her robe and set out for Mouse's lodge, but when she arrived, the lodge was empty. Two Horns or Quick Hands could be in a hundred places, but Mouse was probably with Antelope and Rain On the Lodge, watching the young, unmarried men race horses like they often did.

She strode briskly through camp. Cold air found its way into the gaps of her robe, and she shivered. She kept her head down, out of the icy wind, and peered through her lashes at the ground in front of her.

Voices signaled the approach of men. She stepped sideways, far enough out of the way so they wouldn't have to move to avoid her. Some men would find it a great offense to have a woman block their path, or to cross too close in front of them.

She had only just passed the men when one of them called her name. Her skin tingled, and her blood ran cold. It was a voice she rarely heard, but knew, nonetheless.

She stopped, making her face as blank as untrampled snow before turning to face Lone Wolf. Badger was with him, much less intimidating despite his bulk.

"You dropped this." The silver bracelet hung from the tip of Lone Wolf's finger. He stepped closer and held out the silver trinket, the tiny bells tinkling merrily.

She checked her arm to ensure it was really gone, then reached for the bracelet he held out, but instead of handing it over, he took her wrist with his other hand. She was too surprised to pull away.

"I can fix it for you, so it doesn't fall off again." He wrapped her wrist with the bracelet, closing the clasp with deft fingers. His touch was gentle, so different from when he'd wrestled her to the ground.

She yanked her arm away. "My father will fix it," she mumbled before hurrying away. She put as much distance between them as she could.

As she headed home, she could still feel the warmth of Lone Wolf's hand on her arm. His voice resonated in her ears, and his scent lingered no matter how far away from him she ran. She hated how he'd rattled her, how confused he made her. She could never tell what he was thinking. Worst of all, she hated how whenever she became comfortable with her life, he was there to remind her of all the reasons she felt out of place. This new encounter had made her feel something else as well, something she couldn't name, something unsettling.

11

Summer 1839

"Where are you going?" Pretty Robe asked.

Fire Girl had just quickly gotten dressed and ducked out of the lodge. She poked her head back in, her quiver of arrows behind her. "I'm going to catch up with Father, to hunt with him," she explained.

"I need you here this morning. We're taking the lodge cover down and putting up the new one, remember? There are some final adjustments that need to be made, and we need to paint it." She saw the look of disappointment on her face and added, "You can go hunting tomorrow."

Fire Girl pulled off her quiver and sighed. "Can we use my design?"

"Yes, you sketch it out on the cover, let us know which colors to use, and we'll help paint it."

"Who's coming to help?" She put down her weapons, then searched for her sewing bag.

"Squirrel, Laughing Bird, and Sharp Mouth, of course. Quick Hands and Mouse, maybe others," Pretty Robe said.

She scowled at the mention of Sharp Mouth's name. The woman didn't bother her any longer, but she could never forget the beating she'd endured.

The women took down the old cover and spread the new one out on the ground. Pretty Robe inspected the stitching and reinforced it where necessary. Fire Girl marked her design, a large sun with an eagle in the sky. The others filled it in with paint using brushes made from the porous bone of a buffalo femur or a split stick.

While the women waited for the paint to dry, they played a game of shinny. Fire Girl played on her mother's team. She smiled with pride watching Pretty Robe run through the field chasing the ball with her long-curved stick, then whack the ball into the goal marked by their moccasins.

By early afternoon, the cover was ready. Pretty Robe tied it to the lifting pole, then each of them helped raise it and set it into place. They unfurled the heavy cover around the frame.

When it came time to insert the lacing pins, because she was the youngest, lightest and tallest, Fire Girl stood on Mouse's shoulders to reach the top where the cover met the crossed gathering of poles. The two poles on either side of the opening had been moved inward so the front of the cover hung flat.

She inserted each pin through the overlapping edges of the cover, starting at the top until the openings were low enough to be reached by her mother standing below. When she was about to put in the last of her pins, Mouse squeaked and staggered, causing her to lose her balance.

"Hold still, I'm almost finished," Fire Girl said.

"But you're bleeding!" Mouse said.

"What?" She shoved in the pin and jumped down.

Mouse wiped a drop of blood off her face. "You're bleeding! You dripped on me!"

Fire Girl pulled up her skirt and felt between her legs. Her hand was spotted with dark blood.

Pretty Robe and the other women gathered around. "Daughter, you've started your moon cycle. You're a woman now."

She took in the faces of the other women. Each of them smiled in earnest, looking congratulatory. She crossed her arms. "Does that mean I can't hunt with Father anymore?"

Pretty Robe and the other women chuckled. "No, you can still hunt with him, but not while you're bleeding. Let me finish up here and I'll take you to the Once-a-Month Lodge."

"I'll take her, I'm due to start my bleed any day now," Mouse offered. "You can come later, when you're finished." She grinned at Fire Girl. "Bring something to do, I'll be right back with my things." She ran off happily.

Fire Girl turned back to her mother, arms still crossed, and Pretty Robe's hands came to rest on her shoulders. "Don't look so unhappy. You knew this day was coming soon. You're no longer a child."

No longer a child was exactly why she was unhappy. "Why do people have to grow up?"

Pretty Robe laughed like she'd asked the most foolish of questions, but she meant it. Growing older meant... changes. Changes she wasn't ready for.

When Mouse returned, they walked to the lodge where she would remain for the next few days. It was on the far perimeter of camp where menstruating women couldn't contaminate men's warrior medicine.

Mouse linked her arm with hers. "I'm so happy you start your bleed. If our cycles align, we can go together every month. I started mine before you came to be with the People, and I've been waiting for this." Her white teeth glinted in the sunlight.

Fire Girl couldn't muster a smile if she tried. Her freedom was slipping away. Her old life had been atypical to begin with, as Papa had forced into to a level of independence most white-born girls wouldn't even consider, but with the People, she was completely unrestrained.

Eagle Peak and Pretty Robe never punished or scolded her, and like all children of the People, she was allowed to do almost anything she pleased, though she always strove to make them proud and hated the idea of bringing them shame. But entering womanhood, she would have more responsibilities and obligations. They might even expect her to get married.

She pushed the thought aside. The very idea of marriage made her palms sweat. A husband would put additional hindrances on her autonomy. She tried not to think about the intimate duties she would have to a future husband.

Arms linked, she and Mouse neared a group of men seated under an old blackjack oak. One of the elders was demonstrating his arrow-making. Lone Wolf sat among them, and her palms puddled with sweat. Most days, she hardly felt the pain of loss from her capture, but the dull ache sharpened whenever he entered her consciousness.

Despite Fire Girl's efforts to walk past the men, Mouse herded her closer and sought their attention. "Good day, Lone Wolf." She greeted the other men with equal enthusiasm. "Hello, Badger," she added, in a shyer tone. Most of the men looked up and smiled. Lone Wolf hardly glanced in their direction. Arrogant!

"You two are a refreshing sight on this sweltering hot day," Badger said. "Why not come a little closer so you can keep us all cool."

Mouse hesitated, and Fire Girl's tight shoulders relaxed that her friend hadn't jumped to accept the invitation. Blood stuck to her thighs, catching and pulling on the fine down on her legs every time she took a step. Her back pooled with perspiration. If they stood there any longer, the men would realize where they were headed, and she might die of humiliation.

"Fire Girl," Buffalo Horn's voice shook her out of her thoughts. "Since you like to hunt, come watch Dark Cloud make Badger's arrows." He patted his leg as though offering his lap to her and grinned that crooked grin. She couldn't deny she was interested in arrow-making but was dumbstruck by this new kind of attention.

"We can't come any closer, we're headed to the Moon Lodge," Mouse said.

Lone Wolf looked up to stare at them. Fire Girl's eyes widened in horror and her face flushed with heat. She yanked on Mouse's arm to turn her away.

"Hurry along then, young ladies," the old man, Dark Cloud, called after them, "before your moon medicine weakens these young warriors. Young flower buds like you should be more careful around these busy bees. Next thing you know, one will take you to wife, poke you with his stinger and you'll be swollen with a baby," he chuckled. The other men laughed and even Mouse giggled as Fire Girl pushed her along.

As they approached the Moon Lodge, she whispered to Mouse in annoyance, "I can't believe you told those men where we were going."

"It's not something to be ashamed of. You should be proud to bleed, and the men will want to know which women are ready for marriage," Mouse explained.

"But I am *not* ready for marriage."

"Well, no, not yet, but soon. And I didn't mean *you* anyway," she added slyly.

"Oh, of course." She hadn't missed the lingering glances between Mouse and Badger. Before she could say anything else, they entered the lodge where other women were already inside. She wrinkled her nose and coughed at the overwhelming odor of menstrual blood and unwashed bodies.

"You get used to it," Mouse found them a place to sit. The floor was covered with soft moss and shredded cedar bark, both for absorption and to minimize odor. Never willing to let the subject of marriage drop, Mouse continued, "If you *were* ready for marriage, which of the men would you want to court you?"

"No one," she said. "I don't want to get married."

Mouse shrugged, undaunted. "Maybe in another year or two you'll feel differently."

She likewise rolled a shoulder. "What do you do here anyway?" Her mother had already explained to her about menstruation and the monthly lodge, but it was an easy way to change the subject.

"Sometimes we tell stories, sing songs, make little items for ourselves. You cannot make anything for anyone else, though. Your medicine will be embedded in the item and that wouldn't be good for the receiver. Sometimes moon medicine is negative or brings bad energy. If you're feeling sad, or are in a sour mood, you probably shouldn't make anything at all."

Fire Girl already knew this and had brought her moccasins which needed mending, but with the way she was feeling, she might as well not work on them. "Tell me a story, Mouse. Tell me a funny one, one about Clever Coyote."

A few stories later, Pretty Robe joined them. "How are you feeling?" she asked Fire Girl.

"I feel well." Her belly was cramped, but it wasn't worth mentioning.

"That's good. Mouse, you don't have to stay if you haven't started your bleeding yet."

"All right, but I will most likely be back tomorrow."

After Mouse was gone, Fire Girl said. "*Pia*, you don't have to stay. I'm fine on my own."

Although her mother was still young enough to have a cycle, she no longer bled. Since they had lost their only child, it was probably why Eagle Beak and Pretty Robe chose to adopt. her.

"If you don't mind, I wanted to talk with you," Pretty Robe said.

"Oh?" That uneasy feeling returned, making her cramps more painful.

Her mother rubbed her hands together nervously. "You know what happens between a husband and wife together in the marriage bed?"

She nodded. She'd seen enough to know. There was little privacy in a lodge and the People weren't ashamed to joke and talk about sex. At first, she'd been shocked by that kind of talk, but had become accustomed to it.

"Good, because I wanted to address more than the physical, I want to address the bond between a man and a woman. One day, you might find yourself attracted to a young man. These feelings are hard to ignore, and you may be tempted to act upon them. While it's not forbidden to do so, there are consequences. If you are carrying a child, you will be married."

Fire Girl shifted uncomfortably. Did her mother really think she would be as foolish as to make a baby with someone?

"You must be sure any man you lie with is worthy enough to be your husband," Pretty Robe continued. "Of course, your father and I would prefer that you wait until the right man makes a marriage offer and we approve. We hope the man you marry is someone you'll be happy with, someone who will cherish you."

She sighed. "I'm not even thinking about marriage, and I'm *not* interested in sharing a bed with anyone."

"I know, and I won't say any more until you're older, but you must also be aware that men will start to view you differently now that you're blossoming. Your body is changing, and it's noticeable. *Men* notice these things and they aren't always honorable about what they say and do with their impulses."

She recalled how Buffalo Horn had looked at her only a little while before. Her breasts were growing and showed under her dress. Her skirts were getting snug around the hips. She had been both pleased and self-conscious of it.

"I want you to be careful. Be particular about where you go, and who you go with. Don't let a man convince you to bed with him if there isn't mutual love and respect between you."

Fire Girl considered these words. They sounded like a warning, but also hinted that her mother understood her desire to remain unhindered. Her heart swelled with love for Pretty Robe. "Thank you for always seeing me as I am."

"Of course. Your father and I both see what you are, and we love you for it."

She hugged her mother tightly, grateful to know she had parents who valued her independence.

12

Summer 1839

Fire Girl worked on scraping hides from a recent buffalo hunt with Mouse, Antelope, and Rain on The Lodge. Though they sat in the shade of oak and ash trees, the heat bore down like a blaze. She swatted away buzzing flies attracted by the smell of flesh, fat, and brain fluid.

A group of hunters approached camp through the nearby trees, Lone Wolf, Badger, and their friends. As soon as she heard Lone Wolf's voice, her mouth went dry, and her stomach twisted. The men joked about their success on the hunt while they strode through the wood, leading their horses. Badger did most of the teasing, and Mouse's wistful gaze toward him drew Antelope's attention.

"It looks like you have your eye on one of those young men," she teased.

Mouse turned back to her work, a pink hue on her cheeks.

"Oh, I don't blame you. Badger's a fine warrior. One of the best. Handsome too. But it's your cousin I prefer." Antelope used her chin to point at Lone Wolf.

"You and every other woman in the village," Rain On the Lodge said. "The woman he chooses as his bride will be a very lucky woman indeed." She said that as though the choice was his alone and the woman had no say in the matter. Like she should just count her lucky stars that he'd considered her at all.

"Does anyone have any idea who he prefers?" Antelope asked. "Mouse, you would know."

"Lone Wolf doesn't talk to me about these things," Mouse said, incredulous.

"Yes, but perhaps you may have overheard something," Rain said.

"Oh, you know Lone Wolf," Mouse said. "He hardly says a word to anyone about what he's thinking."

"Maybe I'll visit his lodge one night and find out." Antelope giggled.

"You wouldn't dare!" Rain said.

"Maybe. It'd be humiliating if he threw me out."

"He's a man. He wouldn't throw you out." Rain laughed. "I heard when he's out raiding or with other bands, he's not above welcoming women into his bed."

"That can't be true," said Mouse.

"Maybe not," admitted Rain. "One never knows with Lone Wolf."

Fire Girl gripped her tool with sweaty hands and scraped hard into her hide with disgust. Their stupid banter was always centered around Lone Wolf.

Rain turned to her. "You're quieter than usual. Which of the men do you like best?"

"Buffalo Horn is often looking at you." Antelope's voice lifted in a high singsong.

"Buffalo Horn looks at everyone," Rain said with a note of annoyance.

Antelope shrugged. "I wouldn't mind a poke from his lance."

"What about Lone Wolf?" Mouse raised her eyebrows.

"His too." Antelope grinned.

How could they all be mooning over Lone Wolf? Didn't they know anything? He wouldn't give those girls a second glance. No woman would ever be good enough for him, surely not those clucking chickens. He thought too highly of himself.

Despite her resentment, she couldn't take her eyes off him. She envied the easy and graceful way he rode his horse, fired his bow, or did anything at all. He moved with the sure confidence of one who knew his place in the world. It left her bitter and jealous. He strode past, laughing with the other men, and just as she expected, he didn't even look over.

"I have no interest in any of them," she said with a mouth full of disdain, but the women had stopped listening.

Boys with their small bows and arrows ran up to the men. Round Eyes was among them, playing a mock battle. The boys tried to engage the men in their game. Lone Wolf snatched Round Eyes up and swung him in a circle, making the little boy giggle with glee. The other boys surrounded them, and Lone Wolf gave each of them a turn. As he set the last child down, he tickled him under the arms. The boy squealed and the others joined in a tickle attack on Lone Wolf. He feigned defeat and the group ended up on the ground in a dog pile of laughter.

"See," said Antelope. "Who wouldn't want a man like him for a husband?"

Fire Girl couldn't believe what she was seeing. He knew the women were watching. He *must* have known. Lone Wolf didn't miss a thing. He was only pretending to be kind for their benefit, and it made her loathe him all the more.

The summer days grew long. Laying in a field of bluestem, Fire Girl twirled a blade of grass between her fingers while she watched the clouds. An old hide loaded with buffalo chips lay nearby.

"Fire Girl!" Mouse's voice sang from a distance. "Where are you?"

"I'm here." She stuck her arm in the air and waved.

"I've been looking all over for you." Mouse sat beside her and plucked a tall blade. "Badger and the others are back from their horse raid."

"Hmm," she said, not knowing what else to say.

"You missed the parade. The men brought a lot of horses."

Badger, Lone Wolf, and the other men had often gone on horse raids that summer. She added that to her growing list of reasons to hate Lone Wolf. Horses were all that mattered to him. Didn't he have enough already? What was he trying to prove anyway?

"Badger gave me his lance and shield to hold during the parade," Mouse said softly.

"He did?" Fire Girl stared wide-eyed at her friend. She knew Badger and Mouse liked each other, but this act confirmed his interest in her as a wife. She squeezed Mouse's hand. "I'm happy for you."

Mouse squealed with excitement and hugged her knees. "I was beginning to think he didn't like me."

She sat up. "Are you joking? He's always looking at you."

"But he took so long to *do* anything." Mouse bit her bottom lip. "Are you going to the dance?"

"No."

"You *have* to come. If I don't dance with Badger, I'll be humiliated, and I need you there."

Fire Girl's palms grew damp, but the current cause of her apprehension was a mystery. "Of course, you'll dance with Badger," she said, ashamed of the annoyance in her tone.

"Please come," Mouse said. "You never come to the dances anymore. I thought you liked dancing."

"I do, it's just—"

"Then come." Mouse stood and pulled on her arm. "Let's go back and get ready. I'll braid your hair."

"Alright, I'll come, but I'm not dancing with anyone."

At the celebration, Fire Girl stayed with the older women, and only participated in the women's dances. Mouse ran off to join the young women who gathered to wait for the partner dances. She watched, but only to see if Mouse's hopes were fulfilled. Badger stood with the other unmarried men, sneaking glances at Mouse. When the time came for partners to be chosen, Mouse approached him. He reached for her hand immediately.

She was glad for them. They were a good match. Despite his friendship with Lone Wolf, she'd found no reason to dislike Badger. He was friendly with everyone, good-natured, and lacked Lone Wolf's pretentious attitude. She watched them dance, hands lightly laid on each other's shoulders while they side-stepped in a circle but couldn't shake her feeling of unease. Mouse was her only real friend, but soon, she'd belong to Badger.

Two days later, they were returning from their daily water gathering and slowed when Antelope called down the slope. "Mouse! Come quick. Badger brought horses to Two Horn's lodge. Your father wants to see you."

Mouse grinned and hurried back. Running to keep up, Fire Girl smiled at the cluster of ponies tied outside Two Horn's lodge representing Badger's marriage offer. Mouse disappeared inside with her parents. Fire Girl's smile faded before she headed to her own lodge.

"Did you hear?" Pretty Robe asked as she entered. "Badger has proposed to Mouse."

"Yes, I saw the horses."

"You mean Two Horns hasn't taken them yet?"

"I think he meant to talk with Mouse first, but he's bound to accept. Those two have been enamored with each other for years."

"That's true." Pretty Robe said. She set down the ladle she'd been using to stir a pot. "You don't seem happy for your friend. Is something wrong?"

"No, I'm happy for her. It's just... I don't know. Now everything will change. Mouse won't have much time for me once she has a husband. Then she'll have a baby, and she'll never have *any* time for me." She knew she sounded whiny and childish, but she didn't care.

"Mouse will always be your friend. While it's true she'll have new duties as a wife, with her own household to run, you two will still have time together. You must help her when you can."

"I guess so," she muttered. She didn't say all that had been bothering her. Once Mouse and Badger were married, avoiding Lone Wolf would become even more difficult.

129

By nightfall, the horses were gone. The marriage had been accepted and Mouse went to live with Badger in his own lodge. It was customary for young braves to live in their own lodges, away from their mothers and sisters. Pretty Robe said Badger had received his own lodge at age fifteen, nine years before.

Once Badger and Mouse were married, she avoided making visits to their lodge, fearing to find Lone Wolf there. Instead, she made excuses, or asked to meet Mouse by the river, or came by only after she'd seen Badger leave. Mouse probably wouldn't notice, consumed as she was by her new wifely role.

Days later Fire Girl sat with Round Eyes inside her lodge, playing 'hide the stone.' She covered her eyes while he hid the pebble under one of the three horn bowls.

"Okay, open your eyes," he said.

She lifted one of the bowls.

"Not that one," he giggled. "It's right here." He picked up the bowl in the middle.

"You're not supposed to tell me where it is, silly. You must let me find it."

He stuck out his bottom lip. "I forgot."

"It's alright. Hide it again." As she closed her eyes, someone scratched at the lodge flap.

"May I come in?" Mouse asked.

"Of course."

"Hey, you opened your eyes." Round Eyes pouted.

Mouse entered through the lodge opening. "It's my fault. Can I play too?"

"Yes, but you hide it. I want to guess," he said.

They played a few more rounds until Mouse's expression turned serious and she gave Fire Girl a nudge. "I haven't seen you at my lodge for many days."

She picked up the wooden bowl and rolled it in her palm. If only she could fit inside it, like the stone. "I've been busy making a new shirt for Eagle Beak."

"Yes, but is there another reason you don't scratch at our lodge flap more often?" Mouse peered at her curiously.

Fire Girl fidgeted with her bracelet, making the silver cones dance. "I'm sorry. It makes my heart sad to know I've hurt you. I'll come visit more often."

"Good. Come by tonight and have a meal with us. Badger will be home soon. He's been working on a pipe for my father and wants to finish it tonight."

She spun the bracelet around her wrist. She wouldn't have agreed to go if she knew Badger would be there.

Round Eyes picked up his toy bow and pretended to shoot arrows, but she wasn't in the mood to play dead.

Mouse went on, "I think Lone Wolf will come by..."

Fire Girl froze with her hand on the bracelet.

"I knew it!" Mouse said, slapping her hands on her thighs. "What's wrong? You always act strangely when Lone Wolf's name is mentioned, and you leave if he's around."

"I don't know what you're talking about." Fire Girl gathered up the horn bowls from the game and shoved them into a pouch.

Mouse grabbed the pouch from her. "I know you don't like him, but you've put me between my husband and his best friend. You're *my* best friend. Don't make me choose."

Fire Girl couldn't look at her, unable to find a response.

Mouse grabbed her hand. "Please tell me. *Why* don't you like Lone Wolf?"

It was too much. All the talk about Lone Wolf. He seemed to be the subject of every conversation, along with marriage and courting. What was so important about him that it was all she could think about?

"Don't you know? Or have you forgotten?" she spat, her voice full of malice. "*He* was the one who took me when my family was killed. I hate him! I'm sorry he's your cousin and a good friend of your husband, but I can't stand him."

Mouse's lips drew together in a tight line. It was the first time she showed anger. She whispered to Round Eyes "Go find your grandmother," then waited for him to leave before continuing. "It's *you* who doesn't know. Didn't anyone ever tell you of that day?"

"What do you mean?" Dread built in her gut.

Mouse's expression softened, as though sorry she'd mentioned it.

"Please tell me," Fire Girl said. "This is the first time anyone has ever mentioned that day. I must know." Her stomach twisted with apprehension.

Mouse sighed. "Let's go back to my lodge. Round Eyes will be returning with your mother, and I don't want your parents to know I'm talking to you about this." She led the way back to her lodge with hurried strides. "We don't have much time before Badger returns."

Once inside, they sat. Fire Girl's heart pounded with anxiousness. She was finally going to find out about the raid, maybe even what happened to her father.

Mouse took a deep breath. "You say warriors killed your white family, but it was *our* people who were attacked first. White men fired their guns at a group of women off on a honey hunt. They raped and killed two women, then mutilated their bodies."

She sat frozen. Was Papa with them? It couldn't have been Papa.

Mouse blinked and her eyes shone with wet. "When the women didn't return from the honey hunt, our warriors went in search of them, including Lone Wolf. One of the women was his mother and the other was Round Eyes' mother. Pretty Robe was there too. The white-skins did things to her. Damaged her. That's why she can't have another child."

Fire Girl's belly wrenched in horror. She turned away and covered her ears. "Please, no more."

Mouse took hold of her hands and yanked them away from her ears. "No, you asked me to begin this story and now you must hear *all* of it. Warriors tracked the men and killed them. They followed the trail and discovered the wagon camp."

"I know the rest," she whimpered. "They came for revenge, tried to kill me, and took my sister captive. What I don't understand is why I was allowed to live?"

"No, that's not all," Mouse said. "Our people often take children as adopted members, and you and your white sister were no different."

"But he shot me! He was going to kill me."

"If Lone Wolf wanted you dead, he would've killed you right then. He shot you in the leg to stop you from running, and to stop you from using your gun, but you used it anyway. The man you killed, he was Lone Wolf's father. Haven't you ever wondered where his parents were?"

No. It couldn't be true, but the memory of her shot hitting a man's chest flashed in her mind. "But—"

"The other man you killed was Lone Wolf's brother, who *was* trying to kill you, but only because *you* killed his father. Don't you see? The fact that Lone Wolf let you live shows his mercy."

She shook her head. It wasn't true. Lone Wolf wasn't merciful. He killed Papa.

Mouse's voice softened. "Fire Girl, he had to fight to spare your life. It was his idea to bring you to Red Hawk, and even to Eagle Beak. You should've been dead, but instead, you came to replace the one who already died."

She broke into loud sobs. The doorway darkened as people entered. She raised her head, startled into silence by the interruption. Lone Wolf and Badger stood just inside the lodge.

Badger sighed and looked at Mouse with disapproval. "You told her?"

Mouse stared at the ground. "She needed to know."

Lone Wolf squeezed his eyes shut and turned away.

Grief twisted into rage. Fire Girl jumped up to stand in front of him. "Is it true? You killed him? My father, and all the others? I always believed it was true, but now I know for sure." She sniffed, wiping away tears with the back of her hand. "Of course, it's true. You're a murderer. You *murdered* them."

Lone Wolf faced her, his brow drawn low over his dark eyes, but she was no longer afraid of his glare.

Her voice rose as she continued. "Why didn't you murder me? You should've killed me too. Was bringing me here supposed to add to my pain and your revenge? Am I supposed to be grateful for your *mercy*?" She took a step closer. "Well, I'm not grateful! I hate you for it. I've always hated you and I'll continue to hate you for as long as I draw breath."

"Fire Girl..." Mouse reached out to take her hand, but she yanked it away, keeping her eyes fixed on Lone Wolf.

"You should've killed me, because... because if you think I feel sympathy for what was done to your people, or for the ones I killed, you're wrong. I don't regret it!"

Her sharp words echoed in the lodge. For the briefest instant, she *did* regret them.

Mouse gasped and she caught Badger's shocked glare. Lone Wolf's jaw trembled, fists clenched at his sides. His silence infuriated her. Why didn't he do something, *say* something?

"I'd kill your father and your brother again, if I could," she spat.

It was an awful thing to say, but what happened was awful. Maggie's scream as she was snatched from the ground. All those women and children tortured and killed. She could still see their bodies, clothing torn, limbs ripped apart and the stench of blood. Her father was dead, slaughtered, and it was all Lone Wolf's fault. "As for your mother... maybe she deserved what happened to her."

He charged, growling with rage. He raised his fist, holding a knife, but she stood with her feet planted. Despite her defiance, her heart hammered at the ferociousness of his reaction. She waited for the blow, wishing he would strike and end it. Then she wouldn't have to live with the knowledge of what she had done, and worse, what her father had done.

"Go on, then," she echoed his dare, her tone as sharp as the blade above her.

But he held back, breathing raggedly as he sought to control himself. She swallowed a lump tinged with regret. It deepened when she realized his eyes were wet. He lowered the knife, then bolted from the lodge.

She gasped and pressed a hand onto her drumming chest. Mouse and Badger stood in stunned silence, but their looks of reproach and horror seared her with shame. Too appalled to face them, she ran out.

Part Two

13

Fury smoldered in Lone Wolf's chest, barely contained until he could find solitude. Outside his lodge, he untied his favorite horse, *Hïhkiapï,* Shadow, swung onto his back, and raced away.

The landscape passed in a blur as Shadow's hooves thundered along the ground, matching his heartbeat. He pushed the horse until the gray coat became slick with sweat and lather formed on Shadow's neck.

He charged up a hill, then let the horse slow and slid off. He dropped onto the grass. His heart drummed a rapid beat and his throat flamed. He rested his elbows on his knees and pressed his fists together.

"*Poisá wa'ipu,* crazy woman." The words came out like a curse. He should have killed her. He should have slashed his blade along her throat.

It wouldn't have taken much effort. The skin at the neck was delicate and soft. Her pulse, so visible, her blood warm and thick as it spilled, ending her life. Ending the constant ache her presence caused him. He'd come so close to doing it. Not just now. There were other times. More times than she even knew.

He drew his knife from the sheath at his waist. His father had given it to him after he killed his first buffalo. It had been his grandfather's knife beforehand, taken from an Apache warrior, the first man his grandfather killed. Who knew where it came from before that, or how many lives it'd taken altogether?

He ran his thumb along the edge, pressing down until a bead of blood appeared. He winced and brought his thumb to his mouth to suck off the drop.

It must take courage for women to cut themselves when they mourn the dead. No, not courage. They were driven by grief and a desire to drown out the pain in their hearts with the superficial pain of their flesh. Only once did he grieve openly, at his family's funeral, where all he could do was howl. Fire Girl had almost made him do that again.

"*Poisá!*"

He didn't think it was possible for her to hate him as much as she did, and he hadn't thought it possible for her to hurt him any more than she already had, but that was Fire Girl. Always surprising him with what she was capable of.

He ran his hands through his hair, then lay back, staring at the afternoon sky. His head pounded, thundering like a herd of buffalo. Outrage and anger twisted into grief and shame, then back again. He put his hand over his aching chest.

If only his mother were here. She'd know what to do. The irony of the thought made him laugh, then choke back a sob. The day his mother died had shattered him. It had been early in his seventeenth summer, and his journey as a warrior had already started, full of promise.

His father had been a great war leader, respected by every man in camp. People expected Lone Wolf and his older brother, Hunts Like a

Panther, to become war leaders like their father. Yet, it was his mother, Quail, who had truly understood him. Even Badger didn't understand him sometimes. Like himself, Badger had a strained relationship with his own brother, Buffalo Horn. Half-brother, as Badger was always quick to remind him.

Panther, with his constant teasing and attempts to provoke him. His father, with the endless pressure to gain his approval. Only with his mother had he felt completely at ease. They were all gone now.

He shut his eyes, allowing the memory he wanted to wipe from his mind to come forward.

He'd been the first to find her and the other women, their nearly nude bodies covered in blood, legs vulgarly spread. Quail had still been alive, barely breathing and unable to speak. The others arrived soon afterward. Fox Laugh sobbed over Playful Otter's body and Eagle Beak had to pry him off her so they could bury her.

His mother died moments later, while her men knelt beside her, helpless to save her. Overcome with wrath, he had wanted revenge and blood, and the others had been more than eager to join him.

Eagle Beak tracked the white-skins and found them the next day. Their vengeance had been brutal. They scalped the hair-mouths and hacked off their genitals. Some they burned alive or burned hands and feet before cutting them off and starting again. Panther cut a man's eyelids away, then buried him up to the neck in the dirt, leaving him to wither and die in the hot sun.

They spent two days torturing and killing those men, letting their screams drown out the grief, but he and the others hadn't been satisfied. They followed the trail to the wagon camp and started their acts of retribution all over again.

They had all been there. Fox Laugh, Badger, Eagle Beak, even Red Hawk, along with many others, yet Fire Girl directed her hatred at him alone.

All of it had been justified in his eyes. It was the way of the People, logical and necessary, but now, he wasn't so certain. If they hadn't been so ruthless in their quest for revenge, would his father and brother be alive today? Then there was the matter of Fire Girl.

He remembered her as he first saw her, a wild little thing with flaming hair. He had recognized that hair from one of the men he killed and knew she must be his relative.

From that moment, he intended to bring her back to the People. Whether as a captive slave or someone's adopted daughter, he hadn't been sure. That was for Winged Woman to decide, but he suggested Eagle Beak take her as compensation for his loss. They took several children that day, including Fire Girl and her sister, but in those first few days after the attack, the others had been traded to other bands, or killed.

Why *didn't* he kill her? She killed his father and brother. She deserved death. Perhaps he understood she acted in her own defense. Perhaps it was the knowledge they killed her own father, or perhaps it was the stark fact that she, a girl-child, had killed two of the finest warriors of Red Hawk's camp. It led him to believe she must have great medicine.

He had shot arrows at her, meant to kill, but they failed to strike. That had been reason enough. He needed to understand why the spirits protected her. Another reason there could have been too, but he wasn't ready to follow that path.

At the sound of movement in the grass, he sat up, knife in hand.

Badger rode up on his horse. "Are you done sulking?" He swung his leg over Juniper's head then hopped to the ground.

Lone Wolf sheathed the knife and stood. "I'm not sulking."

Badger huffed. "You have every right to. That woman is—"

"Crazy."

"I was going to say fearless."

He ignored Badger's smirk and stroked Shadow's muzzle. Fearless was right. He'd never known a woman with so much courage. He had laughed when he heard how she beat Sharp Mouth, knowing from experience she was a fierce fighter. He ran a finger over the now invisible line from his temple to his jaw. Fire Girl. She's well named.

"Where is she now?" he asked.

"She took off, ran north into the woods." Badger swung back onto his horse. "Are you ready to talk to Eagle Beak? I sent Mouse to tell him what happened."

He nodded as he hopped onto Shadow. "I hope you didn't scold my cousin too much."

"I'll beat her later." Badger winked.

When they reached the lodge, Fox Laugh was inside with Eagle Beak. No doubt this incident would add more fuel to his stance against Fire Girl. Still deeply mourning, he hadn't yet taken another wife, but it wasn't fair to Round Eyes that he rarely visited Eagle Beak's family. The child had suffered enough.

Pretty Robe sat on the far side of the lodge, her eyes red. Mouse sat with her. She gave Lone Wolf a look of apology, but he'd spare his cousin any additional guilt. It wasn't like she'd done anything wrong by telling Fire Girl something she should have learned years ago, things he'd intended to tell her himself, if she'd ever speak with him.

"You should never have kept that girl in the first place," Fox Laugh said to Eagle Beak. He turned on Lone Wolf. "And you. I don't understand why you didn't kill her for what she said."

Eagle Beak stepped between them. "No one will harm my daughter unless he desires a slow death."

"I'm not going to kill her," Lone Wolf said. "She hasn't returned?"

"No, I'm going to find her. She must have left camp. It'll be dark soon, and she doesn't have her bow."

Fox Laugh scoffed, shaking his head, but they both ignored him.

"I'll go with you," he said.

"No." Eagle Beak shook his head. "If she sees you, she might run further away. In fact, I think it would be best if you kept your distance." He gave him a look which said far more than words could.

Bridget ran through the camp and beyond. The land changed from prairie to forest, but she continued until her legs gave out and she collapsed.

Her mind raced. Guilt and denial divided her into fractured pieces. Her father could never attack innocent women, but in her heart, she knew it was true.

A distant memory came back to her. Her father sat at the table with another man in their old house. An empty whiskey bottle stood between them. It was recently after her mother's death.

"This country would be a lot better once they get rid of all the Indians. That's why they ought to kill their women and children. It's the only way to keep them from spreading like the disease they are."

The words repeated over, and she shook her head to throw them out, wailing and tearing the grass with her fists.

Why would these people keep her alive? Care for her? Mouse was right, she should be grateful to Lone Wolf for sparing her life, but... it didn't make any sense.

The idea of being obligated to him, or to anybody made her sick with contempt. How could she possibly go back there? She could never face him again. And yet how could she leave?

Had she really killed his father and brother? She couldn't even picture their faces. Just painted men on horses. Beasts, she had called them.

How foolish to never wonder who they were or whether anyone grieved their deaths. She was a murderer, too. Worst of all, she hardly gave much thought to the men after they died. Meanwhile, their loved ones had raised her.

She beat the ground with her fists, wishing she could understand. The words she said to Lone Wolf repeated in her mind and she covered her head in her arms. Overwhelmed with disgust at her cruelty, her stomach roiled. She had gotten her revenge but used words instead of knives. So why did it hurt so much?

She took an unsteady breath. It was time to go home and face her parents, who by now had probably heard what she said.

When she reached the grassy prairie, Eagle Beak was headed toward her, leading two horses. She ran to him. "Father." She sank under the weight of all that had happened and collapsed against his chest.

"Daughter," he murmured into her hair as he smoothed it. "It's all right."

She pulled away to look up at him. His daughter was dead. Horrifically killed by her own parent. "Why? How can you call me daughter? You must hate me."

"Fire Girl, listen to me. I loved my daughter very much. I was torn into pieces when she died. I will never forget her. But she's gone now and you're here. You're my daughter too, and I love you. Nothing will change that." He stroked her hair. Papa had rarely shown such tenderness. She couldn't even remember him ever saying he loved her. No wonder. She didn't deserve such kindness.

"Fox Laugh hates me. At least now I know why." Lone Wolf too, but she couldn't even say his name.

He sighed. "It's true he's still grieving, but it serves no purpose to hate you. In time he will see that, just as you must also let go of your grief."

Let go of her grief? Forgive Lone Wolf? It was too soon. She wasn't ready.

"I can't," she said.

"Whatever pain you've felt, whatever awful things have happened, you can't move forward if you're always looking behind you. You have a family that loves you, people who care about you. Your mother and me, Mouse, and Round Eyes. I'm not telling you to forget your white family, only that you let us be your family too."

What he said rang true. Eagle Beak, Pretty Robe, and Round Eyes were the loving family she'd missed. The one she had when Mama was alive, though she'd never imagined they'd be Comanche. And yet, Maggie was out there, somewhere, but she couldn't pester Eagle Beak about her white sister when he was asking for and offering acceptance.

"I do love you. Mother too. You are my family." She pulled away, bowing her head from the lingering shame of her harsh words. "I said horrible things to Lone Wolf. Awful things. I was cruel and wanted to hurt him. I was angry and ashamed, but I didn't mean it."

"Then you must tell him so."

"No, please don't make me. I can't speak to him. Just the sight of him reminds me of everything that happened. You said I must move forward, but when I'm near him, I can think of nothing else but that awful day. *Please*, Father."

"I won't force you to do anything you don't want to do, but this too, you must move past. Lone Wolf is an important member of this band, a close friend of your friend's husband, and a relative of this family. You can't avoid him forever."

Couldn't she though? Perhaps it was the other way around, and he would avoid her. Her face heated from the memory of her harsh words. "At least for now, can I just... keep my distance?"

Eagle Beak sighed. "If you promise me that one day you will apologize?"

She had no idea how or when she would be able to do such a thing, but she promised anyway. "I will."

14

Summer 1840

Lone Wolf brought Shadow to a halt then hopped to the ground. He patted the horse's neck and picked a few burrs from his mane. The gray coat was beginning to spot with white, especially around the muzzle and eyes, but it wasn't from age. Eventually, Shadow would dapple before becoming completely white. He might have to give him a new name.

The camp lay to the north, settled in one of the many small river valleys connected to the larger Washita River, but he rarely stayed in camp anymore. Over the past year since Fire Girl's vicious outburst, he spent his days raiding for horses, hunting, or like today, just riding. Not only to avoid her, though that was a large reason for it, but because he grew restless whenever he was in one place too long.

He couldn't understand why anyone would want to live in the same location, in a house you couldn't move, seeing the same view every day. The world was big, much bigger than he imagined as a child. He would never see all of it, but at least he could go wherever Shadow could take him.

He scanned the landscape. Hills rolled and dipped like water over rocks and the grass rippled in waves, like the ocean far to the south. There was little to break up the view. Well, except for that trail of smoke in the distance. And just when he was feeling at peace.

He swung back onto his horse, strung his bow, and selected an arrow from his quiver. The smoke dissipated, then billowed up again. It was a signal. Sentries would have seen the smoke by now and reported to Red Hawk.

He watched the pattern of smoke, then relaxed the instinctive tension in his muscles. The visitors were *Penateka*, Honey Eaters, from the southern bands. They rarely sent messengers out this way unless there was important news, like war. He pointed his horse back to camp where he'd welcome the arrivals, a tiny seed of apprehension growing in his gut.

Once the welcome feasting had ended, Lone Wolf joined the council in Red Hawk's lodge. The Penateka visitors, Tall Tree and Rolling Thunder, sat in a place of honor next to Red Hawk and Two Horns. Around them sat Badger, Buffalo Horn, Eagle Beak and other lead warriors. After continued polite conversation, the messengers brought up the purpose of their visit.

"We've been fighting the Texians for many years," Rolling Thunder said. "Our warriors have always been able to strike enough fear into them, so they never come very far into our lands, or if they do, they soon leave, but something has changed. The Texians have a new chief. They call him Lamar. His men have attacked our villages, and they've killed women and children along with our warriors. They're trying to drive us from our lands."

"Not only this," added Tall Tree. "The white-man's disease has spread throughout the south. Many people are dead or dying."

"Which disease is this?" Two Horns asked.

"The one that rots the face and body with sores. *Smah puks.*"

Lone Wolf closed his eyes and shook his head. The Penateka had developed a reputation of hospitality which extended to white-skins, and disease was their reward for their frequent contact. Though contact wasn't always peaceful. The Penateka had done their share of raiding settlements. He was grateful the northern bands, like the *Kotsoteka,* had remained unscathed by sickness.

"To prevent further death to our people," continued Rolling Thunder, "our leaders wanted to make peace with the white chiefs. They agreed to meet in the white village they call San Antonio."

Lone Wolf exchanged a glance with his grandfather. News of the council meeting in San Antonio had spread north, but Red Hawk had no interest in becoming involved in negotiations with white-skins. By the mournful looks on the faces of the Penateka leaders, he knew the result of the treaties were grim.

"The white chiefs demanded that we return all captives," Tall Tree said. "Only a few had been adopted, so our people agreed to bring as many as we could, but only to negotiate for goods and supplies. Our leaders went to San Antonio with their families. Our wives and children were curious to see the strange houses and buildings."

Warriors sometimes brought their families with them on raids, but it was a risk. In this case, the Penateka had expected a peace council, and therefore little risk to their women and children.

"Our leaders met the hair-mouth leaders in one of these buildings. They said we had to stop raiding and leave our hunting grounds. Stop raiding? Can you imagine?" Tall Tree's mouth scrunched in disgust while the others murmured in disbelief.

"They may as well ask us for the moon and stars. Again, the white leaders demanded we return the captives. We gave them one girl and a few others, but this didn't make them happy. The whites think we control all the men in every village, and don't understand we cannot tell others what to do."

Many of the men nodded. Lone Wolf watched for Eagle Beak's reaction. If white-skins had demanded Fire Girl's return, surely he would have refused. If news of this came to her ears, what would she say? Would she want to go back?

"Our chiefs became angry and tried to leave," continued Tall Tree. "Soldiers blocked the doors, saying they couldn't leave until every captive had been returned. So our chiefs tried to fight their way out, but they were unarmed and the soldiers had guns. We heard their screams and the gunshots from outside."

The lodge grew quiet as Tall Tree took a breath. His voice lowered. "Almost every chief was killed. The whites also fired at women and children. Many tried to hide in the buildings, but they set fire to their own houses and shot anyone who ran out to escape the flames. Those that lived, they took as hostages. We and some others were able to escape."

Tall Tree paused while Red Hawk and his men reacted in horror to this news. Lone Wolf seethed with rage. The idea that people had been attacked while in council was unfathomable.

"They let one of the chief's wives go. She told us the white-skins wouldn't release the hostages until all captives were returned, but we'll never give into their demands. The Texians are traitors, and we have no trust in them."

"What of the rest of the hostages?" asked Red Hawk.

Rolling Thunder laughed. "Those miserable Texians. They cannot keep our people captive. They all escaped."

"That's good, at least," Red Hawk said.

"It's not good enough," Tall Tree growled. "We must take revenge."

"What do you have in mind?" Two Horns asked.

"*Pochanaquarhip,* Buffalo Hump, is now one of the great chiefs in the south," Rolling Thunder said. "He's gathering warriors. He has gathered many already. After his uncle was killed in San Antonio, he had a great vision where the People drove the Texians into the sea. We will make this vision real. There will be a raid like no one has seen in many years."

Rolling Thunder stood up and raised his hands in the air, his face turned upwards as though he spoke to the spirits themselves.

"We'll drive the Texians out of our lands for good. We'll not forget their treachery and deceit. The Texians will pay for it with many lives. Then *they* will not forget, and they'll know never to cross into the land of the People again."

The room erupted in thunderous agreement. Nothing excited warriors like a revenge raid. Lone Wolf wasn't convinced. He'd feel better knowing exactly what Buffalo Hump planned to do.

"We've come to see if any of your warriors will join us," Tall Tree said. "We know there are many good warriors with the Kotsoteka. We can use as many powerful men as possible."

Several men eagerly volunteered to join the raid, including Eagle Beak and Badger, but Lone Wolf had yet to speak. Driving the Texians into the sea sounded well and good, but how were they going to accomplish that? White-skins had numerous guns while the People had few and killing them was like stomping on an ant, soon they came spilling from their holes.

Rolling Thunder turned to him. "Lone Wolf, your reputation speaks far past the hunting grounds of the Kotsoteka. We were hoping you would join us."

Well, now he couldn't outright refuse. "I'll raid with the Penateka. What the Texians did affects all the People, and they must know such murderous acts won't go unpunished..." He paused.

The Texians might never leave, and retaliation would only lead to further war. Such thoughts made him weary and sad for the future of the People, but he couldn't voice these misgivings. This wasn't a time for uncertainty.

The discussion of captives reminded him of something he'd been wondering about.

"You said captives were returned in San Antonio?"

"Yes, a few," Rolling Thunder responded.

"Was there a girl, about ten summers? Yellow hair, blue eyes?"

"There may have been. I've seen many yellow-hairs. Why do you ask?"

Eagle Beak met Lone Wolf's eyes and spoke up. "He's asking about the white-sister of my daughter. We traded her with another band soon after they came to live with us."

"We heard about this girl." Tall Tree leaned forward. "So, it's true? Your father and brother were killed by a white girl-child?"

He flinched, annoyed that such respected leaders would break taboo in council. "It's true." He gave each man a hard look, daring them to ask any further questions.

Tall Tree cleared his throat and looked away. "We're returning south in two days. We'll join Buffalo Hump's war party in the valley along the Guadalupe, north of the San Antonio village."

The talk continued into the night, as Rolling Thunder explained more details of Buffalo Hump's great raid and Red Hawk's men coordinated their plans. Lone Wolf's doubts diminished, and finally, the council ended.

Rolling Thunder turned to Red Hawk, "I'm glad your men will be joining us. I know Buffalo Hump will be pleased."

As the men departed the lodge. Eagle Beak was the first to exit. Lone Wolf caught up to him and matched his stride. "Are you going to tell her?" he asked.

"No. And I hope you don't plan to."

"Eagle Beak, she has a right to know, especially if her sister was taken back."

"We don't know if she was."

"We don't know if she wasn't."

Eagle Beak stopped. "Do you want her to leave?"

Lone Wolf said nothing.

"That's what I thought." Eagle Beak turned back to his lodge.

He grabbed his arm. "It's best not to hide this from her. If she finds out—"

"I know what will happen if she finds out." Eagle Beak shook his arm free. "She's my daughter. This isn't up to you." He entered his lodge, closing the flap.

———◆◇◆———

Fire Girl and her mother were still awake when Eagle Beak returned from council. He sat at his place and Pretty Robe set some food before him. He only nibbled at it. She watched but didn't press for information. For several moments, the only sound in the lodge was Round Eyes' soft snoring. Finally, Eagle Beak cleared his throat.

"There's going to be a raid. I, and some other men, will join the Penateka in two days. Then we'll head south. We could be gone a long time."

"I'll pack your things in the morning," Pretty Robe said.

"Fire Girl, I'll be counting on you to hunt and provide for your mother and Round Eyes while I'm gone," Eagle Beak said.

Her chest lifted with pride. "Of course," she answered.

"Red Hawk will move the camp further and further south, into Penateka territory. He'll likely move as far south as the Brazos. Then we won't have to travel as far to reunite, if things don't go well."

"I hope you come home to a victory celebration," Pretty Robe said.

The news of the raid wasn't surprising, but Fire Girl was unsure how to feel about it. Gossip had spread about the visitors, about how Texians had massacred the Penateka chiefs while in council.

The chiefs would have been unarmed. They went into the building expecting a peace talk, but instead had been killed. All those bands, now leaderless. Many families left without a husband or a father. They probably killed the women and children as well. It happened again and again. She had heard the stories in her childhood. At the time, such tales had evoked feelings of justice served, of evil and savage heathens meeting a necessary end. But now, she thought of the families and people in mourning.

The memory of the violence at the wagon raid, and the knowledge that similar, if not worse, acts were about to be repeated against the people of Texas made her conscience heavy. And yet, outrage at the injustice that had been dealt to the People also weighed on her mind. The People hadn't asked for this war. This was their homeland. The Texians and other whites had invaded the land of the People. Her people had been betrayed. *Her* People.

But she also heard the Texians had demanded the return of captives. Would Eagle Beak share this news with her?

"Is that all, Father?" she asked.

"It's all you need to know." He rose and undressed for bed.

She went to her own bed and fought tears as she lay deep in thought. Eagle Beak was only protecting her by not telling her about the demand for returned captives, or about the Council House killings, or even to make it clear the raid was against Texas, but it still hurt he would keep it from her. It was especially hurtful after finding out everyone had kept the truth of the wagon raid from her.

But how had she behaved after she had found out that truth? Perhaps they were right not to trust her.

15

Lone Wolf and his companions descended through a gap in the San Saba Hills. Lodges, people, and horses spread along the valley below in such immensity it struck him with awe. It was the largest gathering of warriors he or any of the other men had seen. Not just warriors. Young boys herded and cared for horses. Women cooked or mended clothing but were also present to provide comfort for their men.

Lone Wolf, and the other warriors of Red Hawk's band also brought young herders with them. The boys took the spare horses to the grazing grounds, whooping as they joined other braves in their races and games.

Tall Tree and Rolling Thunder rode ahead to alert Buffalo Hump of their arrival. Warriors from other bands had joined Red Hawk's men along the way. Their party of almost two hundred would bring the total to nearly a thousand.

Eagle Beak's eyes shone with excitement. "The white-skins are in for a surprise."

Lone Wolf's feeling of awe faded as doubt nagged him. Were the people of San Antonio aware of them? Surely, they had sentries who would have alerted the town of their presence and would have sent word to villages further south.

Buffalo Hump planned to attack the villages along the river, all the way to the sea. If the white-skins had enough time to prepare, the People's style of attack would be ineffective, and perhaps disastrous. The People counted on both speed and surprise to ensure victory in battle. Could a party of this size move quickly enough to attack and retreat?

Once Lone Wolf and the others arrived, they had a brief rest before he and his uncle Two Horns joined the gathering in Buffalo Hump's meeting lodge. Representatives from other bands were already seated, and the conversation was well underway. He sat out of the way, feeling somewhat out of place in a group of mostly Penateka leaders.

Most were young, as too many of the older leaders were now dead. Young men would be eager for battle and honor. He frowned. Wisdom and experience were necessary in an endeavor such as this.

Mexican scouts sat toward the rear of the lodge, with hats in their laps and possibly pistols beneath. They looked around nervously, as if they expected a warrior to try and take their scalps. No doubt they had been attacked by the People in the past. What could Buffalo Hump have promised them in exchange for their help?

Kiowa warriors sat among them as well. That didn't surprise him. Kiowa were allies and fierce fighters. Their presence was encouraging. He turned his attention back to the conversation.

"We should attack the white village of San Antonio. It's where my father was killed. I want revenge on those people," said one man.

"There will be soldiers, and many guns. We don't have as many," said another.

"This isn't the time for fear. Look at how many warriors we have. The white soldiers will be fewer."

"There are other villages down the river. We should attack them. They will be unprepared."

Lone Wolf looked to Buffalo Hump for his reaction to this debate. The chief's face was expressionless, but his eyes betrayed frustration. His dark hair was loose and cut to his shoulders in mourning. Long cylinders of silver hung from each ear. Though he still had some years of youth ahead of him, his grief over those lost at the council massacre, and the strain of leadership over so many men showed on his face. A furrow of lines seemed permanently etched on his brow.

As the argument carried on, Lone Wolf tried to listen and ignore his apprehension, but he noticed a warrior seated on the far edge of the lodge. The warrior was unusually tall, which is why he caught his attention, but there was something else about him which captured his interest.

The young man seemed disengaged by the conversation but observed the men with obvious interest. He wasn't much older than Lone Wolf but had the air of confidence and experience of someone twice his age. A knowing smile spread across the warrior's face as he sat back and scanned the room. His eye caught Lone Wolf's and his smile widened as he gave him a nod of greeting.

Lone Wolf leaned over to his uncle. "Who's that man?" he asked, discreetly gesturing to the young warrior. Two Horns glanced over.

"He's *Quahadi*, of the Antelope band, for sure. By his height, I'd guess him to be the son of *Pohebits-quasho*, Iron Jacket."

Lone Wolf stared with admiration at the young warrior. The Quahadi were the most formidable warriors of the People, and a chief's son was likely to be well-respected. A friendship with him would be sure to advance his skills and reputation. It wasn't only himself who would benefit. The Kotsoteka as a whole would be stronger with a working alliance with the Quahadi.

The voice of Buffalo Hump brought him back to the conversation. "As much as I would like to attack San Antonio, we'll have more success if we strike the smaller villages along the river. We'll hit them hard, but fast. Kill as many as you can, as quickly as you can. Take captives, horses, and loot if you must, but do not linger. Do not give them time to gather an army. We'll strike the next village, and the next, and the next, and soon the Texians will know nothing but fear."

Dark-skinned slaves were working in the fields when the warriors arrived at the first town. The line of raiders stretched in either direction, as far as Lone Wolf could see. Hundreds of fourteen-foot lances glinted in the afternoon sun.

Badger, Big Tooth, and the rest of Red Hawk's warriors sat mounted beside him, carrying bows, war clubs and firearms as well as lances and shields. Their bodies and faces were covered in patterns of colorful paint, though black was most common, the color of war and revenge.

"This is a day to remember," Badger said, his face painted in vertical black and white stripes, like the animal of his name.

"The white-skins fear us more than anyone, and if they don't, they soon will," agreed Eagle Beak.

Lone Wolf surveyed the town the Mexican guides had called Victoria. Beyond the fields stood several buildings and houses, but there were few residents visible. To the north, a corral overflowed with a large herd of mustangs, just as the scouts had said. Traders had recently arrived and brought the horses to be sold.

He adjusted himself in his seat on Shadow's back and moved his quiver so he could easily reach his arrows. Shadow shifted, as restless and nervous as himself.

"Any moment now, my friend," he whispered to the horse, stroking his neck.

When he was a child, he assumed he would never know fear or anxiety once he became a true warrior. Now he understood the fear would always be there, as long as he desired to live. What made him a warrior was not a lack of fear, but the ability to use it, to channel the emotion into strength and rage, transforming his energy into something he could use.

He took a breath to settle his nerves and slow his heart. He closed his eyes, recalling his dead mother, the massacred chiefs and their families, the wave of disease destroying the southern bands, everything that fueled his hatred of Texians until he saw nothing but black behind his lids. When he opened them, he was ready.

The call of an eagle cut the silence, Buffalo Hump's signal. Lone Wolf and the others swooped in, their war cries echoing across the sky. The field slaves and their overseers fled in a desperate race to the safety of the town, but most didn't make it.

He rode in the middle of the charge. The warriors at the front released their arrows at the terrified townsfolk. Left with few victims, most of the war party raced off to surround the town. Others headed for the corral. Unable to resist the lure of horses, Lone Wolf joined them.

Other warriors reached the corral before him and released the horses. They came spilling out in a panic. He raced along the herd to keep
them headed northeast. Some of the herder boys rode up and took the
lead. Lone Wolf jerked on Shadow's reins as Badger pulled up beside
him.

"They've surrounded the town, but we need more men on the west
side. Come join us." Badger said.

"How are the townspeople defending?"

"They're armed and firing shots, but sporadically. I think they're
limited in their ammunition. They're building barricades around the
town."

"If we can't break through, let's set fire to the buildings," he said.

"Let's do that anyway." Badger rode off and he followed him toward
the edge of town.

Other men had already lit fires. They used torches to light arrowheads coated with gunpowder and grease, then shot them across
the barricades. The air grew hot from the flames, already heavy with
screams and war whoops.

Lone Wolf spotted a structure which had yet to be ignited. He
tugged on the loop weaved into Shadow's mane to check that it was
secure, then pulled it over his head and under his arms. He grabbed a
torch from a young boy and raced toward the building.

He kept Shadow at a furious pace, knowing he would be within
range of gunfire. Before he dropped to Shadow's side, held only by his
heel hooked over the horse's back and the loop, he launched the torch
over a barricade. It landed on the roof and instantly set the structure
ablaze in the dry heat. Shadow darted away as gunfire erupted around
them.

As the fire spread, men and women fled from the burning buildings. Caught between flames and warriors waiting with notched bows, they dropped as they were hit.

Lone Wolf loosed his arrows, killing two men and a woman carrying a child. His arrow flew with such force it pierced the woman's body as well as her child's, pinning them together as they fell. He rode on, looking for further targets.

The battle—if it could be called that—lost steam. There were far too many warriors and far too few townsfolk within range. Most of the warriors looted empty buildings while others rode off, back to their temporary camp, probably to divvy up the stolen horses. There would be few left for him, and the ones remaining would be of low quality.

He searched for Badger, and found him bent over a few bodies, taking scalps. Big Tooth was with him in the act of slicing off a dead man's genitals.

"I think we're done here," Lone Wolf said.

Badger shrugged. "We could make a few more kills."

Big Tooth stuffed the genitals into the dead man's mouth, taking care to leave the end sticking out, so any survivors would be sure to notice. Lone Wolf looked away. He prayed that when he died in battle, one of his men could save his body from such an insult.

"What's wrong, brother?" Badger looked around. "I know it's not what we expected. Maybe the next town will be more exciting."

"It's not excitement I want." He took a drink from his waterskin. "Attacking a few towns won't send the Texians fleeing from our lands. This isn't the great vision Buffalo Hump promised."

Badger stared at him. "You worry too much. We've just gotten started."

"I heard, once we reach the sea, there is a great town there," Big Tooth said. "There'll be many more horses, maybe guns."

Before day's end, they headed back to camp. Some horses hadn't been claimed, but upon examination, Lone Wolf determined they'd only serve as pack horses. He took them anyway, needing as many horses as possible. He joined the others to rest and gamble for more and better horses.

In the morning, they attacked the town again with little result. The next few days were the same, attacking small settlements, stealing horses, and taking captives. They traveled by night, silent in the darkness. Any metal or ornament was muffled with cloth or hide. No words were spoken except the quietest whisper. The party stretched for miles, small groups of warriors and their women traveling in groups, but still following the main goal of Buffalo's Hump's great vision.

Lone Wolf, Badger, and Big Tooth traveled with Eagle Beak and Two Horns. At times, he wondered about the Quahadi warrior he'd seen at council. The young leader was probably having more success than they were at reducing the population of white-skins.

At times they found small parties of men between settlements, and they passed the days killing and torturing them. Stopping at a watering hole, they found one man hidden among the rocks and dry brush, probably a villager who'd managed to escape. Badger roped him and dragged him out. The man screamed and shouted, while Badger laughed. Lone Wolf drew his bow, intending to kill him quickly, but Two Horns stopped him.

"This one's a screamer. Let's have some fun."

He shrugged and led Shadow to the water. He wasn't interested in torturing the man, not out of any sympathy, but because he wanted to keep moving. He had no intention of denying his uncle's entertainment. They were all frustrated.

Eagle Beak and Big Tooth held the man still while Two Horns sliced off the bottoms of his feet. His shrieks rang out in the dry air. They forced him to stand and walk along the hot prairie ground, leaving bloody footprints in the dust. He and Badger kept their bows pointed at their captive while the group headed south, the man tied to Two Horn's horse by his neck. He would walk or be dragged, and Two Horns took care to take the rockiest of paths, even forcing the man to walk over a bed of spiny cactus.

"Look at him dance," said Badger laughing.

The man's cries wore on Lone Wolf's already frayed nerves. He sighed. "Let me kill him already, Uncle."

Two Horns sighed in mockery. "Does nothing ever amuse you?"

"Watching you try to hit a target always amuses me."

Two Horns notched an arrow and shot it at their captive, hitting him square between the eyes. The man dropped like a rock. Two Horns jumped from his horse to retrieve the arrow, but he struggled to pull it free from the man's skull.

Lone Wolf smirked. "This is amusing, at least."

Two Horns scowled again. He planted his foot on the man's face and yanked the arrow out. The iron head was missing. Lone Wolf laughed, even Eagle Beak was chuckling. After Two Horns dug through the man's brains to find his arrowhead, he took the scalp, then wiped his hands on his leggings.

"How much further is it to the sea?" asked Badger, trying not to laugh. He probably wanted to stay on his father-in-law's good side.

Lone Wolf gazed south. "I think we should be there in another day or two."

By evening, they rejoined the main party, which had condensed back into its full force of a thousand people and three times as many horses. According to the scouts, the port town of Linnville lay ahead. A faint breeze carried the salty odor of the sea, and the landscape had become sandy and white with scattered marshes. They struck a light camp, then would continue during the night to strike the town at dawn.

That night, Lone Wolf lay restless and unable to sleep. In the near distance, a baby cried. By the accompanied female screams, he guessed it wasn't a child that belonged to the People. Men shouted while the woman continued to scream. The men told her to quiet the baby, but the baby wouldn't stop. Then suddenly it did. The woman wailed louder, then broke into heartbroken sobs. He shut his eyes and turned over.

16

As the sun peeked over the big water, Lone Wolf and the other warriors descended upon Linnville. The crescent formation of mounted warriors closed over the town like the mouth of a beast. Their lances and arrows like jagged teeth biting down on its prey.

He and Badger charged through the streets on their horses. Warriors burst through windows and doors, firing guns and loosing arrows as people scrambled to get away. People ran screaming from their homes as he raced Shadow down the main road. They trampled bodies, dodging fellow warriors as they shot arrow after arrow into terrified citizens. He had expected the residents to be armed and ready for the attack, but the war party caught them by surprise.

"The spirits are with us, brother," Badger shouted over the din. "These white-skins are easy to kill."

Lone Wolf couldn't help but smile. It was true. Ever since the attack on Victoria, they'd faced little resistance.

The road opened to sprawling docks. Rows of long buildings faced the shore, while boats with tall posts formed a jagged outline along the horizon, mimicking warrior lances in a battle line. Gulls circled overhead and the big water shone, blue, orange and silvery white in the early morning sun, but there was no time to appreciate the beauty of the sunrise.

Men, women and children filled the open space, climbing over each other as they fled into the water. A long wooden platform stretched into the expanse of the bay, while the citizens of Linnville fled down its path. They jumped off the platform, clambered onto boats, or ran straight into the water, splashing and yelling as they sought refuge from the attack. Boats bobbed and dipped as each one filled beyond capacity. As the boats moved out into the bay, the townsfolk stared, mouths agape at the place they'd once called home, now occupied by the People. Buffalo Hump's dream had become real.

Lone Wolf used the last of his arrows to kill those within range, then glanced around. Only fellow warriors remained. With the town now empty of white-skins, men were looting houses and stores in search of useful items. Their shouts and laughter filled the air as the buildings' contents spilled into the streets before the structures were set on fire.

Men strutted and danced, sporting tall hats and dark-colored jackets with bright buttons. Cloth, lace, dishware, dresses, and hundreds more items, some of which he had no name for, cluttered the ground. He didn't care for white-man's clothes or finery. Guns and ammunition were the only things of value.

Along the waterfront stood several large rectangular-shaped buildings. The doors were too big and the windows too high to serve as homes, and while he'd seen several large houses in the main area of town, those had been richly decorated while these buildings were plain.

"Come on," he said to Badger. "Let's see what's in those buildings." He sped off to investigate, leaving the outraged residents to shout what could only be threats and curses as the town was destroyed.

When he reached the first building, he dismounted. Two large wooden doors, barred with iron, stood between him and whatever goods lay hidden inside. He shook the handle, testing the door's strength, then slammed his shoulder into the wooden panel.

Badger scoffed. "Move out the way." He threw his entire weight against the door. It rattled and groaned but didn't budge.

"So much for raw muscle." His mouth turned up at Badger's grimace of self-disgust.

"Did you bring a hatchet?"

"Yes, but it'll take all morning to get through." Lone Wolf looked up at the window above him. "Give me a boost."

"What are you fools doing?" Two Horns and Eagle Beak rode up, leading spare horses loaded with goods. A couple herder boys held the reins to additional spare mules.

Eagle Beak swept his arm to point out the loaded animals. "We found plenty of iron tools, pretty cloth and lace to give to our wives, but only a few guns."

"Lone Wolf thinks there might be guns in here," Badger said. "But we can't get through."

"Burn it down." Two Horns jumped from his horse and ordered one of the boys to find him a torch.

"A fire is risky," Eagle Beak said. "There could be gunpowder inside." He pointed his horse in the direction of the main area of town. "Let's look somewhere else."

Lone Wolf ignored the debate and examined where the door connected to the wall. Iron plates attached the wooden planks to the stone walls, but they were rusty and worn. He turned to Badger. "Get some rope and bring over those mules."

"How about we use this?" Big Tooth arrived and was carrying a long chain. "I should have known you bastards couldn't accomplish anything without me."

"Good, while you work on the door, I'll climb up and see what's inside." Lone Wolf took a few steps back. "We need to break that win—" Before he could finish the words, the window shattered and shards rained down from above.

"Which of you idiots did that?" Badger picked off pieces of glass from his wide shoulders. A gash on his cheek shone bright red with blood.

"You're welcome," Two Horns said, holding another large stone in his hand.

By now, other warriors had gathered. While they attached the chain to the mules, Badger and Two Horns rolled barrels from the docks and stood them below the broken window.

Lone Wolf hopped onto a barrel. He jumped and tried to catch his fingers over the edge of stone surrounding the broken opening. Humid heat and the stench of tar and seaweed left him feeling weak and weighed down. He landed back onto the barrel. It wobbled below his feet so he planted his palms on the wall to steady himself.

"That was pathetic." Badger eyed him from the ground.

"It was just a test jump." He wiped his sweaty hands on his leggings. Concentrating on his target, he made another attempt, this time grabbing onto the ledge. He braced his foot against the wall and propelled himself upward.

The ledge was covered in broken glass. Pieces cut into his forearm as he pressed down to support himself as he climbed the rest of the way. He removed the shards and crouched on the ledge, peering into the building.

The room was dim with shafts of light angling from the windows facing the water, illuminating motes of dust floating in the musty air. He waited for his eyes to adjust before he could distinguish the numerous crates and barrels piled inside. He hopped to the ground, landing lightly on his feet.

Other men followed, landing behind him. They spread out among the boxes, prying them open with hatchets, knife blades or bare hands in some cases. Lone Wolf found a long iron rod hanging on the wall and used it to pry open a stack of crates in a corner of the large room. Wooden lids clattered to the floor and men's shouts echoed around him. The air filled with sawdust and swirling motes dust. Then a loud crack and a crash, followed by more men spilling through the now open doorway.

Lone Wolf hardly noticed it all. He opened crate after crate, his disappointment drowning what was left of his optimism and hope for the raid. There were no firearms. No ammunition. No powder, nothing that would prove especially useful against the wave of Texians he knew was coming. They might be out there, in the water, but it was only a matter of time before the tide came in.

"Nothing, eh?" Badger came up from behind him and patted his shoulder. "There are still plenty of useful items."

He was right. There were pots, tools, and other metal items they could use. Lone Wolf wasn't especially fond of using things that came from white-skins, but if metal arrowheads and guns could be used against them, then he wouldn't hesitate to take them.

A worthy man could keep several arrows in flight while a hair-mouth reloaded his gun. Arrows didn't jam or backfire, and they were silent, which was especially important when one depended on the advantage of stealth. And while ammunition was scarce, a man could always make more arrows.

White-skins were clumsy while firing from horseback, and they often didn't. All the People had to do was ride in, circle around them, kill as many as they could, then ride out again before the white-skins knew what hit them. But somehow, he knew this wouldn't always be the case. Firearms were always changing, improving, and it wouldn't be long before the People would be attacked by weapons no arrow could defeat.

The firearm that had killed his brother and father was different than any he had seen. It had been his secret hope to find more of those here.

Accepting disappointment, he brought in the pack horses and mules. He grabbed tools and supplies and loaded them onto the animals. He found bolts of pretty cloth to give to Winged Woman, Laughing Bird and Squirrel. Ribbons, sewing kits with thread and those coveted metal needles, more metal pots, and sacks of coffee and sugar. In one crate, he found a pile of books. He took several stacks. Books could be torn, and the pages made excellent stuffing for shields.

After he had taken what he needed, he signaled to the others. It was time to go. Lone Wolf, Badger, and Eagle Beak led their horses and mules back into the sunlight of the dock. Men danced and celebrated in the streets. They were still dressed in bright clothes, black tailcoats, and even lacy corsets. They pranced and spun parasols in parody of the townsfolk watching from the boats.

In the near distance, gunfire popped in a regular rhythm. The sharp odor of blood and beast stung Lone Wolf's nose. Over the din of singing and laughter, he could hear the groans and bellows of hundreds of cattle.

"Before I came here, I saw warriors corralling the animals into a pen. Now they're killing them," Eagle Beak said.

Lone Wolf understood. The warriors would ensure the survivors would have nothing left to survive on.

The shouts and laughter grew sharper, and he turned back to the water. A white-skin stood in the sand, dripping wet with seawater. He waved a pistol in the air and shouted curses. Warriors laughed and taunted him as he staggered and pointed his weapon. Laughter faded and died. The gun clicked, empty and useless.

After a moment of stunned silence, the warriors saluted the man's bravery with war cries and whoops then continued their celebration. The startled man fell back into the water, then scrambled back to the safety of the boats.

"He must be crazy," Badger said.

"Or just stupid," Lone Wolf said, but he was thinking the man was neither. If more white skins were as brave as that man, the People were doomed.

They led the horses back down the main road, collecting loose arrows as they went, distinguishing them by the different designs painted on the end. Several warriors had found barrels of liquor and drank

172

themselves into a stupor. They lay on steps or porches, unconscious, or in the street in pools of vomit.

Buffalo Hump came riding down the road, shouting his disapproval at the drunk men. "Get up, you fools! Every man needs to be ready to fight. We've been here too long." He tried to maintain order, but it was chaos. Too many men were caught up in the frenzy of the raid. It wasn't just the men. Women and families of the warriors, who had camped beyond the town, had come to join the celebration.

"Buffalo Hump is right," said Two Horns. "More white-skins will come. They could be on their way now. We need to go."

Lone Wolf had been thinking the same, but there was still one task he had yet to do. "Badger, will you take my spare horses back to camp? All but this one." He kept the reins to a pack mule with the lightest load and to his favorite horse.

"Where are you going?"

"I need a gift."

Badger nodded. He understood without needing an explanation. While the others headed back, Lone Wolf mounted Shadow and turned him down the side streets, heading toward an area that had suffered the least looting.

He found a house that looked almost untouched. The door at the front was still closed while most of the doors at other houses were broken or missing. He rode Shadow into the yard and dismounted, leaving the horse and the mule by the steps. No one would take his horse or supplies. The People happily stole from white-skins, but they almost never stole from one another.

He hopped up the steps and stood before the door. He had encountered enough houses to know how to turn the knob. Before he opened it, he drew his knife, then slowly pushed on the door. He paused, waiting. There was a chance white-skins were hidden inside, ready with a rifle to blow out his brains. He crouched and crept in, staying low to the ground.

The house wasn't as untouched as he had thought. The room was destroyed. Feathers from pillows coated the broken glass and splintered furniture. He carefully stepped around the wreckage and gave a warning shout, letting any warriors know of his presence. There was no response. Confident the house was empty, he continued through.

He came to a stairway. The bottom floor had been thoroughly looted, so he doubted he would find anything there, but perhaps the upper floor had been ignored. As he ascended the stairs, he tried to fight the overwhelming sense of confinement. The walls were too close together, like a closing trap.

He almost never went into these buildings for that reason. It still baffled him. How could people live in places like this? A lodge was smaller, but its walls could breathe. Light shone through and one could still see the sky through a smoke hole. But one didn't spend all their time inside a lodge anyway. Time was better spent outside, under the open sky. He had to hurry before he couldn't stand it.

He ran his hand along the papery wall, curious about the pattern that covered it. Paintings hung in rows along the walls, scenes of places he'd never see, and of people he'd never know, nor did he care to. He reached the top of the stairs. There were three more doors. He entered the first one on his left.

The room was untouched. A small bed sat in the corner, covered in a white blanket with tiny pink flowers along the edge. One of those tall wooden boxes the white-skins used to store their clothes stood against the wall. On top of it, sat a couple dolls. The ones with faces easy to break. Their black eyes stared at him accusingly.

He stepped in and pulled out drawers, searching through the frill and white linen. He poked under the bed, then sat on it. It squeaked under his weight. The room belonged to a child, a little girl from the looks of it. He ran his hand along the smooth, cool expanse of white, fingering the delicate lace on the pillows and leaving stains from the grease and grime of his fingers.

Had Fire Girl slept in a room like this? Had she owned dolls like the ones on that shelf?

Somehow, he knew she hadn't. The girl that slept in this room would never carry a firearm or use it against grown men. The girl of this room would never hunt and kill a buck all on her own. He wasn't going to find anything for Fire Girl in here.

He rose from the bed and continued down the hall. He skipped the next door and went straight to the room at the end. The bed was much larger, but still, more white and lace. Two more tall boxes full of clothes sat against the wall. But there was something else, a small table with a chair in front. He approached it to examine the items that lay on the table but then stopped. A mirror hung above the table, and he was struck by his own reflection.

Of course, he'd seen it before, hundreds of times, in streams and pots of water. He even owned a small mirror he used when he applied his paint, but he had never seen a reflection like this. The mirror was as clear as a pool on a breezeless day. He could almost see his whole body, as though another man stood in the room.

He laughed. He clearly didn't belong. Dirty, sweaty, covered in paint, grease and even blood. It'd been days since his last bath, and he stank worse than the cattle being killed. Meanwhile, the room was clean and bright. There wasn't even a speck of dust on the furniture. He admired the woman who could keep a home so clean.

Still chuckling to himself, he scanned the items on the table. Bottles of smelly perfume and trinkets of jewelry that were either too delicate or would look as silly and out of place on the prairie, as he did in the house. He picked up a flimsy shawl that lay on the corner of the table, revealing a set of items that made his delay worth the trouble.

It was a hairbrush and matching hand mirror. He picked them up, feeling the texture of molded silver which formed scrolling tendrils curled around flowers, reminding him of Fire Girl's wavy hair. They were fine, and perhaps too fragile and elegant for life with the People, but they were exactly the sort of thing he'd been looking for, something practical, but beautiful to look at. Just like her.

He wrapped them in the flimsy shawl, he could give her that too, then a blanket of wool to protect them. He didn't know how, or when, or even if he'd ever give them to her, but he'd hold onto them, for as long as it took.

He descended the stairs, two at a time, then ran out the door. It was long past the time to vacate the town. The party continued, but there were already fewer men in the streets. The heat of the air had intensified, but it wasn't just from the sun. The whole town was ablaze. He needed to get out. He stuffed the gift into his pack on his mule and hopped onto Shadow. Then he gave the horse a squeeze with his knees. Shadow raced out of town, pulling the loaded mule behind him.

The party continued at camp, against a backdrop of flames as Linnville burned to the ground. Townsfolk still in boats rocked in the water. Even if they could come ashore, there would be nothing to come home to.

Nightfall came and once the frenzy had died down, the men and women packed their belongings onto ponies and travois already heavily loaded with stolen goods. They began the slow trek north.

Lone Wolf had participated in the celebration enough to have woven strips of calico into Shadow's mane. Warriors had found crates full of lead ingots and those had been distributed among the men. His pack horses strained under the weight, concerning him with their slow pace. His anxiety returned, a seed of apprehension now sprouted into genuine worry.

From the corner of his eye, he spotted the Quahadi party. They were lightly loaded and heading further west, away from the main group. He watched them go with regret, then turned to Eagle Beak. "We should break away, and head west."

"What are you talking about?" Eagle Beak said, still giddy with excitement.

"Don't you think we're traveling too slowly? Why are we going back the way we came? The white-skins will be waiting for us."

Eagle Beak looked in the direction Lone Wolf had been gazing. The Quahadi disappeared in the darkness. He turned back, a frown of disapproval on his face.

"We need to stay together. Don't go following those men simply because you admire them. They may be brave, but it's not wise to fracture our group. We have strength in numbers. The white-skins cannot stop a war party of this size."

"Buffalo Hump will lead us into an ambush. We were successful when we surprised them and moved through quickly. Now they're waiting for us and we're slow. We need to separate and take different routes—"

"Do you doubt Buffalo Hump, who is a far more experienced warrior than you? You agreed to his leadership when you agreed to come on this raid."

"I follow a man only when it agrees with my own wisdom. I do not agree with this course." He commanded Shadow to a stop.

"So, you look to follow a man you don't even know?"

"I know him no less than I know Buffalo Hump."

"Who has proven himself a leader already." Eagle Beak moved his horse closer and lowered his voice to a stern whisper. "The reason I like you, the reason I agreed to your offer, is because you're not foolhardy like your brother was. Don't prove me wrong." He started to ride off.

Lone Wolf's face grew hot with fury. He hopped from Shadow, ran in front of Eagle Beak's horse, and grabbed the reins. "This has nothing to do with my brother."

"It does when you refuse to listen to reason and won't take the safer course."

"Is that why you encouraged your daughter to marry Fox Laugh instead of my brother? Because it was the safer course? Did that choice save her?" As soon as he said the words, he winced. He'd gone too far by bringing up Playful Otter's death and her choice of husbands.

Eagle Beak swung off his horse and strode to face him with so much outrage Lone Wolf took a step back. "How dare you? The reason Fox Laugh didn't escort the women on their honey hunt was because he chose to confront your brother. With the women gone, he could talk to him without my daughter knowing. He was trying to save her from disgrace."

Lone Wolf looked away and swallowed his anger. He suspected that Panther's involvement with Playful Otter had been the reason the women had left unaccompanied, but he'd never been sure. He regretted not going himself, but would that have even saved them?

"Your foolish brother wouldn't stay away from her. If he'd only known his place..." Eagle Beak's voice broke in anguish.

Lone Wolf focused on the ground. "It's not my brother's fault she's dead."

"Maybe not, but it's Panther's own fault he's dead."

His head shot back up. Eagle Beak broke taboo by saying Panther's name, but they had both gone far past any code of honor. "Fire Girl pulled that trigger."

"Yes, she did, but you know that's not what I meant." Eagle Beak's voice softened. "You warned him. At the raid. I heard you tell him to stay back. You knew he'd get himself killed, but he didn't listen."

That was because Panther wanted to die. He didn't care to go on once the woman he loved was dead. The fear of death had left him.

Eagle Beak broke the silence. "I am asking you to listen to my warning now. Tell your men to stay."

Lone Wolf remained silent for several long moments. "I will stay, but only because you ask me to. I still believe this is unwise, but I don't speak for anyone but myself. They are not my men to order, and each man will choose his own path."

They both mounted and continued with the group, but Lone Wolf's uneasiness had grown large enough it was beginning to choke him from the inside out.

17

The war party traveled all night. By the time they stopped to camp, Lone Wolf's muscles ached, and he struggled to keep his eyes open. It'd been two nights and a day since he'd slept, and even then, it had only been a brief sleep. Dawn would come soon, and the men would stop and rest until midmorning.

"Tell me again why we didn't bring our women on this raid?" Two Horns eyed the other men's wives as they hastily set up lodges and prepared meals for their husbands and sons.

"Because this wasn't our fight." Badger laid his robe out on the ground. "Red Hawk didn't want to risk everyone's lives just because we wanted to have a little fun and steal some horses."

"Is that why you came, Badger? For fun? Don't you care about Texians killing our people in council and making demands?" Eagle Beak tossed Badger a hunk of the armadillo they had caught.

It wasn't enough to feed the five grown men in their group, so Lone Wolf chewed on a piece of pemmican from his pack. He lay on his robe and stretched his tired legs in front of him.

"I care. But I enjoyed myself too. Didn't you?" Badger asked.

Eagle Beak grinned. "Yes, it was quite a battle."

Laughter and lewd comments carried across the faint darkness.

"Sounds like the fun is still going," Two Horns said.

Lone Wolf and the others glanced over to look. A crowd of men made a circle around something, or someone, on the ground. A woman's screams tore through the men's laughter.

"Oh, I saw that woman," Big Tooth said. "She had huge tits!" He held his hands in front of his chest to emphasize his point. "But they couldn't get all her clothes off. She had a wrapping on her no knife could tear through. I guess they found a way." He chuckled.

"Why don't you go over there and join them," Eagle Beak said.

Big Tooth waved his arm. "I don't have the energy for that."

"If Yellow Bird were here, would you have the energy then?" Badger lay on his robe and crossed his arms under his head, a teasing smile on his face.

"Of course! Wouldn't you if Mouse was here?"

"Yes, but we won't have to wait long. Red Hawk's bringing the band far south. We should meet up with them in a few more days." Badger closed his eyes.

"At least we all have a woman waiting for us, except for Lone Wolf." Big Tooth kicked at Lone Wolf's feet. "You should be over there. When was the last time you had a woman?"

He yawned. "I fucked your mother the night before we left camp." He gave Big Tooth a wink before he turned over. "Now will you all please shut up. I need to sleep."

It was almost midday by the time the party was on the move again. The horses, mules and even some of the cattle from Linnville ambled through the tall grass. The land was flat and marshy, and the noise of thousands of hooves squishing through the wet mud was enough to keep him awake. Even on dry land, the humid air and constant mosquitos pestered him while he tried to doze on his horse's back.

He rode one of his other horses so Shadow could have a break and be at his best if and when he needed him. Both horses were unencumbered. His gear and supplies, except his weapons, were strapped to his mules. All the men rode this way, so they could fight with little burden.

"Lone Wolf." Badger's voice jolted him awake. "Stay alert, my friend. Weren't you worried about an ambush?"

He sat up straighter, cracked his neck, and slapped a mosquito on his cheek. "I was. I am. If we've come this far, I suppose there's less reason to worry."

"At least we aren't traveling the exact same path as before. We're just west of the Guadalupe, and we'll avoid Victoria completely."

"As long as we don't get too close to those stinking people-eaters." The Tonkawa were bitter enemies. They roamed the lands west of the Penateka, although long ago they had once lived in the lands the People now claimed. Everyone knew stories about warriors captured by Tonkawa who ended up as nothing more than bare bones after a feast.

Badger snorted. "Those smelly dirt-crawlers. They're worse than the white-skins. If they spot our war party, they'll run like startled mice."

Lone Wolf smirked in agreement. Nevertheless, he scanned his surroundings. Two Horns rode nearby, the stock of a firearm visible over his shoulder. "Uncle, let me see the guns you got in town."

Two Horns reached behind him and drew from his quiver, a breech-loading carbine. The barrel glinted in the sunlight.

Lone Wolf couldn't help but open his mouth and suck in his breath. "Let me see it."

Two Horns handed it over without a word. Lone Wolf took hold of the gun with both hands and examined it. "It's good we have the lead. We already have bullet molds, but we need more powder and percussion caps."

Two Horns glanced at Eagle Beak, then back at Lone Wolf.

"What is it?" he asked.

Two Horns drew out a package from a pouch at his waist. It took a moment for Lone Wolf to realize what they were. Paper cartridges and percussion caps.

"How many do you have?" He tried to hide the eagerness in his voice.

"There were about fifty of these packages. Ten cartridges in each. I split them with Eagle Beak."

Lone Wolf stared over his shoulder at Eagle Beak, who rode further back and pretended not to notice. He swallowed hard. They hadn't told him, even knowing how much he wanted a gun like this. "How many of these did you find?"

Two Horns hesitated. "Eagle Beak has one, and I have two. There was another warrior with us. He took three more and split them with his friends."

"Where did you find them?"

"In one of the buildings. It wasn't a house. There were other guns too, old ones. But we only took these, and other men took the rest."

"I'll give you ten horses for one."

Two Horns shook his head. "Sorry, Lone Wolf. I planned to give one to Red Hawk."

"Twenty horses. You can choose from my herd."

There was a pause. Two Horns looked at the ground before raising his eyes back to Lone Wolf. "I'll take Shadow then."

His eyes widened, then darkened. He gave Two Horns a hard stare. Then he tossed the carbine back and rode away. A man might hand over his wife before he'd consider trading his favorite horse. Shadow wasn't just a favorite. He was an extension of himself. He had other war horses, good ones. All of them were well-trained, but there were few possessions Lone Wolf held dear, and Shadow topped the list.

18

Familiar war cries sounded a short distance ahead, broken by pops of gunfire. Lone Wolf and the others rode in the middle of the column, but the attack came from the front. Without hesitation, he cut the line to his mules and raced toward the attack.

Warriors circled a group of hair-mouths, shouting taunts and insults while displaying their riding skills. Many stood on their horse's backs at a full gallop or swung under their bellies. It was all a distraction. While the warriors kept their enemies busy, the families and the rest of the party could make their escape.

There was little chance the hair-mouths would pursue. They had foolishly dismounted and ran in on foot. Lone Wolf joined the swirling warriors and drew one of his few remaining arrows. He'd only been able to recover a fraction of them after the attack on Linnville, and he wouldn't shoot unless he had to.

The men were not soldiers or Rangers. The fear in their eyes revealed their inexperience. By the ragtag look of them, they were most likely survivors from the settlements and towns they had struck and had never fought the People before. The hair-mouths waved their guns back and forth, unable to find a target in the swirling mass of riders who darted in two concentric circles. They wove around each other, seemingly random, but in a pattern only they knew. The warriors need only intimidate the hair-mouths enough, and they would retreat.

Lone Wolf gave a sharp war cry, and his fellow warriors took up the call again. Bracing his arm against his horse's withers, he drew up his feet. When he felt balanced, he stood tall. He made faces at the white men, extending his tongue and widening his eyes. His black war paint would make his face hideous to the pale cowards. It wasn't long before the hair-mouths saw an opening, then ran back the way they had come.

He and the others cheered and taunted the men as they ran. For the first time in days, a broad smile of joy crossed his face. If that was all the white-skins could muster against them, then he'd certainly worried for nothing.

The war party continued north. The land changed from flat and brown to sloping green with more trees and grassy meadows. They were nearing hill country and beyond that rose the Balcones that formed the edge of the Edward's Plateau. It wouldn't be long before they would be deep in Penateka territory and would consider themselves safe and home. The party kept their distance from San Antonio, staying far to the east.

While the group crossed the Guadalupe, women started to sing. Their joy was contagious and soon the whole column broke out into song. Lone Wolf joined them, his heart lighter. They may not have driven out all the Texians, but they had accomplished a great feat and had proven the strength and dominance of the People on the plains. And they were going home, triumphant, with no casualties, thousands of horses, and more plunder than they had ever seen.

After they crossed the river, sentries reported another group of hair-mouths hiding in the plum trees and thickets along a creek. Buffalo Hump sent word down the column of warriors that he expected the hair-mouths to charge on the field which lined the stream.

Lone Wolf readied himself for attack. He stripped off his shirt and restrung his bow. Then he brought Shadow up beside him, hopping from one horse to the other. Other men moved into position, herding women, children, and horses to the west side so they could pass while protected by warriors on the east, north and south.

Buffalo Hump rode at the head of the warrior column. He stood on his horse and challenged the men in the creek to one-to-one combat, as in the old way.

Lone Wolf watched from the middle of the guard. The hair-mouths didn't come. Shouts and gunfire announced another charge from the south, behind them. Once again, the hair-mouths came on foot. They ran onto the open prairie and formed lines like a hollow square. As before, warriors circled the foolish men while the rest of the column continued to pass behind.

Eagle Beak rode up beside Lone Wolf. "Those hair-mouths are like children. They don't know how to fight."

"At least these men are firing their weapons," Two Horns said.

It was true. The warriors had a harder time holding the circle. As long as they kept their shields at an angle, the bullets would be deflected against the thick layered rawhide. But as their horses were shot, warriors fell. Other men rode in, gathering the wounded.

Gunfire erupted at the front, from the thicket where Buffalo Hump and his men continued to dart along the line, also using their shields and trying to get off a few shots of their own.

Lone Wolf breathed hard, debating where he was needed most. Either to join the circle at the rear or hold the front, where he was sure another charge would come. He scanned the plum thicket, his eyes widening as he saw dark faces in paint.

"Tonkawa!" He spat on the ground. "Those filthy people-eaters! They must have helped these hair-mouths."

"Why aren't the hair-mouths charging?" Badger asked.

"They know better than to engage us in the open," Lone Wolf said. "Tonkawa must have told them that, but I'm not sure what they're waiting for. They know we won't meet them there."

"I'll get them out," Two Horns said. Holding his new carbine, he rode to join the other warriors, taunting and threatening. The decision made, Lone Wolf and the others followed.

He raced Shadow along the line. He held his shield at his side with his forearm while he shot his bow from below. He killed one Tonkawa before he circled, then raced back the way he'd come.

Two Horns rode along the edge of the creek, close to the line of attackers. Too close. He deflected a few gunshots, then fired off one of his own. A shot hit him in the side. He teetered, then fell off his horse.

For a moment, it seemed the fighting stopped, every man frozen. Lone Wolf caught his breath and released it in a howl. He commanded Shadow to charge. He could see nothing but his uncle's body in the grass. He didn't even use his shield. When he reached Two Horns, he swung down, grabbed him under the arms, and pulled him onto Shadow in front of him. It was only as he headed back behind the line did he realize Badger had ridden beside him, shielding them both.

The air broke into shouts as hair-mouths charged from the creek, this time mounted on sturdy horses. They galloped straight into the line of warriors and beyond, right into the column of retreating women and children. They fired into people's faces. With them came the Tonkawa, their own war cries sounding above the gunfire and yelling.

Mounted attackers came from all sides, mixing warriors, hair-mouths, Tonkawa, women, and children. Screams, gunfire, and groans of death added to the confusion. The line broken, people scrambled to retreat for safety, heading north into the hills.

Lone Wolf weaved through the crowd, keeping his head low while he tried to fight his way through. He swung his war club at any hair-mouths within range. In such close combat and with so few arrows, his bow was useless.

Clouds of dirt, flying arrows, and sprays of blood clouded his vision. He spotted Badger ahead and navigated through the chaos until he was beside him. Without a word, Badger grabbed hold of Two Horns and draped him across his own horse.

The crowd condensed into a mass of bodies as the huge horse herd collided into the fleeing warriors and families, crushing them between the heavy-loaded pack horses and their own mounts. Lone Wolf jerked on Shadow's reins to turn and leap over bodies, trying to get clear of the swarm.

The screams grew louder, accompanied by frightened whinnying, as the stampeded herd forced the retreating crowd into a swamp. Horses fell and others trampled over them, crushing anyone in the way.

"There's Big Tooth and Eagle Beak!" Badger shouted. They raced to join them.

Eagle Beak turned to fire his gun at a mounted hair-mouth who pursued him. His horse stumbled over a body and collapsed to the ground. He flew off and landed in the path of pounding hooves.

"Eagle Beak!" Lone Wolf urged Shadow toward him. Eagle Beak rolled to get out of the way of passing hooves. Lone Wolf leaned down and grabbed his outstretched arm. He swung him onto Shadow behind him.

"Big Tooth, herd a couple of those horses toward us. We're headed for that ravine." They were going to need more mounts if the hair-mouths were going to continue the chase.

They rode through the thicket of plum and bramble, down the slope of the ravine. The sounds of battle faded, but persistent gunfire let him know they were not in the clear. The chase continued along the bottom of the ravine. Eagle Beak took one of the spare horses and climbed onto its back while they continued at a full gallop.

After some time, the gunfire died down and they slowed, giving the horses a much needed rest. Only then was Lone Wolf able to consider their losses.

"Is he gone?" he asked Badger softly, looking at his uncle's body.

"He's been gone this whole time." Badger's voice was strained. "I think he was dead before he hit the ground."

Lone Wolf nodded. There wasn't time to grieve. They needed to get out of the ravine, back up into the hills, and onto the plateau where he hoped Red Hawk would be camped. They had no food, little water, and none of their supplies. Everything was lost. The guns, the lead, all the goods from Linnville, including the gift he had taken for Fire Girl. They each had one horse and Lone Wolf had only a handful of arrows. If they made any mistakes, they were dead.

His thoughts were broken by gunfire. Big Tooth slumped in his horse, blood spilling down his back.

"No!" he commanded Shadow back into a gallop. As he came up beside Big Tooth's horse, he lashed it with his quirt and took the reins. The others raced ahead.

Big Tooth gave him a bloody smile. "I'm fine. Let's go home," he muttered. He wasn't fine but Lone Wolf wasn't about to argue.

He stayed alongside Big Tooth as they continued along the ravine, moving farther from where he wanted to go. Little by little, Big Tooth slumped further and further until he could no longer stay on his horse. Lone Wolf climbed onto Big Tooth's horse behind him and steadied him with his arm around his waist.

Amidst the sound of thundering hooves and his own panting breath, he heard the slow mumble of Big Tooth's death song. His friend's pale and bloody lips stopped moving. His heart faintly beat. Then it stopped.

Fighting tears, he leaned Big Tooth forward and tied him onto his horse, all the while trying to keep both horses at a gallop. The men who chased them had gained enough of a lead that they were now visible. There were six men, two of them Tonkawa. If they weren't going to make it back, he wouldn't let them be eaten. He turned and loosed three arrows, taking out the Tonkawa. A single arrow rattled in his quiver.

Big Tooth now secure, Lone Wolf hopped back onto Shadow. He swung his quirt into Shadow's flank, urging him to unknown speeds. He passed Badger and Eagle Beak, who signaled he should keep going since he was the least armed. No sooner had he pulled ahead, did Badger grunt behind him.

"Brother!" Lone Wolf shouted.

"I'm okay. Keep going! Turn north onto the plateau. We must find Red Hawk's camp."

Lone Wolf rode like the wind.

19

F ire Girl poked her head into Mouse's lodge.

"Are you ready to go?"

"Where are we going again?" Mouse lifted her head from the bed.

She sauntered in and dropped her leather bag on the floor. "I'm taking you hunting." Her grin spread to her ears.

Mouse threw her arm across her face and groaned. "Why did I agree to this again?"

The edge of the bed made the same groan when Fire Girl sat. "Because you love me. Because you have a sense of adventure. Because it's a perfect weather day and I don't want you moping around here over Badger."

Mouse lifted her arm and raised her head. "I've not been moping."

"You stare off into space whenever we're not talking. You're always looking southward. You call that not moping?" She grabbed Mouse's arm to drag her from the bed.

Mouse yanked her arm free. "You should talk! You're the one who's always sour and snippy with everyone."

"Snippy? Maybe I am, but today I'm not. Today, I want to enjoy myself." She tickled Mouse's feet.

She giggled and kicked her legs free. "Okay, okay. I'm coming."

Fire Girl waited until Mouse had dressed before leading the way east from camp. They climbed a small hill overlooking a meadow, then hid behind a rocky outcrop.

The band camped on the southeastern edge of the high plateau. Drier and hotter than their normal hunting grounds, the plateau stretched across the western side of the People's land from north to south, with dull brown grass, scraggly oaks and scattered shrubs that hadn't seen rain in months.

Herds of antelope and whitetail deer frequented the grassy meadows, and she hoped to kill one of those animals for their meal. She kept an eye out for prey, her bow ready, while Mouse opened the pack of food and nibbled on her breakfast.

"How long will we have to wait?" Mouse asked with a mouthful of pecans.

"We'll wait until midday. After that, it'll be too hot for deer to be out in the open." She glanced at Mouse. "We should've been out here at dawn."

Mouse rolled her eyes. "You and your 'up-before-the-sun' mentality."

She grinned. "A lot happens at dawn. You miss some beautiful sunrises." She grabbed a pecan from Mouse's hand. "Speaking of missing things, you need to help me keep watch."

Mouse moved to a gap between the rocks. They remained silent for a while, watching and waiting. After the sun rose past the treetops, when no deer had appeared, Mouse sighed and leaned against the rock.

"This is *quite* entertaining. I'm really enjoying myself, just as you said."

"I guess it's not all that satisfying until there's something to shoot at." She leaned against the rock beside Mouse. "Hand me the water-skin."

After Mouse handed her the water, she sighed again.

Fire Girl took a sip and watched Mouse turn her head southward. "Do you worry about him?"

Mouse was slow to respond, her eyes still gazing in the distance. "I know he's brave, and a good warrior."

"But you still worry."

"I trust he'll return." She smiled, but it was forced.

"At least we're not too far from them."

Mouse nodded and glanced south again.

Fire Girl chewed on her lip. "So... what's it like being married to Badger?"

"What do you mean?"

"I mean... he's so big and you're... not. How do you manage it?"

Mouse's eyes grew wide, and her mouth opened, but she laughed. "We manage just *fine*." She gave Fire Girl a shove. "Look at you, thinking about sex."

She giggled and blushed. She understood the physical mechanics of sex, but it was altogether different to imagine herself participating in it.

"And Badger's not *that* big. He's muscular, not fat."

"I know, I know." She shoved her back. "So, he's not big, huh?"

"That's not what I meant." Mouse giggled. "Oh my, you're making penis jokes now."

They giggled some more, and Fire Girl set down her bow. There'd be no hunt that day, but she was glad for Mouse's company. The sun blazed in sweltering heat, and the sky shone a brilliant blue while locusts buzzed along the tall grass. The day was too lovely to be wasted with disappointment.

She and Mouse slid down the rock and lay on the grass. "Do you *still* not want to get married?" Mouse asked.

Fire Girl stiffened and wiped her palms and the skirt of her dress. "Yes. I *still* don't want to."

"Well, obviously you think about naked men."

"I do not." She tried not to sound defensive.

"You just asked me about Badger." Mouse touched her arm. "Don't be embarrassed, it's normal to be curious."

"I'm not embarrassed." She removed her bowstring so the sinew wouldn't stretch out.

"You're blushing again. Hmm, I wonder *who* you think about?" Mouse poked her with a stick.

"I don't think about anyone." Or at least, not anyone she could name. Faceless men or faces she didn't want to see.

"So you keep saying. But don't you ever want to see for yourself what it's like to be with a man? Isn't there anyone you find handsome?"

"Sure, but handsome isn't what matters." She plucked a blade of grass and twirled it in her fingers. "I don't want to get married because I don't want anyone telling me what to do, or to be stuck at home caring for children while my husband goes off to war." She winced, worried Mouse would take it as an insult.

"Not all men are like that. And there's nothing wrong with those things, you know." Mouse spoke with mild annoyance. "I like caring for my home. I like caring for my family. We can't all go hunting and looking for adventure. Some of us have to stay and raise children."

"So, why haven't you had a baby?"

Mouse rolled onto her stomach and looked away. "We want to. We will."

Fire Girl repented her words after realizing she'd touched another and more sensitive nerve. Women of the People didn't bear many children. Some women were barren, often miscarried, or children didn't always survive to adulthood. But such truths didn't make it any less heartbreaking.

She continued to play with the grass. She put the blade between her thumbs, then put her hands to her mouth and blew, making a bleating noise.

"Watch out with that fawn call. You might attract a mountain lion," Mouse said.

It was unclear if Mouse was still upset. "A mountain lion? That at least would be exciting."

Mouse glared at her. "Exciting? It would kill us."

"Don't worry I'll protect you." She put her arm around Mouse.

Mouse smiled at last. "Ha! Even Lone Wolf couldn't kill a mountain lion."

"Really? That's surprising. I'd think he'd be capable of that." As soon as she said it, she regretted it. She was making a bad habit of saying things she shouldn't.

"That's the first time you've ever said anything even remotely positive about Lone Wolf."

She pretended not to notice the way Mouse was eying her.

"You should have him tell you the mountain lion story, by the way."

"What? No. Why would I ever do that?" Her stomach clenched. Why did they have to talk about Lone Wolf?

"Do you still hate him," Mouse asked softly.

"I don't even think about him."

"That was an awful thing you said. Especially the part about his mother."

"I know." A lump had formed in her throat. Maybe she was ill.

"You should really apologize to him."

She rolled over. "I can't."

"Why not?" Mouse tried to turn her around.

"Because he hates me just as much as I hate him. He probably won't even talk to me."

"I can assure you, Lone Wolf doesn't hate you."

Then what about all those icy looks? But Mouse's tone suggested answers she couldn't consider. She sat up and looked in the distance. The camp was still visible, with tiny dots of people moving. There were a lot more people out of their lodges than usual and they moved much faster than she expected to see. Further south, a large cloud of dust floated upward. Horses.

"Mouse!" She pointed at the dust.

Mouse jumped to her feet and clutched her chest. "They're back!"

Fire Girl scrambled to gather their things then ran to catch up to Mouse who was already running down the hill.

"Something's wrong!" Mouse shrieked. "They aren't waiting for us to prepare a celebration." She looked back. "Someone's been killed."

By the time she and Mouse made it to camp, straggling warriors had already arrived. People scrambled between lodges or helped injured men off horses. Others yelled questions, pleas for explanations, or commands for help. They tried to be heard over the din of crying and wailing, calling for their loved ones.

"They aren't here," Mouse's voice was full of panic.

"There's Pretty Robe and Quick Hands." Fire Girl pointed out the two hugging women. As she and Mouse ran over, Quick Hands pulled away. Her face became visible, distorted by sobs. Mouse collapsed into her mother's arms.

"No! Not Father." They both sank to their knees. "Where is he?"

Pretty Robe answered, since Quick Hands was unable to speak. "He's not here, but Fox Laugh saw him fall."

Fox Laugh stood nearby, looking haggard and worn as though he'd spent a week in the desert without food or water, which wasn't far from the truth. She tried to ignore her discomfort at being near him.

"What happened?" Fire Girl knelt beside Mouse and hugged her shoulders. Her eyes brimmed with tears.

"White-skins shot him and he fell," Fox Laugh said. He winced at his too casual explanation and took on a gentler tone she hadn't heard from him before. "Lone Wolf and Badger took his body, but I didn't see what happened to them after that. I'm sorry."

Mouse and Quick Hands renewed their weeping. Fire Girl's heart ached for them. She hadn't known Two Horns well, but he had seemed a loving father. If he was dead, there was a chance Eagle Beak was too.

Round Eyes ran up to Fox Laugh and hugged him around the waist. "Father, my heart sings at your return."

Fox Laugh placed his hand on the boy's head. "I'm glad to be home. Come, I have a gift for you."

The men departed and Fire Girl went to her mother. "I don't understand. Why didn't they all stay together? Why are only some of them here? Where's Eagle Beak?"

Pretty Robe wrung her hands, distraught. "The men were attacked on their way back. The whole party broke up and many were chased by the white-skins. The groups scattered. Nobody knows where the rest of them are."

Fire Girl grasped her mother's hands. They were trembling. "Then they could still be alive. They could come back tonight." She hoped Badger wasn't dead, too, for Mouse's sake.

"I hope so, but Red Hawk is afraid the white-skins will track and find us. We have to move the camp."

Mouse broke free of her mother's embrace. "But what if Badger can't find us? What if we're too far and he's injured? We have to stay!"

Quick Hands composed herself. "I want to stay as much as you do, but the whole camp is in danger. We must move. We will leave signs for them, like we always do, so they know where to find us."

They settled along a creek which joined the Colorado River to the north. That night, Fire Girl and Pretty Robe sat with Mouse and Quick Hands. By then they'd heard the story of how the war party had hit many settlements and drove the Texians into the water, how they'd come back victorious, until they were attacked by mounted hair-mouth fighters, something that had never happened before.

Drums beat throughout the night, while men demonstrated their shame of defeat and at leaving others behind. They cut their ponies' tails and smeared their own faces with black. But no one placed any blame, except on the white-skins who threatened them, and the Tonkawa who had given aid to their enemies.

When Mouse had stopped crying, she took her skinning knife and cut off her hair in chunks, gathering the strands to scatter in the wind. She made shallow slices in her arms, wincing from the pain.

Quick Hands lay on her robes, not moving. "I will mourn when they bring his body."

Two more warriors arrived that night, and three in the morning. None of them had any word of Eagle Beak or Badger.

"I heard from Laughing Bird that Lone Wolf hasn't come back either," said Pretty Robe. "I imagine they're all together."

"Red Hawk must be worried," Fire Girl said.

The lodge flap darkened as a figure stood before the opening. She scratched at the flap, then poked her head in. It was Yellow Bird.

"Can I come in?" she asked quietly.

"Of course," Pretty Robe answered.

The young woman entered. Fire Girl didn't know her well, as she was even older than Mouse, but she had always admired the woman's petite figure, round face, and luminous eyes.

"Big Tooth hasn't come back," she said sadly. "They tell me he stayed with Badger and Eagle Beak while on the raid, and I know your men haven't returned either. They are some of the last ones still missing."

"Then they'll all come back together," said Pretty Robe. "You are welcome to wait with us."

"No, I'm with my parents. But I wanted to say, I hope your men return soon. And I am sorry about your husband, Quick Hands."

Quick Hands glanced at her, and then back into nothingness.

In the wee hours of the morning, Fire Girl heard shouts. She, Mouse, and Pretty Robe ran from the lodge, headed for the southern edge of camp.

Before she reached the last lodges, horses emerged from the cloud of dust. She searched for the face of her father. She spotted him still on his horse. A cry of relief escaped her lips.

Eagle Beak slid from the horse with great effort, just before Pretty Robe collided into him. They hugged tightly, her mother holding him upright.

Fire Girl could see no obvious injuries. "Father! You're okay."

He looked up from her mother's shoulder and reached a hand to her. "Yes, I'm all right, but many hearts will bleed today."

As he said these words, loud shrieks filled the air. Yellow Bird lay sobbing over a body, which had to be her husband, Big Tooth. Other women and men tried to comfort her, but she was too hysterical to be calmed.

Fire Girl spotted Lone Wolf in the crowd. He pulled Yellow Bird into an embrace. She wept into his shoulder while he whispered to her.

Pretty Robe covered her mouth in dismay. "What happened?"

Eagle Beak ran his hand over his tired face. "Mounted rangers attacked. We fought them, but they overpowered us with their guns and stampeded the herd. We fled, but some came after us. They shot Lone Wolf's friend. We couldn't break free of their pursuit. It took three days before we lost them. We ran into Buffalo Horn and Ferret, and it was a good thing too, as we had no food and ran out of water but couldn't stop to refill or hunt. They had jerked meat with them and shared it with us."

Quick Hands emerged from the crowd and knelt by the body of her husband. Flies swarmed his face, which was so badly decomposed it was hardly recognizable as Two Horns. Quick Hands calmly ripped open the front of her dress, exposing her breasts. She took her knife and slashed at them, then fell over her husband in a flood of tears.

"Where's Badger? Is he all right?" Fire Girl asked.

"He's injured, but alive," said Eagle Beak. "He went to Winged Woman. I saw Mouse go with him. Go see if they need any help."

She hesitated, but it wasn't a time for uncertainty. She hurried to Winged Woman's lodge.

From outside the lodge, she could hear someone groaning in pain. She ducked through the doorway and found Mouse crouched next to Badger, who lay on his stomach staining the pelts with his blood. On his other side, Winged Women dug into his thigh with an awl.

"I feel it." She removed the awl and grabbed a long pair of trade tweezers.

"Can you get it out?" Mouse asked with worry.

"I think so."

Badger's eyes shut and he clenched his teeth while Winged Woman twisted the tweezers into the wound. The muscles and veins of his neck and shoulders rose in thick ropes under his skin. Mouse held his hand, struggling to withstand his fierce grip.

"I've got it." Winged Woman withdrew the tweezers and dropped the piece of lead into a bowl. "You can add this to your medicine." She raised her head, noticing Fire Girl at last. "Have you come to help?"

"Eagle Beak said I should," she answered, her voice unsteady.

"Good, come bind Badger's leg." Winged Woman handed her a pile of ripped cloth strips. "I've got to make a poultice."

The wound looked as though it would need stitching, but she wasn't about to argue with a medicine woman. She came around to where Winged Woman had been sitting. The wound was high up on Badger's thigh and his leggings had been pulled down, but at least he was still covered by his breechcloth.

"Mouse, are you sure you don't want to do it?"

Mouse shook her head. "Oh no, my hands are shaking."

"Okay," she said reluctantly. "Badger, I'm going to need to raise your leg so I can wrap these bandages around it." He nodded and gave her a slight smile, despite his obvious pain.

She took hold of the mass of his thigh and tried to lift. It didn't budge. She strained and adjusted her arms to wrap around his leg for a better grip. Then the limb rose easily.

Badger winked. "You didn't think you could lift any part of me without my help, did you?" he chuckled, then dropped his head back on the ground and took a few breaths.

"You lay still and let the girl do what she needs to do," Winged Woman warned as she mixed herbs and honey into a paste.

Fire Girl rested Badger's leg on her knees. "The wound is bleeding," she said to Winged Woman.

"Then put pressure on it."

She took one of the bandages and tried to wipe away the blood so she could find the opening in his skin. Then she pressed down using the flat of her hand.

"It's higher up," Badger said.

She moved the cloth. "Here?"

"A little higher."

The cloth was already at the top of his thigh, any higher and she'd be on his buttocks. He winked again.

Mouse slapped his shoulder. "Stop it, Badger, you're making her blush."

He smothered a laugh. "Can't a man get a little fun while he's in pain?"

"Who's having fun?" Buffalo Horn entered, holding his arm to his chest.

"What's wrong with your arm?" Winged Woman asked.

"I fell off my horse while we were trying to escape. It's out of place."

"Come here and I'll set it back," Winged Woman answered.

Fire Girl placed her other hand on top of the first and used her weight to add more pressure, leaning onto Badger. He grunted.

Buffalo Horn pointed at Fire Girl with his chin. "Can I have her treat me? It looks like my brother is enjoying her attention."

"You're going... to have to wait... your turn," Badger said between breaths.

"It'd be worth it." Buffalo Horn smiled a toothy grin. "Girl, my ass is sore from riding. Do you think you could rub it for me?"

She tried to ignore their jesting but broke into giggles with her arms shaking.

"Oh... keep that up." Badger moaned. "That feels good."

Mouse rolled her eyes. "You two are the worst."

Fire Girl felt guilty for laughing, picturing Two Horns' rotting body outside.

"Badger, only you could find humor at a time like this." Winged Woman said. "You'd better thank the spirits that the bullet missed your artery. There's a big one right inside your leg. Any closer and you would've bled to death before you reached camp."

"I thank the spirits that the bullet missed my cock and balls, without which, I might as well be dead."

The room erupted in laughter, but they all stopped short when someone yelled for Winged Woman from outside. Lone Wolf rushed in with Yellow Bird in his arms.

"Grandmother, help her." He lowered the woman to the ground.

Winged Woman rushed over. "What happened?"

Lone Wolf was breathing hard, his eyes wild. "She was in anguish over her husband." His voice was shaking. Fire Girl had never seen him so discomposed. "She took my knife. I tried to take it from her, but she cut herself too deep."

His hand was wrapped tight around Yellow Bird's wrist, yet blood oozed from between his fingers in large globs. More cuts covered the girl's arms and chest.

"Fire Girl," Winged Woman said sharply, "let Mouse finish. I need your help here. Put pressure on these wounds."

She hurried over and obeyed, using one of the bandages as a compress on one of the other gashes while Winged Woman tied off the deep wound on her wrist. Blood no longer pumped out, but drained in a slow trickle. The girl lay pale and still, her eyes half open.

Lone Wolf watched in silence. His entire front was stained red. Blood smeared his face and dripped from his hands. He was just as still as Yellow Bird.

Winged Woman felt the girl's neck then took her hands away. "I'm sorry, she's gone."

His shoulders dropped. He closed Yellow Bird's eyes then sat a moment longer before rising. "Thank you for trying to save her," he whispered. He went to the lodge door. "I'll go tell their parents they now have two bodies to prepare for burial."

"Lone Wolf!" Stunned at hearing his name come from her own mouth, Fire Girl stood speechless for a moment. He stopped, equally surprised. "I... you shouldn't go see them, looking like that."

He stared down at himself, as though just noticing the blood coating his body. Though the People were accustomed to violence and Yellow Bird's parents might not be as shocked as she imagined, it seemed wrong to tell them about their daughter's death while covered in her blood.

"She's right," Mouse said solemnly. "You should wash first."

"Give him some water, child," Winged Woman said.

She grabbed a bladder of water hanging near the door and approached him, unsure of what to do next.

"Pour it on him," Buffalo Horn said.

She raised the container to Lone Wolf's shoulder, then froze, too aware of his proximity and the odor of blood on his bare skin. His eyes reminded her of Winged Woman's awl.

Before she could make another move, Lone Wolf took the container from her and stepped outside.

Her face went hot, shamed by his sudden dismissal. Of course, he wouldn't let her help, not after what she'd said to him, not after what had happened. She was nothing more than another *taibo*.

That afternoon, the mourning families took the bodies west of camp to be buried. They dressed them in their best clothes, then ornamented and painted their faces with red and yellow. The bodies were tied into a fetal position, wrapped in robes, and each one lashed to their favorite horse. Women mourners followed the horses to the site, which was part grave, and part cave. They'd have the funeral at sunset, where they would burn their possessions and kill the dead men's horses.

The shots could be heard from camp. They echoed as each horse fell from a bullet through the brain. Fire Girl jumped at each gunshot while she stirred a pot of greasy meat and broth outside her lodge. Her stomach turned. She ran from the pot, stopping to retch in the brush.

The gunshots continued as she sat there, shaking. Memories she'd tried to bury erupted with each shot. People running from wagons, trampled by horses. Her sister's blonde hair flying in the wind. In the silence between, when she tried to push the memories back, images of Lone Wolf covered in blood sprang forward, his hard glare digging its way into her consciousness.

If only it'd been him to die in battle. If only his horses were the ones being killed. He would be erased from her life forever, and no one would ever again say his name.

20

Fall 1840

Lone Wolf sat in Ferret's lodge for a gambling game. Despite the months that had passed and the change of seasons, his mood after the great raid was still grim, but the game was a welcome distraction.

His chest tightened whenever he thought of Big Tooth's last breath, or of his uncle dropping from his horse. And Yellow Bird, her life fading as her blood emptied from her body. He couldn't shake the feeling of guilt over their deaths. What good was he if he couldn't protect the people he cared about?

When he closed his eyes, he pictured Fire Girl's green eyes filled with uncertainty. She had been close enough to touch, but her discomfort in his presence was so palpable he could cut it with his knife. Would she ever look at him without fear?

He added the memory to those already heavy in his heart. One day he'd take his revenge. Not only on the white-skins, but the Tonkawa who had shown the hair-mouths how to defeat the People and turned the tide against them.

He would propose another raid, one with a high chance of success to raise spirits and renew confidence in his fellow warriors. They could strike the Mexican settlements to the southwest and steal horses, like they always did. One day they would strike the Texian villages again, but for now, a familiar victory might be just what he and the other men needed.

The men had gathered in a circle, rolling a set of bone dice on a piece of deerskin, as each man bet horses or other possessions. Lone Wolf eyed the other men in the lodge, considering each of their strengths and how they might perform in his war party. There was no question about Badger. Not only because he was his best friend, but he knew no better man in battle. After years of friendship and raiding together, he could count on Badger to anticipate his thoughts before he knew them himself.

Buffalo Horn could be as irritating as a cactus spine, but he fought well, as did Ferret. Those two always worked well together. But Fox Laugh gave him pause. His skills were not in question, the man was every bit his equal or more, but tension still held between Fox Laugh and himself over his brother and Playful Otter. And because of Fire Girl. He didn't need anyone opposing his lead out of spite.

Maybe he should bring up the raid at a later time. He could find younger warriors to bring along, to help them earn recognition.

Ferret handed Lone Wolf the dice. "It's your turn. Don't be stingy with those horses of yours. I need good horses to get myself a wife." He turned to Badger. "You were lucky to have married one of the last, good, available women."

Badger smiled, too good-natured to take offense at personal comments made about his wife. "What are you talking about? There are plenty of young women in camp."

Ferret scoffed. "Only loud-mouths and gossiping hens. Those are the ones that steal your manhood. I suppose I'll have to find someone in another camp or wait another summer or two until more girls come of age. Like Lone Wolf. He should be married by now. Right, Lone Wolf? Are you waiting on someone or what?"

He gave a half-shrug as he placed his bet, laying two sticks on the deer hide to represent horses. The ends were painted black to show they belonged to him.

Ferret blew out his breath. "I don't know why I even asked."

"What about Fire Girl?" Buffalo Horn said. "She doesn't preen or make a spectacle of herself like the others."

Ferret scrunched his face. "Too skinny and pale for my tastes. And she has that temper. Besides, Looks To the Sky mentioned taking her as his third wife."

Lone Wolf fumbled and dropped the dice he'd meant to toss.

Badger nudged him with his elbow. "That counts as your roll."

"If you don't want her, I'll talk to Eagle Beak myself," said Buffalo Horn. "It'd be a shame to let such a woman get married off to an old bull like Looks To the Sky."

Lone Wolf's jaw clenched as he passed the dice back to Ferret.

"It's only two horses, Lone Wolf," Ferret teased as he collected the sticks into his pile.

"I'm surprised you're thinking about taking a wife," Badger said to his brother. "The only man who's ever had more women than you was Lone Wolf's brother."

Buffalo Horn smirked. "I beat his count long ago, but that doesn't mean once I'm married, I won't continue to add to my score. Then again, I could be content with Fire Girl."

Badger's eyes flicked to Lone Wolf, then back to his brother. "You and Looks To the Sky don't know what you're in for," Badger said. "She's named Fire Girl for a reason. I've spent more time with her than any of you stags. I'm telling you, her kind of woman is a lot to handle. I suggest you find somebody else."

Buffalo Horn raised his eyebrows in jest. "You think I'm not man enough to handle her?"

"I'm not questioning your manhood, brother, just your patience," Badger retorted.

"Eagle Beak has few horses," Fox Laugh said. "If someone made an offer to him, he'd gladly marry her off. She's a burden on that family." His voice was cold and bitter.

"That family is *your* family," Lone Wolf reminded him. "Not that you spend much time with them," he added under his breath.

"You of all people should know why that is." Fox Laugh leaned forward with a hard glare. "Because of *her* and her kind, we both lost everything."

That was true and yet, it wasn't. "She's one of us now," he said softly.

"Is she? Why do you care so much?" Fox Laugh demanded. "We all know she hates you, and yet you sit there and defend her. Is she the one you're waiting for? If so, you're not only a fool, but a disloyal one." The brittle edge in his voice threatened to crack, unmasking all he kept hidden beneath his anger. "Your own brother, Lone Wolf. How can you betray him like that?"

The way he spoke of betrayal, it was as though he was asking the question for himself more than in regards to Fire Girl.

Lone Wolf returned the glare. "I have betrayed no one. And neither has she. Eagle Beak and Pretty Robe are at peace with their loss. Fire Girl looks after Round Eyes as if he were her own. It is you who betrays the memory of those you loved by carrying so much hatred in your heart."

The pain in Fox Laugh's eyes made him regret his harsh words, but it needed to be said. How many years would he mourn? How long until he let go? Fox Laugh and Fire Girl had more in common than either of them would admit.

Fox Laugh took his winnings and stormed out. Lone Wolf looked down at what was left of the sticks he had brought to wager. The lost horses were little compared to the herd he had accumulated, but somehow, he knew they would never be enough. Perhaps Fox Laugh was right. The dice had been tossed and he was already losing.

They soon moved camp. Lone Wolf helped Squirrel, Laughing Bird and Winged Woman set the main poles in the ground for his, Red Hawk's, and their own lodges. Men rarely took part in setting up a lodge, and if they did, it was only to help to lift and place the heavy poles. It was something Lone Wolf had done for his mother.

"Move that one more to the left." Laughing Bird eyed the spacing and balance of the poles, tightening the rope which tied them together at the top. She could always tell whether a pole was off center. Lone Wolf shifted the pole with his foot.

"Stop right there. It's good," Laughing Bird said.

"No, now it's too far over. It should go back to the right." Squirrel walked between the poles while counting her paces.

"It's perfect," said Laughing Bird in annoyance.

"It's not."

He ignored their argument and went to get another pole. Once the four main poles were set, the others would be set in between. He bent down to grab one and scratched his palm on a jagged piece of wood. He inspected the pole until he found the offending splinter. It was small but could snag or tear the cover in a heavy wind. He withdrew his knife and used the edge to smooth out the surface, then ran his hand along the wood to feel for further imperfections. The pole now smooth, he stood and shivered from the cool morning air. Loud voices caught his attention.

Eagle Beak and Pretty Robe were unloading gear from a pack horse, and he watched for a moment, then forced himself to turn back to his grandfather's wives and their bickering.

Fire Girl then appeared from behind the partially set-up lodge where she'd been lashing the cover. His gut stirred with abandoned hopes. She noticed him and her posture became stiff and wary. He should look away, give her the space he would if he'd startled a fawn in the meadow, but he was likewise stuck under her gaze.

Buffalo Horn walked up, taking the reins to their horses in an offer to lead them back to the pasture. He wore that crooked-toothed smile of confidence, immune to Fire Girl's distrust even if she gave him the same uncomfortable glance. But he must have made a humorous comment to break past her shield, because she laughed, flashing Buffalo Horn a bright grin.

Lone Wolf grew hot with jealous regret by the show of friendliness she had never shown toward him. Until Fox Laugh said it, he hadn't realized how obvious her disdain was to everyone else. How much had he made himself the fool?

As if he knew Lone Wolf watched, Buffalo Horn turned and smugly grinned as he walked to the pasture with Eagle Beak's horses. Lone Wolf resisted the urge to shove his fist into that smile.

After a restless sleep, Lone Wolf rose before dawn. He went outside to say his prayer of gratitude and greet the day. Shadow waited outside, loosely hobbled. He flicked his ears in greeting and gave Lone Wolf a nudge on the shoulder.

"Yes, we'll go riding today," he told the horse, unhobbling him and strapping on a bridle. "Maybe go down the river first and collect pigments." He'd need the paints if they were to go on a raid. And make more arrows, many more than last time. There was the new shield he needed to paint. Lots to do and little time before the cold of winter arrived. Taking his weapons with him, he led Shadow to walk along the water.

The faint glow of the rising sun appeared while Lone Wolf scanned the water's edge. With the muted light coming in, his vision improved, and he plucked a few chunks of oxide for pigments from among the shale and even a few well-worn skipping stones. While Shadow munched on wild rose hips, he flicked the stones into the water, counting the skips and challenging himself to beat his own high score.

It had been a pastime since his boyhood, when he did his best thinking. He should be planning his raid, but his thoughts kept being invaded by the smile of a certain fire-haired woman that was never meant for him.

When he ran out of stones, he walked along the bank, picking up more pigments and storing them in his pouch while collecting more stones for skipping. Shadow followed as he worked his way further from camp. A brownish black rock caught the first rays of light, casting a glittery silvery sheen. He picked up the jagged piece, examining the triangular crystals clustered in red oxide. It was an unusual rock, not one he'd ever seen before. Perhaps it could be crushed and made into black paint, or maybe he'd just save it as an oddity.

Before he could add it to the collection in his pouch, Shadow snorted and raised his head. His nostrils flared at the odor of smoke, coming from a direction away from camp. From the same direction came a yell. Alarm sprouted in Lone Wolf's gut, but the sound was so faint, he questioned whether he'd heard anything at all. He paused, stone in hand and listened. The yell came again, vaguely familiar, like a little red-haired girl fleeing across a river.

Alarm spread into panic. He tossed the stone aside and drawing his bow, he charged downstream, becoming desperate as he heard a bellowed growl carry across the dawning air.

21

Quiver slung across her back, Fire Girl made her way to the pasture to take one of Eagle Beak's horses. It was dark enough that the birds were not yet awake, and the rabbit-eared mare flicked its ears and made a grunt of annoyance that she'd awoken it. There were better horses to take, but the old nag had proven useful and good luck on her first solo hunt. She needed that luck now.

After the defeat at Plum Creek, Eagle Beak had all but forbade her from leaving camp on her own, but they'd moved far from those lands. No enemies would dare walk so deeply within the land of the Kotsoteka.

Leaves rustled in the breeze. Many had lost their green and had changed to brown, gold or rust orange, while others had fallen and littered the ground. They crunched under the hooves of her horse as she rode away from the pasture and the lodges behind her disappeared in the darkness.

She crossed the river where it was shallow, but water splashed up the horse's sides and she drew up her legs to keep her feet dry. The weather was too cold for wet moccasins. Past the tree line, the ground opened into a meadow of dry bluestem and dead wildflowers. She slid off the horse, letting it follow as she stepped lightly along the edge of grass, staying hidden within the trees. Burdock pods clung to the fringe of her leggings and the nag's shaggy coat, but she ignored their itch and kept her eye on the meadow. Across the field, a grove of hazelnut and oak stood like generous old grandmothers, offering the perfect fall food for deer.

A shadow of movement caught her eye, and she drew an arrow with swift confidence. The winds were in her favor as she took aim at the hungry doe. It was over quickly, and she marched over to her kill with a wide grin. Perhaps there'd be no hunters to compliment her, but Eagle Beak and Pretty Robe would be pleased at the fresh meat for the morning meal. And she'd learned her lesson from before, having brought supplies to build a proper travois.

After hobbling the nag, she bent down to say her prayers over the dead doe, then took out her knife and got to work. The few bites of raw liver didn't satisfy her sudden hunger, but it was early enough that she could manage a longer delay.

A small fire caught quickly with the abundance of dry fuel, but she was sure to clear away the dead leaves so it didn't spread. It would only take a few moments to char the few chunks of meat she'd speared with a stick. The smell of roasting meat hit her nose so hard her belly rumbled. She tested it with her fingers, licking off the juice and then took a bite into the nearly raw venison with crispy edges.

She had only finished the first chunk when she heard a rustle in the brush nearby. Two furry shapes tumbled down a slope, scattering leaves as the bear cub siblings tussled in the dry oak litter. The hair on her neck raised in alarm. Bear cubs meant a bear mother.

Dropping the stick of meat, she reached over her shoulder for her bow, drawing it slow and steady. "Get back, little ones!" she yelled, hoping they'd flee back to their mother.

The cubs came straight for her, the dead deer, and her meat stick. She backed away, taking slow steps just as the large she-bear appeared behind the cubs. The bear spotted her immediately, letting out a bellow of warning. Fear gripped her by the spine as the charge came, sudden and fierce.

Huffing clouds of hot breath, the bear leaped forward with a growling grunt. With a yelp, Fire Girl took a single leap to the side, but the bear knocked her over and her face hit the ground with a leafy crunch. She tasted autumn earth as the weight of an angry bear pressed onto her back. Her lungs failed to take in air and her ribs threatened to snap, but she was cushioned by the thick layer of leaves beneath her. She lay limp in a farce of death while the bear snorted and sniffed, surrounding her with musky breath. Teeth tugged on her hair and clothes. Claws dug into her side, tearing through the cloth of her hunting shirt as the bear tried to flip her onto her back. On instinct, she covered her neck and tried to draw up her legs and roll into an armadillo ball.

"Keep your legs spread wide," a voice hissed from the trees. She knew that voice, but it was impossible for Lone Wolf to be there. It went against all reason to trust him, but she obeyed all the same. His advice made sense. It would be harder to flip her that way.

She wasn't the only one to notice Lone Wolf's arrival. The heavy weight lifted from her back as the bear pounced after him. Fire Girl heaved a breath as she turned to the side. Unlike her, Lone Wolf managed to let loose an arrow and it struck the bear in the neck. The she-bear skid to a sudden stop, snapping its jaws at the protruding shaft. With his bow drawn, Lone Wolf side-stepped deeper into the trees. "Get up!" he commanded. "Get behind me."

When their mother charged, the bear cubs had retreated up the slope, but now they were back again yanking on the deer carcass with their teeth. Fire Girl was in between them and their mother, the worst place to be. She scrambled to her feet, picking up a piece of wood from her fire as the bear spun for another charge. She held out the flaming branch, sweeping it from side to side as she backed up and out from between the mother and her cubs. Her puny fire should have done nothing, but the bear halted again with a chuff. It raised itself onto hide legs, above her flaming branch and roared.

This was it. This was the end. Once she had begged for death and now the spirits would fulfill her wish. How foolish she'd been. The bear would finish what Lone Wolf couldn't, but he would witness it.

Lone Wolf roared back and hollered at the bear in an attempt to redirect its attention. He released another arrow, this one striking the bear in the side. The bear made a sound like a whimper. The cubs scrambled up an oak tree and moaned for their mother.

Fire Girl swallowed. The bear was protecting her young. She'd been the fool to linger after butchering her kill, releasing the smell of blood and roasting meat to any nearby predators. The bear dropped to all fours. Fire Girl continued to brandish the fire as she backed toward her frantic horse, still hobbled and unable to flee.

The bear made another half-attempt at a charge and Fire Girl made a wide and wild wave with her torch. "Watch out!" Lone Wolf shouted, too late. The flames caught in a low-hanging branch and the dry wood came alive with orange heat. She sucked in a breath and in her surprise, dropped the torch. The leaves at her feet took flame. She skittered back and then turned to run. The bear bounded in the opposite direction, her cubs following to escape the fire.

The old nag screeched and yanked at the ties while the flames licked closer. Fire Girl dodged flying hooves as she drew her knife to cut the horse free. Dark smoke filled her vision and she coughed.

"There's no time!" Lone Wolf was suddenly at her side, gripping her elbow. "That old horse isn't fast enough. Get on Shadow." Around them the forest had become a wall of heat and flames. In another moment, they'd be surrounded.

"Let me at least free her." She slashed blindly at the ties. The nag snapped free and was gone. She had no time to react before Lone Wolf grabbed her and thrust her onto his horse with the same force he'd used three years prior. He was in front of her in an instant and the iron gray stallion took off at a bolt.

"Can your horse outrun a fire?" she yelled at Lone Wolf's back. How was he there? *Why* was he there? Those were questions for a later time.

"Maybe not, but we have to try."

At a barked command, Shadow thundered across the meadow and toward the creek. Fire Girl squeezed her eyes shut against the sting of smoke and the wall of heat. She covered her mouth and nose with her shirt, clutched Lone Wolf's sides, and hid her face against his back, fear overcoming her timidity at touching him.

His hair whipped into her face. It smelled like smoke and burning wood, but also that familiar underlying fragrance. Her head spun in circles. The world had become a roar of flames as they flew at impossible speeds. They weren't going to make it.

"Take a breath!" Lone Wolf shouted.

She did, even if her lungs burned with ash. She cracked an eye open in time to see the river before they splashed into the water. The sudden cold shocked her senses. They dove into the deepest part and the current swept her forward. She lost her grip and slipped off, sinking underwater. She thrust her legs and fought to break the surface. The river spun her in circles, and she lost track of Lone Wolf and his horse.

Taking another breath, she tried to swim to the opposite shore, but it was useless. A boulder jutted out ahead and she reached to grab it, but her fingers slid along the slick surface, and she was back to spinning. Her head submerged again, and she thrashed to gain purchase and propel herself up again.

Strong hands gripped under her arms and pulled her up. She gasped for breath, clutching his shoulders and forcing him down.

"Grab the mane!" Lone Wolf yelled and sputtered.

She clung to Shadow's neck, pulling herself up until her head was free of the water. Lone Wolf held on from the other side, the long reins to his horse gripped in his teeth. She blinked and wiped the water from her face, shivering and she coughed.

"We h-have to g-go back! The camp! The f-fire will reach them!" she chattered.

He looked at her like she'd gone mad, not far from the truth. Behind her, the fire raged on, racing alongside the river, each tree and bush becoming alight like a vanguard of flame. The winds shifted in their favor, pushing the flames away from shore. Onward they floated. Her shoulder and sides throbbed, and she noticed the thin swirl of red leaking from her side. A wound from the bear's claws, ones she hadn't felt until the brief calm, but it would have to wait.

"The river gets shallower ahead," he said, breaking the roaring silence. "Shadow can pull us out." At the next bend, he swung the reins at an extending branch, catching at a loop. Shadow bobbed his head and the horse braced to a stop. At Lone Wolf's encouragement, the horse swam forward to shore. The cold made it impossible to move her arms and swim, so she clung to the horse until her feet touched bottom, then clambered up rock and earth, finally to collapse on the bank.

She lay only a moment before those same hands pulled her up. "Come on, we have to get warm."

"Not another fire," she mumbled, but she let him guide her up the bank and onto dry land.

"I would agree with you, but it's absolutely necessary right now."

He was right. Her wet clothes clung to her chilled skin, and she couldn't stop shaking. Behind her, the landscape raged, orange flame and smoke reaching to the sky in angry clouds of black. A ruin of her own doing.

She didn't know how long they walked before Lone Wolf called his horse to a halt. She crouched into a ball, hugging her knees and shivering into them while Lone Wolf dusted his hands and his flint in the sand to dry them. It was then she realized he was shivering too, his face pale. Several attempts later, the spark took hold of the small pile of kindling he'd gathered.

She couldn't look at the flames and shut her eyes.

"Fire Girl, you need to get closer to the heat."

She choked out a sob. "I hate my name." Her lip blubbered like Round Eyes when he fought tears. "It's all my fault." Lone Wolf said nothing, which she took as agreement, but it was true. The she-bear

223

and her cubs were probably dead. The nag, dead. All the game and wildlife, plants and food to gather before winter, dead. If not for Lone Wolf, she'd be dead too, and deservedly so, but that was true even before the bear.

"You're hurt," he said after a moment. "Once we're both warm enough, you need to let me see to those wounds."

"They're just scratches," she said bitterly, closing the rips in her tunic with a fist and pressing against her side. Despite her effort to hide it, her face scrunched in a wince. "I have my medicine bag and I can put a salve on it later." Why let him help when he wouldn't even let her wash away blood from him?

He stared into the flames, back to ignoring her. Never a single clue to his thoughts, as usual. Only then did it sink in that of all people, she was sitting with the man she hated and who was supposed to hate her. "How did you find me?" she asked.

He rubbed the heat from his outstretched hands onto his face. "I smelled your fire."

It was a simple answer, but it explained plenty. He must have also smelled the roasting meat, probably wondering who would be so foolish as to start a fire among dry leaves and in a place where bears were known to hunt for food before the winter sleep. He should have let her burn or drown in the river.

"I need to know if my parents are safe."

"Red Hawk will have moved the camp once they saw the heavy smoke. We can find them later." He sat back on his heels and peeled off his hunting shirt. His wet leggings came next, revealing prickles of goosebumps on his bare skin.

She looked away with a shiver. "Eagle Beak won't know where I am. Pretty Robe will worry."

He finally met her eyes directly. "They will, but there's nothing you can do about that right now." There was an edge to his tone which he softened with a look of sympathy and concern.

What did that even mean? How long did he expect them to sit and do nothing? And yet she was too cold to move. It would be smarter to peel off her wet clothes so her skin could properly dry off and she could tend to her injuries, but she had nothing else to wear. Lone Wolf might have stripped down to his breechcloth, but she wasn't about to do the same and sit with him in the nude.

Another wave of cold rattled her bones. She removed her soggy moccasins and warmed her feet with her leggings yanked up to her knees. Lone Wolf fished into a damp pouch, pulling out stones and setting them by the fire. "If you won't take off those wet clothes, at least put these hot stones against your skin. Not only will they warm you up, but your clothes will dry faster."

Rather than asking why he had a pouch full of rocks, she followed his advice, taking the heated stones and tucking them under her shirt where she hugged them to her chest and belly. Why did he care? Why not just leave her to suffer and freeze? But he hadn't left her to the bear, nor to the fire she created, and not to the river that swept her away.

With her free hand, she opened her soggy medicine bag. Moving aside pouches of wet herbs she found the little horn container with the salve Pretty Robe had taught her to make. Opening it with one hand proved difficult, but she managed without having to ask Lone Wolf to assist. She scooped out the fragrant ointment of honey and yarrow and smoothed it onto the open skin. The yarrow helped with the bleeding and the honey would stop festering. She found a strip of willow bark and chewed on it, as much for the pain as to fill her empty stomach.

Lone Wolf opened his pouch again and emptied the rest into his palm. He poured out rose hips and dried cherries, now swollen with river water. He offered her half and she took them gratefully, adding the lost deer carcass to her list of regrets. Silent and still they chewed, and after the meager meal, she lay on her side and closed her eyes.

"Are you still shivering? Are you warm enough? If not, you shouldn't sleep," Lone Wolf said.

"I'm fine," she lied. Although still cold, she doubted she was at risk of death. Too bad. It would be better to shut out the world, forget the bear, and the fire, and almost drowning.

The sun was high when she opened her eyes, and Lone Wolf was dressed again, standing with his horse. He noticed her as she sat up. "Can you walk? Can you ride?"

She gave him a quick nod and stood in her now dry moccasins. There was no more conversation as they headed back upstream on the unburned side of the river. Across the way, as far as she could see, the ground was swathed with black, smoke rising from a thousand pockets of ash and smoldering flame.

He made no accusations or chastisement of her mistake, just kept his eyes focused on the path in front of them as he guided Shadow back to camp. For once, she was grateful for his silent manner and the distance he kept between them.

She made no attempt to hold onto him this time, letting her legs do the work as Eagle Beak had taught her. Her hands rested on her thighs.

She'd lost all her arrows in the river, but at least her bow was still in its case. Hopefully her father would forgive the lost nag.

As he had predicted, the last site had been abandoned, leaving only the remnants of early morning cook fires and scattered refuse, evidence of their rushed departure. Lone Wolf kept his horse moving through the empty campsite, heading in the direction of the tracks left by horses and trailing travois. They passed near where Pretty Robe's lodge had stood, and she scanned the spot where she had slept that morning.

"Stop!" she told him and slid off the horse. She rushed over to pick up a bright and colorful object which stood against the brown flattened earth and dust. She turned the painted wooden top over in her hands. "It belongs to Round Eyes," she said half to herself.

Her hand went to the bracelet on her wrist, now well-fitted. Eagle Beak had been endlessly generous, but her thoughts strayed to Lone Wolf when he had found it in the snow. The way he looked at her, the way he touched her skin, the way he sat looking at her now, patiently waiting for her to return to the horse so he could take them both home. She swallowed and climbed back into her seat behind him, clutching the toy in her fist.

It was late in the day when they reached the new site. Lodge poles stretched in silhouette against the setting sun. Riders raced out to meet them, Badger for Lone Wolf and Eagle Beak for herself. She hopped off the horse and ran to her father.

"I'm sorry! I'm sorry," she blubbered out. "I'm so glad the fire didn't reach you."

"I've been out searching for you all day," Eagle Beak said before wrapping her in his arms. "I only just returned. Come, your mother is worried."

As if to make his point, her mother came riding up along with others. Red Hawk rode at the center of the group, flanked by more warriors. She huddled into the safety of Pretty Robe's arms.

"You're wet and cold," Pretty Robe scolded. "And you're hurt." She took the robe she was wearing off her own shoulders and wrapped it around Fire Girl.

"We had to jump into the river to escape the fire," she explained.

"You saved her? Oh, thank you, Lone Wolf." Pretty Robe clasped his hand to show her gratitude.

It was hard to hear it put in those terms, but it was true. Lone Wolf had saved her. She pulled the robe up over her head and Pretty Robe put her arm back around her shoulders. "Let's go back to the lodge. I'll warm you up with hot stew and tea to ward off illness. You too, Lone Wolf," but he was already surrounded by warriors and men, including her father.

Fire Girl followed her mother to the lodge, leaving Eagle Beak to hear from Lone Wolf what had happened, and what she had done.

She sat huddled by another warm fire, dry clothes on, a bandage around her torso, a hot bowl of broth cupped in her palms, and wrapped in the furriest robe. Eagle Beak ducked into the lodge, his expression a mix of stern admonishment and worry. Although he'd said nothing to her, she could imagine the ridicule from Lone Wolf as he explained her foolish behavior with the bear and the fire.

"If not for those favorable winds, the whole camp would have burned. We'd have had no time to escape, not for the young and the elderly. Not everyone has a horse like Shadow, and even if they did, we would have lost everything. Lodges, food, supplies—"

"I know. I *am* sorry." She looked up at him. It used to be rare to see him angry or exasperated with her, but that was beginning to become more common lately. Would he see her as Papa had? Reckless. Impulsive. The echo of Pretty Robe's words played in her mind. *Burn strong, but steady. Don't let the fire consume you.* Maybe she hadn't meant a literal fire but she was doing it in all the ways it could be interpreted. "I was trying to scare away the bear. It was an accident."

"Lone Wolf told me about the bear. Did you really think you could scare it away? I hate to think what could have happened to you if he wasn't there."

She ducked her head into the robe. It might have been possible to survive without Lone Wolf, but she'd never get the chance to know.

"As I understand it," Pretty Robe spoke up. "The bear didn't fully attack her. Her injuries will heal." She grasped Fire Girl's hand. "Do you understand the significance of the bear's visit?"

"Visit?" It was too casual a word for the encounter, but she let Pretty Robe explain.

"The bear spirit is a symbol of personal strength and healing."

She rolled a sore shoulder. "Seems like it wanted to do the opposite of healing."

Pretty Robe made a brief chuckle. "You're more like the bear than you think. Whether you want it or not, the bear will become a part of your personal medicine."

It was unclear how to make the bear a part of her medicine, but Eagle Beak refocused her attention. "I take it you didn't thank Lone Wolf for helping you?"

She hugged the bowl to her chest. "No, I didn't... a lot happened."

He nodded. "You need to make this right, daughter. Not only to show your gratitude for today, but to apologize for what you said to him last summer. Tomorrow we will visit with him and you will show the respect he deserves. Have a gift ready."

He left again, probably to sulk about his reckless daughter with the other men who despised her.

Pretty Robe gave her a sympathetic smile. "Don't worry, daughter. I know just what we can make."

22

Mouse stuck her head into the open doorway. "Pretty Robe asked if I'd stop by and see if you needed any help cleaning up from the morning meal."

Fire Girl tugged the yoke of her dress back into place after rewrapping her wound. "Sure, I could use some help."

Mouse dropped to her knees and collected dirty bowls and rawhide trenches onto her lap. "Did Lone Wolf really toss you into the river to save you from the fire?" Her grin spread from ear to ear, like what happened was no more than a juicy bite of gossip.

"He didn't *toss* me. We dove in on his horse."

"I can't believe you got to ride Shadow. Lone Wolf never lets anyone ride him. Not even Badger. Well, okay *once* he let Badger ride him. Maybe twice."

She didn't even remember that part. It was all a fiery blur. "It's just a horse."

"Not to Lone Wolf it is. And you should know by now the value of a good horse."

She did. Even the nag was a loss and Eagle Beak had not been happy to hear it.

Pretty Robe returned to the lodge, carrying a large container of hackberries. "Here, this shall be enough." She dropped the basket.

"Enough for what?" Fire Girl asked.

"To make the candy."

"Oh, hackberry candy!" Mouse said. "It's my cousin's favorite. Great idea."

"This is for Lone Wolf then?" Fire Girl bit her lip. It didn't look like there was going to be any way out of making that apology.

After the tedious task of removing the pits, they boiled the berries in a large pot with plenty of honey and precious white sugar Pretty Robe had bought from the trader last Spring. The berries cooked until they broke down and became a sweet, sticky paste. Then Pretty Robe scooped the mixture out onto a large sheet of rawhide.

"It will take some time for this to cool and harden," Pretty Robe said. "While it does, why don't you use some of the spare rawhide to make a case to carry it? You can paint one of your pictures on it."

"Paint a picture?" What sort of picture could she paint for Lone Wolf? His horse? Nothing to do with fire, that was certain.

The rest of the morning, Mouse and Pretty Robe worked beside her, mending her hunting clothes while she painted. After a while, Mouse broke the silence. "People are saying your name fits you even better than before, Fire Girl."

She snapped her head up. "What are people saying about me? And why do you listen to their gossip?"

"I'm sorry," Mouse stammered. "I didn't mean..."

Pretty Robe shot Fire Girl a warning look and she drew back, softening her expression. "No, *I'm* sorry. I didn't mean to jump on you like that. It's just, I feel terrible about the fire, and I know it gives people reason to dislike me more than they already do." Even that morning Fox Laugh had declined to join them for the morning meal, giving Fire Girl another one of his scalding looks.

"It's fine," Mouse said with a smile. "I don't think as many people dislike you as you think. They're also saying it's admirable how you took on a bear like that. Besides, I doubt your prospects for marriage will be affected by this."

"Marriage?" Fire Girl set her brush down and wiped at her damp palms. "Why are you even talking about marriage?"

Mouse was undaunted. "Well, you're fifteen summers, right? Many girls get married at your age. I wouldn't be surprised if you begin to have suitors." She glanced at Pretty Robe, who didn't look up.

"Maybe this summer, maybe next summer," Pretty Robe said calmly.

"Maybe never." Fire Girl smothered her annoyance and got up to check the candy. "It's cooled now. What next?"

"Now we'll cut off pieces and roll them into bites," Pretty Robe said. As they worked, Pretty Robe mused. "Lone Wolf's mother taught me this method, you know. She and I used to be good friends." She smiled sadly. "She was a fine woman, quiet, like her son, but she could have a wicked sense of humor." She laughed softly while Mouse made a wistful smile.

Their shared grief left her feeling awkward. It wasn't often the People spoke of the dead, but their memories had nothing to do with her.

When the candy was done, they packed the candy in the painted box and saved the extra for later. Eagle Beak returned from his day spent collecting wood to make new arrows. He set bundles of wood

233

down and stood, holding out her skinning knife. "Lone Wolf asked me to return this to you. He found it buried in ash."

She took the knife. The handle had been replaced with a fresh piece of smooth bone and the blade sanded and sharpened. "He went back there?"

Eagle Beak gave her a mysterious smile. "Obviously so. Did you prepare a gift?"

She nodded, her palms freshly damp. "Yes, it's ready."

"Good, let's go see him now."

Holding the box of hackberry candy, Fire Girl followed Eagle Beak as they approached Lone Wolf's lodge. She swallowed nervously when he came into view. He sat against a backrest, painting a new shield. He set down his bone and horsehair paint brush among his bowls of pigment, then raised his hand in greeting. She blushed when he stood. He was still wearing nothing but a breechcloth, but the weather had turned unusually warm. The sun blazed with heat and sweat trickled down her back.

Eagle Beak and Lone Wolf exchanged greetings and spoke about the horse raid Lone Wolf was organizing. "When are you leaving?" Eagle Beak asked.

"In two days. Will you join us? We could use your tracking skills."

"Maybe next time. Where do you plan to go?"

Fire Girl stopped listening. She focused on anything but Lone Wolf and tried not to fidget or scratch at her itchy wounds. Her mother made her wear her best dress, even though she'd outgrown it since spring. It was a two-piece gown, in the newer style, with a V-shaped neckline. If she raised her arms, the skin at her waist showed. The skirt hugged her hips. Her mother had also fussed over her hair and jewelry, tying the ends of her braids with strips of blue cloth and making her wear long earrings that brushed her shoulders.

She tugged on the skirt self-consciously. Life would be easier if she'd been born a man. She could walk around in a breechcloth and not feel the least bit exposed.

The conversation had stopped. Eagle Beak waited for her to speak, and she tried to remember what she planned to say.

"Lone Wolf..." It was odd to say his name to his face. "Thank you for... for helping me escape the fire." She found the courage to look at him. He stared back with great intensity.

Her voice faltered, but she continued. "I also want to apologize for what I said to you last summer. It was abhorrent and cruel. I hope you know I didn't mean it. I was angry and... well... It doesn't matter why. I shouldn't have said those things." There. She did it. She'd rushed through the end, but it was done. She was about to step away, but his soft voice held her captive.

"Thank you, Fire Girl." Why did it hurt when he said her name? "I know you didn't mean what you said, and I've already forgiven you." His words were rushed, as though he didn't wish to discuss it any more than she did. "As for the fire and the bear, I know you blame yourself for all of it, but it isn't all your fault."

She wanted to pretend he sounded arrogant or haughty, but his voice rang sincere.

He continued, taking a step closer. "When we were warming by the fire yesterday, I should have said this. You were brave and handled it well, under the circumstances. You didn't panic. If the bear didn't survive, that's my fault. I was the one who put arrows in her. I was the one who startled her into a charge, which then put you between her and the cubs." Did she only imagine the pain in his eyes? "She probably would have only bluffed until you backed away or let you play dead. The fire... it couldn't be helped. I'm just glad we both survived."

He had such an edge of earnestness to him, she couldn't look away. Strange that the one person she expected to blame her the most was now telling her it wasn't her fault. Did it really matter to him?

Eagle Beak nudged her from behind until she handed Lone Wolf the gift. "My mother and I, and Mouse, we made this for you, to thank you," she stammered.

He took the package, pausing to run his fingers over the design on the case. She'd ended up painting a single wolf in black silhouette beneath the moon with a star-studded sky, not sure where that image of him had come from. Was he was pleased or amused?

When he opened the box, his face brightened into a wide grin. Her breath hitched, stunned, having never seen him smile so broadly before. She instantly recalled overhearing a group of women talk about his appearance. They'd used words like, "severely handsome," and "so good-looking it hurts to look at him." She understood the meaning of those words now.

He took a piece of the candy and put it in his mouth. He closed his eyes, seeming to savor the flavor before his expression became forlorn. "It tastes just like I remembered. My mother used to make this for me when I was a child." He smiled sadly. "Thank you. This is truly a wonderful gift." The wistful look in his eye gave her goosebumps. He opened his mouth, about to say something else, but glanced behind her and his face became sober once more.

She had forgotten that Eagle Beak stood at her back. "Pretty Robe wanted me to ask you to join us for our evening meal," Eagle Beak said.

Fire Girl blinked in astonishment. No one had told her about the invitation.

"I'll be there," Lone Wolf said.

After they said their goodbyes and she and her father returned to their lodge, Fire Girl sensed Lone Wolf watching. It gave her a strange, warm, but fluttery feeling in her stomach.

She begrudgingly helped her mother prepare a large meal for their guest. They'd had visitors before, like Red Hawk and his wives, Two Horns and Quick Hands, and Mouse. Those meals were casual affairs, and her parents hadn't expected her to do much besides her usual help.

It was clear, by her mother's and father's behavior, that this occasion was different. The lodge was cleaned and tidied, her parents wore some of their better clothing, and they had enough food to feed at least ten warriors.

The food had been laid out in the center of the lodge. A wooden platter filled with roasted deer and buffalo meat sat in the middle. Beside it stood a large pot of antelope stew which Pretty Robe had insisted was Lone Wolf's favorite meal. Fire Girl had prepared it with wild onions, radishes, yampa roots, corn, and herbs. Around the meat sat bowls of plums, wild grapes, cherries, mulberries, persimmons, and prickly pear, as well as bowls of nuts and seeds. Flat cakes made from ground corn and crushed pecans lay on a cloth with a jar of precious honey, and of course, more hackberry candy.

It all seemed more than necessary just to thank Lone Wolf, even if he had saved her and she wondered if there was some other reason.

The worst part about it was she wasn't going to be able to ignore him like usual.

They sat in the lodge and waited for him to arrive. Pretty Robe did some last-minute arranging of the food and slapped away Round Eyes' eager hands. Eagle Beak cleaned his pipe, while Fire Girl tried to think of some excuse to be anywhere but in the lodge. Then came the faint tinkle of metal cones from Lone Wolf's leggings.

He scratched at the open lodge flap and Eagle Beak shoved his pipe away, then gestured for her to stand as Lone Wolf entered. She was relieved he wore his everyday clothing, although he did look as if he'd taken more care than usual with his appearance. His hair shone smooth, and his clothes and face appeared fresh and clean.

He greeted each of them, then Eagle Beak directed him to sit at the place of honor. She stood out of the way as he moved past. She smelled his scent, redolent of sage, pine, and some other pleasant smells her nervous mind couldn't untangle.

The men sat and Pretty Robe motioned to Fire Girl and then at the pot. She dolefully complied, ladling out the stew her mother had instructed her to make a point of serving.

"Fire Girl prepared the antelope stew," Pretty Robe said to Lone Wolf, smiling.

Resisting the urge to roll her eyes, Fire Girl thrust the bowl at him, then took her seat out of the way. She stared at her lap, wishing she could make herself sick.

I could've poisoned it before I served it to him. The vicious thought filled her with guilt.

The conversation was mostly between Eagle Beak and Lone Wolf, and her mind drifted back to the wildfire and his quiet observance while they sat to get warm. His concern over her comfort and wounds revealed a manner that was almost kind. But now, she might as well be invisible. Hopefully it wouldn't be long before Eagle Beak retrieved his pipe, the signal for the men to talk alone, and for women to leave the lodge.

Four-year-old Round Eyes moved to sit next to Lone Wolf and leaned on his leg. He smeared his leggings with sticky fingers, but Lone Wolf didn't seem to mind. He smiled at the boy and stroked his hair absently while he talked with Eagle Beak. Round Eyes hung on his every word, trying to join the conversation whenever he could, and pleased whenever Lone Wolf would acknowledge him with a smile or a comment.

They talked more about horses and horse raids and guilt over the dead nag stirred her gut. She liked horses, but it was all Lone Wolf cared to talk about. Then again, it would be good to have a real horse of her own, one she could ride whenever she wanted, one trained to follow only her signals, once as fast as Shadow. She could have escaped that fire on her own, riding to freedom...

"Fire Girl, did you hear Lone Wolf? He said your stew was delicious and he would like another helping." Pretty Robe gave her a tight annoyed smile.

She swallowed hard. She was being childish and ungrateful. Her parents had gone to a lot of trouble, and she was being rude. Even if it was Lone Wolf, she didn't want to shame her parents by her behavior. He *had* saved her life.

She poured stew in another bowl. Lone Wolf wore that look from earlier, the one that made her stomach flutter. She stepped closer to hand him the bowl. He smiled gently and said, "Thank you." Again, there was a quality to his voice that seemed almost plaintive.

He took the bowl, but somehow her fingers touched his. It was like touching a hot coal. She startled, jumped back, and let go. The bowl upended and landed on the ground in front of him, spilling steaming hot liquid onto his lap.

Lone Wolf gasped and stood. Splatters of stew hit Round Eyes and he cried. She covered her mouth with her hands, unable to move. Her mother offered Lone Wolf a rag, then pulled Round Eyes into her lap to comfort him. Her father leaned against the backrest and shook his head, muttering under his breath.

Lone Wolf attempted to clean the stew from his clothing. "It's fine," he said, but he didn't sound fine. His voice had lost its softness, gaining a strained edge, and he wouldn't look at her.

Humiliated, she dashed out, running as hard as when she'd set Lone Wolf ablaze with her words. Maybe Papa had been right about her. Even from wherever his bones lay, she could hear him laughing. Reckless, impulsive and impossible. She would always be too much, too difficult. Anyone who gave her kindness would soon regret it. There wasn't anywhere she could go where folks wouldn't eventually tire of her. She could have a new life, a new family, a new existence, but it would always turn out the same.

A new vicious thought flashed in her mind. Had Papa gotten what he deserved? No, it was a sin to think such things. Everything that had happened was wrong, even she was wrong. But Lone Wolf was worse, so much worse. Out of breath, she sat in the tall grass in the dark and covered her head with her arms. She couldn't imagine what he must think of her. Clumsy and foolish.

Why had he saved her? Why had he even come? How could he forgive what she did, what she said? She could never speak to him again. Now that she made that stupid apology, maybe she wouldn't have to.

The moon had shifted from its position in the sky by the time she came back to the lodge. Lone Wolf was gone. Round Eyes slept with a bandage on his burned hand. Her mother and father said nothing when she came in.

She stood, fighting tears. "I'm sorry. I didn't do it on purpose."

"I find that hard to believe," Eagle Beak said, but Pretty Robe remained quiet.

"I'm telling you the truth. I know I was being awful, and it seems like I meant it, but I didn't. It was an accident."

"You *were* being awful, Fire Girl," said Pretty Robe at last. "Then you ran out without a word. Honestly daughter, I don't understand you. A man risked his life for you, saved yours, and this is how you behave toward him? And it's not the only time Lone Wolf took a risk on your behalf."

She frowned. She resented being reminded of the raid and Lone Wolf sparing her.

"Are you ever going to get over this grudge you have against him?" Pretty Robe asked.

"No! I mean, yes. I don't know. Why *did* he risk his life? That's what I don't understand. I don't *want* to be obligated to him. I don't *want* to owe him my gratitude. I just want him to leave me alone."

Pretty Robe bit her lower lip. She exchanged a look with Eagle Beak, who shook his head. "I can't explain that for you, daughter," she said.

"Then explain this," Fire Girl said. "I made the apology, we made him a gift, but why parade myself in front of Lone Wolf like a piece of meat?" She pulled on the silly dress to prove her point. "I don't know what else you want from me."

Pretty Robe took a deep breath. "You're right. I'm sorry we pushed you." She pulled Fire Girl into a hug.

Eagle Beak's knees cracked as he stood and moved closer to them. His hand rubbed her back. "I'm sorry, daughter. It was too soon for any of this."

Too soon for what? But she was exhausted and worn, so sought the comfort of her bed and escape from her thoughts. Lone Wolf was leaving on a raid in two days. If she could avoid him until then, she wouldn't have to see him for at least a month.

23

F ire Girl sat outside the lodge chewing on a hide from the last of the fall hunts. Misty air cooled her face as she gazed at bare oak trees. The camp would move for winter soon. She welcomed the change, the end of a painful year.

Round Eyes rode to her on a donkey, his small bow and arrow slung across his back. He even had the solemn face of a warrior. "Raiders have returned. Sentries saw the signal and Grandfather said we should get ready for them."

Just as he finished his words, the camp crier shouted the same announcement. She frowned. She'd never been expected to formally welcome returning warriors. That honor was reserved for family members and close friends. They would have done so after the Penateka raid, but that return had been disastrous.

Sometimes she stood off to the side and watched the men parade through the camp, their finery on display as well as their scalps. She would linger with the crowd and listen to the men recount their honors, her heart divided by conscience and custom. Eventually, she'd lose interest and return to her task while others continue their celebrations.

But now, Lone Wolf and his men had returned, and Eagle Beak expected her to greet him. A feeling in her chest like the flick of a bird's wing came and went, quick as a hummingbird.

"Hurry down to the stream to take a bath, then get your grandmother," she told Round Eyes. Her mother was gathering willow branches for a new backrest.

"I already took a bath. And Grandmother is on her way here."

"You did?" She examined her nephew. Dirt smudged his cheeks and dust covered his bare feet. She rolled her eyes. "Come on."

She took Round Eyes into the lodge to get him dressed. He was young enough that he often went about naked, though he sometimes wore a breechcloth. For special occasions, such as this one, he would wear fancy leggings and a decorated shirt. Once she dressed him, she struggled to comb his long tangled hair.

"Ouch, that hurts!"

"Well, if you let me braid it, it wouldn't get so tangled." She grabbed the old tin that Eagle Beak used to store his bear grease.

"Are you going to braid it now?" he asked.

"Yes." She parted his hair.

"No! Don't!"

She sighed, exasperated. "Why not? Don't you want to look like a warrior?"

"I will look like a warrior! I'll look like the best warrior in camp. I'll look like Lone Wolf."

His words struck her silent. She fiddled with the hair tools, trying to hide her discomfort. "Fine. Leave it loose then. Just don't complain to me when it gets all tangled again."

"How come Lone Wolf's hair never gets tangled?"

"I'm sure it does." She shoved the tools back into their cases. "He's just too proud to ever let anyone see it like that."

"You shouldn't speak ill about Lone Wolf. He *should* be proud. Did you know that he once—"

"Round Eyes, please go outside and wait for your grandparents. I need to get dressed."

"So what? I've seen you without clothes before."

She blushed. "Yes well, if you're going to be a warrior, then it's not right for you to spend so much time alone with an unmarried girl. Now go!"

Round Eyes left and she sat for a moment, trying to compose herself. Her nervousness at seeing Lone Wolf again was different than before, edgy and sharp, like a blade in her chest.

The crier made another round of announcements, saying the parade was about to begin. She'd better hurry.

She took off her everyday dress and put on a deeply smoked gown, heavily quilled on the yoke and shoulders with designs in white, yellow, green and blue. She had just finished it and hadn't worn it yet. It would satisfy her parents if it looked as though she put in some effort, but without looking like she was trying too hard. There was no way she would wear the too-revealing, two-piece dress from before.

After rebraiding her hair, she put on a pair of earrings which matched the colors of her dress. She hadn't yet made a pair of moccasins to match, so slipped on her better pair, then went out.

A crowd of people gathered along the main route of the welcome parade, which would pass right by her lodge. Her mother and father came over and she gave them a weak smile. Round Eyes stood with a group of young boys, who tried to look fierce and solemn. The sound of drums grew louder while people chanted and sang. Then came the faint sound of bells, signaling the approaching warriors.

Her heart pounded in time with the beat. She shifted her feet and clasped her hands. The tips of the men's lances glinted white in the sunlight, bobbing in rhythm over the heads of the oncoming crowd. Dust rose from their horses, then the riders themselves appeared.

Lone Wolf rode at the front. Despite the cool air, he wore no shirt, but his upper body and face were painted black, red, and white. Black paint decorated his horse's rump. Strips of cloth and feathers waved from Shadow's bridle and tail, and from Lone Wolf's lance and shield. Also from his lance hung a string of bloody scalps.

Badger rode behind Lone Wolf, with Mouse proudly beside her husband. She wore her best clothes and held Badger's lance and shield, an honor for a first wife. A younger warrior stopped before a young woman, then handed her his own lance and shield. The girl blushed deeply and accepted the honor as her friends and family smiled their approval.

Her mind flashed with panic as the warriors came closer, about to pass her. Her parents smiled, eagerly awaiting Lone Wolf's arrival. It was hard to tell because of the black around his eyes, but he seemed to watch her as he approached. His stern face reminded her of the way he looked when she first saw him, his bow pointed at her while she hid and watched people die.

She backed up behind the crowd.

Her father grabbed her arm. "Where are you going?"

She pulled her arm free. "I can't."

Eagle Beak tilted his head in confusion, but she couldn't explain and fled into the lodge. The figure of Lone Wolf on his horse filled the doorway before she closed the flap. Did he stop? She heard talking, but the noise of the crowd drowned out any words or familiar voices. Singing and drums receded as the crowd followed the procession. Instead of relief, a pang of regret twisted the knife in her chest.

After evening fell, her father came in. "Are you coming to watch the celebration?"

She shook her head.

"Then I guess you won't be coming to the dance later."

"No."

Eagle Beak pursed his lips, then left. The door flap closed behind him.

She sat alone in the dark lodge. She tried to continue to work her hides, but restless thoughts distracted her. The dance had started long before, but the drums and singing were still going strong. Her foot tapped in rhythm. Everyone was having fun without her. Her solitude served no one, not even herself.

The pain in her chest from earlier had faded to a dull ache. Perhaps she had just been paranoid. It was silly to think Lone Wolf would actually offer her his lance and shield. The idea was absurd, and she'd acted a fool once more. She put her tools away and rose to join the festivities. She would show Lone Wolf once and for all he couldn't intimidate her.

Light from the fire illuminated the figures of the crowd against the moonlit sky. She circled the onlookers, finding a gap where she could stand and watch. Mouse stood with her arm around Badger who was coated in sweat from dancing. They both glowed in their happiness.

She felt eyes on her and glanced to her side, expecting to see Lone Wolf, but it was Buffalo Horn. He smiled, but she looked away.

The music changed, signaling a new dance, woman's choice. Mouse grabbed Badger's hand and they were the first to join the circle. Loud laughter carried across the dance arena, and Fire Girl instinctively turned toward it. Antelope was tugging on Lone Wolf's arm. She led him to the circle and put her hands on his shoulders, as he put his on her waist. She grinned, looking thrilled. Lone Wolf's smile appeared forced, but Antelope must have said something funny because he smiled that broad smile and broke into a laugh.

Her skin grew hot, and her chest tightened. For reasons she couldn't explain, she went to Buffalo Horn and took his hand. "Dance with me."

"Of course!"

They joined the circle of dancers and Buffalo Horn put his hands low on her waist. She couldn't see Lone Wolf anymore from the direction she faced, so she tried to concentrate on the dance, sidestepping with Buffalo Horn around the circle.

Being this close to him felt awkward. She'd never been close to a man in that way, and she was aware of nothing but his presence. It dominated all her senses. He smelled of sweat and bear grease. It either had gone rancid or he rarely bathed and rubbed a new layer over previous ones. She could feel the oiliness on his hard shoulders. His eyes roamed over her, but she tried not to look at his face. His hands slipped lower and further down her hips, pulling her closer despite the expectation they keep an arm's distance away.

He whispered in her ear. "I hoped to dance with you."

She smiled weakly, fully regretting her choice and wondered what to say to get away.

"You never dance with anyone, so I'm honored you picked me." He leaned further into her neck. She could feel and smell his hot breath. "You know, there's at least one other person here who would do anything to trade places with me right now."

What was she supposed to say to that? "I want to go—"

"Let's take a walk."

"What?"

"A walk," he repeated. His chin gestured toward the piney woods.

Her eyes grew wide, and she pulled away. "No, I can't. I have to go." She spun on her heel and walked away, searching the crowd. The song ended and the drummers switched to a new song with new dancers, but it was no use. Lone Wolf was nowhere to be seen and Antelope was missing as well. The implication of this left her feeling hot in her chest again.

Who cares? Those two deserved each other.

She left the dance and wandered along the edge of wood. The full moon lit her path. Warm tears ran down her face and she angrily wiped them away. She was moving through the trees when she heard a sound. Her skin prickled with alarm. Not another bear, and yet...

The noise continued as she went toward it, stepping silently, her hand on her skinning knife. A figure stood in front of her, moving in a strange way. She peered closer, then paused when she realized what she was seeing.

It was Buffalo Horn. With a woman. She couldn't see who it was because the woman faced away from her, braced against a tree, her dress hiked up to her waist. Buffalo Horn stood behind her with his hands on her hips. By the movement of his pelvis, it was obvious what they were doing.

She couldn't help but watch, horrified and yet curious. Whenever her parents had sex, they did so quietly under the cover of a robe. The noise she heard was the wet slap of bodies as Buffalo Horn rutted her. The woman groaned and Fire Girl wasn't sure if it was in agony or pleasure. The sound brought her to her senses, and she fled.

She headed to the stream with the intention of following it back to camp. Drums were still beating in the distance, but she had no desire to return to the dance. Buffalo Horn had asked *her* to go with him into the woods, but now he was with someone else. Lone Wolf was with Antelope, or maybe that was Antelope with Buffalo Horn? Either way, why did she even care?

Her confusion and anger threatened to bring more tears. As she reached the ridge above the riverbank, she stopped short. Again, someone stood ahead of her, by the shore. His back was to her, but she knew him immediately. Her heart beat faster than the dancing drums.

Lone Wolf's head turned up, watching the stars. She was reminded of that night when she'd tried to escape, and he had stood in that same way, staring up at the night sky, silent and still. He crouched, picked up a stone, then tossed it into the stream. It bounced across the surface several times before it sank to the bottom.

So that's why he was carrying stones. Were those the same ones she had used to warm her skin, or had he collected more? For reasons unknown, she had the urge to go to him. She took a step closer, then paused. What would she even say? What if he had nothing to say? She couldn't bear the humiliation.

Backing away, she left as quietly as she could. Once she reached the woods, she ran to her lodge. It was still empty, and she crawled under her bedding, not bothering to undress and buried her face in her robes.

Two days later the band took down their lodges and headed to the winter camp. She rarely saw Lone Wolf all winter. His lodge door was always closed. When she visited Mouse, he didn't stop by. She only caught glimpses of him at a distance as he returned from a hunt or from riding with Badger, but he never looked her way.

One cold afternoon, she sat alone in the lodge when a man entered through the open doorway. By his youthful face and lithe body, she thought it was Lone Wolf. The relief it was Fox Laugh was shadowed with disappointment.

"Round Eyes isn't here. He's playing with the other boys," she said without looking at him.

"I'm not here to see Round Eyes," he answered hesitantly. "I came to talk with you."

She sat straighter, wary and stiff. Fox Laugh took a few steps closer but kept his distance. He didn't sit.

"I wanted to say, I've done you a great wrong. I've never been kind to you, but you don't deserve my bitterness."

A wave of shock left her speechless.

"In being cruel to you, I've dishonored the memory of my wife." He paused and gazed sideways. "I loved her very much. Every day, since she's been gone, I've wished she was here and it hurts me to see you in her place." His throat moved as he swallowed. "When I see you, I can only see what happened to her. But if Pretty Robe and Eagle Beak, and

251

even Lone Wolf, can forgive and move forward. If *you* are able to, then I should too.

"I'm sorry for how I've treated you, because in truth she would have liked you." He smiled. "You're like her in some ways. Different, but the way you are with Round Eyes, it's how she was too. I'm grateful to you, for spending time with him, for being like a mother to him. It makes me sad that he doesn't remember her and never will. But your presence is a comfort to the both of us."

Never in a hundred lifetimes did she expect to hear such words, least of all from Fox Laugh. She managed to speak. "Thank you for that. It makes my heart glad to hear it. I accept your apology," she said. "And I offer mine as well, for whatever it's worth."

He started to leave but stopped again. "Did you know he was my friend? My best friend?"

"Who?"

"Lone Wolf's brother. He was like a brother to me, like how Lone Wolf is to Badger."

"No," she said breathlessly. "I didn't know that."

"He was nothing like Lone Wolf. Lone Wolf is quiet and he's always thinking, but his brother acted without thought, always into some trouble or another."

Fox Laugh seemed lost in his memories, speaking more to himself than to her, a different man entirely. She'd always wondered how a woman as sweet as Eagle Beak's daughter was said to be could ever marry a man as cold as Fox Laugh, but now she saw it. This was the man inside, the man under all the pain, grief and bitterness. The man from before that day.

He went on about Lone Wolf's brother, his best friend, the man she killed. "He was brash and loud and always the center of attention. He was fond of women too." He brushed his hand over his face. "In fact, the only time we ever fought, it was because of a woman. You see, he fancied her, my wife I mean, before we married. He even tried to court her. I'd been in love with her since we were kids and he knew it. I felt like someone had handed me the moon and stars when she chose me. We were very happy."

She could hear the emotion in his voice but dared not interrupt.

"She picked me, but I know she loved him too. Now they're both gone. My time with her was brief, but I'll treasure those memories for the rest of my days. The men think the best things in life are war, earning honors, and stealing horses, and those things are great, but there's nothing better in this world than to love a great woman, and to be loved by her in return."

Before she could answer him, he ducked out and disappeared from the doorway.

Her winter nights were restless and plagued by dreams. She saw Lone Wolf's brother and father die at the end of her gun. She dreamed of Maggie being carried away and of a dark shadow ringed with sunlight. She had visions of Buffalo Horn in the woods, only sometimes it was Lone Wolf.

She dreamt of Lone Wolf standing before her, smiling, as he did when she'd brought him the hackberry candy, or of him looking at the stars cast in moonlight. Somehow, those dreams were worse, and she'd wake up covered in sweat and an ache in her belly that sometimes extended lower. She didn't want to think of Lone Wolf in that way. She didn't want to think of him at all.

24

Spring 1841

Loud voices and ribald laughter came through the opening of the lodge door as Fire Girl sat with her parents finishing their morning meal. Such behavior was common, so she ignored it, but Eagle Beak snickered, "Sounds like someone is about to take a wife."

Pretty Robe peeked from a crack. "It's Looks To the Sky. He tied five horses outside."

Fire Girl dropped her sewing and scrambled to the door to see for herself. Five sturdy looking horses were hobbled in the clearing beside the lodge, one stallion, two geldings, and two mares. Looks To the Sky's stocky figure walked away through the crowd of onlookers, his long braids swinging behind him.

She spotted Lone Wolf in the crowd and felt that hummingbird flutter, then someone moved in front, and she lost him as people headed to their lodges. She shut the flap.

Eagle Beak's hadn't moved from his seat. His brow furrowed. "Has Looks To the Sky spoken to you, daughter? Did you know of his intentions?"

"No. I've never spoken to him. I don't know why he's asking me. I don't want anyone to ask me," she rambled out. Marriage was bad enough without some man she hardly knew trying to become her husband. "Are you going to accept the horses?" She trembled as she waited for his answer.

"I know what needs to be done." He gave her a reassuring smile.

The family stayed in the lodge while she waited to see what Eagle Beak would do. Noon passed. By then, if he intended to accept, Eagle Beak should have taken the horses to add to his meager herd.

Looks To the Sky arrived to tie two more horses to the group outside. It was unusual for a man to increase his offer. Either he was persistent, or more likely, was unused to taking no for an answer. Eagle Beak might change his mind. He had so few horses as it was.

That afternoon, when Eagle Beak still hadn't accepted, Looks To the Sky came to the lodge. He was older than her father, and his large belly protruded over his belt. His braids were so long they hung past his knees, extended with horsehair and wrapped with otter skin, a sure sign of vanity. He swung them both behind him before he sat across from Eagle Beak, not even waiting for an invitation.

She grimaced. She'd run away to the Apache before being forced to marry such a man.

Pretty Robe took her hand and led her outside. "Let's go work while your father talks to Looks To the Sky."

"He's not going to accept, is he?" She searched Pretty Robe's face for clues.

"Trust your father to do what is best."

She wanted to trust him. Eagle Beak knew better than to make her marry that man, but perhaps she'd made herself too much a burden and he'd be happy to be rid of her.

She and Pretty Robe worked on scraping hides, then Squirrel and Laughing Bird came and sat nearby. Squirrel whispered to Pretty Robe, "How has Eagle Beak not accepted the horses? Surely, he will not refuse a more than generous offer?"

"Only the daughters of chiefs hold out for more. Eagle Beak must think highly of his daughter to decline," agreed Laughing Bird.

Fire Girl wanted to punch those fat cheeks of hers. If only she had done so years ago.

"We all think highly of Fire Girl," Pretty Robe said. "Eagle Beak will decide in our daughter's best interest."

"I don't want to get married anyway," she said.

The two older wives looked at her with wide eyes and open mouths.

"Perhaps not to Looks To the Sky. Perhaps you're waiting for someone young and handsome?" Squirrel said.

"Or he's waiting for you," added Laughing Bird.

"Tsk," said Pretty Robe, sounding like a scolding bird. "Stop your gossip and let us work in peace."

Squirrel and Laughing Bird exchanged looks, eyeing her with knowing smiles. She ignored them but their expressions didn't help her discomfort.

A short time later, Looks To the Sky came out of the lodge. She watched his face for any sign of her father's answer, but his expression remained flat. When Pretty Robe told her it was time to return home, she leaped to her feet to follow.

When they entered, she strode up to Eagle Beak. "Well?"

"You will not marry Looks To the Sky." He sighed heavily, his face worn out.

Her heart lifted in relief, then she threw her arms around his neck. "Thank you, father." He returned her embrace.

"He was in here a while," Pretty Robe said. "Did he say why he wanted to marry our daughter? He's never spoken to us about her before."

Eagle Beak pursed his lips. His eyes darkened. "The pompous bastard. I won't even repeat what he said about Fire Girl... but he thinks no one else will want her and we should be lucky he'd be willing to take her off our hands. I told him if he had such a poor opinion of her, he could take his horses and shove them up his ass."

Her eyes burned. She'd escaped marriage, but this confirmed that others considered her a burden.

The next day, Fire Girl started her daily chore to collect water. Once her water bags were full, she started home. As she rose to the top of the slope, Buffalo Horn headed toward her. She tensed at his approach.

"Is it okay if I walk with you?" His voice was unusually hesitant.

She quickened her pace, but he walked in step beside her and cleared his throat. "I wanted to say, I'm glad your father didn't marry you to Looks To the Sky." He glanced sideways at her, expecting her to respond. She clutched her water bags. They were about to enter the clearing of the camp. Buffalo Horn stopped and grabbed her arm.

"Fire Girl, I like you. I wasn't sure how you felt about me, but when you asked me to dance last fall, I thought maybe you might like me as well—"

"No." She pulled her arm free. "I mean... I'm sorry." What had she done? By asking him to dance she had given him the wrong idea. Is that why men were offering marriage? She finally met his eyes, finding his confusion and perhaps even a little hurt. "I don't want to get married. Not to anyone. I'm sorry." She turned and hurried home, not daring to look behind her.

Her mother wasn't in the lodge when she delivered the skins of water. There was no one to tell about Buffalo Horn's offer, but maybe it wasn't an offer after all. She hadn't let him finish what he was going to say. It would be better to pretend nothing had happened and spare herself the humiliation of refusing two proposals. She could only imagine the gossip.

At Mouse's lodge later that evening, Fire Girl cooked flatbread on hot stones while Mouse stirred the boiled meat.

"I can't believe your father let those horses go," Mouse said. "I heard Looks To the Sky offered double the initial amount."

Fire Girl stifled a groan. She wasn't going to escape the topic of marriage. "I'm happy he refused them. I didn't want to marry Looks To the Sky."

"Well, it was a lot of horses." Mouse glanced at her husband. "Badger didn't offer so many for me."

Badger opened one eye from where he lay against the backrest, dozing as he waited for his food. "I gave as much as I could afford. Looks To the Sky is a rich man. Horses are like pebbles in his moccasins to him."

"Others have more." Mouses turned back. "If a young man were to offer marriage, would you want to?"

"No," she said. "I've told you already, I don't want to marry anyone."

"Not anyone? What if he was handsome and a brave warrior?" asked Mouse.

Fire Girl blew out her breath and set down the last cake. "It wouldn't matter to me if he was handsome, ugly, poor, rich, old, or young. I will not ever marry."

"Your family may need you to marry," Badger said.

"I don't think Eagle Beak would make me if I didn't want to."

Mouse and Badger exchanged looks, "Well, he might, if he really had to," Mouse said.

Exasperated, she stood up, "If all you two can talk about is marriage, then I'm going home. I won't change my mind. I'm not getting married. I knew that even before I came to the People."

She stormed from the lodge, running straight into Lone Wolf, the first contact with him in months. It was one thing for her to avoid him, but quite another for him to pretend she didn't exist, especially after the incident with the stew. A surge of anger and hurt made her flush red, bringing tears to her eyes.

He stared at her with concern. "What's wrong?" His eyes had the same soft look as they did after the fire. When he wanted her to get warm and take care of her wounds. *Now* he was worried about her? After avoiding her all winter? The wounds on her back had healed. It was elsewhere that hurt. She bit back a sharp retort and hurried past.

"What's happened?" Lone Wolf asked when he entered Badger's lodge.

"She's just being Fire Girl," Badger said.

Mouse shot her husband a sharp look. "She's mad because she doesn't want to get married."

Lone Wolf tensed. He expected that was true, but it still stung to hear it put so bluntly.

Badger gestured for Mouse to leave so they could speak alone. After she left, Badger sat back on his bed. "What's the matter, my friend?"

"That's what I wanted to talk to you about," Lone Wolf said.

"What is?"

"Marriage."

"Oh, ho." Badger sat up and slapped his knee. "You're finally ready to settle down and stop torturing all the wooing women. So, who's the unlucky girl?"

Lone Wolf sank to the floor. "Quit fooling around. You know exactly who I want." He leaned against a backrest, staring out of the smoke hole. It seemed like everyone but her understood that. Or perhaps she understood it too well. He was a fool to continue to have hope, even if he'd spent the winter trying to bury it.

Badger reached out a hand to pat his shoulder. "Sorry, I couldn't help myself. I know you care for her, but she... you know? This is a delicate situation."

"Yes, I know. She hates me."

"Does she?" Badger asked.

Lone Wolf lifted his head, hope springing to life from the grave. "What do you mean? Has she said anything to you or to Mouse?"

"Yes, but only that she hates you, but it's what I mean. By avoiding you, by refusing to talk about you, by making a point not to look at you even though she often does, she's trying to convince herself she hates you, but I think she's hiding something. If she truly cared less about you, then she would be indifferent."

It's what Lone Wolf had also believed, but he wasn't so sure anymore. "Badger, I touched her hand, and she dumped a bowl of soup on me. She hates me."

"Oh, how I would have *loved* to have seen that." Badger laughed, ignoring Lone Wolf's look of insult. "No permanent damage done though, eh?" He winked and gestured to his groin. "I still think she's hiding something. She's so used to pretending to hate you, she doesn't know how to stop. As soon as she realizes she has feelings for you, she does something to keep up the pretense. But if I were you, I wouldn't go about it the way Looks To the Sky did, and just wander over one day with a bunch of horses."

"I've already spoken with Eagle Beak. I did that long ago."

"That's not what I mean. You should speak with her first."

Badger was right, but he dreaded asking only to have her scorn him. More than she already had. Telling her how he felt would be the hardest thing he would ever do. He sat up. "Badger, I need your help."

"What would you have me do?"

"Speak with her first. Just to break the idea. My approaching her will set her immediately on the defensive, but if you brought it up, and she had time to think it over, then I could talk to her afterward, convince her if I have to. But I don't want it to come as a complete surprise."

"Why don't we ask Mouse to do this?"

"Because, then it will seem as no more than idle gossip. Besides, Mouse is my cousin while you're like a brother to me. From you, there can be no question of my sincerity."

Badger sighed, "I will do this. For you. But we cannot wait. Someone else may decide to ask her."

Lone Wolf groaned and sank back again. "I know. I didn't expect anyone to make an offer yet." He picked up a piece of kindling and snapped it in half. "For a moment there, I was afraid Eagle Beak was going to accept the horses from Looks To the Sky." He sighed. "Our deal was never settled. Eagle Beak said he wouldn't allow it unless she accepted me on her own."

"So, in other words, never?" Badger laughed.

Lone Wolf flicked a piece of broken wood at him. "Anyway, I hadn't planned on asking her yet. I need at least another year, but if I don't do something now, Eagle Beak might run out of patience and give her to someone else."

"Yeah, like Buffalo Horn," said Badger with a sly grin.

He grimaced. "Don't remind me. I can't stand the thought of your brother's greasy hands on her."

"So, you saw the way Buffalo Horn pawed her at the dance last fall?"

"Of course, I did. I was about to shove my knife in his throat." He ran his hands over his face, trying to erase the image of Fire Girl in Buffalo Horn's arms. She looked so lovely in that new dress. It brought out the color of her eyes and hair, like a bright flower in a field.

"Good thing you didn't. I don't think the council would see that as anything but an act of jealous rage." Badger winked. "She *did* ask him to dance, you know?"

Lone Wolf scowled. "You're not helping."

"I know." Badger grinned. "Besides, *you* were dancing with Antelope—"

"I danced with Antelope because the whole celebration was in my honor and I didn't want to be rude. I waited all night for Fire Girl—"

Badger kicked his foot. "I know that, but she doesn't. Don't you think she hears talk from the women?"

"I don't care about any of those women."

"I know, but while you've been twiddling your thumbs, Buffalo Horn is making his move."

"You don't think your brother's intentions toward her are sincere, do you?"

"First of all, he and I may share a father, but you're more of a brother to me than he is. Secondly, anything is possible with Buffalo Horn. And third... well, I don't really have a third."

Lone Wolf chewed on his lip.

"Hey," Badger added, giving Lone Wolf's foot another nudge, "don't worry about Buffalo Horn. He might be a horse's ass, but he's decent enough to know when to stand aside. He doesn't care about her like you do. I don't believe Buffalo Horn is capable of seeing a woman as anything more than a bed warmer."

"I know. It's not him I'm worried about."

Badger nodded. They were both quiet a moment.

"When you do make the official proposal," Badger said, "you're going to have to make an impression."

Lone Wolf gave him a wicked smile. "I've already taken care of it."

25

F ire Girl returned from gathering wood for her cooking fire when
Badger approached. "Can I speak with you?"

His request left her unsure. They didn't often speak unless she was
with Mouse, but it sounded urgent. "All right."

"Let's go into your lodge."

She hesitated. There was no one in the lodge, and it was improper
for her to be alone with a man who wasn't her relative.

"It's fine, your father knows I'm with you." He smiled, but she
wasn't reassured.

He entered first and she followed, apprehensive and afraid of what
he might have to say. Badger sat but kept shifting positions, and he
wouldn't look directly at her. She was about to question him when he
began.

"There's something I must ask you, but it won't be easy."

"Badger—"

"Please, don't speak until I've finished talking. It'll be easier if I
say what I've come to say first. And please sit already." He motioned
impatiently at her spot.

Her mouth went dry, but she held her tongue and sat on her heels.

"You've said you don't want to marry anyone, and I want to know why. You see, there's someone who is interested in marrying you very much—"

"Is it Buffalo Horn? Did he send you to talk to me?"

"What?" Badger drew back and shook his head. "No, not him. Why? Do you *want* to marry my brother?"

"No!" She shook her head. "Nevermind."

Badger took a breath and continued, "So... as I said, please let me talk." He rubbed his forehead. "There's someone who wants to marry you and if there was any way that I... I mean, that *he* could change your mind, he would do whatever possible."

Her heart pounded loud in her ears. Did Badger really speak for someone else, or did he speak for himself? Did he mean that *he* wanted to marry her? Was that why he and Mouse talked so much about marriage? How did Mouse feel about all of this? To share a husband with Mouse would be strange, but then again, maybe it wouldn't be so bad. They'd be like sisters.

Badger had stopped talking.

"Are you done? I thought I wasn't supposed to talk."

"I want to know why you don't want to get married."

If he was nervous about proposing, if this was truly what Mouse wanted, she should make this easier on him. "It's true I don't want to get married, but there is one person I would agree to marry."

"Really, who?"

"You."

"Me?" He stared, thunderstruck.

"You don't have to pretend." She put her hand on his knee to reassure him. "I see how happy you and Mouse are and I know you're a good man, but I'll only share a bed with you in order to make children—"

Badger slapped her hand away. "Wait, wait, wait. You misunderstand me. I don't want to marry you."

"Oh. Then who does?" she asked, then remembered she didn't want to know.

"Lone Wolf."

"What?" Her heart leaped like a jackrabbit, threatening to escape through her throat. Lone Wolf couldn't want her. She had insulted him. Multiple times. He ignored and avoided her all winter. And even if it was true, she couldn't marry the man who killed her father.

She jumped to her feet. "Is this some kind of joke?"

"No, this is not how I meant..." Badger rubbed his face. "Lone Wolf, you bastard, you owe me for this," he muttered to himself.

She headed for the door.

Badger put his hand out to stop her. "Wait, listen," he said. "Lone Wolf cares about you. He's been waiting to marry you for a long time. He thinks you hate him."

She spun on her heel. "I do hate him!"

"Do you really? You two make a good match, and you're always looking at him, and I think you like him as much as he likes you—"

She couldn't take any more. She threw open the flap, terrified and angry, and some other emotion she couldn't place.

Near the edge of camp, Fire Girl slowed to a brisk walk. She already had a habit of running away whenever something went wrong, and she didn't want anyone to suspect something was amiss. In fact, she wanted no one to know what had happened. If only she could erase it all. Why had Badger said that Lone Wolf wanted her? It didn't make sense, but when she pictured his smile, that feeling returned and she couldn't shake it.

Lone Wolf called her name and her stomach flipped. She hurried back into a run. As she approached the river, he came up from behind. She had a long head start, but he was fast. Entering the stream, she drew her dress above her knees. The water forced her into a fast wade. She recalled the swirling river as a fire raged behind them.

He splashed in behind her. "Stop. I want to talk with you."

She clambered up the bank on the other side. The memory of that day when she had run from him as a child flashed in her mind, bringing hot tears with it.

He spoke again, but she wouldn't hear him, or didn't understand, like that day when he'd shouted in a language she did not then comprehend.

As she crawled up the bank, his hand grazed her foot, but she got to her feet and hurried into a run. Branches whipped at her face, blocking her view. She didn't know where she was going but stopping meant having to face him. He was right behind her. She could hear him breathing, could almost feel him. Then came the sudden breeze of his scent and her mind wheeled.

"Fire Girl, stop." He touched her arm, but she shook him off. He tried again and took hold, a strong insistent grip. She tried jerking him free, but her foot caught on a root, and she lurched forward, taking him with her.

She hit the ground hard, her momentum carrying them through two full rolls down a slope until she stopped, out of breath and stunned in a grove of cottonwood with fluffy wisps of white floating above.

He lay half on top of her. As soon as she regained her senses, she struggled to push him off. As he'd done years before, he grabbed her wrists. A surge of panic filled her.

"Get off of me, I hate you!"

"Please listen—"

"No, I don't want to listen to you. Let me go!" She tried to twist out of his grip. He raised his body and lay on her, pinning her arms at each side of her head.

"I'm not going to hurt you, but I won't let you go until you listen to what I have to say." His voice was stern, as though she was still a child. "Look at me," he pleaded, his voice softer.

She clenched her eyes shut and turned her face away. His weight was stifling, and she heaved for breath. One of his long lean legs rested between hers and his hair fell around her in a heavy black curtain. That same queasy feeling returned along with something warm.

"Let me go, you're hurting me, and I can't breathe."

He relaxed slightly, as though considering her point. "Will you listen if I let go?"

She nodded weakly.

He lifted his weight and released his grip, just barely, but it was enough. She yanked her arms free, then rolled out from under him. She was up before he could stop her.

"Wait, you said you would listen."

She ignored him and stumbled away.

He groaned in annoyance and grabbed her arm, pulling her toward him.

"Let go!"

He did, but it was too late. At the peak of her indignation and terror, she balled up a fist and struck him in the face.

He stepped back, wavering. His eyes were wide as he reached up and touched the blood on the corner of his mouth. "I'm sorry, I shouldn't have grabbed you." He stared at the ground between them, not moving.

She stood back, similarly aghast. She clutched her hand, biting her lip against the numbing pain in her knuckles and the throb that traveled up her arm.

"Go," he whispered.

But her feet wouldn't move.

He glanced at her. "You should put that hand in the stream."

He was right, her fingers were starting to swell. She walked away, cradling her arm. When she reached the river, she knelt by the shore and lowered her injured hand into the water. It was ice cold. A thin red trail ran from her hand into the water, swirling like smoke, like the wounds she wouldn't let him touch. The skin on her knuckles was broken, most likely from his teeth.

Brush and leaves rustled behind her, then Lone Wolf appeared in the reflection of the stream. Somehow, the sight of him was as soothing as the water. He sat beside her then dipped his hand into the stream, cupping it and bringing it to his face where she had punched him.

She pulled her hand out and gathered handfuls of cottonwood fluff that lay around them. She dipped the cotton in the water and watched it become saturated, turning from white to gray.

"Here, let me." She moved closer and pressed the soft fibers against his bleeding mouth.

He had the same expression on his face as when she had run into him years before and pointed a knife at him. She swallowed and focused on the dirt on his leggings.

He took her hand, pulling it away from his face. The cotton dropped to the ground. Cradling her hand, he fingering her palm, tracing the lines, and carefully stroking each of her swollen fingers. She didn't pull away.

"Fire Girl," he said.

Her heart skipped. The unasked question hung in the air between them, her answer caught in her throat. She couldn't say the word. He released her hand and his arms wrapped around her. She let herself lean into his embrace.

His scent surrounded her, a heady reminder of all her reasons for running. She found her voice. "I can't marry you."

The embrace tightened. His cheek brushed against hers. "You can. Don't be afraid. All you have to do is say yes."

Her fingers, crushed against his chest, uncurled and rested on bare skin. His heart raced through his chest and hers matched its pace. He raised his head and she turned hers to meet it. It was as though her muscles moved on their own, but her lips glanced on his face as they sought his mouth. Their lips hardly touched, but she tasted blood, and it sent a spark. She jerked her head away and jumped to her feet. This time, Lone Wolf didn't follow.

The next morning, Fire Girl and her family were still getting up when they heard the trilling, "Li li li li li," from women and the stampede of hooves as a large group of horses was brought to them.

None of them bothered to look out the opening. They all knew who was there.

Round Eyes couldn't resist. "There has to be at least thirty horses out there, maybe fifty!"

"Don't exaggerate, Round Eyes." Pretty Robe peeked out. "It's not fifty, or even thirty."

"How many?" Eagle Beak asked.

Pretty Robe raised a finger to count. "Twelve."

Fire Girl's palms began to sweat. Twelve was still preposterous. No one paid that amount for a wife, but Lone Wolf was making his point very clear.

Eagle Beak cleared his throat. "Fire Girl—"

"I can't." She shook her head.

"I know you think Lone Wolf—"

"I won't do it. I won't marry him."

"Stop interrupting. How can you refuse to marry such a fine warrior as Lone Wolf? He's young, he's handsome, he's brave, and he's sure to be chief one day. No one could ask for a better husband."

He was all of those things and more, but he was supposed to be her enemy, not her husband.

"I know the rift between you two runs deep. I hoped you would get past your resentment toward him before this day occurred, and I wouldn't have to make this choice for you."

She faced him, fists at her sides. "Father, do you hear yourself? You're really going to make me do this? Marry me to someone against my will?"

"You don't know what's right anymore. You belong with him."

"No! How can you..."

He rose to take the horses.

"Please. You can't do this." She grabbed his arm. "I beg you. Don't make me do this."

Eagle Beak stopped. He sighed deeply but remained inside. Round Eyes couldn't be kept indoors, so he ran out to play with the other boys, listen to gossip, then come back and report what he'd seen or heard.

She didn't care what people said about her, she couldn't be Lone Wolf's wife.

By noon the horses were still there, but Round Eyes reported that Lone Wolf had arrived with five more. All afternoon, he added more horses to the herd, waited for a response, then brought more. By late afternoon, more than thirty horses stood outside, filling the spaces between lodges and knocking over drying racks.

Round Eyes ran inside, "Grandfather, I spoke with Lone Wolf. He asked me if I thought you'd change your mind." He looked proud to have been given the honor of go-between. Older brothers were usually the messengers between a girl and her admirer.

"*His* mind? What about my mind?" she snapped.

"That's what I told him, that it was really you who was the problem. He asked to speak with you, Fire Girl."

"How is Lone Wolf?" Eagle Beak asked. "Is he angry?"

"No, well... maybe a little angry, or just sad. Are you going to talk to him, Sister?"

She shook her head.

Round Eyes pouted. "Why not? Why don't you want to marry Lone Wolf? All the other girls want to marry him. They think you must be crazy."

"You wouldn't understand," she said softly.

"This is all wrong," Eagle Beak said. "Lone Wolf and I made a deal. He brought more than the agreed upon amount, and now there are many more than that. I don't want to be the one to renege."

"You're doing this for horses? Is that all I mean to you? Is that the price for me? Twelve horses?"

"It's forty now," Round Eyes reminded her.

"That's not what I meant." Eagle Beak reached for her, but she pushed him away.

"I thought you understood me," she said.

He sighed again. "This is ridiculous. You don't know what you're doing. I cannot refuse these horses."

"You refused the horses from Looks To the Sky."

"That was different. You and Looks To the Sky don't care about each other."

"And I don't care for Lone Wolf either. Why does everyone think I do? I hate him, remember?" But she didn't sound the least bit convincing, not even to herself.

Pretty Robe pursed her lips. "I've seen the spark between you and Lone Wolf. It's true, when you were younger, there was fury in your eyes whenever you looked at him. But now, there is longing. How can you not see what everyone else sees?"

She couldn't believe her ears. "You too, mother? Why is everyone telling me what I feel? You don't know what I feel."

"Listen to me. Lone Wolf is a good man," Pretty Robe said.

"No, you're wrong. How can I marry the man who killed my father? And whose father and brother..." but she couldn't say it. The doubt and the memory of their encounter at the river made her heart race and her face flush. She pushed it away.

"Remember what I told you," Eagle Beak said. "You must look forward. He will become your family now."

"No. Please no." She sank to the floor.

Round Eyes ran out again, probably to relay this latest conversation to Lone Wolf and anyone else who wanted to know.

Then came shouting. It had been too long since Lone Wolf had brought the last offer. Round Eyes burst back into the lodge.

"Grandfather! Lone Wolf is herding in more than fifty more horses!"

She had to look, and it was true. His offer was now close to a hundred.

"It's his entire herd," Round Eyes said.

She scanned the horses. Every one of Lone Wolf's stallions, mares, colts and fillies stood outside. He sat mounted on his favorite war horse, his face hard and unreadable. The gray mustang couldn't be part of the deal. He would never give him away.

Horse and rider rode up and down along the herd, keeping them clustered together. Badger and Ferret were mounted too, helping to control the horses.

Then Lone Wolf did the unthinkable. He dismounted from Shadow, removed the bridle, and stepped back. He reached out a hand to stroke the horse's neck, then closed his eyes and walked away, leaving his horse with the rest of the proposed payment.

"He's offering Shadow for you," Round Eyes said in an awestruck whisper. They all stared. She didn't need to see their faces to know their disapproval.

She closed her eyes and recalled how it felt when Lone Wolf held her. The way he'd touched her. His warmth and scent while her lips searched for his. She felt faint.

"Don't let him do it," she said. "Not Shadow."

Eagle Beak glared at her, then pushed past her to go out to meet him.

She looked out to listen.

"You don't have to do this," Eagle Beak said as he strode toward Lone Wolf. "I'll take the first twelve you offered, and you can take back the rest as *my* payment to take that stubborn woman off my hands." He took a breath. "That includes Shadow. We won't take him from you."

"I don't do this for you, I do it for her." Lone Wolf must have sensed her watching, because he looked in her direction. "Take the horses, all of them. I don't care, but tonight, I'll come for her."

Tonight? He was coming tonight? It was already late in the day, but tonight she'd have to sleep in his lodge. With him. Her heart pounded while something stirred low in her belly.

"Don't be stupid, Lone Wolf. How are you going to hunt and provide for my daughter without a horse? Take Shadow, take Fire Girl, and be stubborn fools together. I wish you better luck at managing her than I had." Eagle Beak stormed back to the lodge. "And get these horses out of here before they do any more damage!"

Lone Wolf stood a moment before whistling to Shadow, who followed his master back to his lodge. She wasn't sure, but she thought she detected a smile on his face.

Part Three

26

Pretty Robe put the finishing touches on the vermilion stripe of
paint in the part of Fire Girl's hair. It hung in two long plaits,
wrapped with otter skin and the ends tied with blue ribbons.

She wore a buttery soft deerskin dress, dyed the palest shade of blue,
and decorated with elk's teeth and blue and yellow quills. The dress
hit her knees and elbows with long luxurious fringe that swayed with
every movement. Her bracelet of bells dangled from her wrist, and
bells had been added to her matching tall moccasins came up just past
her knees.

"When did you make this dress?" she asked.

"I started making it three years ago, when Lone Wolf came to
arrange the marriage."

Three years? He'd asked for her three years ago? Her legs could
barely hold her up.

"I used the skin from that buck you killed, remember? Along with
the other deer you killed that summer," Pretty Robe said.

She remembered how her pride in the kill had been clouded by
resentment toward Lone Wolf.

Pretty Robe put her hands on her shoulders. "You look like a true
bride, a woman of the People."

She forced a smile. The dress was beautiful, but she probably looked as miserable as she felt. She tightened her sweaty hands into fists to keep them from shaking.

Eagle Beak still seemed angry but gave her a hug. "Be happy, my daughter. Lone Wolf will make a good husband, and he couldn't ask for a better wife."

She couldn't make sense of it. Lone Wolf had given up his whole herd, for her? Had he really been waiting for her all this time? After everything that had happened? After the things she had done and said?

Her heart sank to her legs when footsteps shuffled outside, accompanied by the gentle tinkling of bells. Then came a pause and a scratch at the lodge flap. Eagle Beak took her hand and led her to the door.

He opened the lodge flap, and she stepped out. She turned to face Lone Wolf, but because of the glare of the setting sun she couldn't see his face. She tried not to squint.

He dressed up for the occasion, wearing his best leggings and shirt. His hair glistened in the sun. The cluster of eagle feathers tied to his scalp lock, representing his coups, stood straight and proud. A pipe bone necklace with tiny gray shells and blue beads circled his neck. Around his wrists were the copper and silver bracelets she often saw him wear. If he'd been anyone else, she'd have been impressed and flattered by his good looks. She swallowed and wiped her damp palms on her dress.

Lone Wolf and her parents exchanged words, but all she could hear was her pounding heart and a buzz in her ears. Before she knew it, he took her hand and led her from the lodge. She looked back at her family standing in the doorway. They smiled encouragingly. He was leading her away and she wanted to stop it, to go back, but her legs wouldn't obey. Was this really happening? Was she really married to the man she'd hated for the past four years?

They arrived before his lodge, one she had always avoided. The outer cover displayed a wolf against the night sky. Beside it, shield and lance rested on a stand, absorbing the last rays of the sun. His magnificent gray horse munched on sweet grass nearby.

He opened the flap and led her inside. The sudden darkness blinded her.

She stood frozen as a statue, her eyes cast down and body rigid. After a moment, she nervously looked around at her surroundings, at his belongings against the lining, his fire pit and altar, the various tools and decorations hanging from the poles.

A huge painted buffalo robe hung at the rear of the lodge, but she hadn't the right mind to examine it closely, too aware of the bed below it. Large, and comfortable looking, with several furry robes, the raised platform supported a well-stuffed mattress sewn from trade blankets and a couple pillows against the backrest. For all its luxury, it was a source of dread.

He sat at the fire, which burned low and steady. "Please sit."

She hesitated but obeyed, sitting across from him and wiping her hands on the skirt of her dress.

"Have you eaten? I have food if you're hungry."

She shook her head, but he reached for a basket of corn cakes and a container of honey and placed it nearby, taking one for himself, though he didn't eat.

"You don't have to be afraid of me. I won't force you to my bed."

She lifted her head and raised her eyes to him. Maybe that was true, but he tackled and pinned her down. He pressured her into marrying him, which amounted to the same thing.

He stood, moved closer, and sat beside her. She tensed, leaning ever so slightly away, but he placed his hand on the side of her face, hardly touching her.

"I won't force you," he repeated, "but that doesn't mean I don't desire you." Heat radiated from his touch.

How could it be that he desired her in that way? And yet the way his eyes grazed over her, she knew it to be true. His hand dropped to her shoulder and stroked one of her braids before brushing it back over her shoulder. He paused, then caressed her collarbone, exposed by the wide neck of her gown. His touch sent shivers. Her stomach made those flips again, and her body became warm. Every inch of skin became hyper aware of his touch. If she spoke, she might break the spell.

"We're husband and wife, Fire Girl, and when we lay together," he continued, "It's my hope that you're as eager to have me as I am to have you." His hand slid from her shoulder to her chest. "But if you're afraid, I will lead you through it." He grazed the curve of her breast, his thumb caressing the peak of her nipple through the supple suede of her gown. She sucked in her breath at the sudden and intense sensation. Encouraged by her response, he repeated the motion. "I want to make you feel good," he said.

It did feel good, and for the moment, she didn't resist. She couldn't help but submit to the pleasure of his touch. She breathed deep and inhaled his fragrance, a scent which had haunted her ever since the day he took her, faint, but pleasant. She had to concentrate to hold it in her mind, searching beneath the outer smells. His leather clothing, the metal tang from his nearby weapons, the musk of his sweat, the surprising sweetness of his breath, and there it was. A breeze that carried with it juniper and sage, wildflowers and honey. She closed her eyes, transfixed.

He leaned over her, gently pushing her back. She came out of her daze, with a yearning anticipation mingled with fear. Warmth spread from her center and her muscles tensed with ache. She could refuse, but then he might stop touching her.

He lay beside her, his breath shallow on her cheek. His hand moved to her leg, then slid up her gown. As if acting by their own will, her legs parted as his fingers raked fire along her skin.

She panted out breaths. "You said you wouldn't force me."

"Do you want me to stop? Tell me so, and I will." His voice was heavy with longing. His hand reached the top of her thigh, then his fingers brushed the cusp between her legs. It was like that hot coal existed at her center.

She gasped, grabbed his wrist, and pushed him away. "Stop, please stop." She sat up. She couldn't look at him, ashamed she'd let it go so far.

He sat up and took a few deep breaths. "Okay," more to himself than to her. "I'm sorry." He stood and went to the bed. She heard the rustle of fabric and dared to look. He removed his shirt, carefully folding it and laying it down, before he kicked off his moccasins and began to remove his leggings.

"What... what are you doing?"

He half turned toward her. "I'm going to bed." He continued to undress.

She watched, dumbfounded, but unable to look away as he became nude before her. She couldn't help but admire his body. He was lean, and every muscle defined beneath smooth brown skin. She even dared to gaze on his backside. He turned to face her, and she caught a glimpse of the rest of him before meeting his eyes as he spoke.

"There are plenty of extra robes and blankets over there, if that's where you prefer to sleep," the slightest edge of disappointment in his tone. He gestured to a sleeping area on one side of the lodge, then slipped into his bed. She had yet to get up and sat for a moment.

Seeing her hesitation, he lifted his blanket and shifted to make room, "You are welcome to join me." His voice was now flat and emotionless.

In answer, she rose and moved to the other sleeping area. She didn't undress and lay under the robes in her gown. She felt him stare before he turned his back to her to sleep.

Fire Girl awoke to the sound of dogs barking, a sign the village was awake and she had overslept. She snuggled further into the buffalo robe, wishing she could sleep in a little longer before starting her daily chores. Then she remembered.

She squeezed her eyes shut, hoping it had all been a dream, but her senses argued the truth. The lodge was too quiet. She couldn't hear her father snoring, Round Eyes' chatter, or her mother softly singing. The room smelled different, the robes and bedding. Everything smelled like Lone Wolf. And she was still wearing her dress. Her wedding dress. She was married and Lone Wolf was her husband. She opened her eyes.

He sat at the fire, already dressed and eating his morning meal. She sat up, unsure of what to do. Most wives would go straight to work, taking on the daily running of the home. Her mother would chide her to know that she had let her husband rise first and have to make his own meal.

His low voice interrupted her thoughts. "Come, sit with me and have something to eat."

She rose from the sleeping pallet, straightened the bedding, then smoothed her hair and the fabric of her skirt. She sat across from him, and he set food down for her, roasted meat and dried fruit, with a couple of the corn cakes. She nibbled at the fruit while he finished his own meal. He poured coffee from a metal pot into two trade mugs.

"You have coffee? I thought I smelled it." She couldn't help but be delighted. Eagle Beak and Pretty Robe rarely had coffee, as they were usually frugal when making deals with the Mexican traders, but she knew other families had it often and had been envious.

He smiled. "I always have coffee." He handed her a mug.

She took a sip and held in a sigh. It was sweetened with just the right amount of sugar. Then she set the cup down. She'd dropped her guard again. He wasn't going to win her over with coffee.

"Thank you." She eyed him cautiously. He'd finished and seemed to be waiting for her, but she stalled, unsure what was supposed to happen next.

The huge painted buffalo hide hanging above the bed caught her eye. Battle scenes covered the pale canvas of the hide. Some looked as though they had been painted long ago, the colors faded. Others seemed fresher and the style of the artwork differed.

He looked over his shoulder. "That's my father's robe. My grandmother made it for him."

She stifled a shudder at the mention of his father, hearing the note of sadness in his voice.

He walked over to it. "She painted most of the designs when he was a young warrior, noting each of his war honors. My mother was adding to it." He stroked the fresher designs with tenderness. "It's the only thing left of his belongings. I refused to burn it with the rest of it."

She swallowed hard, remembering the wails of grief she had heard on her first night in camp, one voice rising above the others, howling into the night, grieving the loss of an entire family suddenly gone.

"I'm sorry." The words sounded weak compared to his loss.

"No, I shouldn't have brought it up. Now isn't the time to speak of such things." He turned. "If you're done, then come outside with me. I have something to show you." He gathered supplies and she followed him out.

Shadow stood outside. Lone Wolf threw a blanket and buffalo robe across the horse's back, then strapped a surcingle to the horse and tied packs to it. Another blanket and two bridles lay on the ground. Shadow kept turning his head, nipping at Lone Wolf, probably not too pleased about being used as a packhorse.

So, he was going to take her away from camp? She'd be alone with him. Her knees grew weak. They'd been alone before, after the fire, but that had been different. Now she was his wife. "Are we going far?"

"No, not far, less than half a day's ride, but I want to be prepared."

She nodded faintly.

He stepped up to face her. "Remember, you don't have to fear me. I will never harm you. Do you believe me? Do you trust me?"

She was amazed that she did. "Yes."

He gave her a hesitant smile. His hand moved up, as though he was about to touch her, but he dropped it again and returned to his horse. She stood awkwardly, her mood discolored with regret.

Squirrel and Laughing Bird sat outside next door, scraping hides from a recent hunt. Squirrel glanced in her direction, then nudged Laughing Bird and murmured words to make her look up.

She smiled out of politeness but inwardly seethed at their curious watching.

Just beyond, Mouse left her lodge. She grinned and waved. Could the others tell that she and Lone Wolf had failed their wedding night?

He stood by Shadow, stroking the horse's muzzle and speaking affectionately while he fed him the leftover fruit from breakfast. Eagle Beak often spoiled and sweet-talked his own favorite horse, but she was still unused to seeing Lone Wolf behave in any other manner than taciturn.

"What is it you wanted to show me?"

He didn't answer right away, slipping a bridle over Shadow. "Your wedding gift."

She blinked in surprise. He had a gift for her? She wanted to ask more, but it was clear he meant it to be a surprise.

He slung his quiver with its bow across his back, then picked up the extra blanket, bridle, and Shadow's reins. She followed him as he led the way to the horse pasture.

When they reached the edge of the pasture, he made a quick, melodic whistle. Soon a brilliant looking filly cantered over. She ran her hand over the strawberry roan coat. "She's beautiful," she said in an awestruck whisper.

"She's yours."

Her hand froze, stunned. "But you gave all your horses to my father."

"I kept this one for you."

She stared at the filly. She never had a horse of her own. She rode her father's horses, when necessary, but there had never been any she was particularly attached to. Not one as splendid as this one.

"I bred Shadow with one of my best mares," he explained. "When she was born, I knew she had to be yours. She's three years old so I'm still training her, but she's as smart as Shadow is. She'll serve you as well as he does me, perhaps even more so"

She swallowed thickly. "Thank you, thank you so much."

Three years ago, she'd actively avoided and hated him. She had wished him dead. Meanwhile, he'd been thinking about marrying her and giving her this spectacular horse.

"Do you want to ride her?"

"Yes," she answered eagerly.

He laid one of the blankets on the horse's back, then attached the bridle. He helped her mount, as her dress was cut rather slim. When she sat, the skirt exposed much of her legs. She pulled it down self-consciously, noticing how his gaze lingered over her bare thighs.

He nimbly mounted his own horse. "I'll have to teach you the commands. She knows some verbal ones, but you will mostly control her using your legs and heels."

"My father taught me those kinds of commands."

"I know he did, but I have a few of my own that are unique, and I think work better, especially under duress."

As they rode, he explained what he'd taught the filly, and what she would continue to work on with her. Fire Girl only half-listened,

287

focusing on the ride and the changing landscape of rolling hills, oak and timber. Then he called to her, bringing her out of her reverie.

"Have you thought of a name?"

"A name?"

"For your horse."

She thought for a moment, admiring the smokey red coat of her new horse. "I'll call her Smoke."

He smiled. "I think it suits her."

She grinned back.

"If I'd known all I needed to do was give you a horse to get you to smile at me, I would have done that years ago."

She blushed and looked down.

They rode for the rest of the morning, mostly in silence. He asked her about hunting and told her a few of his own experiences.

"Mouse told me you once had a close call with a mountain lion."

"Did she? I don't know why she likes that story so much. I think she enjoys hearing about my failures."

"In that case, she and Badger make a good team," she quipped.

He burst into a laugh. "That's very true."

She liked his laugh, its clear sound. She liked his mouth in a grin, and the way his eyes crinkled in the corners. He had dimples in his cheeks. Why hadn't she noticed them before?

"So, what happened? With the mountain lion, I mean. I assume you didn't have to start a fire to escape it."

He laughed. "No. I was hunting deer and killed a fawn. I barely looked up before the mountain lion pounced. Luckily, I'd already drawn my knife to butcher the fawn, or else that would have been the end. I was able to stab her before she could take out my throat, but she ran off."

"Do you think she lived?" The bear and her cubs likely didn't, which made her sad to know it.

"Maybe. She probably bled to death or was hindered enough to be unable to hunt. I regret not killing her right then. I'd like a mountain lion to hang in... our lodge."

Her cheeks became warm again, but she pretended not to notice the hesitation. "I'm sure you'll get another chance to kill a mountain lion someday."

"Perhaps. They're one of the hardest animals to hunt. It's more likely they'll hunt you. By the time you realize one is there, it's already too late."

Their horses had moved closer together and Lone Wolf was almost knee to knee with her. He stared at her again, smiling in that avid way that made her stomach flip. She'd always assumed his eyes were black, but they were a warm, deep brown with flecks of amber and caramel, far more complex than she'd ever imagined.

The landscape changed. Bright green grass covered the ground, dense with trees. A narrow valley lay ahead, lush with vegetation.

"We should walk the horses from here," he said.

He navigated their way through woods and shrubs, and down into the valley. Although spring had pretty much ended on the prairie, here the foliage was as fresh as the start of the season, with wildflowers painting the tall grass in splashes of colors. They came to a grove of redbud trees, their blossoms still in bloom. Branches spread over them like a pink canopy. As she ducked under a low hanging branch, she broke off a piece and nibbled at the sweet-sour buds.

"Why do we never camp here? It's so beautiful."

"That's precisely why. If we camped here, the trees would be cut down, the fruit and plants over-picked, and ground covered in our refuse. Instead, we preserve it as a place to visit, to celebrate life, heal the soul, or to impress your new bride," he grinned shyly.

That time she didn't look away.

"We're almost to the stream. The water's path curves back on itself and there is a small beach. We'll stop there, water the horses, and have a meal."

"I can hear the water." Heat and thirst had worn her out and she looked forward to the respite. The sound of water grew louder, like a roar.

She followed him and sure enough, the land opened to a small beach. It wasn't just a stream, more like a pool. The roar came from a waterfall cascading from the rocky outcrop above, sending up droplets of mist that floated toward them, cooling her instantly.

"You didn't say there would be a waterfall."

"Call it another wedding surprise." He smiled that dimpled smile, which made her stomach flutter. "This whole area is full of underground springs, and there are other falls and caves. This one is the largest."

They arrived at the beach. It was rocky, but he led them to a spot with enough soft sand and soil. He unbridled the horses and spread their blankets on the ground while the horses walked to the edge of the water to drink.

"Go ahead and rest. Eat if you're hungry. Despite the beauty of this place, there isn't much game, but I'm going to try and find us some meat. It's safe here, so you can relax." As an afterthought, he removed the knife sheath from his waist and tossed it onto the blanket. "Just in case." He took his bow and arrows with him, then disappeared into the trees.

She sat on the blanket and picked up the knife. The weapon had always terrified her, not only because its violent danger, but its owner. Twice he had threatened her with it, and she'd never seen him without it. Its personal significance could only be surpassed by the private medicine bundle he and all the other men wore inside their breechcloths, his pipe, and his horse. But now he'd left it with her with hardly a thought.

She examined the sheath, with its fringed leather case, quilled design, and brass studs for reinforcement. The case was worn in places that bore evidence of its frequent wearing. The bone handle was also worn down from his hands. She gripped it to match the marks of his placement. Holding it felt odd, like a stranger peeking into someone's medicine cabinet. She felt that way about everything to do with Lone Wolf.

She drew the knife. The blade was long and wide and had been sharpened so many times its edge was wicked thin. She ran her thumb along the edge. It wouldn't take much pressure to cut through skin. How many scalps had he taken? How many throats slit? How many bodies stabbed? It was better not to know. She put the knife back in its case and set it down. She was done being afraid.

After opening his pack to eat a few pecans, she lay back and looked at the sky. Birds flew overhead, too small to distinguish against the cloudless deep blue. The sun had already risen past its midpoint, but it was only early in the afternoon.

A pair of purple martins flitted overhead, circling and dancing before swooping over the water to catch insects, then landed in the trees above her, filling the air with their song. After they darted away, she could only hear the sound of water while she watched dragonflies dip and skim the surface before taking flight.

She lay there for what seemed a long time, almost dozing, but couldn't be sure how much time had passed. If Lone Wolf came back with some meat, she should have a fire ready. After gathering sticks and dry grass, with extra care, she used the flint from his pack to build one.

Hot and sweaty again, she drank from the waterskin which was nearly empty. The refreshment of the pool called to her, so she took off her moccasins and waded to her knees in the stream, taking the skin to fill. While she stepped through the water, small fish swam about and tickled her legs. It had been so long since she felt so peaceful and at ease.

How quickly her impressions of Lone Wolf had changed. Why had she insisted on believing she knew him better than the people who'd known him his whole life?

After all the events of the past year and beyond, she'd been so blind to see how he cared about her. No, not blind. In denial. Deep down she knew the truth but had been afraid of it. Afraid to admit she cared in return.

27

Lone Wolf treaded through the grass back to the beach, clutching two dead rabbits by their ears. It had taken longer than he intended. He couldn't focus on tracking game when his new bride waited for him. Fire Girl waited for him. Not running away, not turning away, not pushing him away. He had to stop to catch his breath.

He had never been able to think about her without an ache in his heart. It had become as familiar to him as the grief for his family. He couldn't separate the feeling any more than he could his heart and mind. But the ache was fading. Perhaps the grief would too. Now that she had become relaxed and even friendly with him, he didn't know how to behave around her.

Lone Wolf arrived at the lagoon but had to stop again. She waded in the water with her back to him. Her dress hiked almost to her hips, revealing those long legs he had only glimpsed. The afternoon sun shone in her hair. A breeze sent wisps to blow around her face, giving her a golden aura. The sight stole his breath and his heart raced in his chest so fast it would outrun Shadow if it had legs.

He watched her, not wanting to break the spell. She must have sensed his presence, because she turned his way. She smiled but lowered her dress. As she came closer, he imagined gathering her in his arms, holding her, and telling her the words he had yet to say. He imagined other things too but had to tread carefully.

She made a fire, a good sign of her regained confidence and that she considered him a companion. Maybe she didn't yet love him like a husband, but at least she no longer despised him.

He held up the game. "I have our meal."

"Good, I was getting hungry." She reached out to take the rabbits, but he only handed her one.

"We'll each clean one."

Another smile lit up her face. He would never tire of seeing it. A glow brightened her cheeks and light flashed in her green eyes before she lowered her lashes. Beautiful. If he said the word out loud, how would she react?

After the rabbits were cleaned, he staked them next to the fire. While the meat roasted, they ate the food from his pack. Their horses wandered to their temporary camp. Shadow leaned over his shoulder as he fed him the leftover corn cakes.

"How long have you had Shadow?" she asked.

Her interest in his horse warmed his chest. "I was twelve when he was born. My father had this black mustang, a fierce and dangerous horse. I was determined to tame him, but that horse taught me many lessons in humility. That's when I became interested in breeding. I thought, if I raised one of his offspring from the start, I might gain a horse with the same ferocity, but one I could control."

"He seems like a puppy to me," she teased as the horse nudged him for more food.

He laughed. "Right now, he does, yes, but not in battle. He's as much a weapon as my lance or bow. That's why I rarely leave him in the pasture. He's too aggressive with the other horses, but he's calm if I'm close by. He doesn't like anyone but me, though he'll tolerate Badger." He paused. "He doesn't seem to mind you though. When most people are this close, he often stamps and snaps his teeth." He laughed as Shadow nibbled his ear.

His smile faded as her expression changed, so intense and focused. She was watching him. Something about her look made him think about things he'd been trying not to think about, like the soft skin of her thigh, or the swell of her breast, and how it had felt under his hand. The way she had responded to his touch, letting him know the desire he had for her wasn't one sided. Such thoughts were like blowing on smoldering embers, starting a fire he knew wasn't ready to burn.

"I'm glad you kept him," she whispered.

"Your father said you insisted I take him back. I love Shadow dearly, and his loss would have hurt me, but it would have been worth it."

Her cheeks flushed pink like a rose. "Should we head back before it gets too dark?" she asked.

He considered how to respond, as the answer might raise her guard. Focusing on the fire, he spoke. "I thought maybe we could camp here for the night. Perhaps even take a swim." He dared to check her reaction.

"Are you sure it's safe?" Her voice wavered with doubt.

"Nowhere is truly safe, but this place is as protected as we could hope for."

"When you say, take a swim—"

"Yes, I mean taking off our clothes and getting in the water." He kept his voice even, feigning confidence though his heart was pounding.

She stared at her lap and played with the fringe of her gown. "I— I couldn't do that."

"Are you sure? The water is cool and pleasant. We didn't come all this way not to enjoy it."

Her lips drew tight, contemplating, then she shook her head.

He glanced at the pool. "I understand, but I hope you'll change your mind. As for me, I'm going in."

As he removed his clothes, he could feel her eyes on him. Last night, he'd accepted he wouldn't be bedding her, and had taken her stare as no more than curiosity. Now he sensed interest that could lead to something more.

His body responded to her gaze, though he tried to ignore it. He needed to get into the cold stream. Brisk water tightened his muscles as he strode in. Then he dived below, staying under until he calmed, leaving a dull ache in his groin.

He surfaced, facing the shore. She'd been watching but looked away and took a long drink from the water skin.

"Are you sure you won't join me?"

She shook her head.

The pool was tempting her, he was sure of it. Beads of sweat glistened on her temples, and they both had been coated with dust from the ride. She said she trusted him, but he hadn't done much to earn that trust.

"What if I turned around while you undressed and didn't look until you were in the water?" Her long pause left him hopeful.

"All right, turn around."

He spun his back to hide his eagerness.

While she undressed, he resisted the urge to sneak a glance. She made a soft splash as she entered. He waited until he was sure she was deep enough to cover her before turning, grateful the water also covered him. "Do you feel better?"

She arched her head back, dipping her long wavy hair in the water. "Mmmm," she murmured, "it is nice."

He had to look away. "Do you want to see what's behind the waterfall?"

"There's something back there?"

"It's one of the reasons I brought you here."

He swam to the far edge, where the water was less turbulent, and she followed. They swam along the deep edge of the pool, ducking below the outcrop of rocks covered with moss and intertwined with roots from the trees and brush above.

He took her hand to guide her, sliding his fingers between hers. "The pool becomes shallow, and the rocks are either slippery or jagged, so be careful." He glanced at the sun, hoping he had timed their entry well, then ducked through the curtain of water and watched her do the same.

Behind the fall, the stone wall slanted inward, forming a small cave. The rock was worn smooth where the water had eroded it, but deeper in the cave, the surface was rough and uneven. Stones glimmered with quartz. As the light from the setting sun shone through the water, it hit the crystal, making the cave shimmer and sparkle.

She gasped, her head arched high as she looked at the cave. "It's like being under the stars. Have you been here often?"

Since the water was so loud, he had to move close to hear. "Not in many years, but my mother used to take my brother and me here. It's one of my favorite memories of her."

As much as he hated to mention his mother, he wanted her to know how special this place was to him.

"Thank you, for bringing me here," she said.

The soft tone of her voice drew him closer. Her wet skin glistened, like droplets of crystals on her body. Her damp hair curled in ringlets around her face. A bead of water ran along the spiral of an amber curl beside her cheek. It hung for a moment from the tip, stretched until the tension could hold it no longer, then landed on her collarbone. His eyes followed it along the angle of bone until it reached the hollow below her neck, then down her chest until it joined the water.

He released his breath, not realizing he'd been holding it. Close to succumbing to his urge to pull her against him, he focused on the sound of crashing water. Holding her in this place of his childhood memories would fulfill this moment. But he didn't want her to recoil from his touch. He'd waited this long for her, he could summon more patience.

———◆———

Time stilled and the rest of the world seemed to vanish behind the roar of the waterfall. Nothing and no one existed but herself, the glittering cave, and Lone Wolf. His silent but intense stare made that warm feeling return.

It was clear he intended to bed her, but he promised to respect her refusal. Picturing him naked in the sun, she wasn't sure if she would refuse. She never thought a man's body could be beautiful, but his was. He had dived under the water, as sleek and as graceful as an otter.

He squeezed her hand. "I can see you're uncomfortable, and I promised I wouldn't make you do anything..."

"Yes?"

"Will you let me look at you?"

She nodded but couldn't meet his eye. They would lie together. It was inevitable. And it would happen tonight, soon. Right now, even. But she feared it. When he had touched her before, she felt vulnerable and exposed.

He led her into shallow water. She tried not to pull back when the level dropped, and her breasts met the crisp evening air. Goosebumps prickled her skin, and she shivered. They stopped when the water was at her navel, then he turned, standing less than an arm's reach away.

His eyes drifted over her body. Her nipples hardened from the cool air, sending tingles through her nerves. He reached for her face, lifting her chin. "You're so beautiful."

She trembled. The backs of his fingers stroked her jawline until he reached behind her neck, fingering the curls of baby hairs that grew at her nape. "Will you let me touch you again?"

"Yes." It came out hardly more than a whisper. Her heart raced as she anticipated his fingers on her skin, recalling the acute pleasure it had given her.

He put both hands at her waist, then slid them up, cupping her breasts, before grazing his thumbs across her tender peaks. She sighed, almost whimpering, and gripped his forearms to steady herself.

He stepped closer, pulling her closer as his arms wrapped around her. Afraid to move, she lost herself in the sensation of his bare skin, cool in the darkening dusk and growing starlight. She rested her head on his shoulder and he leaned his face down to hers.

Instinctively, she kissed him, soft and hesitant. Kissing wasn't common among the People, so Lone Wolf pulled back a moment before responding. He caught on quickly, parting his mouth while she drew his lip between hers. He tasted like fresh water and moonlight.

She leaned her whole body against his, feeling his hard arousal against her belly. Although she should have expected it, it caught her by surprise.

He sucked in his breath with a hiss, taking hold her hips with both hands. His fingers dug into the flesh of her buttocks, then lifted her up, wrapping her legs around his waist as he waded to shore.

Her arms shook, clutching his shoulders. It was happening. He intended to take her right on the shore. She ducked when they passed through the waterfall and when her breasts grazed his face, his mouth closed over her nipple. She gasped, shocked at the pleasure, more intense than his fingers had produced.

The last of the sun slipped below the horizon casting them in dusk's faint light. When they reached the blanket, he lowered her down. She let him take in the full sight of her, fighting the instinct to cover herself.

"So beautiful," he said again. He moved down her body with his hands and mouth.

She kept still, flushing not just from the heat of his touch, but the sounds he elicited. Once it happened, that was it. They'd be truly married. There'd be no more running away or escape, she'd be his and he'd be hers and she'd be a part of this world forever. Part of her felt an urge to stop it, but the rest of her was too mesmerized, too enticed by the pleasure he created.

As he continued to tease her breasts, her whole body clenched. The ache in her center deepened. His hand ran along her belly, then down. She tensed but her hips tilted upwards, as though offering an invitation. He made a sound in the back of his throat as his fingers found their way to her heat. He parted her and began to caress, circling her throbbing nub at the apex.

She squeezed her eyes shut, amazed she was letting this happen. Her knees trembled as he continued to stroke, spreading her slickness around swollen flesh. He pressed up until one of his long fingers slipped inside, a feeling that was less painful than it was strangely fulfilling. Her body responded by contracting against him and he moaned.

He nuzzled the smooth flesh of her belly and breathed deep. "I want to taste you," his voice low and husky.

She shut her eyes and gripped the blanket on either side. She rode on a wave of ecstasy, rising and building toward a great peak. Racing upward. It was happening too fast. It felt too much. The wave broke up, her pleasure scattered by doubt.

"Wait," she called out softly. Too softly. He didn't hear or didn't want to. "Wait." She said it louder and scooted away.

He raised his head, breathing hard, then rolled onto his back.

"Sorry." She touched his shoulder.

He clasped her hand. "No, don't be sorry. I forgot myself and I rushed you." He moved to lie level beside her.

She shifted closer. "I want to, but what you were doing felt so strong. I couldn't take it."

He smiled. "That's how it's supposed to feel. It takes you higher and higher, and just when you think you can't climb any higher, you fly. Let me show you. I promise, you'll be glad I did." He reached between her legs and the hunger in his eyes returned.

She tilted her head to see his erection. "Some of the women say there can be pain." She meant it as a question.

His expression grew serious. "I can't promise it won't hurt, but it won't last." He resumed his skillful stroking, his voice dropping lower. "If you let me finish what I was doing, it may hurt less when I take you."

His touch resumed that earlier enticement, making up her mind. She brushed her lips against his. "I want you to feel good, too. Is it okay if I touch you?"

"My sweet wife, you never need to ask permission for that. I get pleasure from touching you." His fingers made a motion to make her whimper, while his erection pushed against her hip, proving his point. "But yes, I would greatly enjoy it."

His eager reaction made her grin. She roamed her hands over his chest, marveling at his sculpted body. She reached to caress his back, grazing along the dip of his spine, then over the arch of his buttocks. His thighs were hard, solid muscle. The power in them reminded her of his galloping mustang. His strength had once frightened her, but she now knew he would never hurt her.

She reached his belly and felt sparse hair growing below his navel. His breath became shallow, and the muscles of his abdomen twitched as she caressed him.

"I must warn you, if you continue, I'm not sure I could stop again if you asked me to." His words came breathless in her ear.

"I know." Eager and willing, he'd said. It had seemed unlikely, but now, here she was.

Reaching the base of his rigid cock, she encircled it with her fingers, sliding her hand upwards along its length and over the head, drawing forth his moan into her shoulder. He swelled in her hand. Such a contradiction of texture, solid and hard, and yet covered with skin so delicate and tender.

His comment about deriving pleasure from touching her became clear. She loved his reaction, his moans and sighs. Fierce One, the warrior who had once terrified her, was now weak and lost by her touch.

She continued to stroke him, amazed when a drop of moisture slipped under her thumb as it rubbed over the tip. He clutched her, muttering into her ear. He repeated the words, louder, more urgently.

"I need you now, Fire Girl."

She answered by rolling onto her back, wanting what he'd offered. He wasted no time in moving over her. Leaning on one elbow, he used his other hand to guide himself. The pressure both shocked and pleased her, but as he continued, the pain deepened. She cried out into his shoulder, but he didn't stop, and she didn't want him to.

His movements were slow at first, and she held still, adjusting to the feel of him. Hurt soon warmed to hot pleasure, and her ache finally filled, she met his movements with her own. She rocked her hips so she could reach that spot of delight and bringing her arms around to clutch his hips, she met him with equal force, their noises filling the night air.

She could climb no higher and whispered his name, letting him know she was ready to fly. He embraced her and together they expelled the built-up tension with furtive thrusts. A sky full of stars twinkled above, but it felt as though their bursts of light had spread through her body. She soared as the waves washed over her, rhythmic pleasure dying down to a steady, small contraction of muscles as the pulses of afterglow faded.

Still warm and tingly, she tried to catch her breath. Lone Wolf breathed deep against her neck, then sighed and traced her ear with his lips. A final spark shot from where they were still joined, making her shiver.

He loosened his hold and rested his weight on his forearms. "Are you all right?"

She smoothed his hair away from his face. It was like seeing him for the first time. His handsome features, the sharp jawline with full lips, his high cheekbones with smooth brown skin, and thick brows with shining eyes beneath.

"I'm wonderful."

As soon as she said it, he kissed her. The sensation was as exciting as their lovemaking. His lips were warm and soft, and his tongue exploring her mouth thrilled her, reminding her of what their bodies had just done. He broke the kiss and rolled her on top of him. "You are wonderful," he murmured.

His words of affection, still so unexpected, kept her elevated with the stars. She hid her smile and settled into him, resting her head on his shoulder while he pulled a robe over them.

It took her a long time to fall asleep. Sensations lingered throughout her body, her mind recalling every pleasurable touch. The sound of Lone Wolf's even breathing and the steady rise and fall of his chest under her cheek soothed her enough to relax and close her eyes.

28

F ire Girl sat up and looked for the horses. They stood several paces away, munching on a patch of young grass. Meadowlarks and thrushes serenaded the morning. The sun had risen past the treeline along the edge of the riverbank, sending rays of light through their branches and highlighting the waterfall's mist. The pool of water sparkled white and gold.

She sighed in contentment. Everything still felt like a dream. "I don't want to leave this place."

He stretched languidly beside her, clearly in no hurry. His fingers ran up her back and toyed with her hair, wrapping around her russet curls. "It has been wonderful." He sat up. "In fact, I cannot think of a time when I've been any happier than I am right now." He clasped both hands around hers. "Together, we start a new life. Will you do that with me? Will you let me make you happy?"

Her chest swelled. "Yes." She kissed him.

"Good," he smiled. "Now, perhaps we should bathe again."

She gratefully agreed. They had joined again during the night and her insides felt sore and raw, and her thighs were sticky from his seed.

Once in the water, he pulled her close. "Let me wash you." He stood behind her, rubbing her breasts with his wet hands, then circling her nipples until she grew weak in the knees. His hands moved down, and she squirmed against him, feeling him hard against her backside while he worked magic with his fingers. When they were finished, they dressed, packed their belongings, and began the ride home.

Since they had a late start, the sun was almost overhead, but they were still less than halfway back to camp. She spotted a grove of wild plums. The last time she had food was the evening before, and her belly rumbled with hunger.

"Let's stop and eat," he said.

She placed a hand over her abdomen. "You heard that?"

"Heard what?" He smiled and slid down from Shadow.

While she gathered an armful of plums, he stomped the tall grass so he could place a blanket. His sweeping motions, hopping and shifting from one foot to the other, were like a dance.

"Is our camp now blessed?" she asked, grinning at his exuberance.

"Not until you sit with me." He pulled her down beside him.

They ate, sitting cross legged in silent enjoyment. As he bit into one of the ripe plums, he made a sound of pleasure so similar to his restrained noises during their lovemaking.

An urge overcame her. So far, he'd been the one to initiate their coupling, but that didn't mean she couldn't as well. He belonged to her as much as she belonged to him, and she wanted to do what they had done earlier but had no idea how to ask for such a thing.

She watched him, marveling at the signs of his contentment and remembering the moments over the past day. His quiet humor, his kindness, his patience, all the signs she'd outwardly ignored despite being drawn toward him.

Before she could lose her courage, she moved into his lap and put her arms around him. She buried her face in his neck, smelling him, but also embarrassed at her forwardness.

He dropped the plum. "Just when I think I couldn't be any happier, you surprise me," he whispered. "I wanted this for so long." His arms tightened around her, hands running along her back, hips, and thighs. "For you to feel the same way about me, as I do you."

"I do, Lone Wolf. I want you." She nipped at his ear.

He pressed against her, hard and urgent. The sensation gave her a rush of warmth. She shifted to sit facing him, raising her dress. He reached down to loosen his breechcloth, then pushed into her. It hurt again, but it felt good too.

The look in his eyes, one she hadn't recognized before as desire, love, and longing, turned her insides into liquid. She gripped his shoulders as she climaxed, thrusting down hard. She wanted nothing more than to have him fully inside her as she rode wave after wave of flight. She slowed her movements, nuzzling his neck as she calmed.

He rose to his knees, lifting her with him before laying her on her back. Crouching between her legs and clutching her waist, he drove into her. She gasped, taken aback by his zealousness, then roused by it as he worked himself to an urgent finish.

He made a series of deep, slow thrusts, shuddering and letting his breath out slowly as he came. They lay for a few moments, relaxed and reeling. His head rested beside hers, their chests pressed together, hearts beating in unison, and his body still joined with hers.

Her eyes open to the bright blue above them. She had opened herself completely, past all her defenses. She could no longer pretend or hide her feelings. Instead of being vulnerable, she was as free as the endless sky.

"Will it always be like this?" she asked.

He lifted his head, wearing a smile of self-satisfaction. "I hope so. There's nothing I want more than to keep you happy, but that depends on us, I suppose." He kissed her softly. "This is still very new to both of us. Who can say what we'll be like when we're both old and gray."

She giggled at the thought, still amazed at the idea they were married. She was reminded of a comment an older woman had once made about wishing she had a younger man in her bed, missing his endless energy. "It's new to me, but not to you."

"You are new to me, and I have waited for you for a long time."

She looked to the side, afraid to meet his eyes. "My father said you asked for me three years ago. You haven't been with anyone in all that time?"

He turned her face back to his, but the amused grin staring back at her made her frown. He laughed, then rolled off her onto his side. "I'm sorry, I don't mean to laugh. It's surprising to see you jealous."

"I'm not jealous." She raised herself to her elbows. "I was just... curious."

He plucked at the fringe of her sleeve. "I know and it's fine. There's much about me you don't know, but you're welcome to ask me anything."

She lay back, focused on the sky. He was right, she knew very little about him, but what should she ask? She wanted to know about his childhood. It was hard to picture Lone Wolf as a boy, but such questions would lead to talking about his family, and that would be too painful. Maybe one day they could talk about such things.

"Tell me about the others, the first one," she blurted. Her face flushed. It had seemed a safe question in her head, but it made her sound nosey. It was a question Antelope would have asked.

He gave her a mischievous smile. "The first didn't last long enough to be worth telling."

She covered her mouth to keep from laughing.

He made a look of mock offense. "I'm serious. I was young, eager, and stupid."

"How old were you?"

His brow lowered as he reflected. Pretty Robe kept track of the seasons and passing years on a piece of deerskin, much like Lone Wolf's buffalo robe over his bed, but she knew the People didn't celebrate birthdays like she had when she was a child, although most people knew the season of their birth. Eagle Beak had once told her he was born in the Winter of Great Snows, which Pretty Robe had explained was forty-six years ago.

"It was seven years ago, so I was fourteen. It was the year of my vision quest and my first buffalo hunt. My brother said it was time I became fully a man." His mouth smiled though his eyes didn't show it. "He took me to another camp where he knew some women."

"So... the woman..."

"Was older and experienced? Yes."

She hid another smile.

"Are you mocking my humiliation?" He tickled her waist, still bare. She squirmed and laughed. "And now you're laughing?" The tickling stopped as his hand slid further up and caressed her breast. "I want you to know, there has never been anyone who mattered. Most of them were women my brother had lain with himself." His fingers were hard and rough, but his touch was gentle, lightly circling her nipple until her breath quickened. His expression changed, as though mesmerized by the view of her body in the sunlight. "Then, when I was older, I decided to find a woman I would be happy to spend my life with."

His kiss was lingering and slow, while his hands pushed her dress up higher, exposing her breasts, then he leaned down to cover her nipple with his mouth. She reached under his shirt to trace his ribs. His skin rose with goosebumps under her fingers. He gripped her hip and shifted her body closer to his. She raised her leg to wrap around him, ready to join with him once more.

Then he snapped his head up and rolled to his feet in a movement too quick to follow, bow in hand and arrow drawn.

<hr>

Lone Wolf tensed as he watched the approaching cloud of dust. He'd been alerted by men's voices carrying across the prairie, and beneath that sound, the creak of wagon wheels and the jingle of harnesses.

He could see the men now, six of them, dark skinned and murmuring in Spanish. Mexican traders. They were headed toward him, as they had likely seen Shadow and Smoke grazing while he and Fire Girl lay in the grass.

He moved to stand in front of her while she pulled down her dress, cringing at the possibility the men had seen her.

"Stupid fool," he muttered to himself. It wasn't her fault he'd been so beguiled, but he should have taken better care than to lose awareness of his surroundings.

"*Lobo*, is that you?" One man called out in the People's language. "I see that horse of yours."

He released some of his tension, lowering the point of his arrow. He was on friendly terms with José Ortiz, but it would be careless to trust him. Alone with a woman, and lightly armed; José and his men would likely have guns.

"It's me," he shouted to the men. "Fire Girl, get my knife," he added under his breath.

"Who are they?" She leaned over his shoulder as she pulled his knife free, tugging closed his breechcloth as she did so.

He gave a quick nod of thanks. If he died, he'd die with dignity. Although it wouldn't be terrible to die knowing he spent his last day making love to his wife, his cock still coated with his seed and her wetness.... *Focus, you fool!*

"They're Comancheros. Stay behind me and be ready to ride home if I tell you." He glanced at her. "In fact, get onto Shadow."

"But, what if—"

"Shadow is faster and stronger, and he'll know the way. Don't look back if I tell you to flee."

"But—"

"Do it." He hated speaking so curtly to her, but she had to understand their vulnerable situation. If José or any of the men wanted to, they could easily kill him. He might be able to take out two, three, or even four of them before he died, but then she'd be alone with the others. She'd put up a fight, that was a given, but they'd overpower her.

311

Once they were done, if they didn't kill her, they'd take her with them to trade or ransom to some other man.

José and the others reached them. All but José were mounted on horses, rifles held loosely in their hands, surrounding their mule-led cart. José sat in the cart's only seat, the reins draped across his lap.

As Lone Wolf feared, their eyes strayed to Fire Girl sitting on Shadow. His jaw tightened as the men's eyes roamed over her, openly staring. At least she had laid the blanket on the horse's back first, using the excess to cover her bare legs. She might have the knife hidden in it too. Shadow shifted his hooves, snorting and shaking his head while he flicked his ears. Smoke followed his lead, hiding behind her sire.

"Why do you point a bow at me, *Lobo*? Is that how you welcome a friend?" José asked.

Lone Wolf forced a smile, hoping to lighten the mood. "A man can never be too careful, *Ho-say*. What brings you out here?" He had switched to Spanish as a show of courtesy.

"We hoped to find your camp." José pointed at Shadow. "I see that horse, and I say to César, 'Isn't that Lone Wolf's horse?' Lucky for me, I was right." He grinned. "I also see you have taken a wife." He exchanged knowing looks with his companions.

"Yes, I was ready to start a family." He tilted his head. "How are your wife and children?"

José's grin faded. "They are well." One man shifted his rifle, then spat on the ground.

Lone Wolf took on a relaxed posture. "What reason do you have to seek me?"

"Did I say lucky for me? I meant, lucky for you, *amigo*." José hopped from his cart and pulled back the canvas cover. "I tell César,

'That Lone Wolf is always asking for guns.' Well, today I have some."
He reached into a crate and drew out two gleaming rifles. Breechload-
ers. "I have ten saved just for you."

Fire Girl made a gasp. Lone Wolf kept his face blank but couldn't
help lifting his chest in eagerness. "You are giving them as gifts?"

José laughed so hard he coughed. "You are such the jokester, like
your *coyote*. I am a greedy man, and I will not take less than four horses
for each."

"Then you will leave with your ten rifles. I have no horses to trade."

"No horses? But you are the richest man." José put one of the rifles
back and held the other out to Lone Wolf. "Come, take a look. These
are new models. I have cartridges and caps for them too."

He resisted taking a step. "I told you. I have nothing to trade." He
said it in the People's tongue, so Fire Girl would know the direction
the conversation had headed.

José nodded, but his eyes flicked to his wife. "Is she why you have
nothing?" His laugh was mocking as he took another leering look at
her. He also switched to Comanche. "Only a fool would give up so
much for a single woman, but I see why she was worth it. She is special
to you, no? She wears that bracelet you haggled me for three years ago."

He winced. The bracelet jingled as Fire Girl lifted her arm to inspect
it. Their eyes met, hers showing confusion and maybe hurt.

"I'll tell you what, *amigo*, because I like you, I will make you a deal."
José gestured with the rifle at Shadow. "You have a fine horse, and a
fine woman. I will take either one, and you can have three of these rifles
and all the ammunition you can carry."

Fire Girl shifted, rustling the blanket. He hoped she wouldn't brandish the knife. Heart hammering in his chest, he gritted his teeth. "No deal."

José waved his hand. "Don't be like that, *Lobo*. I come all this way for you. I give you good deals. Now you dismiss me like a fly on your meat?"

He scanned the men. Their rifles were held low, but all pointed toward him, fingers loosely at the trigger.

"Come back next year, *Ho-say*. I will have many horses to trade."

"Next year I may not have these rifles."

"That will be my loss, but I will have the horses ready for you, if you wish to trade then. As for now, Red Hawk expects me in camp, so we'll be on our way." He hoped José would catch the reminder that if he killed him, his grandfather and every worthy warrior would retaliate. Viciously.

The silence stretched for many heartbeats.

Finally, José nodded. "As you say, *Lobo*. I will be back next year."

He grabbed Smoke's reins then swung up onto Shadow behind Fire Girl. He put his arm tight around her waist. "It was good to see you, *Ho-say*." He gave Shadow a squeeze with his knees and the horse took off at a quick trot with Smoke following.

At each hoofbeat, he expected a bullet to hit his back.

29

Fire Girl kept silent until they were far enough away from the Comancheros. She leaned against Lone Wolf, letting him control Shadow's reins while she tried to keep her hands from shaking. His heart beat against her back, almost as fast as hers.

When it slowed, she tried to relax, but her muscles ached with tension. She took a deep breath. His grip on her waist loosened, but she clasped his arm to keep it around her. Months ago, they'd ridden together on this horse, and she'd done as much as possible to avoid touching him, now she didn't want to be without his hold.

"It's all right. We're safe," he whispered in her ear.

She shook her head. "I was so afraid."

He commanded Shadow to stop and turned her face to him. "I know, but you did fine. You are a brave woman, and you didn't show fear." His voice was low and calm.

Strange how the man she once feared she now looked to for safety and reassurance. "I don't understand. I thought they were friends." She handed back his knife.

"No, not friends," he said as he sheathed the blade. "They seek opportunity. They will trade with us but also trade with our enemies. There is no loyalty beyond the best price."

She glanced down, fingering the bracelet. "Why didn't you tell me?"

He clasped his hand over her wrist, just as he had done after she dropped it in the snow and he put it back on. "You wouldn't have accepted it if you knew it was from me, would you?"

Her eyes welled. He was right, but she'd been deceived. She wore the bracelet thinking it was a symbol of Eagle Beak's love, but all this time it had been Lone Wolf's.

"It was still a lie."

He let go of her wrist. When his body pulled away, her back felt cold. "Don't blame Eagle Beak. I had to convince him to give it to you on my behalf."

"How did you...?" Then she knew. The other items Eagle Beak had brought home that evening. Purchased by Lone Wolf, with *his* horses.

He reached for her again, touching her shoulder. "Don't be angry. Many times, I wanted to tell you, not about the bracelet, but how I felt."

All his moments of kindness and hers of scorn came back to her. "You're right. I didn't make things easy." She smiled and touched his cheek. "Thank you." His expression of relief doubled her guilt.

He urged Shadow forward, and they rode for a while until she remembered there was another matter she needed to set right. "I'm sorry you had to give all your horses to my father."

"I'm not."

"You could have traded them for those guns. It's my fault you gave up your herd. Maybe we can ask Eagle Beak."

"No, I will not ask your father to return a single horse." His tone implied no argument, but she couldn't let it go.

316

"If the Comancheros come to camp, my father could buy guns with the horses you gave him." She waited for his response.

His face was drawn and troubled. "*Ho-say* won't be coming to our camp. He'll either take them to another band or sell them to the Apache."

Her heart grew heavy. Lone Wolf and the others wanted revenge for the deaths of Two Horns and Big Tooth, and guns would have made all the difference in a raid against mounted soldiers. The weight of his sacrifice felt like a rock in the pit of her stomach. At least he still had Shadow.

"Are we going to ride together the rest of the way?"

He smiled at last. "Do you not want to? I like you sitting in front of me." His arm pressed her body against his.

She liked it too, the hard planes of his torso against her back, his strong legs aligned with hers, feeling each twitch of muscle as he guided his horse toward home.

"Would you like to race on Shadow again?"

"Yes!" The first time she'd been too terrified to appreciate a war horse's speed, but Shadow was supposed to be faster than any of them and now she'd get to be in front.

He grinned, seeming more excited than her. "Hold tight with your legs. You should grip his mane too, but I won't let you fall." He dropped the lead to her horse and put both arms around her while holding Shadow's reins.

"Wait, what about Smoke?"

"She'll follow and keep up. I've done this with her before."

"Wait," she said again as she gathered her loose hair into a twist and quickly tied it. "I don't want it to fly in your face." Then she grabbed

Shadow's mane. At a command she neither felt nor heard, Shadow sped forward.

The horse's speed increased with every thundering heartbeat. Her hands dug deeper into Shadow's gray coat and mane, exhilaration filling her chest and tightening her throat. The ground beneath them became a blur of green, brown, and gold, while Shadow's hooves drummed the earth in a rhythm beyond song.

Her eyes teared from the wind in her face, but she smiled wide. Lone Wolf whooped, then Shadow galloped even faster. Her heart leaped. Compelled to release her own joy, she let out her own cheer of delight.

He dropped the reins. Shadow slowed until at last he eased into a walk. Smoke appeared alongside them, keeping up as Lone Wolf had promised.

She twisted around. "That was breathtaking."

"I'm glad you enjoyed the ride." He smoothed her wayward hair.

"I did. Shadow was great too." She smirked.

His eyes widened before he broke into a laugh. "Wife, if you make any more jokes like that, we'll never get home."

It was late afternoon when they arrived in camp. Lone Wolf sat tall as he rode Shadow past clusters of lodges, his lovely wife in front of him. Neighbors gave knowing looks and smiles and he made a great effort to keep his own proud smile from creeping onto his face.

Everything had changed. Two days ago, Fire Girl wanted nothing to do with him, now she was his wife. She had smiled at him for the first time, let him make love to her, an experience that would forever be burned into his memory, and she wasn't just letting him, she enjoyed it. She spoke his name, not with malice or bitterness, but in the throes of ecstasy, and it had heightened his pleasure beyond comprehension. He couldn't have hoped for a better outcome. Perhaps soon his seed would take root. He would like to have a child, a family once more.

When they arrived at their lodge, he helped her dismount and removed the packs and surcingle from Shadow. "I'm going to water the horses. Then I need to see my grandfather."

"I'll do it."

He touched her cheek. "Are you sure? You should rest."

"I'm fine." She was so confident, so stubborn.

He glanced at Shadow. "I know he's been good with you, but if he shows any signs of aggression, let him be. I don't want you to get hurt."

"We'll be fine. Go see your grandfather."

He brushed his hand against hers. "I'll be back this evening."

"I'll be waiting." Her loving smile was hard to resist. He wanted nothing more than to take her inside and onto the bed, but he gathered his weapons, and headed to Red Hawk's lodge.

His grandfather sat against his backrest, eyes closed as though asleep but Lone Wolf knew better. He sat and waited for his grandfather to address him.

"I'm surprised you've peeled yourself away from your bride long enough to visit me." Red Hawk peered at him with one eye.

"Something happened on our way back."

Red Hawk opened both eyes and sat up. "Tell me."

After he finished explaining what had occurred with José and his men, Red Hawk sat in silent thought. "*Ho-say* will not hold a grudge for long. He has been trading with us for years. You are not the first to offend him," Red Hawk said at last. "He'll be back."

"When he returns, I'll buy many guns, but I need horses."

"Maybe you shouldn't have given so many for that girl." Red Hawk winked. "I know you weren't thinking with your mind." He grabbed himself to make his point. "Now that you've satisfied those needs, are you ready to start thinking like a warrior?"

Lone Wolf smirked. "Tell me again how many horses you gave for Winged Woman?"

Red Hawk laughed. "Not nearly as many as you did."

"It doesn't matter. I will raid and get more horses. Then, when we have the guns we need, I'll make war on the Tonkawa and strike the Texian villages."

Red Hawk waved his hand in the four directions. "Lone Wolf, you've stolen all the horses to be had from the Arkansas River in the north to the Guadalupe, and just as far east and west."

He shrugged. "Then I'll go to Mexico."

"Mexico will take many months. Will you have time to do that and raid the Tonkawa before winter?"

"Then I'll get my revenge next summer. It might work out better that way. I don't want to go unprepared."

Red Hawk stared. "I admire your determination."

"Will you come with me when we make war on the Tonkawa?"

"No."

Lone Wolf sat straighter. "They killed your son."

"So did your wife."

He flinched, an old ache squeezing his heart.

Red Hawk sighed and patted his knee. "I am old. The raid for your mother was my last. I intend to spend my remaining years in comfort. It is you who is a warchief now. Men look up to you. There are few with enough experience to lead. You're brave but you keep a cool head." His eyes twinkled "Except when it comes to your woman."

<hr />

Fire Girl led the horses to the stream on the other side of camp for water and then to the pasture. She removed the bridles and rubbed the horses down with handfuls of sweetgrass.

Shadow remained calm and docile throughout. "I guess you're just like Lone Wolf," she said. "Tough and scary when you have to be, but sweet otherwise."

"You're back."

She spun to find Mouse dragging a load of buffalo chips. "We just returned."

Mouse grinned. "How do you like being married?"

She stroked Shadow's muzzle. "I don't know much about it yet."

"You two were gone for a while." Mouse's grin widened.

"Do my parents know?"

"Everybody knows."

She blushed. "I suppose I should see them and tell them all is well."

"They know, but you should see them anyway." Mouse pointed at Smoke. "Is that the horse Lone Wolf gave you."

She beamed as she stroked Smoke's neck. "Isn't she beautiful?"

"She is. You are very fortunate."

Mouse was right. Her heart felt like bursting. "I don't understand how it all happened. I didn't know I would feel this way about him, but it seems this is how I've always felt."

"Took you long enough." Mouse smirked.

"You knew, didn't you? All this time? Why didn't you say anything?" She took the other edge of the hide with the load of chips and helped Mouse drag it to camp.

Mouse shrugged. "It wasn't my place. I already got in trouble for speaking out of turn, remember. Besides, I was never sure, just had my suspicions. I was convinced after seeing his reaction to your insult."

She swallowed. She had yet to make a real apology for that. "Did you know he gave me the bracelet?"

"Yes."

She frowned. "I wish someone had told me."

"I guess we all thought you knew. I mean, didn't you? Didn't you know in your heart?"

"I guess so." She blinked back tears." I should have realized it after he saved me from the fire. I just didn't want to."

"That's what made it so hard. I saw him right after that happened. You should have seen his face, how he was so worried for you." Mouse sucked her teeth. "It reminded me of when his mother died."

She wiped her face. "You still should have told me."

Mouse grabbed her arm. "That's not fair. Don't blame me for your stubbornness. Would it have made a difference if I told you? Would you have been kinder to him?"

"I... I don't know."

"Besides, it's done. You're married and you're happy now, right?"

"I am."

After leaving Mouse, she went to see her family. Round Eyes ran to hug her and she picked him up.

"You're too big to carry around."

"I know, but I miss you. I wish you'd come live with us again."

She laughed. "I thought you wanted me to marry Lone Wolf."

"I did. But I didn't think it'd mean I wouldn't see you as much."

"You'll still see me every day. Lone Wolf and I just left camp for a while." She put him down and entered the lodge. Eagle Beak sat against the backrest, watching her with eyes of amusement.

She joined his side, sitting until she could work up the words. "I'm sorry I was so difficult."

"I understand all this wasn't easy for you, but I hope you see why I did it. Are you happy?"

It was the second time someone asked if she was happy, third if one counted Lone Wolf's question at the stream, but she supposed it made sense that everyone wanted to be sure. "Yes and thank you."

"It's good to hear, my daughter." He handed her bundles of her belongings, along with her bow and quiver. "You're his family now, but you'll always be our daughter and I hope you will bring your husband to sit by our fire."

Pretty Robe entered and Fire Girl rose to meet her. "Mother, I'm sorry about everything." She hugged her and the words rushed out. "You were right about Lone Wolf. He's everything you said a husband should be."

Pretty Robe pulled away and clasped her cheeks. "Of course, he is."

"How did you know?"

"I knew his mother, remember? I know the boy she raised. Also, it was the way he talked about you."

Her heart quickened. "What did he say?"

"When he came to ask for you," Eagle Beak said. "I asked him why he chose you, but if you really want to know why, you should ask him."

She nodded. There was so much they hadn't said.

Once back in Lone Wolf's lodge, she stood to take in her new surroundings with a fresh eye. It was her lodge now. The duties and responsibilities she had to her new husband sank like a weight. Her chores used to be no more than bothersome necessities, but she was the wife of the band's greatest warrior and everything she did would reflect upon him.

Ashamed that she'd been so idle, she searched for something to clean. Typical to his nature, the lodge was uncluttered and tidy. His eagle fan suspended from a pole above the bed, and his pipe bag and tobacco pouch hung from a pole on his backrest. The rest of his tools and belongings were packed in parfleches stacked neatly against the lodge lining.

It seemed presumptuous to go through his things, to look for items that needed repair or replacing, but she was his wife, wasn't she? She tentatively opened a few cases and poked at his folded clothing.

Winged Woman, Squirrel, and Laughing Bird had taken over the duties he couldn't do for himself once his mother had died, so she wasn't surprised to find everything clean and in good condition. She sat and sighed, her attention drawn to his weapons.

They made up most of his possessions. Aside from the everyday bow and quiver he had taken with him, there were two other bows, one short and one a bit longer. Both appeared sturdy and well made. He had an extra quiver with several bundles of arrows. His long war lance and shield stood on a frame outside, but resting against the lining was another stouter lance, and beside it, his stone war club and coup stick.

Her gaze landed on his firearms. The stock of an old flintlock musket and pistol protruded from hide cases. At closer inspection, she spotted another. Nearly hidden behind the other weapons, a wooden stock peeked out from pale yellow leather. Heart pounding, she recognized it immediately. Her breath came hard and fast.

Ignoring the other weapons, she crept to the familiar firearm. Somewhat ashamed for snooping, she hesitated, but no. That carbine was hers.

She slid it out and unwrapped the leather case, revealing the smooth wooden stock and shiny barrel. Her throat tightened. With trembling fingers, she fingered the initials of her father's name etched into the stock. E. M. C. Emmet Mitchell O'Connell.

Through tears, she spotted her old powder horn and the tin of percussion caps sitting where the gun had been hidden. Her heart beat like a wild colt as she lifted the carbine, surprised at how heavy it seemed to her. Had she really carried it around?

She examined the barrel, stock, and firing mechanism, pulling back the lever that lifted the compartment where powder and lead were loaded. Lone Wolf kept the mechanism well-cleaned and oiled. He wanted guns, but all this time he had hers. How many men had he killed with it?

Her arms shook as she raised the stock to her shoulder and sighted down the barrel. Would her aim still be true? Sudden bursts of memory flashed like a shot, seeing Lone Wolf's brother and father die at the end of the barrel.

She lowered the weapon. After returning it to its wrapping, she placed it back in its hiding place. She sat, her mind filled with doubt. The time with Lone Wolf at the waterfall felt like a dream, another reality, apart from her memories and fears. What would it be like to live with him every day? Like he said, she barely knew him. In the back of her mind, there was a nagging notion of something yet unresolved.

The sun was setting but Lone Wolf hadn't returned. She made a fire outside and heated water flavored with wild bergamot for drinking. Yampa roots and flat bread cooked near the fire on a stone. She burned sage and waved the fragrant smoke to the four corners of the lodge. After a quick bath, she wore a fresh dress and moccasins but her hair, though clean, hung loose and free.

She sat and brushed it out to braid, when footsteps shifted outside. A doe carcass dropped beside a pair of blue-beaded moccasins. Unsure how to greet him, she didn't move.

Lone Wolf ducked his head in and gave her a quizzical look. She stood and searched for something to say. After a brief pause, he stepped inside and pulled her into his arms. Funny how all her fears drifted away when he held her.

"You were so quiet I wasn't sure if you were inside," he said. "I was afraid you might have left me."

The words added to her guilt. "I'm not going anywhere," she murmured into his chest.

"Good," he said with his face in her hair. He pulled back and examined the lodge. "My wife is not only beautiful but knows how to care for her husband."

Pleased by his compliment, she kissed him. "My husband knows how to provide for his hungry wife."

"You don't need anyone to provide for you, though I will happily do so. Next time we will hunt together."

She grinned. "I'd like that."

She poured him a bowl of mint water and put on her heavy buffalo hide apron, then went out to dress the doe. He joined her, and together they skinned and butchered the animal. There was little light left, but they worked by firelight. She tacked down the hide for cleaning, while the meat roasted.

While they ate, she sat with him until the moon rose. There was little conversation, but her earlier fears were eased by their quiet comfort and harmonious efforts. The fire covered and the extra meat laid out for drying, he took her hand and led her inside.

Seeing the bed again, her nervousness returned. The previous night she'd been in a daze, but they would sleep together from now on. The bed had seemed large before, but it was hardly big enough for two. They would have to lie close together. What if she snored or kicked him in her sleep? What if *he* snored?

He touched her shoulder. "Is everything alright?"

She turned around. He was already undressed. She should kick herself. What woman wouldn't want to lie beside a man as splendid looking as him? "I'm fine."

"We don't have to do anything if you don't want to." He stood there as uncertain and hesitant as herself. It made her want to chase out those shadows she let creep onto his face.

Pressing her body against his, she kissed him, deepening the kiss as she traced his spine with her fingertips. He gathered her dress to her hips then slipped his hands underneath, working the dress upward and over her head. They tumbled onto the bed.

When they were at rest, she lay on her side, caressing the muscular planes of his torso. His eyes were closed, but he wasn't breathing deeply enough to be asleep. She stared until he must have sensed her gaze. His eyes opened and looked at her as if ready to listen.

"Why me?" The words came out with more emotion than she intended.

He didn't respond right away, as if needing time to find his answer. "Because there's no one else like you, and not because of where you come from." He raised himself to lean on his elbow. "No matter where you lived, you'd be extraordinary." He paused and she waited.

"Ever since our paths crossed, I was drawn to you. I didn't like it at first, but it wasn't long before I couldn't see my existence without you. You and I are linked. Like darkness and light, joy and pain, or even hate and love." He touched her face. "One is meaningless without the other." He sighed. "I know you hated me, and a part of me hated you too, before I was aware of my love, but now I believe those feelings are more alike than they are different."

She swallowed. "I don't know any more if I hated you. I was afraid of you, but there were moments I felt as you described, that our lives were connected in ways I couldn't understand. Each time you looked at me, I thought I hated you more. You made me feel exposed. Everyone else was looking *at* me while you were staring *inside*, like I had a hole in my chest, and you could see right into it."

He brought her hand to his lips. "You see, we are of the same mind, a match made by the Creator himself. I may not have known what was to become of it when I took you that day, but I believe it was supposed to happen."

She flinched when he mentioned her capture. He put his arms around her, "I've been saving something for you. I'm afraid to give it to you, because I don't know how you'll feel, but I want you to have it again."

He crouched beside his weapons and picked up the long bundle wrapped in leather. He removed the casing, then held the firearm out to her. "I admit, I meant to keep it for myself, but after a time I decided I would one day return it. I've never used it."

Swallowing the lump in her throat, she lifted the carbine from him, then held it unsteadily. The painful memories of that day edged into her mind. "Fox Laugh said he and your brother were best friends."

His body tensed and a shadow returned to his eyes. "They were."

"Did he love her?"

The knot in his neck moved as he swallowed. "He did." Lone Wolf moved to sit beside her. "There's something you need to understand. Do you remember firing it?"

She laid the gun across her lap and stared at it. "Sometimes it comes like a flash of light, like when the sun reflects off the water, but I blink, and it's gone. It happens when I use my bow... or when I hold the carbine."

He picked up the gun and handed it to her. "Take it. I need you to remember."

His voice was so serious, she was afraid to refuse. She took the carbine and slowly lifted it to her shoulder.

"Do you see his face? Picture it."

She sighted down the barrel, then closed her eyes. A man swinging a club rode toward her. She had never remembered his face, but now it was clear. He looked like Lone Wolf, the same stern face, but with red around his eyes. They were hard, unflinching, even as her gun pointed at his head. His mouth was moving, as though he was murmuring something.

Hands shaking, she lowered the gun.

"What did you see?"

Her eyes burned. "There was no fear. No hesitation." She wiped her face. "But why should he have been afraid? He was a warrior, and I was just a little girl."

"A girl who killed a man, a man who was the greatest warrior in camp."

"I still don't understand."

He clenched his eyes shut. "My brother was ready to die, but he wanted a warrior's death. Who better to take him to the afterworld than one who had defeated the best?"

She gasped. "He was singing his death song."

Lone Wolf hung his head. "I'm glad to know he did."

After a long moment, he took her hand and broke the silence with a question she never expected. "What did they call you? Your white family, what was your name?"

She told him and watched him feel the sounds in his mouth before he tried them out loud. Then he said it, her white name.

"Bridget."

It had been difficult to say that name, to recall it from the recesses of her mind. Even stranger was it to hear it repeated, especially from one who wasn't white.

"What does it mean?"

She thought of a way to explain so he would understand. "It's a name of strength, and honor. My ancestors worshiped a spirit with that name. She was the spirit of fire, song, and wisdom, and the protector of a land my grandfather came from."

"Where?" he insisted.

"Far to the east and over the big water. It's surrounded by water, smaller than this land, and very green."

"Like your eyes," he whispered.

He seemed interested in hearing more, then frowned. "It's a good name. Fire Girl doesn't suit you as well, not anymore. You should have a name like this, but in the words of the People. I will ask my grandfather to give you a true name, one with great power and medicine."

30

Lone Wolf's arms slipped around her waist from behind, cradling her and waking her from her dreams.

"You have no idea how much my heart sings to wake up with you next to me in this bed," he whispered.

She snuggled against him. "You'd better get used to it. No more having this bed all to yourself."

"I don't want to get used to it." He leaned over her. The weight of his eyes intensified his tone. "I don't want to ever forget how grateful I am to have you as my wife."

The words filled her, expanding her heart to the edge of bursting. She never expected anyone, especially a man like Lone Wolf, to speak such devotion. Her father's insults echoed in her mind. *Unworthy. Unlovable.* And after the things she had done...

Unsure of how to respond, she kissed him and rolled out of bed.

"Where are you going?"

"The sun's almost up. I'm going to bathe, get water, make us something to eat," she shrugged to hide her awkwardness.

"Not so fast," he pulled her into the bed. "All of that can wait. The only thing I am hungry for is you."

That way of loving him came easy and required no words. She wrapped her legs around him and let him take her back to a place where she didn't have to think, only feel.

The sun now past the horizon, she walked to the stream, leaving her husband snoozing in the bed.

Mouse met her on the path. "I remember being newly married," she said with a wistful sigh. "Staying in bed late. Walking around in a constant state of flushed joy."

"Are you saying you don't feel that way about Badger anymore?"

Mouse tugged at a stalk of grass until it snapped. "Oh, we have our moments. Just wait until you have your first fight."

She scoffed. "I think Lone Wolf and I have done our share of fighting already."

Mouse laughed. "That's true. Now you two can just enjoy each other for the rest of your days."

They reached the riverbank, undressed, and waded into the stream. As they bathed, the cool water made her think of the waterfall. Mouse was right. She should stop overthinking and just enjoy her new marriage.

"We should cook our evening meals together today," Mouse said.

"All right."

Mouse splashed her. "This worked out so well. Our husbands are best friends. We're best friends. It's perfect."

She nodded. Perfect.

"I better head back," Mouse said. "Badger was already grumbling for his meal. Are you coming?"

"Go on ahead. I'm going to collect some sweet flag I spotted down-stream."

Mouse left, but Fire Girl floated in the stream a bit longer. After dressing, she walked along the shore until the water pooled in a shallow, muddy pond. Sweet flag was rare but useful for colds. She broke off several stalks, breathing in their pleasant aroma before adding them to her medicine bag.

She looked up at the sound of approaching male voices. She had gone too close to the are where the men often bathed. Not wanting to be caught invading their privacy, she scrambled up the uneven ground along the tall grasses, hoping to get far enough ahead before they spotted her, or she offended them by being in their way.

"Hey, Fire Girl!" Badger shouted. "Is Lone Wolf's not enough for you? Did you want to try out the rest of the stock?" His deep laughter followed.

She glanced over her shoulder. The men were nude, carrying their breechcloths in their hands. Stifling an embarrassed laugh, she shouted back, "I just checked out the selection, and I think I picked the best stallion of the bunch." The men made sounds of mock insult.

"Your loss," Badger said. "Where is that lazy husband of yours anyway?"

"She's probably worn him out." That was Buffalo Horn's voice. She took faster strides.

"Wait, I want to talk to you." He came running up from behind. At least he'd put on his breechcloth.

"What is it?" Her voice sounded more annoyed than she meant to. As the others passed, she stepped back, being sure to keep her distance in case Badger was watching. Being alone with Buffalo Horn was probably not something Lone Wolf would want to hear.

"Why so venomous?" he said. "I wanted to wish you the best in your marriage."

"Thank you." She managed to make her voice kinder.

A smug look spread across his face. "So, you and Lone Wolf. I mean, I knew he was sweet on you. We all did, but I thought he didn't have a chance since you hated him. I guess I was wrong."

She shifted her weight from one foot to the other. "Buffalo Horn—"

He waved her off. "No, it's fine. I'm happy for you both. Lone Wolf is a good man and I know he loves you. I've never been in love, so I don't know what that's like..." He rubbed the back of his neck. "He deserves to be happy, so do you. I wish you both a great deal of happiness."

It *sounded* sincere. "Thank you." She started to walk away.

"Watch yourself, though."

She stopped short. "What do you mean? You just said he was a good man."

"Oh, he is. He's honorable and a great warrior. There are few men I'd trust with my life, and Lone Wolf is certainly one of them. What I meant is that he tends to overthink things. He gets his heart and his head mixed up. And you can be difficult to get along with. I don't want either of you to get hurt."

Her face went tight. "Thanks for your concern, Buffalo Horn, but I can assure you we'll both be fine." She spun on her heel and continued home. Although her words sounded confident, his comments weaseled under her skin.

"Fire Girl," he called and hurried toward her again. "You're always walking away from me," he muttered. "I have one question."

She took a breath and turned around. "What?" she said, exasperated.

He faced her directly. "Did you ask me to dance so you could make him jealous?"

Her mouth dropped open, struck silent with guilt.

He nodded and pursed his lips, looking off to the side. "I thought as much. See, that's what I mean. I know I have a reputation with women, but I never mess with anyone's feelings."

She stared at her feet. "Buffalo Horn, I'm sorry."

"No, you don't understand. I don't mean *my* feelings. It's not for *my* sake you should be sorry. That's what I'm trying to say about Lone Wolf. He's kind of a fool when it comes to women. He's not as thick-skinned as I am." He thrust a finger at her. "*Don't* break him." He turned and strode away.

She choked on the lump in her throat as she hurried back to the lodge.

Lone Wolf sat before an altar formed by a buffalo skull, saying his morning prayers. He smiled when she entered. She said nothing, to not interrupt him, but started to prepare a meal.

"Are you all right?" he asked.

"Yes," she said without looking up. She tried to smile, but it was useless.

"I can tell you're not. It's fine if you don't want to tell me, though I wish you would, but can we at least agree to always be honest with each other?"

She stared at him, thinking hard. Up until that morning, she'd never considered how much her behavior may have hurt Lone Wolf, apart from the times she actually meant to. Was it really possible that *she* could break *him*? "I... I was thinking about how much I regret not being friends with you before." It wasn't the whole truth, but it wasn't a lie either.

He moved to her side. "I don't blame you for that. I didn't like it, but I understood it." He waited, as if he sensed the words she left unsaid. "Remember, the past is behind us."

Did he hope she would say something else? Why was this so hard?

"I'm lucky to have you." They kissed softly and she went back to preparing their meal while Lone Wolf completed his prayers.

She had just served him when the doorway darkened as several men entered the lodge, talking and laughing loudly. Badger entered first with Buffalo Horn behind him. She looked away, but not before he winked at her. Ferret and Turtle followed, greeting her politely.

"So, Lone Wolf, you're finally up," Badger's grin spread from ear to ear as he sat against one of the backrests and stretched his legs in front of him.

Buffalo Horn made a show of sniffing the room. "It smells like sex in here."

Heat rose to her cheeks. She made a mental note to burn sage as soon as she was awake from then on.

Lone Wolf stood by the bed strapping on his belt "Shut up, Buffalo Horn." He sounded only slightly irritated, as though he was used to this sort of teasing.

Deciding she'd better play host and dutiful wife, at least for her husband's sake, she set out more food for the visitors. The men

337

sprawled about the lodge, stretching out or leaning across bedding and items while they ate and talked. Lone Wolf sat with them and took out his pipe and a pouch of tobacco.

Their conversations picked up from the middle, continuing from before she became a part of Lone Wolf's life. More talk of horses, jokes she didn't understand, and stories about people and events she knew nothing about.

Feeling like an invisible intruder to their gathering, she got up to go find Mouse.

Mouse was working outside her lodge. She chattered and moved about, stirring a pot of food, laying out strips of meat, or grinding fruit until she settled with Fire Girl to make pemmican from yesterday's dried meat. They made several pounds before their husbands strolled over.

Badger entered his lodge with Mouse behind him, and Lone Wolf sat next to her. "I'm sorry we didn't have our meal, just the two of us." He reached for her hand.

She squeezed his fingers. "It's fine."

He eyed her. "And I'm sorry about Buffalo Horn."

Those shaming words brought fresh heat, but she hid it by giving Lone Wolf a playful smile. "He's just jealous I turned him down then went ahead and married you."

"He asked you to marry him?"

She froze. "Sort of, I didn't let him ask before I told him no. I thought you knew."

"No, I mean... I thought he might." He chewed on his cheek. "That makes things awkward. I should say something to him."

"You don't have to. He and I already talked about it," she said too hurriedly.

"Is that why you were upset?" He toyed with the bells on her bracelet.

"He said he was fine, but..." She caused enough hurt already, which meant there was no need to create conflict with his friend. "He was more worried about you. I guess when it comes down to it, his loyalty to you surpasses anything he might have wanted with me."

Lone Wolf leaned back and crossed his arms. "I'm not so sure about that. I should be glad I don't have to worry about him trying anything with you, but I don't want him planting doubt."

She touched his leg. "I'm sorry I let him get to me. Like you said, it's all in the past."

After a few moments, Badger came out of the lodge with his hunting gear and Mouse giggling behind him. They appeared flushed and out of breath.

"I'm going to join the others for a while." Lone Wolf stroked her hair before he stood and followed Badger. She watched him leave, wishing she could regain the feeling of peace from their first night together.

—◇—

In the pink glow of dawn, Lone Wolf lay in bed with his wife, reluctant to get up and leave her embrace. He twirled her hair, as he often did. They'd been married nearly a month, most of that time spent in the bed. His plans for Mexico were set, but he hadn't shared them with Fire Girl yet.

He kissed the top of her head. "I spoke with Red Hawk. We will have your naming feast in two days."

She squeezed him tighter. "Do you know the name he's picked for me?"

He smiled. "No, and even if I did, I wouldn't tell you."

She poked him in the ribs. "It's not nice to keep secrets from your wife."

His smile faded. "There's something else. I'm going on a horse raid."

"A horse raid?" She sat up. "Is this to get those guns?"

He nodded, unsure if she was upset or not.

"I should have expected you to plan a raid." She smirked. "You were always obsessed with getting more horses."

"Obsessed? Is that what you think?" He tickled her under her arms, using the opportunity to caress her breasts. Her nipples were the color of spring blossoms.

She pried his hands away. "Ever since I've known you, you were always off on a horse raid, coming back from a horse raid, or preparing to leave on a horse raid." She threw both hands in the air. "You never seemed to have enough horses."

"And now I have none. Besides, I was always raiding because I was trying to get enough horses to marry you."

"Really?" She grinned.

"Yes, really, but I don't just need horses for guns. There are young men ready to prime their skills and they expect me to lead them. Everyone is restless. I am restless."

"So, being with me is not enough for you, then?" She opened her mouth in mock offense.

He pulled her down beside him. "Being with you is everything and more." He kissed her deeply. Kissing had been strange at first, but now it made his heart race. He broke the kiss before he got too aroused.

"I like being with you, too," she whispered.

As small as it was, it was a comfort to hear her say that. She didn't often express such feelings, and he savored each word.

"When will you leave?" She leaned in to kiss him again.

"In a few days."

She pulled away. "That soon!"

"This is the time, my love. There are only so many days of summer left."

"How long will you be gone?"

"A month, maybe two or three months. It's hard to say." He played with her hair, waiting for her to respond. He'd seen her angry enough times it was all he could do to brace for it.

"Bring back many horses." Her smile didn't reach her eyes. Half of her smiles were like that, but when he did get a full smile, the light in those green eyes warmed him like nothing else. But she was trying to be agreeable, and he could appreciate the effort. He also appreciated the way she pressed her body along his. She moved on top, hips swirling. The slow gyrations stirred him.

His half-hardened cock swelled as it lay in the crook of where her hip met her thigh. He reached for her breasts again, rolling her nipples until he drew out a moan that made him as solid as iron. The sight of her, naked and aroused, wanting *him*, left him breathless.

As she straddled him, he cupped her buttocks and arched his hips to slide into her warmth. Each time he entered her was pure ecstasy, and he was grateful he would get to do so for the rest of his life.

His brother had once said, "Loving a woman is like a curse," but that was after Playful Otter had married Fox Laugh. It was only a month or so afterward that Panther's demeanor had changed, disappearing at unusual times and returning looking pleased with himself, though he would never explain the reason for his happiness. Now he knew it was because Panther was secretly bedding her.

For a long time, it seemed his brother had been right, and that loving Fire Girl would only bring him pain, but now he was surrounded with immense pleasure. It pulsed from his cock and throughout his body, far more powerful than he had experienced with previous women. Laying with them had been nothing more than satisfying an urge, but sex with a woman he loved was an altogether different experience. If this was what it had been like for Panther, then he couldn't blame his brother's betrayal. Nor his eventual self-demise.

31

Under the soft glow of the sun's descent, Lone Wolf led his new wife to Red Hawk's lodge for the naming feast. Fire Girl fumbled with the gifts they had brought, and he caught one of the packages before it hit the ground. "Don't be nervous. Red Hawk likes you."

"Are you sure?"

"Of course. He's told me so many times."

She glanced at the carbine in her arms. "Do you think he will accept it?"

He stopped and put a hand on her shoulder. "He will."

Outside the lodge, Laughing Bird and Squirrel prepared food for the feast. They greeted him with smug smiles, a reminder of the times his grandfather's wives would tease him or try to get him to reveal his feelings for Fire Girl.

She stopped again. "Are you sure it doesn't bother you that I'm giving the carbine to Red Hawk after you just gave it to me?"

It was true he'd prefer she'd keep the carbine for herself, but it made him proud that she was willing to give up something so valuable, especially since she had little to contribute. The act proved the links to her past were fading. "My grandfather will be honored by your gift, as am I."

Her mouth turned down, and he was tempted to kiss away her pout, but they had an audience. Instead, he took her hand, gave it a reassuring squeeze, and led her inside.

He seated himself next to Red Hawk and Fire Girl circled the lodge until she reached the women's side. She set the gifts beside her, and as a sign of respect, kept her eyes lowered, her knees together, and hands folded on her lap.

Pressing a fist to his mouth, he hid his amusement at her attempt to be demure.

"How is my favorite grandson and his young bride?" Red Hawk said.

"We're well, but don't tell anyone I'm your favorite." He winked at the old man. "How are you feeling? Do you still have that pain in your hips?"

Red Hawk groaned. "It hurts more and more each day. Soon I'll hardly be able to ride Arrow."

"That's a shame." Lone Wolf kept his face like a stone. "What good are you if you can't ride your favorite horse? We'll have to leave you at the bottom of a hill next winter."

Fire Girl's eyes widened with shock, but Red Hawk slapped his knee and chuckled. "The poor girl isn't used to your humor. It's about as dry as these old bones."

"Or maybe he's just not as funny as he thinks." She raised a brow.

His grandfather laughed. "I knew I liked you." He turned to Lone Wolf. "You better treasure this girl, but you know that already. You've been thirsting after her ever since she came here." He snickered then began to cough.

Lone Wolf struck him across the back.

Red Hawk nodded his thanks and cleared his throat. "Speaking of," he continued, "have you planted a baby in her yet? I know you've spilled enough of your seed inside her— "

"That's enough, Grandfather," Lone Wolf said.

Fire Girl looked away and tried to hide her giggles behind her palm.

"Fine, fine," said Red Hawk. "I just like babies and this girl needs one. So when you get back to your lodge, get busy planting. If you need advice, let me know." He winked and Fire Girl's giggles turned into full out laughter. "See, she thinks *I'm* funny. She's smart enough to know a *good* joke!"

"Or she's just laughing at the idea of you giving me pointers."

"Oh, ho! You think I don't know more about pollinating flowers than a young man like you?" He wagged a gnarled finger. "I'll remind you, I fathered three sons and four daughters. My wives can tell you they're satisfied. Let's bring those two inside so you can ask them. I don't know where Winged Woman is, blasted woman." He muttered to himself and tried to stand.

"Sit down, Grandfather." Lone Wolf laughed. "I have no doubt of your virility or potency."

"Don't you forget it." Red Hawk sat. "You should also remember it runs in the family. Your father sired two sons..." Immediately after the words left his lips, humor fled the room, and the lodge grew quiet. Red Hawk took a couple deep breaths. "Well, the others will arrive soon."

He lifted his head and ceased being Lone Wolf's grandfather, becoming his chief.

Eagle Beak and Pretty Robe entered with Round Eyes. As they greeted one another, Mouse plopped down next to Fire Girl, and Badger seated himself beside Lone Wolf. He elbowed him in the ribs. "Marriage suits you, though it's nice to see you every once in a while."

"You'll be seeing plenty of me soon."

"Right, and then after a month I'll be sick of your ugly face."

As Lone Wolf laughed, he stole a glance at his wife. Tomorrow he would prepare for the coming raid and a pang of regret played on his mind. He had never before worried about missing someone while he was gone.

One Eye, Lone Wolf's eldest uncle, came through the door, with his new wife, Quick Hands. He'd never been married before and rarely raided but was a decent enough hunter. Nevertheless, he had fulfilled his duty to marry his brother's widow.

Winged Woman, Laughing Bird, and Squirrel joined the group with containers of food and settled around the fire. Each of the families had brought gifts for Red Hawk and for Fire Girl, and they set them down near the altar. Lone Wolf noticed a few sticks representing horses. They must have come from Eagle Beak.

"Fire Girl," said Red Hawk. His tone had become formal. "It makes my heart glad you've become one of the People. Now that you have joined my grandson, my heart is happier still."

"Thank you, I am happy too." She held out the carbine.

Although Lone Wolf had no doubt his grandfather had spotted the gun when they entered, Red Hawk's eyes widened, and he smiled proudly. He took the carbine and made a show of examining it. Her gift was more symbolic than practical, but his grandfather would know what it meant that she had presented it to him.

"Did you know we are people of the Wind as much as of the Earth?" Red Hawk asked. "Wind touches everything. Even the strongest rock cannot resist the wind. Where once it was brittle and sharp, ready to cut an unsuspecting creature, wind will wear it down, smoothen and soften the edges. Our people came from the mountains. We knew the way of rocks and stone."

He set the carbine down. "When we left those mountains, we shed everything, like newborn children, our paths lay open and boundless like the prairie we had entered. Only a few stories and legends came with us, but we created a new People. We befriended the horse. Like the wind, the horse is always on the move, racing across the prairie. So, like Horse and Wind, moving is our life, never still, never in one place for long. And though we move forward, we never forget where we come from." He extended his hand toward Fire Girl. "Such is your life."

Her eyes welled, but she smiled. "I am ready."

"Lone Wolf tells me you would like a new name. That's good. Sometimes it's hard to know when a name has outgrown its use, but when a big change comes in a person's life, we should mark it with a new name."

The lodge fell silent as Red Hawk took his pipe from its bag and laid the stem and pipe bowl on a piece of deerskin on the ground. Lone Wolf emptied his mind of his fears and worries, seeking to connect his heart with balance. Red Hawk lifted the bowl in the palm of his left hand and the stem in his right. He brought them together and paused before inserting the stem into the bowl. Male and Female, Earth and Sky, Sun and Moon were now joined. A sense of wholeness filled him with peace.

Red Hawk held the pipe facing East and took out a small pinch of tobacco. He sprinkled it on the ground as an offering to Mother Earth, then added some to the bowl. "The East is yellow for the rising sun which brings us a new day. We thank the Creator for each day we are allowed to live upon Mother Earth." He then faced south as he repeated the act of sprinkling tobacco on the ground and then into the bowl. "South is black for the spirit world. We seek spiritual wisdom and pray for help from our Spirit Guides."

The ritual continued for the rest of the directions: red west for the setting sun, white north of winter, green ground for Mother Earth, and blue for Father Sky. Then Red Hawk lifted the pipe as an offering to the Creator.

"Great Spirit, Creator of all creatures, those that crawl on the earth, swim in water, or soar in the sky, the four-legged and the two-legged, the earth and sky, wind, water, earth and fire, the sun and the moon, the four directions, all of us here and our ancestors before us. We offer this pipe to you, in unity of all things."

He brought the pipe to his mouth while Winged Woman handed him a long, thin piece of wood to light it. Once lit, he drew the smoke into his mouth and blew it into each of the four directions, then handed the pipe to Lone Wolf.

He took the pipe, cradling the bowl as he brought the pipe to his lips as though taking a sip of water. He inhaled, letting the smoke merge with his breath before blowing it out in a long fragrant stream. The smoke billowed up to the opening at the top, taking with it his prayers for a long and happy life with Fire Girl.

The pipe continued around the circle, following the path of the sun as each man took his smoke and sent forth his prayers. Once the pipe reached Red Hawk, he took another inhale and set it on a buffalo skull that served as his altar. He turned his attention back to Fire Girl.

"Come here, granddaughter." She moved to kneel beside Red Hawk as the old man used a weathered hand to take hers. Lone Wolf shifted to make room for her. If she were a baby, Red Hawk would have lifted her to the sky.

"I have thought for many days on this, and I have decided on a name for you, one that connects you to your animal spirit."

A flicker of confusion passed over her face and Lone Wolf fought a feeling of regret for not giving his wife more warning.

Red Hawk lifted her hands four times as he repeated her new name.

Eka Wasápe,

Eka Wasápe,

Eka Wasápe,

Eka Wasápe.

Red Bear Woman. He smiled with pleasure. Not only was the bear a part of his wife's medicine, as dictated on that day, it was a good symbol. Solitary, powerful, playful at times, but ferocious when provoked, just like his wife. The bear had no predators. It was a good name.

She thanked Red Hawk then turned to the rest of the guests, who repeated her name as she returned to her place. Eagle Beak and Pretty Robe patted her shoulders as she sat, but a shadow of uncertainty hid behind her smile.

The feasting began and good humor conversation returned as Red Hawk's guests relaxed into the informal atmosphere.

Lone Wolf shared more about his plans for the raid with Badger and Eagle Beak. "We will travel deep into Mexico. I suspect most of the settlements won't have many horses."

"That will take more than a month or two," Eagle Beak said.

"And we'll pass through Apache lands," Badger added.

"I know, but we'll be ready." He glanced again at Red Bear, who was immersed in conversation with Mouse and Pretty Robe. She wouldn't mind if he took longer than he initially planned, not if he came back with numerous horses. He would speak with her later that night.

The moon rose and moved across the sky when at last the feast ended. Lone Wolf's friends and family had returned to their lodges, but he and Red Bear were the last to leave. Before he reached the door, Red Hawk whispered to him, "Remember what I said. You are the son of my son. You take after your father and me in more ways than your skills on the battlefield. Combine that with Red Bear's... ripeness, I have no doubt you two will make many children."

"I hope you're right, Grandfather."

Red Hawk patted his shoulder then Lone Wolf ducked out of the lodge and joined Red Bear outside. She was wearing that look on her face, the one that said she was thinking hard and not about anything good.

He brushed his hand along hers. "Is something wrong? Do you not like your name?"

Her lips twisted. "It's not that. The whole incident with the bear, I was so ashamed. I was glad I would finally be rid of Fire Girl, like maybe that girl was dead and I could be someone else."

He swallowed. "You shouldn't be ashamed, Red Bear." He liked saying her name out loud. "Remember what I said. You handled it well, and the bear, she was challenging you, but not in the way you think. It was a message of healing, and I think you've done that now. I wanted to tell you all of this and more, that day and everyday afterward."

He hoped so about the healing part. There was nothing he wanted more than for her to be happy. Even right at this moment.

She took a breath and stared at the ground. "You're right. I'm sorry." A quiet moment passed. "I just wished you had warned me about the name. And I overheard what you and Badger were talking about. You're going to be gone longer than you told me."

"I thought maybe you'd like to get rid of me for a while." He said it in jest but failed to make her smile.

"You said we should always be honest with each other, but there are things kept hidden from me. The men I killed on the raid. The carbine you've had all this time. The bracelet. The fact that you loved me. What else is there that I don't know?" Her look burned into him and he tensed at her harsh tone.

"If there's anything you want to know, ask and I'll tell you."

"I don't even know what to ask! That's not the same as you being forthcoming."

He closed his eyes and swallowed. "What you ask of me isn't easy, but I will do my best to tell you anything as it occurs to me." He reached for her hand. To his relief, she let him take it and squeezed his fingers. He sensed her fiery mood cooling.

"What else would you have told me? You said you would have told me more things that day."

He pulled her closer. "I would have told you that I loved you, and that there was nothing you could say or do to change it." In truth, he hadn't been sure at the time what he would have said to her, but the words would have come.

"I still don't understand how you could love me, after what I did, after what I said."

"Red Bear Woman, the little girl I found on the prairie is not the same person in front of me. That little girl, despite all odds, killed two great warriors and saved her own life. An act of great strength, power and spirit. But she's not dead, she's just become an even stronger woman." He brushed her cheek with his fingers. "I won't pretend I don't miss my father and brother, but if you hadn't done what you did, or if I had taken my revenge against you, then I wouldn't know you. My love, and my wife." He drew her into a hug, but she pulled free.

"I know what I want to ask. Where is my sister?"

His heart skipped. It was an unexpected question and he still worried that finding her sister would give her a reason to leave. "She's with the *Yamparika*, a northern band. She was adopted soon after you both arrived." He hoped his answer was still true and that the sister hadn't been returned when the hair-mouths made their demands.

Her head turned to gaze north. "I saw her once, she seemed happy."

"She's with a good family." He didn't know the couple that had taken the sister, but Red Hawk had said they would care for the girl, like Eagle Beak and Pretty Robe cared for Red Bear. Maybe the Yamparika didn't hear about the demand to return all captives.

"I'd like to see her again. Will you take me to her?"

"I will, but it will have to be next summer."

32

The next day Red Bear helped Lone Wolf prepare for the horse raid. She packed extra clothing, tools for repairing weapons, medicine for illness and injury, and plenty of dried meat, dried fruit, and pemmican. As she packed, her stomach twisted with nausea. She paused and clutched her belly.

It could be dread. Lone Wolf's journey would be long and dangerous. She had confidence in his warrior skills, but there was always a risk he wouldn't come home alive. The nausea surged, sending bile into her throat, but she swallowed it down.

Her husband sat on the edge of the bed, attaching turkey feathers to a stack of newly made arrows. He stopped and stared at her. "Is anything wrong?"

She took a sip of water from her drinking bowl. It might offend him if she expressed her worries about him being hurt or killed, appearing like she doubted him. And it might bring bad luck. "I was thinking about how empty this lodge will feel without you."

He flashed his dimples while he continued to wrap sinew coated with glue around an arrow shaft. "Don't worry, I'll be back before you break for the winter camp. By this time next year, we'll have twice as many horses as before."

"I know." She forced a smile and continued to pack.

After a round of fervent love-making, she lay panting. Lone Wolf rolled off and lay beside her, equally drained.

"Woman, you almost make me regret I paid so many horses for you." He stroked hair. "Then I wouldn't have to go on this raid, and we could do this every night."

She laughed. "We already do this every night, and not just at night."

"Sick of me already, are you?" He leaned on one elbow and used his free hand to trace the curve of her breasts. Her skin tingled. "I can't help myself. My want for you never ends."

She leaned and nibbled on his neck, tasting his sweat. "I wish I could go with you."

"It wasn't so very long ago you ran from my presence." Along with his teasing words, his fingers danced around her navel.

She breathed deeply, taking in his scent, his presence. "All that time, I could have known you. We could have been friends. Now I understand what I've been missing, and you have to go." She traced a finger along the center of his chest, finding his heartbeat. It was still racing. "Will you let me come with you?"

His eyes shone with pride. "You have great courage, but I can't allow it. Not this time."

The idea of joining him wasn't unusual. Plenty of women followed their husbands on raids. Not only would she get to spend more time with him, see what he was like in battle, she might have a chance to earn her own honors.

She sat up to show him she was serious. "But why? I can help. I can shoot, I can probably shoot better than some of the men you're taking with you, like Turtle."

The hint of a smile came and went. "That's true, and I don't doubt your skills— "

"Then why can't I come?"

He sat up. The humor vanished from his face. "My love, I can't bear to lose you. It's taken so long to get us here. I can't let someone take you from me." His voice was tinged with irritation, or perhaps worry.

She stroked his cheek. "No one is going to take me, Lone Wolf."

"There may be whites along the way. Even the Mexicans try to secure captives to trade. If they see you, they'll come after us. It will put everyone in danger."

He made a good point. She stifled a shudder at the memory of José and his men. "I could stay hidden."

He shook his head. "It's too risky."

"I'm not afraid."

"No, Red Bear."

"But—"

"I said no." His eyes darkened in a flash of anger.

She drew up her knees and wrapped her arms around them, fighting the urge to deliver her own sharp retort.

He rolled onto his back and rubbed his face. He sighed. "No one knows you're here, and I don't want that to change." His voice returned to its low, soft tone. "Besides, you're too noticeable to hide." He reached for a lock of her hair, curling it around his fingers. "Can you forgive me?"

She wasn't sure what he meant. Forgive him for getting angry? For denying her a chance to join him on a raid. For killing her father? For taking her? Whatever it was, she would forgive anything.

"All right. I'll wait for you."

"It won't be too long. I promise."

The next day was given to ceremony and dance to ensure a safe and prosperous raid. Lone Wolf had very little time alone with Red Bear, but she said no more of her desire to join him, permitting him the solitude he needed to ready his mind for the journey ahead.

Before dawn, he prepared to leave. His supplies had been packed on a pony lent by Eagle Beak. All that was left was Lone Wolf's personal rituals. He sat at the edge of the fire, naked and recently bathed, with his damp hair against his back. He opened his private medicine bundle and took out a small leather pouch filled with dried herbs and plants, then rubbed it on his body.

Wolf spirit, guide me. Lend me your keen eyes so that I may find my enemy.

Wolf spirit, guide me. Lend me your sharp nose so that I am always aware of my enemy's presence.

Wolf spirit, guide me. Lend me your strength so that I can defeat my enemy.

Wolf spirit, guide me. Lend me your wisdom so that I may lead with honor.

Help me guide my brothers on our journey, so I can bring us home.

When he had finished his prayers, Red Bear helped him dress. He relished feeling her touch before he would leave for the rest of the summer.

"Now I know what that scent is." She attached his leggings while he straightened his breechcloth.

"What do you mean?"

"That scent, it lingers on your skin. It's perplexed me for years. I smelled it that day and I've been haunted by it ever since."

"Haunted?"

"Well, it used to put me into a panic." She unfolded his war shirt.

"Is it bad? Does it bother you?"

"No, it's nice. I mean, before I was bothered by it, but only because I didn't want to be reminded of that day. But it's always been sort of... alluring."

"I like the sound of that." He grinned.

"Why do you do it?" She handed the shirt to him.

"I can't tell you exactly why I use this particular medicine in this particular way. That's too close to telling you about my vision quest." He pulled his shirt over his head. "But I will say that I only do it when I need my medicine to be extra powerful."

"So, like that day on the raid."

"Yes, and for some time afterwards." The raid wasn't as tender a subject as it used to be. He could mention it without immediately being sorry, though they didn't talk about it unless they had to.

"And when you married me?"

"Pretty much any time that had to do with you." He smirked as he sat.

She knelt behind him to comb his hair. "When exactly did you ask my father to marry me? Are you leaving your hair loose or braided? Do you want the roach headdress?"

"Loose. No roach." Lone Wolf turned his head to see her. "You mean you really don't know?"

"No, should I?"

"I thought maybe after everything, you might have figured it out."

"Well, I didn't, and now I want to know." She handed him the case holding his eagle feathers. They were attached to a small loop which he would use to thread in his scalplock braid. Two of the feathers were painted red on the tips, signifying he'd been injured while acquiring his coups. From one quill hung a rattlesnake rattle, and it clattered as he removed the case.

He straightened the feathers and smoothed the barbs before raising his arms to attach the loop. "Do you remember the day you killed the stag?"

She held up a mirror for him. "Yes."

"I saw you when you came out of the woods with the travois. I was impressed and proud. I convinced the others to turn back because I wanted to talk to you, but I was nervous to do so. We raced instead."

"I remember. You and Shadow were showing off," she teased. "Was that for my benefit?"

He tried not to smile. "I suppose it was. I picked that flower for you, anyway, but I was too afraid to give it to you."

"It still amazes me to hear that," she said. "*You* were afraid of *me*? I was terrified of you." She lowered the mirror.

"When the other men were talking to you, I could see they were looking at you in that way. Even though you weren't a woman yet, they were aware of you." He shrugged. "I suppose I was no better, but it made me feel protective. That's why I stayed back. I could tell you were nervous, and I was trying to get them away from you."

"I thought you were arrogant."

"I know, but it was better than making you more uncomfortable. Besides, you didn't want to talk to me anyway." He chuckled, but she turned away as though ashamed. "I wish I had said something," he added. "I wanted to tell you what I thought of you, to express my admiration." He ran his hand down her arm. "So, the next day I went to see your father. I know you remember it because that was when I came from your family's lodge and you were standing there, with your skinning knife." He touched her cheek. "I suppose it confirmed everything. You unable to do what I was unable to do."

"*That* day?"

"Yes, I had just finished talking to him." He lifted her hand so he could see into the mirror again and applied his paint, swiping his finger in a shell case filled with bear grease before dipping it into pigment. He put black around his eyes and red on his forehead and cheeks.

"What did you say to Eagle Beak?"

"I told him how much I admired you, and a lot of what I told you before, about you and I sharing the same spirit. He didn't agree right away. I had to do some convincing." He cleaned his fingers on a damp cloth. "Then I just waited. Waited for you to grow up. Waited for you to stop hating me. But then I couldn't wait anymore." He smiled.

She looked into the mirror. "I wanted to kill you, and you wanted to marry me."

He took the mirror from her hand and lifted her chin. "That had a lot to do with why I wanted you. Of course, I didn't want you to kill me, but I admired your courage to challenge me. Very few have dared to do so. No one but you is still alive."

She kissed him, pressing her mouth hard against his while touching him beneath his shirt, then under his breechcloth. Her warm hands heated his blood. They were soon on the ground. It was rushed and over too quickly, leaving him feeling somewhat dissatisfied and abashed at taking her while dressed for battle.

"Dances and ceremonies are one thing, but there's no better way to send a man off than to remind him of what he gets to come home to." He gave her a final kiss.

He hated to leave so abruptly, but the other men waited for him. He straightened his clothing before hurrying outside with her.

Badger, Buffalo Horn, Ferret, and Turtle were already mounted, encircled by family and friends who had gathered to see them off. He gave a quick farewell to Pretty Robe, and his grandfather's wives before giving his attention to Eagle Beak and Red Hawk.

He clasped Eagle Beak's forearm. "Thank you, for everything."

"I should thank you. I've never seen my daughter so content." Eagle Beak smiled. "I'm happy for you both."

Red Hawk patted his back. "May the spirits ensure your safe return."

He embraced his grandfather's thin shoulders. "Only after I've fulfilled my task." He mounted Shadow, and before turning to leave, clasped Red Bear's hand. "You won't forget me while I'm gone?"

"Go on, husband, then hurry back so I can welcome you home." Her playful smile, all the way to her eyes, made his heart leap.

"I look forward to it." He took in the sight of her, the love in her expression, the shape of her face, then spun his horse and the party rode off.

33

Red Bear curled into a ball under the buffalo hide blankets. Without Lone Wolf beside her, the bed felt huge, making it difficult to sleep. The lodge felt empty as well. Too quiet and the absence of company made her feel unprotected. It was too bad she no longer had the carbine, but she slipped her skinning knife under the buffalo hair-stuffed pillow.

After a restless sleep, she rose and went to the stream for her morning bath, eyeing the still visible moon. Lone Wolf had departed the morning after a gibbous moon, but it had waned to the thinnest crescent. The soonest he would return would be the next full moon, but she knew it was likely he'd be gone longer than that.

As she waded out, her stomach lurched, and she bent over to vomit. She stood straight with her hand over her belly, trying to gain her sense of balance. Her thoughts of Lone Wolf's long absence must have driven her to sickness, but then she knew. More than a cycle had passed since her last visit to the once-a-month lodge, before she married Lone Wolf.

She bent a hand to cup water to wash the taste of bile from her mouth. Her heart raced with this new knowledge, her condition obvious though she hadn't considered the possibility before. How silly of her to never think of it, considering the frequency at which she and Lone Wolf had coupled.

Though it was too early to feel anything, she pressed on the skin below her navel. Her sore breasts, which she had assumed was a sign of her moon bleed, now registered as another symptom she had missed. The reality of her life set in. She was a wife of the People, married to a young leader off on a horse raid, and she carried his child. What would he say when he returned and saw her swollen belly? Would he be pleased?

Her birth mother had also been sixteen when she married Papa, then had Bridget less than a year later. The memory of her mother reminded her of her failed promise to care for Maggie.

Lone Wolf said he would take her to her sister. Maybe she'd have the baby by then. What would Maggie think of her married and with a baby?

She hurried to dress so she could tell Pretty Robe and Mouse, but after she tugged her moccasins over her feet and headed home, she had second thoughts. Lone Wolf would return before her belly was large enough to notice. If she could keep the baby a secret until then, she could share the news with him first. He was her husband, after all.

Days passed, and the camp moved to follow the buffalo herds to the south. Her bleeding failed to come, confirming that life had sprouted inside her.

Mouse pounded stakes into the ground with a rock, securing her lodge cover while Red Bear helped to arrange parfleche pouches inside.

"We should share a lodge." Mouse set down the heavy stone. "I'm always lonely whenever Badger leaves, so I often sleep with my mother, but it will be much more fun to live with you."

Red Bear paused in the doorway. It would be harder to hide her pregnancy from Mouse if they were living together, but she didn't want to offend her by choosing to remain alone. "I'll bring over my belongings."

For the next month, she ate a small amount of food when she first awoke, finding it prevented her from becoming sick and raising suspicion.

The heat of late summer bore down as Red Bear, Mouse, and Pretty Robe prepared the evening meal. Red Bear ground pecans to mix into the flatbread but paused to catch her breath.

"Are you alright?" Pretty Robe asked.

"I just needed a moment, that's all." She returned to her pecans.

"Are you sure, I've noticed you seem more tired than usual."

"I'm fine."

Pretty Robe exchanged a quick glance with Mouse, "We should go see Winged Woman about this. She'll know."

Red Bear ground the pecans until they became a fine powder. Feeling her mother and Mouse's eyes on her, she frowned. "Why are you smiling?"

"No reason," Mouse said, losing the smile.

Pretty Robe stirred an iron kettle of water and chunks of buffalo meat. "Do you have anything to give Winged Woman? We should make an offering, to ask for her assistance."

"I don't need her assistance. I said I'm fine."

"Red Bear," Pretty Robe's tone changed from amused to concerned. "You should talk to Winged Woman. She'll have advice for you and can tell you when to expect the baby."

She sighed and set down the grinding stone. "I wanted to wait for Lone Wolf."

"What for?" Mouse frowned. "He can't help you with this."

She couldn't explain it. She wanted to have that time with him, where the secret was theirs alone, but now it was too late. She handed Pretty Robe her bowl of pecan powder to add to her mother's corn mixture.

"Do you have a gift?" Pretty Robe took the bowl.

"I do have something." She went into her lodge and came out with a quilled suede bag. "It's for herbs and plants, but I meant it as a gift for Winged Woman's past troubles with me. If I give this to her now, how will I show her my gratitude for all she's done?"

Winged Woman was Lone Wolf's grandmother, and essentially his mother. She ought to behave like a proper daughter-in-law. Tomorrow, she'd offer to help with their meals.

"You should give her the bag now, and tell her how you feel," Pretty Robe said. "You'll think of something later if you want to give her another gift."

Additional disappointment weighed on her shoulders. She set the bag aside. "Why can't *you* tell me what I need to know?"

"I can tell you some things, but it's best to have a medicine woman's advice."

The next morning, Red Bear, Mouse and Pretty Robe went to see Winged Woman.

The elderly medicine woman sat outside her lodge boiling plants for dyes. She smiled as they approached. "It's good of you to visit." She gave Red Bear and Mouse a pointed glance. "I hope you bring comfort to one another while your husbands are gone."

"Yes, grandmother," Mouse said, "We often are in each other's company, but we've come because my friend needs your guidance."

Winged Woman stared hard at Red Bear and nodded. "Let's go inside."

Once they entered, they continued to make minor conversation, before Red Bear steered the conversation back to their intended visit.

She withdrew the suede bag from beneath her robes and presented it. "I made this for you, for your troubles, and because you've been kind to me since I came to the People. I wish to thank you for it."

Winged Woman took the gift and inspected it. "This is fine work. Pretty Robe, you have taught your daughter well. Thank you, I will use it. Now tell me what is troubling you?"

"It's been more than two moons since my last bleed."

Winged Woman smiled. "That's not something unusual for a girl like yourself, newly married and in love. You carry a child in your womb."

She nodded. She knew that much already but dared not be rude.

Winged Woman explained what to expect in the coming months and how to ensure a healthy child and safe birth, but Red Bear hardly listened.

She had missed her chance to tell Lone Wolf first, and now Winged Woman knew, and soon Laughing Bird and Squirrel would know, which meant the whole camp would hear about it by tomorrow. But it was done. It wasn't as though Lone Wolf would care if she had told him first or not. She was being silly. In another month or so she'd begin to show. Perhaps Lone Wolf would return in time to feel the baby's first kicks.

As fall approached, Red Bear looked each day for a signal announcing the party's return.

"Is there anything?" Mouse asked as she returned from the edge of camp.

She shook her head. "Why don't you seem concerned? When the men were on the big raid, you were anxious and miserable."

Mouse shrugged. "That's because the men were led by someone I didn't know, traveling in lands less familiar to us." She squeezed Red Bear's hand. "Lone Wolf leads this raid and he always brings his men back safely. Badger won't let him do anything stupid anyway."

"Do you think Lone Wolf would do something stupid?" She followed Mouse back inside the lodge.

Mouse poked at the fire with a stick. "When it comes to horses, Lone Wolf can become consumed. But you know that, you've seen it yourself."

"This isn't helping to console me."

"I'm sorry, but you needn't worry. Like I said, Badger has always been good about keeping Lone Wolf on the right path. Besides, we're *numunuu*. We are proud when our men raid, proud when they return, and proud when they die in battle. You're the wife of a war leader, Red Bear. You need to be an example of strength for other women. This is the way."

Mouse's confidence, even after losing her father, and everything else that had happened inspired her spirit. Ignoring her fears, Red Bear focused on preparing for the baby and Lone Wolf's return.

She tracked her pregnancy on a piece of wood, cutting lines for each day and carving a circle for each moon that had passed. After four circles, her belly developed a swell. It was barely noticeable, only a slight roundness, as though she'd eaten too much.

As she ran her hand over it, a strange sensation fluttered below her navel. It reminded her of butterflies held in her palm, or small fish tickling her ankles. The feeling gave her a sense of peace. This was something she could keep to herself, something no one else could see or feel, at least not yet.

Red Bear sat with Mouse in front of her lodge, making pemmican in preparation for the hard winter months. Round Eyes and other boys played with the camp dogs, chasing them and running while the dogs chased them in return.

Round Eyes fell to the ground and the dogs swarmed him, licking his face, hands, and feet as he giggled and thrashed his legs. He stood, laughing and covered in dirt. He threw a stick he'd found on the ground and the dogs chased after it.

A wide grin grew on Red Bear's face as she set her hand on her belly. The other boys gathered around Round Eyes. He was younger than most, but taller than all of them. He smiled again, a dimple in each cheek, and swept his long, loose hair from his eyes. Eyes that were warm and brown with flecks of gold.

Red Bear's grin faded as she sucked in her breath. He couldn't have...

Even the way he moved and carried himself, his natural skill, brought to mind the image of Lone Wolf as a young boy. Her chest tightened. She wrapped her arm tightly around her waist. The nausea, which had long stopped, came back with a rush.

Then the words Fox Laugh had confessed to her echoed in her mind. *"She picked me, but I know she loved him too."*

She grabbed Mouse's arm. "Lone Wolf's brother. Did he and Lone Wolf look alike?"

Mouse lifted her head. "Oh yes. Once Lone Wolf came of age, he was like a reflection of his brother. When they were kids, they used to play pranks on everyone, tricking people into thinking one was the other, but after a while, they both grew tired of being mistaken for each other." She shaped a brick of pemmican with her palms. "Lone Wolf especially hated it. It's one of the reasons he was so opposite to his brother, and why he keeps his hair loose."

"To be different?"

"To be himself, and not just someone's brother." Mouse wiped her hands on her hide apron. "Why do you ask?" She gazed in the direction Red Bear had been staring, at Round Eyes. Her faded smile confirmed Red Bear's suspicions.

"Lone Wolf wasn't the only one who lost both his parents that summer, was he? Does he know?" she asked.

"Who, Round Eyes?"

"Yes. And Lone Wolf." If Hunts Like a Panther was Round Eyes' father, that made Lone Wolf his uncle. No wonder he made particular efforts to be kind to the boy.

"I think so." Mouse pursed her lips. "I think everyone knows, except for Round Eyes, of course. It wasn't obvious at first. There were suspicions, then after he was born, there were little things."

"Like what?"

"Well, Fox Laugh doesn't have a brother, and since Lone Wolf's brother was his best friend, he was eager to take the role of uncle."

Red Bear bit her lip. Panther would have been uncle to her own child, teaching and training him to become a warrior, as was tradition, but it was her fault he was dead. Then again, if Panther were alive, she wouldn't be. The whole thing made her head spin.

Mouse continued, "Whenever he held the baby, and he wanted to hold him often, there would be this look on his face. He was in love with Round Eyes, but there was also a look of regret."

"Wasn't Fox Laugh angry? I mean, he treats Round Eyes like his own."

"Does he?" Mouse raised her eyebrows. "I think he's kind of torn. He didn't outwardly show anger or hurt, but it was a betrayal. His wife, whom he adored, and his best friend? But I think he accepted it, too. And now? Well, Round Eyes is all that's left of both of them."

She kept silent, watching the boys play.

Fox Laugh approached. He called to Round Eyes and the boy ran to the man he knew as his father. He ruffled his hair and said something to him, holding up Round Eye's bow and his own weapons before they walked off together.

34

The weather turned cold, and Red Bear continued to watch for Lone Wolf's signal. While she made a new shirt for him, she pictured quiet evenings by the fire, cuddling the baby. For his sake, she hoped it would be a boy. She imagined him teaching their child to ride and shoot a bow, and one day going on a hunt together.

She made the shirt using her best antelope skins, softening the leather until it would be the most supple shirt he would ever wear. The design she planned for it used colors she knew he liked, displaying horse prints in black across a field of green with a red sky.

Pretty Robe ducked into the lodge, carrying a large bundle. "Look what your father made." She unwrapped the bundle to reveal a cradle-board. "It's the same frame from Round Eyes' board, but we made new bindings for it."

Red Bear sucked in her breath and took the board from her mother. Memories of her first days with Pretty Robe and Eagle Beak returned to her mind, when she had cared for Round Eyes as a baby, not knowing she had played a role in the death of his parents.

She examined the smooth wood and willow frame, with finely beaded binding straps attached. "It's beautiful."

"I made this too." Pretty Robe held up a set of lining with a hood sewn from rabbit fur. "It will still be cold when the baby is born, so this will keep him warm."

She ran her hands through the soft fur, perfect to lay against delicate baby skin. "If you have any scraps, I could make a pair of moccasins."

Her mother withdrew pieces of rabbit hide from inside her sleeve. "I was going to make them myself, but I figured you'd want to."

She hugged her. "Thank you." A painful lump in her throat made it difficult to speak. When she pulled away, she left wet spots on Pretty Robe's shoulder.

Pretty Robe touched her cheek. "Are those happy tears?"

She wiped her face. "I'm grateful for all you've done for me..."

"But you worry about Lone Wolf."

Before she could answer, a sharp movement against her ribs made her gasp.

"Is that the baby?" Pretty Robe placed a hand on her swollen bulge, then smiled as the baby shifted. "He's a strong one."

"I wish Lone Wolf was here to feel it." Saying the words aloud brought further ache in her chest. He had missed so much.

"He will be here."

"I wish he hadn't left. I should have asked him to stay with me."

Pretty Robe frowned. "Would you ask your husband to stop being a warrior?"

She chewed her lip. "He didn't have to leave so soon. He could have waited. And why take so long?"

"He gave nearly everything he had for you."

"Only because he knew he could get more." She wished she could take back the spiteful words as soon as they left her lips, but Pretty Robe's stern face softened.

"You must have hope."

Red Bear made two more circles on her stick, bringing the total to six. There was no sign of Lone Wolf or his men. They should have moved to the winter camp, but Red Hawk still waited. She wrapped a large buffalo robe around her shoulders before heading outside.

She stood in front of Red Hawk's lodge, trying to summon the courage to scratch at the flap.

"Come in, Red Bear," Red Hawk called out. "I see you standing out there."

She ducked her head and stepped in, supporting her bulge.

He smiled at her when she sat. "How is my lovely granddaughter today? You must miss my grandson?"

His words brought a smile. It pleased her to hear Red Hawk speak affectionately toward her. She knew Lone Wolf respected him, not just because he was his grandfather and his chief, but because he believed him to be a great man. For all those reasons, she desired his approval.

"I do, Grandfather."

The old man eyed her with narrow eyes, little more than slits behind his wrinkled face. "You have grown in many ways. A young woman, bearing a child of your own. I knew I was right about you." When he chuckled, his eyes disappeared.

"What do you mean?"

"When you first came here, well, I'm sure you know, there was much dispute about what to do with you."

Though his tone was cheerful, the words were solemn. It hadn't been the purpose of her visit, but now questions begged to be asked. "Lone Wolf has explained it to me, but I still cannot grasp it." Her voice lowered to a whisper. "Why wasn't I killed?"

Red Hawk sat back against his back rest. "Lots of people were killed, across several days. We took our revenge many times over." He sounded pained.

She hated to make him revisit his loss, but she had to know.

"I killed your son—"

"And would ending your life have given back his? Or my other grandson? Would I have felt any less grief?"

She stared at him.

"You're trying to understand forgiveness, but I didn't forgive you. That isn't what happened here. You have to remember, our people are warriors. We value courage above all else." He leaned closer. "How could I not take the chance to find out more about you?" He lifted a finger. "There was little risk in delaying your death. If you turned out to be nothing special, we could have ended you at any time afterward." He sat back with a smile. "We almost did."

She blinked, surprised his talk about killing her didn't bring any fear.

He reached out a hand and placed it on her shoulder. "Now you've become so much more than I could have imagined. It didn't surprise me at all when Lone Wolf confessed his love for you. I couldn't see it happening any other way."

Her eyes welled at hearing her husband's name. "Where is he, Grandfather? Why hasn't he come back?"

"It's impossible to predict what will happen on a raid. There are fewer and fewer good horses to be found nowadays. Perhaps he traveled deep into Mexico."

"You're not worried?"

Red Hawk sighed. "I am, but Lone Wolf wouldn't have gone too far if he knew he couldn't return in time for the winter move."

"So, you think he'll return soon?"

"I hope so. We'll wait a little longer. If he doesn't return by the time we leave, then it's likely he's gone straight to the winter camp, and we'll meet him there."

She hadn't thought of that. The idea renewed her hopes. She stood, but a dark thought came to her. "Grandfather?"

"Yes?"

"Were you there? At the wagon camp? Did you see?"

His face softened as he stared at his fire, the way Lone Wolf often did. "No, I wasn't."

In the same way she had recognized Lone Wolf in Round Eyes, she saw him in Red Hawk, his features revealing the handsome youth he'd once been. Would Lone Wolf reach such an age, or die in battle as all the men hoped would be their fate.

"But you were there at the other attack?"

"Yes, I helped my son and the others get their revenge, but I didn't go on to raid the wagons."

"So, did you... did you see my father die? He had hair like mine."

Red Hawk took a breath. "Yes. I saw him die." He raised his head to face her.

She wanted to ask, needed to know. Did he suffer? Did he die quickly? But she knew what the answer was.

Another month passed, and the band packed up for winter. Red Bear tried to take comfort in believing Lone Wolf would know where to meet his people.

Eagle Beak lent her ponies for a travois and to carry her gear, but she needed help to mount Smoke with her swollen belly. Pretty Robe laced her fingers so Red Bear could step onto them and get a boost.

"This would be easier with a saddle and stirrups," she said.

"I'll tell your father to make you one."

He wouldn't finish it in time before the baby was born, but maybe she could use it for the next baby. Unless there wasn't another baby. She forced away the thought. Everyone kept telling her to have hope, so she clung to it like the fruit of the buttonwood in winter.

They began the slow trek to the mountains in the north, but when the band arrived at the winter site, Lone Wolf and his party weren't there.

Each day, she shuffled out of her lodge to check with the sentries for any sign or signal of the returning warriors, but each day yielded nothing. She wouldn't let herself believe he was dead, but the thought lay dormant as a tiny seed in her mind.

Red Bear marked another circle on her stick, then went out into the cold morning to the edge of camp where she looked for any sign of her husband. She stood on a rocky edge, searching for a whiff of smoke, or a puff of snow kicked up by horses, but there was nothing.

Snow drifted on her face, stinging her cheeks and nose. The wind picked up, forcing her to retreat from her perch. Her heart felt so heavy she shuffled her feet, but they were too numb to notice the snow filling her moccasins.

The seed of doubt dug into her mind, edging its way through her hopes, like a knife prying her heart open and bare. He wouldn't die and leave her, not now, not when she had his baby.

On her way back, she passed an old sycamore. A buttonball dropped from above her, the last seed fruit leaving the tree bare and empty.

Inside their shared lodge, Mouse poked a dead fire. She took one look at her, then turned back and sat in silence. There was nothing to say. They were both widows.

The nights were bitter with cold. In less than two months, she expected to deliver her son. She had no doubt it would be a son, but Lone Wolf would never see him. No one openly mourned, as there had been no definite word, but the air hung thick with gloom, making the hardest month of the year even more unbearable.

She lay on her side, in the bed she used to share with him, her hand over her round, hard belly. She glided her palm over her stretched skin, meeting the child's hand or foot whenever it pushed upwards against her flesh.

Staring at the empty space beside her, she tried to recount the number of words spoken between herself and her husband. They had been married nearly a month before he left, and before that, she had hated and avoided him.

How could he leave her? How could he have broken his promise? He didn't love her. He cared only for himself. He was obsessed with horses and raiding, with no consideration for anything else, least of all her. He had used her, taken his pleasure, and when he had tired of her, gone off to amuse himself elsewhere. He said so himself, saying he was restless.

She ran her hand along the cold surface of the bedding where he'd once slept, the depression of his body still visible. His scent lingered on the blankets. She buried her face in them, breathing in the aroma of her husband, while her eyes brimmed. She squeezed them shut, letting the tears fall and make spots of wetness in the buffalo hair.

Raising her hand from the bare spot, she placed it back on her belly. Her eyes shut as she pictured Lone Wolf's hand on her own, letting him feel the movements of the son he'd never meet. Her fingers slid between his, feeling his hard knuckles and joints, the calluses of his palms as their hands intertwined. She ran her hand up his arm, tracing the lines of his muscles and veins as she reached his shoulder. His arms wrapped around her, pulling her to him, embracing her with warmth and reassurance. She felt his lips meet hers, tender and comforting.

"Lone Wolf," she whispered in the darkness.

Her eyes opened and the image of him was gone.

She awoke in the early morning with a stabbing pain in her lower back. The pain swelled and rushed like a knife drawn forward in her womb to the front below the swell. She cried out and bit her hand.

The pain subsided, so she tried to stand to get Winged Woman or Pretty Robe. She took a couple steps, then it returned with a fierce rush, tightening and clenching until it stole her breath. She dropped back onto her knees. She felt between her legs, finding warm wetness. Pulling her hand away, it was covered in blood. She threw her head back and wailed.

Mouse sat up, took one look, and rushed out. She returned with Winged Woman and Pretty Robe in her wake.

She squatted on the ground, her arms and legs shaking. She couldn't stop them from trembling, couldn't move. Everything Winged Woman had told her was lost. It was too soon. If the baby came now...

"I'm here. Lean on me." Pretty Robe pushed her hair out of her face. Turning to Mouse, she said, "I've got her. Help Winged Woman."

"Heat some water," Winged Woman said, her voice calm and even. Mouse set the trade kettle over the fire with a shaking hand.

The pain retreated. She sat back on her heels. "I can't have this baby."

"It's going to be fine," Pretty Robe said.

"No," she gasped. "It's not. Lone Wolf's not here. I need him here."

"Fathers are never around for the birth of their children," Winged Woman said. "Even if he was here, it would make no difference."

"No!" she shouted. "He has to be here." She had to hear his voice, see his face. She closed her eyes and tried to picture it, but nothing would come.

"You must calm down." Pretty Robe smoothed her forehead.

A stab of pain took her breath. She gritted her teeth while her body punished her. Streams of red formed a puddle between her feet.

Winged Woman stared and worry flashed in her eyes before she felt between Red Bear's legs. "The head is there."

"It's too soon." Mouse's voice trembled.

"I can't stop it," Winged Woman said. "We have to deliver it."

"No!" Red Bear shuddered with sobs. "We have to wait for Lone Wolf!" She couldn't do this without him. He had always been there, even when she hadn't realized it. He had always been there for her, but he *left* her.

Pretty Robe's face was drawn, as though holding back the words she knew to be true. He wasn't coming. He was never going to come.

"We can't wait. There is no waiting," Winged Woman said.

"No..." Another spasm of pain took over.

Lone Wolf, please! Where are you?

There hadn't been time to dig a pit, but Mouse laid rabbit fur pelts on the ground between her legs. Winged Woman waved an eagle wing, letting the plumes graze her body. She chanted a low prayer, while Pretty Robe murmured whispers of instruction and encouragement.

Red Bear didn't listen. She went limp as the truth of her loss sank in. The pain in her body was nothing compared to the ache of her grief.

Mouse wiped the sweat from her brow, then helped to lift her. Red Bear's limbs didn't feel like her own, like the weak arms and legs of a doll. She could hardly stay on her knees. If only she could sleep and pretend none of it had happened, but the pain refused to let go.

"When it tightens again, push. Push hard and don't stop until I tell you," Winged Woman said.

The cramping spasm came again, but she did nothing. Her belly squeezed tight, on its own. Caught by the momentum, she pushed, weakly at first, then with force.

"Breathe, child. Breathe and take a rest. The head is almost out." said Winged Woman.

She shoved Mouse and her mother away so she could lie down. She had nothing left.

"No, you mustn't lie down," Pretty Robe said. "You must let the earth pull the baby out."

She sank deeper to the ground. Maybe the Earth Mother would take her too. The cramps returned, fierce and unrelenting. Despite her exhaustion, she tightened, ready to push.

Pretty Robe lifted her into a squat. "That's it, Red Bear, don't give up."

"Again. Push now. Push hard. PUSH!" shouted Winged Woman.

She pushed. She was dying. Her body was ripping itself apart from the inside out. She pushed and she screamed.

"Lone Wolf!"

When she opened her eyes, she was lying down. Robes covered her. She touched her belly. It was still large, but soft and achy. The room was dim, shapes blurred like underwater.

She raised her head, blinking until the figures took form. Mouse sat beside her, her eyes rimmed with red. Her mother and Winged Woman sat in the shadows. They held something between them, wrapped in a blanket.

"The baby?" she said with a rasp.

Her mother looked up. Her face was streaked with tears.

Red Bear's heart shattered. She had no strength, and everything hurt, but she reached out and pleaded, "Let me see him. Let me see my son."

No one moved.

"I know he's dead. Give him to me."

"It wasn't the right time. It wasn't meant to be," Winged Woman said. "The spirits took him back."

"His father is dead." Saying out loud made it real. Lone Wolf was gone. Her broken heart grew numb. "How could I have raised him properly without his father? My son knew this, so now they are both gone." She tried to stand. "Give him to me."

Winged Woman held out the tiny bundle as she brought him over. Red Bear took him and pulled back the robe to reveal the wrinkled face of her dead child. She saw a familiar mouth and nose, a dark swatch of hair like Lone Wolf's but with a bit of curl like hers. Despite his bluish tinge, the child would have had the rich chestnut skin of his father, but the eyes were fair like her own. She didn't need to see them to believe it.

She touched his tiny fingers, caressed his legs and held his foot in her palm. They had once pushed and prodded inside her, but now lay stiff. He would never hold a bow, run in the grass, or ride a horse.

She hugged the tiny body to her own. He would never know his father, but now he would never call her Mother.

35

A cold night wind scattered dried brush and branches along a near frozen landscape, edged between rocky desert in the east and rising mountains to the west. His face half covered by the hood of his buffalo robe, Lone Wolf watched a tiny farmstead from his position behind a bluff. Smoke wafted from a pipe on the sod roof, nearly invisible in the darkness, but it was the odor of burning wood that had led him to the farm.

There had to be at least one man inside, possibly women and children, but he wasn't concerned with the occupants. A corral held six fine-looking horses. Three paints, two red sorrels, and one black stallion, crowded together for warmth beneath a canvas run-in. The corral looked in better shape than the dilapidated sod and clay shack beside it.

With such a prize to guard, the man was likely armed, but Lone Wolf and his four men could easily defeat him. Better yet, they could steal the horses without ever alarming anyone inside.

He turned Shadow and joined Badger, who waited with his own horse, Juniper. Down the other side of the bluff and in a shallow valley, Buffalo Horn, Ferret and Turtle guarded the seventy-six other horses they'd already stolen.

"We'll steal these last six, then go back," he whispered.

"That's what you said the last time. Only it was nine horses." Badger swung onto Juniper.

Lone Wolf shot Badger a glare. "If you want to go home, then go."

"You also said *that* the last time, and did I leave?"

He tightened his grip on Shadow's reins as he looked back out at the farmstead. If they turned back, he might miss other farms like this one further south, with even more horses.

Badger poked him with his bow. "I want horses as much as you do, but we've been gone for months, and we'll be gone for months more. Winter is here. We may not be able to get home before Spring."

Badger was right. The raid hadn't gone as planned. Other bands had hit the Mexican ranchers sooner and there were few horses. He'd urged his men further and further south in hopes their luck would improve. Now they were far from their homeland, deeper into Mexico than he'd ever traveled before. The unfamiliar land made Badger and the others nervous. Even Lone Wolf felt ill at ease, but he had yet to give up.

"Lone Wolf?" Badger poked him again. "Are you even listening to me?"

He pushed the bow aside. "I hear you."

"Didn't you promise Red Bear—"

"I know what I promised." He faced Badger. "That's why I can't go back. We don't have enough horses to justify this raid."

"Are you listening to yourself? Justify this raid? We don't have to justify anything. We raid. We get horses. We go home. We've done the raiding and got the horses. Now it's time to go home." Badger started toward the others.

"After these six," he repeated. "I promise."

Badger called over his shoulder, "Your promises don't mean what they used to."

"She'll understand," he muttered, but he wasn't sure he believed it.

Ferret agreed to guard their existing herd while Buffalo Horn positioned himself near the doorway to the house, ready to strike down any occupant coming out to stop them. Although the fire inside still burned, no sound emitted from inside the little sod-house.

Lone Wolf and Badger headed to the corral gate, while Turtle rode around to the opposite side so he could drive the horses toward the opening. Badger stopped his horse several paces from the fence. He would herd the horses to Ferret once they were out.

Lone Wolf dismounted and approached the gate. Although he moved silently, the black stallion lifted its tail and tilted its ears in alarm. With its well-muscled, compact body, the stallion would make a suitable alternative to Shadow.

"*Puki nebaep*," he whispered to calm the horse, referring to it as though it already belonged to him.

The horse snorted, warm breath from its nostrils visible in the cold air. The other horses shifted, and one whinnied.

"*Nebaep, nebaep*," he repeated. He glanced at Buffalo Horn, watching for any signal if the occupants stirred. Buffalo Horn sliced the air with his hand, palm down and near his chest, signaling all was well.

He lifted the wooden gate from the gate post and let it swing wide. He moved out of the way, but the horses didn't run out. They skittered to a corner of the pen.

"Hurry," Badger hissed.

"Move further back," Lone Wolf hissed in return. "Your big ugly face is scaring them." He gave an impatient wave to Turtle, who then shook a blanket to encourage the horses to run.

At the same moment, Buffalo Horn called out and a gunshot rang into the night, echoing against the nearby bluff.

The horses ran. Spooked as they were, they nearly scattered, but Turtle raced from around the corral to keep them grouped and Badger steered them away, bow drawn. He shot an arrow at the house, but Lone Wolf couldn't see anyone in the doorway.

The men and horses disappeared in the dark and Shadow followed the group. Lone Wolf ran to catch up, whistling a command for his horse to slow, but it was drowned out by another report of gunfire. He dropped to the ground and scrambled behind a fence post. It wasn't wide enough to hide him, but it was a moonless night, and perhaps the farmer hadn't seen him. Where was Buffalo Horn?

His friends wouldn't leave without him, but they might not return in time before the Mexican killed him.

"¡Malditos indios, robando mis caballos! ¡Hijos de perras!" The voice had a distinctly feminine quality. Lone Wolf raised his head. The silhouette of a woman stood in the doorway, reloading the firearm. She hissed when an arrow struck her in the gut, then leaned against the doorframe.

Checking the direction from where the arrow had flown, Lone Wolf drew his own.

Buffalo Horn called to him from the darkness. "Go!"

Lone Wolf stood with his bow and raced past the house. He caught a glimpse of the barrel as it raised and pointed at him. He let an arrow fly. The gun went off again, but into the air above his head. The woman dropped to the ground.

Turning on his heels, Lone Wolf loped up to the house, another arrow ready in case she wasn't dead.

The woman lay gasping, sprawled across the threshold so her upper half lay inside the house while her legs draped onto her porch. The gun lay by her bare feet, out of her reach, but Lone Wolf kicked it behind him as he crossed the doorway. His arrow had pierced her neck and blood trickled from her mouth as she tried to breathe. More Spanish curses came out as mumbled gurgles.

He frowned with the slightest sting of regret. The woman had shown courage and it was unfortunate he had to kill her, but if he hadn't shot the arrow, his brains would be splattered outside.

Buffalo Horn stopped in the doorway. "You have a habit of encountering brave women with guns." He stared at the woman, who still lingered, eyes wide and filling with tears. "Too bad you had to kill this one. She's beautiful."

Lone Wolf knelt and placed a hand on the woman's forehead. She flinched and tried to move her head, but either she was too weak, or he'd pierced her spine and paralyzed her.

"You honor me with your courage. Die with grace, for yours is the death of a warrior." He drew his knife, put it to her throat above the arrow shaft, and ended her suffering.

Buffalo Horn retrieved the gun and headed outside. The sounds of horses and men's voices carried through the doorway. Badger and the others had returned.

Lone Wolf stood and scanned the tiny one room house. A bed made of a wood and reed platform similar to his own, sat in the corner.

A single chair rested beside a simple wood table, and across the bed was a round iron stove. Baskets of wool, dried corn and other items hung on the clay walls. By the doorway hung a woolen shawl and wide-brimmed hat. Did the hat belong to her husband? Where was her man?

As he took another step inside, a small gasp and a whimper followed the crunch of his foot. The sounds came from under the bed. Looking at it again, he noticed a doll made from corn husks lying on the cover. Children.

Still holding his knife, he crouched and peered under the bed. Two wide-eyed faces stared back at him. He inwardly groaned. They had seen.

He shoved the bloody knife back in its sheath. He'd clean it later. Gesturing with his hand, he said, "*Ven, no les haré daño.*"

As expected, the children scooted further into the corner. They had little reason to believe he wouldn't harm them after seeing him kill their mother. One of the children was a girl, about seven or eight, holding a small boy, no older than Round Eyes.

"What are you doing in here?" Badger asked as he stepped inside. The children made muffled screams.

"There are two children under the bed. I was trying to get them to come out, but now that you're here," he waved at Badger's hulking form, "they never will."

Badger scowled. "You're the one with black on his face and blood on his hands." He smirked. "What do you want with them anyway? We should leave them here and go."

"I'm going to bring them with us." The boy could be a playmate for Round Eyes and the girl could be of help to Red Bear.

388

Badger rubbed his face. "We don't have enough food for the five of us. It's a long way back. They won't make it."

That was probably true, but if these children were anything like their mother, they might survive the journey. "I don't think they have a father, so they'll die out here. They have a better chance coming with us."

"Fine." Badger strode closer to the bed. "I'll move it and you grab them.

As the sun lit the winter sky in pale gray, Lone Wolf and the others left the farmstead with their stolen horses and Mexican captives. The children hadn't said a word, simply staring in fear as he bound them to one of the horses, not one from their own herd in case they were able to use commands.

Once enough distance lay between them and the farmstead, he and the men found a dry arroyo with enough flat land and grazing grass for the herd. They would rest for the morning. The meat they'd brought was nearly gone, and game had been scarce, so Buffalo Horn mixed heated water with dried, crushed corn for their meal.

He passed each man a bowl, saving a small amount for the children, which he handed to them on a strip of bark with a grunt. "We should have brought women with us if we were going to look after infants."

Lone Wolf eyed the pair. He had given them a blanket, but they shivered with cold.

"At least we can go home now," Badger said. He still sounded peeved.

Lone Wolf's gaze drifted to the stolen horses. The black stallion grazed on the few tufts of grass left on the frozen ground. It was a splendid looking horse, not as splendid as Shadow, but a great prize.

He smiled. "We don't have to go yet. If we head just a little further south, we might find more horses like that one?" He raised his brow at Badger.

Badger sighed and shook his head but said nothing.

He knew Badger well enough to know his silence meant anger. Badger was rarely angry, but when he was, he didn't like company. Lone Wolf let him stew while he went to examine the horses.

He hated to admit it, but he hadn't only gone on this raid to get horses to trade for guns. Before he and Red Bear married, he had been the wealthiest man in camp, with a herd larger than any chief. Now he was poor. He wanted to make her proud, to ride into camp followed by numerous horses, and see the look on her face when she welcomed him.

He stroked the stallion's shiny black coat. It'd been well-cared for. A healthy horse would last him several years, one he could breed with other good horses. He approached Shadow, who stood by himself, his tail swishing back and forth, just as peeved as Badger.

"You're not jealous, are you?" He patted Shadow's neck. "Know this, I'd be willing to trade that horse if it meant I had guns to take my revenge, but I'd never do the same with you."

That wasn't exactly true. He had been willing to trade Shadow for his wife, but she hadn't allowed it. That alone had ensured he had chosen the right woman. He smiled to himself. Although he missed having her by his side at night, the memory of her touch had kept him warm. Another month, and he'd feel her again.

When he returned to the camp, everyone but Badger was asleep. Even the children were cuddled under their blanket, breathing softly. He moved to sit beside him.

Badger still hadn't said anything, just held a bowl of corn mush in his hand and used a stick to scoop it into his mouth. He didn't look at Lone Wolf.

"So, what do you think?"

Badger set the bowl down and dragged the stick in the dirt. "You *know* what I think."

"The others will stay if you will."

"You think I'm going to leave you here alone?" Badger broke the stick between his fists. "Mouse would kill me. Red Bear would too, though, it wouldn't be a bad way to go." The smallest hint of a smile played at the corner of his mouth.

Lone Wolf grinned and poked him with a piece of the stick. Badger had never been able to stay angry for long. "You'll stay?"

Badger sighed again. "I'm only going to say this once, and I say it because I'm your brother and I love you. Someday, you're going to have to learn how to let go."

"Let go?"

Badger scooped up a handful of mush. "When your mind is set on something, you hold onto it with everything you have, no matter the consequences." He clenched his fist until it shook. Mush oozed out between his fingers and plopped onto the ground. "First it was horses, then guns, then your woman, now horses again."

Lone Wolf's chest grew hot as he imagined a thousand sharp retorts.

"I'm glad things worked out with your woman," Badger continued, "but if they hadn't, would you have ever let her go?"

Lone Wolf stood. "I'm heading south at midday. Come with me, or don't." As he stormed off, he heard Badger curse and kick the bowl.

The noonday sun did little to bring warmth, despite his fur-lined moccasins and heavy buffalo hide robe. Jagged mountain peaks grew larger as he led his raiding party southwest, but he wouldn't take them into the mountains. It was unlikely he'd find a ranch or homestead in there.

The Mexican captives rode behind him, between himself and Buffalo Horn, their hands bound and tied to the horse they shared.

The boy whimpered and cried, saying *mamá*, but the older girl shushed him.

"*Por favor, agua*," she said.

Lone Wolf held out his waterskin and sat back on Shadow until the horse stopped and the children's mount ambled up alongside him. The girl raised her joined fists and took the waterskin, but instead of drinking from it herself, she lifted it to her brother's mouth.

The boy gulped the water while his sister maintained a wary eye, like a mother with her cub. She handed Lone Wolf the waterskin, but he waved his hand. "Keep it, *Matzóhpe*, Wildcat." He urged Shadow on.

Her fearful stare, tinged by hatred, followed him, burning into his back, like Red Bear's when she was a child. The Mexican girl was younger than Red Bear had been, more like her yellow-haired sister.

He'd promised to take his wife to her sister. What would she say if she was no longer with the People? Would Red Bear leave to find her?

A knot twisted in his gut at the idea of losing her and Badger's words pounded like a drum: *Would you have ever let her go?*

He'd given almost everything to be with her, waited years, not only for her to grow old enough, but to stop hating him. Letting her go was not an option.

But what if she wanted to go?

He thought back to the moment he had learned about captives returned east, and the possibility that Red Bear's sister could be one of them. He wanted to tell her, even if it meant her leaving. Because of Eagle Beak's insistence, he hadn't said a word, but he should have. She deserved to know.

His shoulders sank. Red Bear had asked him for the truth, and he had withheld it. She had made him promise to return and he had broken it.

Easing Shadow into a stop he turned to the men behind him. "We're going home."

36

Mouse approached the bed where Red Bear lay with a bundle in her arms. Only her face peeked from the blanket. She looked as though she had aged more than twenty years, her eyes sunken in shadows, the rims edged with red. Despite the haggard face, she looked very much like the child Mouse had met more than four years before, weak and exhausted from weeping.

She pushed Red Bear's hair away from her forehead and tried to keep her voice even. "It's time." Red Bear retreated further into the blanket, pulling the bundle tighter around her. The faintest whiff of decay hit Mouse's nose, but she held back any reaction. "You have to let him go."

Red Bear stared at the beyond, as though watching ghosts move in the shadows. "I can't. He's all I have left of him." Her voice was raspy, like dried leaves on stone.

Mouse's throat burned, but she had to be strong for her friend, like always. "It won't be all you have." She wanted to tell her that she still had Pretty Robe and Eagle Beak, and herself, but it would do no good. "Please let me take him. We need to send him on."

Red Bear blinked, her eyes suddenly alert. She pressed her lips to the bundle in her arms, murmuring words Mouse could hardly hear. "Will they look after him?"

"Who?" Her chest had gone tight, dreading the words to come.

"Round Eyes' mother and father. Since he's here with us, his parents can take care of my son instead. That's why the spirits took him, isn't it? As punishment for what I did. They took my husband too, so I would know his grief." She rolled onto her back, leaving the bundle for Mouse to take and stared at the sky through the smoke hole. "It hurts that I can't say his name. I want to shout it from the mountains. I want to tell him that I love him. I don't think I ever said it."

"He knows you love him." Mouse reached for the bundle, but Red Bear wrapped her arms around the baby's body, arms that were scabbed with long cuts.

"Let me hold him a little longer."

Mouse took a shuddering breath. "Red Bear, please. I need to take him." She slipped a hand under the bundle, gentle but firm, and pulled the baby from her.

Red Bear lifted her head, letting the blanket fall away and revealing her cropped hair. "I'm coming with you." She threw the blanket off and tried to stand but fell back onto the bed.

"You need to rest. Winged Woman said you lost a lot of blood. You're still bleeding." Her dress showed a dark blotch between her legs, and her chest was stained with dried milk. "I'll send Winged Woman in. Lie down, Sister."

"I want to bury my son." Red Bear's voice broke.

Mouse stared at the baby in her arms, the face hidden beneath a blanket. They had already prepared his body, gently washing him and covering his eyes with red clay. But after he was wrapped, Red Bear had taken him and wouldn't let him go. That was two days ago.

"He will go into the earth as if he were my own. I promise you."

Red Bear curled back into a ball and pulled her robe over her. "Take him, then. Take him and put him in the ground."

Mouse shivered while Eagle Beak and Red Hawk formed the grave, removing rocks and soil to form a narrow crevice in the mountain side. Red Hawk used a hatchet blade to break through the top layer of frozen earth while Eagle Beak scraped with a buffalo shoulder bone. She wiped her runny nose with the back of her hand before placing her arm back beneath the bundle in her arms.

The knot in her stomach tightened. She couldn't stand seeing Red Bear so lost in mourning. It was hard to say who she mourned most, her husband or her son. Even though the men hadn't returned, Mouse was sure Badger was alive. If he was dead, she would know it. Something in the wind would speak to her heart and it would crumble like a withered leaf, but her heart beat strong and sure.

It was no use trying to reassure Red Bear. Mouse had tried, many times, but she had sunk into her cavern of grief, unable and unwilling to climb out. As fiercely as Red Bear held to the belief that Lone Wolf was as dead as her child, Mouse held onto her sureness that he and Badger still lived.

Even if she could prove it, it wouldn't ease the grief over the baby.

She clenched her eyes shut. She wasn't sure what was worse, losing a child, or never having one. She'd been secretly jealous of Red Bear, a baby after no more than a month of marriage while she and Badger had been married two years with nothing to show for it.

There had been times when her bleeding came late. The first time she had shared the news with Badger, glowing from his look of pride, but days later, her moon time came. After seeing how crushed Badger had been, she no longer told him. They rarely spoke of it now.

When Badger returned, she would ask him to take another wife. She had no doubt the fault was with her. He was strong and his seed plentiful. If it hadn't taken root, it meant her body could not support it. Another woman would give him the son he longed for. She would bear the shame like she did her other burdens.

The men stopped digging. The crevice was long and wide enough to hold the tiny stillborn and his belongings, and deep enough to prevent scavenging animals from finding him.

Pretty Robe joined her, holding the items they had made for the baby. Mouse placed the body inside, while Pretty Robe laid the toys, moccasins and other items they had made around him.

Mouse put her hand over his head and whispered, "Go on to the Spirit World, little one." She paused and willed herself not to cry. "And if your father and my husband are there, send them our love, for our hearts are with you." She spotted one of the tiny moccasins and snatched it. It would be something Red Bear could hold onto.

She stepped back and let Pretty Robe, Eagle Beak, and Red Hawk murmur their own prayers before they covered the body with soil and piled rocks back into the crevice. Then she and Pretty Robe headed home.

Winged Woman tended the fire with Round Eyes' sleeping head in her lap. Red Bear's form remained hidden under the blankets.

"Has she gotten up or spoken?" Pretty Robe asked.

Winged Woman shook her head.

"She spoke earlier," Mouse said. "When I came to take the baby."

Pretty Robe sat on the edge of the bed. She stroked Red Bear's back. "I wish I could take away her grief." They all feared she might do as Yellow Bird had done, and let death take her. Quick Hands entered, carrying a pot of stew which she set beside the fire. She crouched, leaned down, and whispered to Red Bear.

Mouse felt a pang of sadness for her mother. Although One Eye was kind, their marriage was nothing like the close bond she had shared with Two Horns. There was little of the laughter and affectionate teasing Two Horns had displayed. Sometimes Mouse would catch her mother staring off into nothing, as she had done in the days right after his death.

Perhaps once Red Bear recovered, she would do the same.

The early spring sun brought warmer days, and the wintry sky grew from pale gray to soft blue. The land showed signs of waking. Red Bear left the bed on occasion, but she rarely spoke. Mouse remained in the lodge with her, to help her friend complete the necessary chores of living.

"I'm going to go collect firewood," Mouse told her one morning.

Red Bear sipped broth from a bowl. She had grown so thin and gaunt, but broth was all she would eat. Her cropped hair, ragged and uncombed, gave her a wild look. At least the cuts on her arms and breasts had finally healed and milk no longer leaked. "Fine," she answered hoarsely.

Mouse headed to the outskirts of camp, but there was little wood left on the ground. She walked further, searching the ground for any remaining scraps. After climbing a small rise, she approached a grove of oak trees, where she collected fallen twigs and branches. Once she had a large handful, she turned back to descend the hill.

As always, she scanned her surroundings before leaving the shelter of the trees. A faint wisp of gray disappeared into the sky. With a racing heart, she gasped and watched, holding her breath, unsure if her eyes had fooled her. It took several moments, then a thin trail of smoke billowed and rose once more.

She dropped her load of wood and ran through the camp. Sentries had spotted the signal as well, and Swift Foot, the camp crier, took up the announcement, yelling the news behind Mouse as she ran.

She burst into Red Bear's lodge. "They're back!"

37

Red Bear lifted her head when Mouse entered the lodge. The words she said weren't making sense.

Mouse dropped to her knees and grabbed her hands. "Did you hear me? The warriors are back. Lone Wolf has returned."

Her numb heart shuddered to life. "He's here?"

"Yes." Mouse's eyes shone with wetness. "They're here, Red Bear. They've come back to us. Come and see, let's go meet them." She stood, pulling on her arms.

He was alive. He was home.

Like frozen fingers warming by a fire, her heart stung. If Lone Wolf was alive, then why had she suffered? Had it all been for nothing? No, not nothing. His child had grown inside her. Grown and died without him.

She yanked her hands free. "I don't want to see him."

"You can't mean that."

"I do." She returned to the bed and covered herself.

"I don't understand. You should be happy." Mouse tugged at the blanket.

"Please go."

Mouse stood, her small stature as imposing as Badger's. "I can't tolerate this anymore. Get up! Stop feeling sorry for yourself and go meet your husband. This is not the People's way."

Red Bear shrank under the covers. Maybe it was wrong, but she couldn't pretend to be joyful when it hurt so much. Why hadn't he kept his promise?

After lighting the signal fire to announce their arrival, Lone Wolf mounted Shadow. He had little interest in waiting for a parade or celebration. There probably wouldn't be one anyway.

The stolen horses spread behind him, less than a hundred in all. It wasn't what he had hoped to gain, and only a portion of them were his, but it was enough, for now.

Riders approached, Red Hawk in front with Eagle Beak following and someone sitting behind him, bundled in a robe. Was it Red Bear? Being in her arms again would ease the burden of his guilt and frustration.

While the riders were still some distance away, the person behind Eagle Beak jumped down and ran the rest of the way. The robe fell back, revealing Mouse's face as she called Badger's name.

Badger leaped from his horse and raced toward her. When he reached her, he picked her up and swung her around.

Red Hawk and Eagle Beak were still approaching, a pace too slow for Lone Wolf's comfort. He searched their faces as dread crawled through his gut. Red Bear would have come with Mouse, unless she was hurt, or worse.

"Where's Red Bear?"

Red Hawk stopped. "Grandson, my heart dances to see you again. I'm sure you've had a long journey, and there are many questions, on both sides. Come and rest, then we'll talk." He stared at the children behind him. "You brought captives."

"They're for Red Bear." The lack of answer to his question sent his heart up his throat. "Where is she? What happened?"

Eagle Beak exchanged worried looks with Red Hawk, as though he couldn't decide whether to explain, or follow the chief's subtle direction to wait.

"Eagle Beak, where's my wife?" Any attempt to keep his voice calm failed.

Before Eagle Beak could respond, Badger came forward. His drawn face, brows turned down in sympathy, was a change from the angry expression he'd been wearing for months. He must know what Lone Wolf didn't.

The other men of his raiding party continued on toward camp, all but Badger, Eagle Beak and Red Hawk. Lone Wolf swung his leg over Shadow's neck and landed on the ground. He strode toward Badger, but Mouse met him halfway. She took his hand. "Cousin, I have something difficult to tell you."

"Is she dead?" Even saying the words cracked his heart.

"She's alive."

He released his breath. Nothing could be worse than her death. "Then, is she ill?"

"Something like that." She stared at her hands gripping his.

His relief had come too soon. "Tell me."

Her eyes lifted to meet his. "It wasn't long after you left that Red Bear learned she was growing a child."

A baby? Any joy he felt was cut short by Mouse's pained expression. "The baby died."

He pulled his hand away. His gut twisted. Guilt pressed on his chest with the weight of a mountain, and he strained to breathe. The rest of Mouse's words tangled together in his head, but he slowly pieced them together.

"She thought you were dead. We all feared it. You were gone so long. She's been in mourning for you and her son."

A son? A son he never knew existed, now gone.

"Lone Wolf, listen to me." Mouse yanked on his arm, forcing him to look at her. "She's not herself. She didn't... she didn't want to come see you."

As he raced Shadow into camp, he planned what he would say. Although he hadn't spent enough time with Red Bear to predict how she might react to him, everything he knew prepared him for the worst.

At the door, he paused before grasping the edge to open it. He entered into darkness. Cloth rustled, then his eyes adjusted, and her figure took shape, a bundle of blankets on their bed.

She sat up as he stepped closer. Her beautiful hair, once long enough to reach her waist, hung in ragged clumps to her chin. Beneath pale skin, her cheekbones jutted out, creating shadows around her sunken eyes. If he hadn't seen her heart beating under her thin chest, he would have thought her a ghost.

Whatever words he planned faded into nothingness. Even if he had something to say, he couldn't speak through his burning throat. He crouched beside her. She lowered her head in her hands, shaking with silent sobs, her arms marked with red lines. When his hands touched her, she pushed him away, mumbling words he couldn't understand.

"Red Bear, please." He clasped her skeletal shoulders and she fell against him, weeping into his shirt. Her cry cut into his chest. He hugged her tighter, as though he could fill the emptiness of his shame with her body. Without thinking, the words fell from his lips, "I'm sorry."

She broke free, moving to the other end of the bed, and glaring with more spite than she had ever shown before their marriage. "Don't you *dare* tell me you're sorry." Her icy tone froze him in place.

"Red Bear—"

She threw an object at him. "He *died*. He died because you weren't here."

In his lap lay a tiny moccasin, beaded to show a dark blue sky and white stars. His vision blurred. He slid closer and reached for her, but she shook him off.

"Don't touch me! Don't ever touch me again." She gasped for breath. "I waited for you. I looked for your signal, every day." Her voice broke, but she swallowed. "When he was dying inside me, that's when I knew you were dead." Her eyes met his. "Where were you, Lone Wolf?"

All his reasons were useless. There was nothing to say to excuse his absence.

"Were you in danger? Captured by enemies? Injured?"

He shook his head. Although their journey had been hard, slowed by winter storms and efforts to keep the herd together and the captives alive, it wasn't enough to explain his broken promises.

Her face slackened with the weight of understanding. "It was just horses, wasn't it?" She spoke hardly above a whisper.

"Yes."

She sank back. "Now I know the truth. You're everything I thought you were."

His heart sank as her meaning became clear. "Please, listen—"

"No! I won't. I hate you. I hate you more than anyone. No, not anyone. The person I hate more than you, is me." Her voice rose as she continued. "I hate myself for being fooled. You tricked me into loving you."

He blinked. She couldn't mean it. "Red Bear—"

"Everyone tried to convince me you were this great, honorable man. Even you believed it. You thought you showed honor by not forcing me to your bed, but you arranged it all so I had no choice but to marry you. How is that any different?"

"That's not—"

"You didn't care about what I wanted. You thought only of your own desires."

Her words were twisted truths. That wasn't what he'd done, was it? Doubt dug a hole in his gut, but she wouldn't let him speak, wouldn't listen to reason. "You don't know—"

"I *know* what you are. Our son knew it, too. He knew it so well he refused to be born into a world where *you* would be his father. I only wish I had known the same before I agreed to be your wife."

Heat flared through him. The last time she had raged against him, he wanted to use his knife on her throat. Now she used her words like a thousand knives to cut him apart. But her accusations were unfounded, fabricated through grief. He couldn't believe she meant it.

"Red Bear, I never meant to hurt you."

She laughed, a hoarse cough that jolted him with shame. "You brought me here, Lone Wolf. All you ever did was hurt me." All previous emotions, the rage and grief, were gone. She was calm and still, proving she meant every word. "Just go," she whispered. "I can't even look at you."

There was nothing he could say. He couldn't fix this. She hated him, as much now as before, and maybe she never really stopped. Maybe she never really loved him at all. He gathered his robe around his shoulders and ducked out the door.

Red Bear was surrounded by emptiness. The words she had said to Lone Wolf echoed in her mind. Her fury subsided, leaving loneliness and doubt. Had she really meant what she said? Did she really want to send him away? Was this like before, when she raged at him because she was ashamed of her father and of herself?

But she had nothing to be ashamed of. It wasn't her fault their baby died before he could take a single breath. Meanwhile Lone Wolf had nothing to say, nothing but excuses. Did he even care? How could he when he never knew? He never felt their son move inside her, never watched her belly grow and change. Never held his stiff body in his arms.

Her eyes welled with fresh tears, but through them, she spotted the tiny moccasin on the ground. She picked it up and clutched it to her chest. All the hours she spent preparing for a baby that would never be, imagining a future that would never happen. It had all been for nothing.

She wasn't sure how much time had passed but it was dark when Eagle Beak and Pretty Robe entered. "You need to speak with Lone Wolf," Eagle Beak said.

She shook her head. "There's nothing left to say."

Pretty Robe sat beside her. "That's not true. You need to make amends with him."

Red Bear sat up straighter. "How can you be on his side? You've always defended him."

"It's not a matter of taking sides. You're both upset and you need each other," said Eagle Beak.

"I don't need him."

"He needs you," Pretty Robe said. "I thought you loved Lone Wolf."

Did she? It seemed like years ago since she did, and it had been brief. Perhaps it had never been real.

Eagle Beak lifted her chin with his finger. "Go to him, Red Bear. He's been in Red Hawk's guest lodge, but he won't see or talk to anyone. I think he's waiting for you."

She swallowed. Lone Wolf was always waiting for her, but she should never have given in. "Then he'll wait forever."

While he was alone, Lone Wolf came to a decision, one he didn't want to make. When he was sure, he went to see Red Hawk and Eagle Beak and told each of them his plans. They listened, tried to sway him with pleas and reassurances he could no longer believe. Once the ties had been cut, he stood outside and looked up.

Endless stars hovered above, twinkling souls of lives now gone. His parents. His brother. What would they think of his choices? Part of him wanted to believe they would understand why he loved and married the woman responsible for their deaths, but perhaps he'd been wrong. Perhaps it wasn't her forgiveness he needed, but theirs.

He sighed. It was time to see Badger.

His friend was sitting against his backrest, Mouse beside him, leaning on his chest. Their quiet affection stung his throat. Mouse sat up when he entered, and as she walked past, touched his shoulder. "It's good to have you home, Cousin."

The sting deepened. He wouldn't be home for long.

After Mouse was gone, he sat across from Badger, unsure how to begin. "I'm leaving."

Badger recrossed his legs. "I could try to talk you out of it, but I'm sure Red Hawk and Eagle Beak already tried and failed. Where will you go?"

"I'll find Peta Nocona, get revenge on the Tonkawa. After that, I don't know."

Badger leaned forward. "You're not the only one who needs revenge. He was my friend too. And your uncle was my wife's father. What about Red Hawk?"

"Red Hawk isn't interested in revenge."

"Then what about me?"

Lone Wolf nudged his foot and managed a smile. "You could always come with me."

Badger sat back with a grunt. "You're a bastard, you know that."

"Yes, I do."

Badger smirked and drew out his pipe. They smoked in silence, the years of their friendship sealed within the words not said.

After leaving Badger, Lone Wolf was ready to face Red Bear. As he entered the lodge, she stood, with effort. Had she been expecting him?

He stared at her before he spoke. For a single heartbeat, he saw the woman who loved him, but he resisted the instinct to take her in his arms, unable to bear it if she pushed him away again. A moment ago, he'd been certain of his decision, but now, seeing her, doubt crept through his resolve.

"Red Bear." His voice faltered, saying her name louder than he meant to. He tried again. "As you said, I've been selfish. I thought to do well for your sake, to make you proud, and..." Those were just excuses. He wasn't here to defend himself. "I was wrong. It wasn't horses you needed but a husband. I see now that I acted by my own wishes."

He paused, his gaze straying to the floor. Breathing became torture, as though his lungs were pierced by the shards of his heart.

"You never wanted to marry me in the first place, and I know you more than regret it now. I should have never... I wish to make it right. So, I release you from me. You're no longer my wife, and no longer will you have to suffer the faults of an unfit husband. It'll be as though our marriage never was, as it never should have been."

He couldn't bear to see her reaction. If she was remorseful, she would have apologized or at least greeted him with some affection, but she stood like a stone, saying nothing. It was clear she wasn't going to try to change his mind. His last bit of hope vanished like a wisp of smoke.

"The lodge is yours. Keep anything you need. I'll only take what's left of my weapons, riding gear, and medicine."

He knelt to gather the items he had mentioned. Among his clothes, he found a shirt feeling the superb softness of it. He admired the quill design, unsure whether to take it. She had made it for him. Regardless of how she felt about him now, it was evidence she had once loved him, however briefly. He added it to his things, leaving the lodge to load his horse.

When he finished, he stood near the door, waiting for her to say something, to repair this undoing. All it would take was one word, but her silence shattered whatever was left in his chest.

He had one last thing to say. "When the next group of traders come, if you wish to leave with them, no one will stop you."

38

It had been three days since Red Bear last saw Lone Wolf. He ended their marriage. It was all over. So why did it hurt? Why did it feel like part of her had been ripped in half?

Pretty Robe stepped through the doorway. "It's time to leave the winter camp. I'll help you pack." Her mother spoke with sadness, deepening Red Bear's guilt.

Everything was like it was before, when they had all wanted her to marry Lone Wolf and she had resisted. She had been a fool. Maybe she still was.

As she packed, each movement stole her breath. She stared at her arms, surprised at the wrist bones showing under her skin. She needed to eat, to get strong again, then maybe she could talk to Lone Wolf.

The thought surprised her, emerging from somewhere deep inside, but it eased some of the pain. He'd looked so stricken, so broken, but she'd wanted to make him hurt, to make him feel all the anguish she carried. He should know what it feels like to be shattered. She'd certainly done that.

Pretty Robe took down the cover, revealing the camp as people dismantled lodges and loaded horses While Red Bear folded the dew cloth, a small girl took items from around the lodge and piled them onto travois. She had skin as brown as one of the People, but Red Bear had never seen her before.

"Who is that?" she asked.

Pretty Robe glanced at the girl. "Oh, I forgot you haven't met Wildcat. Her brother, Cub is off playing somewhere with Round Eyes."

"But where did they come from?"

Pretty Robe made a wistful smile. "Lone Wolf brought them."

Captives. He probably killed their parents too. A feeling she couldn't quite describe crept through her. Anger, mixed with guilt and sympathy.

The girl kept glancing at Red Bear, probably surprised to see someone who looked like her with the People.

"Does she speak our language?"

"She's learned a few words, but Eagle Beak and I use what little Spanish we know to help communicate."

"You said her name is Wildcat? Did you name her?"

Pretty Robe shook her head. "Lone Wolf did."

Despite everything, that made her smile. What could the girl have done to earn such a name? She would have to ask Lone Wolf.

Her heart thudded to a stop. She clenched her eyes shut. It was time to talk to him.

When the ponies were loaded and her travois tied, she mounted Smoke and joined Pretty Robe and Eagle Beak. Her parents rode ahead, their presence bringing comfort. She had yet to see Lone Wolf with the warriors flanking the group, but maybe he rode at the front with Badger and Red Hawk.

Glancing around, she spotted Mouse with Badger and Buffalo Horn. If Lone Wolf wasn't with them, where could he be?

Mouse brought her pony beside her. "You look better."

Red Bear nodded. "I feel stronger, but it will be a while before I can hunt again."

Mouse frowned. "I didn't expect to see you so... calm," she said sourly.

She chewed her lip. "I know. I'm sorry I was so bitter." She swallowed. "I don't know what to say when I see him again. Will you tell him that I want to talk with him?"

Mouse stared at her. "You don't know?"

Her stomach clenched. "Know what?"

"I can't believe he didn't tell you."

"Tell me what?" But she guessed what Mouse was about to say.

"He's gone."

"What do you mean, *he's gone*?"

"I thought he told you. He left the band."

"He left?" Her chest burned. "Where did he go?" She glanced at Badger.

He glared at her, misery beneath his anger. "He went to live with the *Quahadi*, the fiercest warriors of our people. On the Staked Plains."

He was gone. She struggled to catch her breath. She did it. All these years she had wished for him to vanish from her life, to be free of him, and she had finally pushed hard enough to send him away.

"Don't let the fire consume you. Don't ruin him." She had done that ten times over.

She dug her heels into Smoke, urging her into a gallop. There was still a chance she might find him, stop him. Each hoofbeat brought

413

her closer. She headed west, searching the horizon for any sign of Lone Wolf. Reaching the top of a hill, the land spread below her, but without a rider in sight.

She was too late. Her chest ached, fierce and punishing. She darted Smoke in every direction, searching, turning in circles, but it was useless. After years of death, heartbreak, and revenge, the man she blamed for all of it was gone, but nothing hurt worse than the emptiness of his absence.

"I didn't mean it. I'm sorry," but there was no one to hear.

The prairie stretched, endless, tinted by the glow of the rising sun. Tall grass rippled in the breeze, like flames caught in a wind.

Upcoming Books by Veronica Castillo

End of Days (coming soon)

Smoke and Shadow Series
Embers in the Dark (March 2025)
Ashes in the Wind (coming soon)
A Lasting Flame (coming soon)

Want more Red Bear and Lone Wolf? Keep reading for an exclusive sneak peak at the next book in the Smoke and Shadow Series, *Embers in the Dark*

Sign up for my Newsletter and get exclusive updates on upcoming books!

Embers in the Dark

1

Spring 1842

The steep drop made Lone Wolf's stomach plummet and set his teeth on edge. Barely hidden by rock contours and scrubby mesquite, the trail narrowed as it scaled the steep canyon walls. His horse paused and nickered in protest.

"Let's go, *Hihkiapi*, Shadow." He gave the horse a small kick in the flank, urging him to continue, confident in his horse's nimble steps.

Reddish waters ran at the bottom of the Palo Duro Canyon, its meandering path like Red Bear's wavy hair loose in the sun. Layers of rust-colored rock, sandstone, and shale formed the graded inclines of the gorge stretching behind him, while above awaited the flat-topped Staked Plains. The sun made long shadows of the few spindly tree limbs stubborn enough to take root in cracks along the rocks. He needed to make it to the top before nightfall.

Just as the sun dipped too low, leaving the canyon in darkness, Lone Wolf reached the summit and stared wide eyed at the infinite abyss of *El Llano Estacado*.

The large expanse of the plateau loomed before him, with nearly nothing to measure its distance nor to mark its progress, and therefore, nothing to relieve the eye from the monotonous flat. Few set foot upon the plateau, except those wishing to die a slow death from heat and thirst, and the *Quahadi*.

The Antelope band were the toughest and fiercest of all the People, and Lone Wolf hoped to join them. The elusive group might be difficult to find on the plateau, but if he didn't come across them, they would surely discover him.

Leading a pack mule and his spare pony, he rode west toward the setting sun. Its light cast an eerie fire along the far-reaching grass. He watched until the sun disappeared beyond the edge of the world and the moon rose above. The overwhelming emptiness of the plateau, and the flood of memories with no obstacle in sight to stay them, filled Lone Wolf with a sense of hopelessness. He had chosen to live on the fringes of existence.

Once night came, Lone Wolf threw his robe onto the hard soil, and his body on top of it. Each tiny rock and sharp pebble dug into his back through the thin buffalo hide. He should have brought more supplies, or at least another robe to provide more cushion between his body and the dry packed earth. Pulling the edge of the blanket over him, he rolled onto his side.

Shadow stood still in the darkness, already asleep beside the spare horse, *Sumu Naki*, One Ear. They had ridden throughout yesterday's daylight and the moon's rise, so the horses had earned their rest. He closed his eyes and listened to the sounds of the desert night.

Insects chirped, rodents scurried, and even birds scuttled in the stubby brush scattered along the flat earth. An owl hooted and swooped over him, close enough that Lone Wolf could hear his wings shift in the still air. A mouse squealed, then the owl took flight, disappearing into the night to consume its prey. Coyotes yipped in the distance, their howls diminishing as they moved further away.

Most nights, such noises worked like a mother's lullaby to lure him to sleep, but his eyelids snapped open and he rolled over onto his back again. Infinite stars studded the blackness and filled his vision. A thick cluster of them swept in an arc across the sky, the path of souls to the spirit world. The souls of his parents and brother walked that path.

The starry sky forced an image of the waterfall's sparkling cave he'd shown Red Bear after they married. It was under the stars and upon the shore where he first made her his woman. He squeezed his eyes shut again and tried to forget the memory. That was a lifetime ago. Red Bear never really wanted him, and she wasn't his woman anymore.

The night passed, and Lone Wolf slept little, but the sun stubbornly made its rise. He tried to shut out the light by pulling his robe over his face, but the hot air of his breath became suffocating. Shadow's hooves shuffled closer, then a muzzle pressed against Lone Wolf's head, urging him to get up. He reached an arm out and pushed the horse away, but the gray mustang insisted.

"Are you in this much of a hurry to find the Quahadi?" His voice sounded rough from lack of use, so he cleared his throat. The horse snorted in response. "All right, I'm up, I'm up."

He threw off the robe and rose to his feet. Pain shot through his stiff back and his limbs ached with each movement. He stretched his arms above him and twisted his waist until he heard cracks in the joints, then staggered off to a nearby bush to piss.

While he stood there, he scanned the horizon, seeing nothing but dust and spindly vegetation in every direction. After straightening his breechcloth, he packed his things. The sun warmed his back, so he pulled off his shirt, carefully folding it before sliding it into his bag. It was the shirt Red Bear had made for him while he'd been gone on his last raid. The raid that cost him his wife and perhaps his son. Maybe even his best friend.

It didn't matter anymore. He needed to forget the past and focus on his new purpose; to join a new band and make new friends. If he could only find the Quahadi.

The rhythmic sway of Shadow's gait lulled Lone Wolf into drowsiness. Bright afternoon sun shone relentlessly on his face and the black charcoal he'd smeared around his eyes did little to reduce the glare.

As he rode, he fought sleep, slumping his shoulders. He tried singing to keep himself alert, but his eyes shut regardless. A voice in the distance shot his head up, and he squinted in the sunlight.

Three mounted figures appeared, seeming more like an illusion caused by waves of heat on the ground, but Lone Wolf knew better. He reached for an arrow and drew his bow. Before he could see the figures clearly, the voice came again.

"Stop there!"

He stopped while the others came closer. By their dress, he could see they were of the People and cursed himself in his stupidity. He hadn't feared facing an enemy, but hoped to make a better impression on the Quahadi than to be caught unawares and singing like an adolescent boy.

Holding his arm parallel to the ground, he wove it like a snake moving backward, the sign of *Numu*, telling them he was a friend. The men approached until they were several paces away then paused. Their horses moved into a half-circle around him. Lone Wolf remained calm, but kept his bow in hand.

He recognized one of the riders immediately. A young warrior sat upon a black mustang, taller than the others, his long legs revealing his unusual height. He had broad shoulders and his face was young with sharp cheekbones and heavy-lidded eyes. His thick black hair hung over his chest in two long braids wrapped with otter fur, and between them rested a necklace of bear claws.

Lone Wolf knew him as *Peta Nocona*, Wanderer, the son of *Po-hebits-quasho*, Iron Jacket, who was lead war chief of the Quahadi. Wanderer was the man Lone Wolf hoped to find, and he grinned with his good fortune.

Before he could speak, one of the men turned to Wanderer. "This man must be crazy. We should be wary of him." The speaker was small, but the bear grease smeared on his chest and arms highlighted his muscles and tattoos. His face bore a stern expression.

"Only a crazy man would ride alone on the Staked Plains, and he must truly be insane if he's singing so carelessly," agreed another. The third man's fluffy hair bounced as he moved. His features reminded Lone Wolf of the dark-skinned slaves he'd seen working the Texian's farm fields. From under thick brows, large green eyes stared out, not as green as Red Bear's, but more the color of sage.

Wanderer ignored his companions and rode closer. *"Maruawe,"* he said in greeting. His brow lowered as he eyed him, as though he recognized Lone Wolf, but couldn't place him.

"Haa maruawe, haitsii," Lone Wolf said, referring to the men as friends. "I'm glad to have found you on my journey across the plateau."

"Do I know you?" Wanderer asked.

"No, but I know you. I'm Lone Wolf of the *Kotsoteka*. I raided with you and Buffalo Hump on the Great Raid two summers ago."

"Ahh yes, I remember seeing you." Wanderer turned to his friends. "Here is a man worthy to know. I asked Buffalo Hump about him, and he told me Lone Wolf showed much promise as a warrior."

"He must be resilient to travel so far with so little, but such a fine horse," said the green-eyed man who eyed Shadow with admiration.

Lone Wolf didn't miss the subtle inquiry. As a stranger, the man used an indirect manner to question the purpose of Lone Wolf's arrival, but he had no desire to tell these men why he had left the Kotsoteka.

"I plan to live with the Quahadi for a while and learn what I can."

The men exchanged glances and Lone Wolf could tell they were neither amused nor impressed with his vague response.

Wanderer seemed the least suspicious and changed the subject. "This is War Raven and Mullido." He gestured first to the smaller man, then to the green-eyed one. "We're on our way north to raid the first trade caravans of the season. They probably think we're still sleeping off the winter and won't expect us."

"We could use an extra man," Mullido said. "You're traveling light, with only a spare mount and a pack animal, like us." He motioned to

Lone Wolf's other animals. He'd left the rest of his horses in the care of his grandfather back in his homeland. They were the ones he'd gained in Mexico the previous fall in the raid that ruined his marriage.

He hesitated. He hadn't expected to join a raid so soon, nor to return to the lands he'd left, but it would be the perfect opportunity to earn the respect of the Quahadi.

"I'd be honored to join you."

Wanderer grinned but the other men only nodded in acceptance. War Raven seemed the least happy. Lone Wolf noted that earning his respect would take longer than the others. Nevertheless, his hopes rose with the prospect of proving himself with his new companions, and with the excitement of a raid.

The journey north passed quicker than when Lone Wolf had traveled on his own. Along the way, he learned more about his new companions.

"My people came from every part of the world," Mullido said. "I have ancestors across the big water, from Africa and one of my great-great-grandfathers was *taibo*, a white-skin. I also had a grandmother who said her people have been living in Mexico since the beginning of time."

Lone Wolf smirked. It was only fitting the man had a Spanish name to describe his fluffy hair.

"Mullido is a little bit of everything." Wanderer winked.

"And at the rate he spreads his seed around, the People will be as mixed as he is," War Raven added.

Mullido shrugged. "It's not my fault there are so many irresistible women."

"You shouldn't talk," Wanderer said to War Raven. "You have almost as many lovers."

War Raven shrugged. "It's not my fault women can't resist me."

After they descended the plateau, Wanderer led them northwest until they found a trade caravan headed along the Cimarron. Lone Wolf stifled a pang. He was near to where he had raided the wagon camp almost five years ago, where he found Red Bear Woman as a child, and where his father and brother died. He forced the memory aside.

The slow moving wagons rumbled along the ground. Patches of snow filled the banks of the shallow river they followed. From their position atop a bluff, Lone Wolf counted eight wagons and sixteen men. White men.

His grandfather, chief of Lone Wolf's Kotsoteka band, avoided whites as much as possible and usually traded with the Mexican Comancheros. Jose Ortiz often made a special trip to meet with Red Hawk's band since he knew he'd be paid with good horses and furs, but the caravan Lone Wolf now watched wasn't Jose's.

"I thought only Mexican traders used this pass." He scanned the mounted men riding alongside the wagons for rifles, counting each firearm that glinted in the sun and doubling the number as a precaution.

"These whites are the first of the Santa Fe traders to make the journey for the season," Wanderer said. "White traders usually use the northern pass through the mountains since the river is often dry, but in the spring they'll risk coming through here."

It was a stupid risk. If those traders knew anything about the People, they would know warriors would be anxious to roam about raiding or warring now that the weather warmed, especially young men, who were a year older and hoped to earn more honors to elevate their status.

"Do you think they'll have guns?" Lone Wolf asked.

"Maybe. Traders these days are reluctant to provide guns to our People, or if they do, they're usually old muskets."

Muskets were useless compared to arrows since they took too long to reload. It was newer firearms Lone Wolf hoped to find. Ones like the breechloader Red Bear had as a child, the first he'd seen of a gun that might compete with his arrows. Eventually, firearms would improve until they were superior to anything the People could make, and he was determined to not let whiteskins get the upper-hand.

War Raven made the shrill call of his kin, and they rode in a wedge formation toward the wagons. Their whoops and war cries echoed off the sides of the bluff as they swept around the wagons. The traders dove for cover or scrambled for weapons.

The blur of horses, dust from pounding hooves, and colorful feathers waving in the rush filled Lone Wolf with exhilaration. They had ridden in so fast the traders hadn't time to move the wagons into a defensive circle. Wanderer led the line until their horses cut between the group of wagons, isolating one.

Lone Wolf and the others circled the rest of the wagons, darting out of range when the traders aimed their guns. The traders outnumbered them, but it didn't matter. They weren't here for blood. Their purpose was to distract the men long enough for Mullido to gain access to the lone wagon and load the spare animals with whatever loot he could find. Without a full war party, it wasn't worth openly attacking the traders and risk losing a man. That was far worse than leaving empty-handed.

War Raven taunted them further by standing with both feet on his horse's back. He reached into his breechcloth and waved his cock.

While the traders were distracted, Lone Wolf kept an eye on Mullido, but no guns emerged from the wagon he searched, only the ones already in the traders' hands. A shot fired in Lone Wolf's direction, but he kept his shield at an angle and the lead round deflected off the thick layers of dried buffalo shoulder skin.

The white-skin who shot at him shouted and raised his rifle in frustration. He started to reload. It was a breech-loading rifle. Eyes fixed on the gleaming stock, Lone Wolf swooped in from the circle. The trader wore a face of terror as Lone Wolf spurred Shadow toward him. As he reached him, Lone Wolf dropped to the side of his horse, swung under his horse's belly, and came up the other side, but not before snatching the man's hat from his head and rifle from his hand. Waving his prizes triumphantly in the air, Lone Wolf spun on his horse to ride backward and faced his horror-struck victim.

Wanderer whooped a cheer, then War Raven made another call. The warriors broke their circle and rode their horses hard to the south, out of range and out of sight. Lone Wolf draped the new rifle across his lap, admiring the sheen of the wood and the oiled metal. His luck had turned.

"What did you find?" Wanderer asked Mullido once they were safely out of sight of the traders.

"Just bolts of cloth, lace and a few kitchen tools."

"I guess we could use them as gifts," War Raven suggested.

"The only valuable gain is Lone Wolf's new rifle, and maybe the hat," Wanderer said.

Unable to erase the grin of satisfaction on his face, Lone Wolf tipped the brim, as he'd seen Texians do. The others laughed.

"We plan to summer with the *Penateka*. Will you join us?" Wanderer asked.

"The Penateka? Why them?" Lone Wolf asked. The Honey Eater bands roamed further south, near Texian villages.

War Raven smirked. "Wanderer wants to see someone who lives with them."

"Who?" Lone Wolf asked. "Buffalo Hump?"

"No, Buffalo Hump no longer lives with the Penateka. He's become disgusted by them, saying they no longer live like the People," War Raven said.

"The Penateka are too influenced by the whites. They wear trade clothing and some groups have even signed treaties. Their head chief, *Pahayuca*, The Amorous Man, is excessively large."

"That's because he stopped raiding and eats too much white sugar," Mullido said.

Lone Wolf frowned. "Then why are we going there?"

War Raven and Mullido exchanged smiles. "You'll see."

Wanderer gave each of them a glare. "Pahayuca is my relative, and I want to visit him. Everything else is secondary."

Lone Wolf could tell he was being left out, but didn't press the issue. Wanderer's men seemed to trust him and their company worked to chase away his loneliness. The sky hovered in a brilliant blue, and the wide landscape swept in every direction as they rode on fresh mounts. Best of all, he had a new gun.

He removed the hat and threw it over his shoulder, letting it roll along its brim in the breeze behind him, the only sign that he or anyone had passed through.

Acknowledgements

This book would not be possible without the love and support from my husband, Eric, and our family. Thank you for all the days and nights I spent writing, editing, planning, researching, and back again while you gave me the gift of time. I wouldn't be following my dreams without you by my side. You are the Badger to my Lone Wolf.

Thank you mom and dad for inspiring my love of books and history. I first learned of Cynthia Ann Parker because of my mother and the books we read together. My journey into the world of the Comanche started when I was Bridget's age and I never left.

What is a writer without writer friends? It can be lonely behind a keyboard, especially when one is shadowed by doubt and frustrations. Many writers read drafts, critiqued, offered feedback and advice, but I want to extend special thanks to Krista, Lori, Immy, and Claudia. Red Bear and Lone Wolf (and Fox Laugh) wouldn't be who they are without you. You loved my characters as much as I did, read everything I had, and never stopped believing in me. There are so many times I would have given up if not for you. Plus there was that special shared joy we had in breaking our characters and testing their limits. Also special thanks to Cass, Caroline, Poppy, Rebecca and Jackie for your endless support and encouragement. You let me rant, let me fall apart, and listened with patience even when I could not read a scene without tearing up.

To Gabriel, Robin, Ben, Suzanne, and Carrie who read my earliest drafts and helped guide me from newbie to confident writer. And to Remi who first saw the potential in Fox Laugh. To Tim for sprinting with me so often, and all the folk who played a part in developing my characters and story, I thank you.

I'd also like to thank Rebecca Ferrier from History Quill and her editorial expertise. My book would not have made publication without her wisdom and the confidence she inspired.

I also extend sincere appreciation to the Comanche Nation and their language resources. My trip to Texas and Oklahoma may have ended in a broken leg, but the research and knowledge I gained was invaluable to telling a story that I hope is sensitive and honest to both the history and a culture I hold with deep respect.

Thank you to Whittier Public Library and librarians everywhere. One cannot write history without research, and loving research makes the journey all better. But it sure helps to have guidance and direction.

This acknowledgement would not be complete without including my dearest Aunt Maria. The first and most significant kindred spirit I have ever known. Your soul and spirit lives on in every character, every story, and every word I write. I miss you every single day.

And to Cynthia Parker and Peta Nocona, whose lives inspired me in the first place. May you forever roam free.

About the author

Veronica Castillo is a middle-aged educator who grew up in California loving books and history, and existing in her dream world. Many of her stories are inspired by history and her family's roots in Mexico, Texas, and Arizona. She didn't decide to become a writer until the stories in her head became too intense to ignore.

While she attempts to put her dream world onto pages, she resides in the Midwest with her husband, sons, cats, and an adorable dog. She is a 'sometimes artist', enjoys playing with yarn and needles, and you may catch her on weekend mornings spinning wool on an antique spinning wheel. Veronica will always be a California girl and one day, she will return to the redwoods and rocky coasts of her youth.

Meanwhile, there are still so many more stories to come.

Email: veronicacastilloauthor@gmail.com
Instagram: @veronicacastilloauthor

Printed in the USA
CPSIA information can be obtained
at www.ICGtesting.com
LVHW041206081124
795950LV00001BC/51

9798991687218